THE BRIDLED TONGUE

THE BRIDLED TONGUE

Catherine Meyrick

Courante Publishing

Published by Courante Publishing, Melbourne, Australia
courantepublishing@gmail.com

Author website and blog: catherinemeyrick.com

Cover Design by Jennifer Quinlan, Historical Fiction Book Covers

A catalogue record for this book is available from the National Library of Australia

ISBN-13: 978-0-6482508-3-8

For Gabrielle

Characters

Norwich, Norfolk
Alyce Bradley, a waiting woman
Hugh Bradley, Alyce's father, a mercer
Joan Bradley, Alyce's mother
Isabel Sutton, Alyce's sister
Will Sutton, Isabel's husband, a grocer
Sir William Sutton, Will Sutton's father, a wealthy grocer
Katharine, Lady Sutton, Sir William Sutton's wife
Robin Chapman, a journeyman mercer
Edith Chapman, Robin Chapman's mother
Wat Simpson, an apprentice mercer
Marieke Thompson, Alyce's childhood friend
Grietje de Jong, Marieke Thompson's mother, a lacemaker
Lettys Rowe & Martha Powell, Isabel Sutton's friends
Bess Godfrey, Ruth Williams & Harriet Brewer, midwives
Maude Middleton & Agnes Hall, town gossips
William Reynes, curate of the church of St Peter Mancroft

Ashthorpe, Northamptonshire
Thomas Granville, a privateer
Cecily Beaumont, Granville's sister
Kit Watkins, Granville's serving man
Marian Haines, Cecily Beaumont's waiting woman
George Haines, Granville's steward, husband of Marian Haines
Jack Stokes & Nick Price, grooms
Sir Philip Rossiter, Granville's neighbour
Margaret, Lady Rossiter, Sir Philip Rossiter's wife
Eloise Wyard, a neighbour
Elizabeth Jefferies, the wife of Ashthorpe's rector
Peter Marston, a yeoman farmer
Beth Marston, Peter Marston's wife

London
Giles Clifton, a gentleman of means
James Foster, a privateer
Lucy Foster, James Foster's wife

Part 1

Whoso keepeth his mouth and his tongue keepeth his soul from troubles.

Proverbs 21:23

1

August 1586

Alyce Bradley climbed down from the wagon and turned slowly, gazing past the impressive market cross and over the bright awnings of the stalls to the tall houses and shops surrounding the square. The church of St Peter Mancroft dominated one end, the Guildhall with its chequered stone the other. Behind the houses to the side of the market square stood the solid bulk of Norwich Castle. She had glimpsed the walls of the keep, stark in the bright sunlight, as they had made their way through St Benedict's Gate and on towards the square.

The air was alive with the buzz and rumble of a busy town and the smell of many things combined: bodies living close, cooking, animals, the tang of the river Wensum. And over it all, the endless pealing of church bells.

Welcome or not, Alyce was home.

'Mistress Bradley?' A sturdy lad of sixteen or so pulled off his cap. 'I'm Wat Simpson, one of Master Bradley's apprentices. He sent me to carry your things home.'

'Thank you.' Alyce had to raise her voice against the clamour of the bells. 'I hope it's not too heavy for you.' She glanced towards the pannier on the ground beside her.

'Nay.' He grinned, pulling his cap back on. 'It cannot be heavier than half a dozen of the Master's bolts of damask.'

'Wat, why are the bells ringing?'

'Have you not heard, Mistress? A group of Catholic traitors have been captured in London. They were plotting to kill the Queen and set the Scottish queen in her place.'

Alyce shivered and silently prayed those taken were truly guilty.

She touched Wat's arm as he bent to lift the basket. 'Wait one moment.'

Alyce walked over to where Jack Middleton stood directing his apprentices as they unloaded the wagon she had travelled on to Norwich. His wife, Maude, supervised from the doorway to their shop.

'Thank you for your company Mistress, Master Middleton.'

'We were happy to have you with us.' Maude smiled. 'It is not easy for a woman travelling alone.'

Alyce dropped a shallow curtsy. 'Good day to you both.'

Maude opened her mouth but her husband spoke over her. 'Good day to you, Mistress Bradley.' Amusement gleamed in his eyes.

Alyce grinned back at him.

Maude's shrill voice followed her. 'I thought she said her name was Banbury. You knew I had it wrong, and you said nothing.'

'Wanted to spare the woman your interrogation.' Jack Middleton's voice faded as Alyce moved away, Wat Simpson behind her, the pannier high on his shoulder.

They wound through the market-goers, around St Peter Mancroft and along the street to her father's shop. Alyce paused at the entrance, settled her shoulders and stepped inside.

Light from the large window glowed on the wooden presses at the back where damasks, chamlets, velvets, silks, satins and taffetas were stored. Baskets of varying sizes were arranged around the room. Lined with soft linen, they held laces, French garters, knitted hose and gloves, brass and thread buttons. A journeyman stood sorting through the boxes kept in the compartments of the tall wall cupboard in the far corner. Alyce knew exactly what was stored there and in what order—glass buttons from Murano, gold thread, silk lace, silver points, fine silk thread from Bologna and other expensive wares.

At one of the tables, another journeyman was berating a young man she assumed was near the end of his apprenticeship as if he were a green lad. The journeyman turned, taking Alyce to be a customer.

Robert Chapman. He had been an apprentice when she left Norwich twelve years ago.

As Chapman approached her, recognition lit in his dark eyes.

Without acknowledging him, Alyce hurried towards the back of the shop to the stairs leading to the floor above.

'Alyce.' Her father's voice boomed out as she entered the

hall. He sprang up from the settle beside the window and clasped Alyce into a bear-like embrace.

Alyce stood still, her arms at her sides, blinking away tears.

He stepped back, his hands resting on her shoulders. 'Look at you, Alyce. You have grown to be a fine woman.'

She smiled at him, startled by the compliment. Her father was the same effusive man despite the grey now in his once dark hair and clipped beard, the pouches beneath his smiling eyes.

'It is good to have you home at last.'

'Ay, it is.' Her sewing set aside, Alyce's mother had risen from the seat.

Alyce stepped forward and kissed her, a dry brush of lips upon her cheek.

'I have waited long for this day.' Her mother caught her hand and squeezed it.

Surprised by her mother's glistening eyes, Alyce could think of no reply.

'I trust you had an easy journey?'

'For certain, it was slow.' Alyce forced a smile. 'The wagon was heavy-laden.'

'By wagon!' Her mother's eyes widened. 'Could Lady Faulconer not have lent you a horse and ordered one of her men to escort you?'

'Lady Faulconer died over a month ago. I was no longer of any use.' She looked towards the window, away from her mother, her jaw tight. 'I was told to consider myself fortunate I was permitted to travel with her notary as far as Lincoln.'

'Who told you that?' her mother snapped.

'Lady Faulconer's nephew, the *gracious* Sir Christopher.'

'We would have arranged something more suitable had you sent your message sooner. It arrived only last night. When we heard that a train of riders and wagons were heading towards the town, your father sent Wat to the square.'

'I travelled in good company—Master Middleton and his wife. They were in Lincoln settling his brother's estate.'

Alyce's father raised an eyebrow. 'I'll wager Maude Middleton questioned you close for the whole journey.'

'She did not recognise me.'

'And you did not tell her.' He gave a barking laugh. 'That's the spirit.'

'She knows who I am now, sure enough. Master Middleton recognised me but said nothing until we arrived.'

'Jack Middleton learnt early to keep his own counsel. News of your return will be spread across the town by nightfall. Maude Middleton will only have to tell her friend, that common scold Agnes Hall—she is better than any town crier.' He glanced at the gilded timepiece on the cabinet at the end of the hall. 'I have a shipment of cloth unloading. We will speak this evening, Alyce.' He embraced her again and walked towards the stairs.

Alyce followed her mother to the upper floor of the house to her old bedchamber.

The afternoon light streamed through the open window, giving the small chamber an airiness at odds with Alyce's memories.

Her mother went to a press opposite the window and opened it. 'Eliza, my maid, sleeps in here too. She has made room for your things.' She glanced at the pannier Wat had set down beside the curtained bed at the end of the room. 'When will the rest of your belongings arrive?'

'This is all I have.'

'But...' Her mother jerked her head, clearly displeased. She took a deep breath, putting the matter aside. 'I will send Eliza to help you unpack.'

'There is no need, Mother. I would like a little time alone—the journey was tiring.'

'Of course. You will want to change and rest.' She stood at the doorway, her hand on the latch. 'Eliza will bring a jug of warm water for you.'

'Thank you.' Alyce gazed at her mother. She was as elegant as Alyce remembered. Her golden hair was not as bright, her face was lined and her clear blue eyes not quite as vivid, yet she was still a beautiful woman. It was a beauty she had bequeathed to Alyce's sister, Isabel, but, Alyce knew too well, not to her.

As the door closed behind her mother, Alyce walked to the window. This was the view she had remembered through the long years away. Light still played across the rooftops, and the road… She knew where it led now—to a life as difficult as it had been here.

The noise of the town, of the lives of the thousands who dwelt in Norwich, carried on the air, and hope, that unruly weed, thrust aside the worries that had beset her on her journey home.

~

Alyce pushed open the door to the parlour where, under her mother's direction, Wat was arranging bolts of cloth in a display of bright colour across the parlour table.

Her mother smiled. 'Alyce, you are up at last.'

'I am sorry, Mother. I will ask Eliza to wake me when she rises tomorrow.'

'Do not apologise, you were tired after your journey. And there is no need to rise when Eliza does. You are not a servant here.' She waved Alyce forward. 'Now choose two or three of these and we will make them into gowns for you.'

'But I have enough.' Alyce spoke without thinking. Other than what she had worn yesterday, all she had were two unadorned gowns of a sombre frieze.

Her mother nodded to Wat. 'This will do, Wat.' She winced as he slammed the door behind him and thumped down the stairs. 'That boy needs to learn to move more quietly.' She turned to Alyce. 'If all you possess was in that pannier, you have two or three gowns at most, and you were wearing the one gown of any quality you own yesterday. And it looks to be one that you took with you when you left here. As for what you are wearing—'

'What is wrong with what I am wearing?' Alyce interrupted, glancing down at her modest gown of brown wool frieze covered with a clean apron.

'You are dressed as a serving maid! Even your hair is hidden away beneath that coif.' Colour flared in her mother's cheeks. 'You were to have a new gown every year.'

'And I did.' It was not Alyce's fault she did not have clothing in bright colours or rich fabrics. She had not chosen the life she had lived these past twelve years.

'What of the cloth we sent each New Year? We knew Lady

Faulconer would only provide one gown. You should have brought home more.'

'My lady considered the fabric unfitting for one of my station as I am not of gentle birth.'

'Not of gentle birth!' her mother sniffed. 'In this town, you are the daughter of a mercer of high standing and you must dress accordingly. Your attire reflects your father's business.' Her brow furrowed. 'Surely you want new gowns?'

'But...' Alyce stared at the colours and textures of the cloth laid out on the table, 'I suppose.'

Her mother touched a bolt of damask the colour of marigolds. 'This is a beautiful colour.'

'It must be worth a fortune with a dye like that. And it is silk.' As she gazed at it, the long-repressed yearning for gowns in bright colours threatened to overcome Alyce's studied care not to draw attention to herself. 'Father would never—'

'Your father said we may have whatever we wish.' She held out a length of grosgrain. 'What about this?'

Alyce ran her fingers across the pink-tinged yellow cloth but shook her head.

Her mother exhaled and pointed to another bolt of cloth. 'That chamlet is not so bright, but it is changeable—take it to the light and see.'

Alyce picked it up and moved over to the window. The cloth shimmered reddish, blue in the clear light. 'It is still too eye-catching.' She blinked back unbidden tears. Fabric in its varied colours and textures had delighted Alyce as a girl, as had the skills she had learnt from her mother to transform flat cloth into shapely garments. These skills had been of use to Lady Faulconer, but the dull colours and sober styles had given Alyce no pleasure other than a task completed well.

'Oh, Alyce, I do not want my daughter wearing plain workaday colours.'

Nothing was to be gained by clinging to the dullness of the past. Alyce returned to the table and pointed to a russell worsted in tawny. 'I would wear this.'

Her mother watched her, thoughtful. 'If you choose cloth for two gowns, plainer colours you are content with, I will decide on a third, something brighter you will like once you are used to pretty gowns again. But, and there will be no arguing, you are to have a bright red taffeta petticoat—a flash of colour to make up for the dullness of your gowns.'

Alyce almost laughed aloud. Her mother would have her way, and why should Alyce resist?

'If you do not mind,' Alyce said, 'I will visit the de Jongs today.'

Her mother glanced up. 'You and Marieke wrote to each other?'

Alyce gave a quick shake of her head. 'Nay.'

'I believe they still live where they did.' She seemed no happier at the thought of Alyce's friendship with Marieke de Jong than she had been when Alyce was a girl.

'I do not have time to come with you, and I cannot spare Eliza.'

'It is not far, Mother, and most will not know who I am, so you need not worry about talk of me wandering the town unaccompanied.'

'Very well.' It was said grudgingly. 'But wait until after dinner. Your father wants a word with you. He is in his office.'

'And after, how would you have me help you? I cannot be idle.'

Her mother blinked, surprised. 'This is your home, Alyce. You are not here to serve. You may spend your days as you please, but I would welcome help with the sewing and preparations when we have guests to dine.'

'I could tend the garden. It looks to be in need of some attention. And the stillroom.'

Her mother frowned, and Alyce glimpsed the woman she remembered from her childhood.

'If you wish,' her mother's voice was harsh, 'but any remedies are only for use in this household. I want no line of strangers at the gate with all sorts of outlandish requests.'

'Of course not, Mother. My only skills are in the basic physic any housewife uses.'

Her mother stared at her as if she were trying to read her thoughts. 'Make certain you always remember that.'

Alyce watched as she tidied the bolts of cloth away. Her mother may well be glad to see her, but if Alyce were to bring shame by her behaviour, she was certain the angry woman of her memory would reappear.

~

Her father looked up from the ledger on his desk when Alyce came to the door of his office.

He beckoned her in. 'I'll only be a moment more—a few items I should have entered yesterday,' he said, carefully copying details from scraps of paper into the ledger. 'I had forgotten your mother is reckoning the accounts this afternoon.'

Alyce walked to the window. Townsfolk made their way up and down the street to the haberdasher, the tailor, the mercer, the sun catching a bright feather on a hat or the satin lining of a cloak, glistening on a jewelled clasp or a brooch, flashes of colour among the workaday browns and blues.

'Alyce, sit down.' Her father indicated a chair at the other side of the desk.

The room had changed little since Alyce had last been here. The panelling, the ledgers, even the mementos of her father's travels were as she remembered them. A small brass urn decorated with enamelled figures and a box inlaid with polished stones sat on the desk; a series of small beakers of coloured glass intricately painted with gold were arranged along the shelf —artefacts from a world Alyce could only imagine.

'I have always loved this room.'

'Not always, surely.'

'Most of the time.' She thought of the perfunctory beatings her father had given her here; his heart had never been in them. 'When you were away, I would creep in here and shut the door. I could read, undisturbed, for hours.'

'Was there much time for reading with Lady Faulconer?'

'I read aloud to her each day, but the books were all of her choosing.'

'No travellers' tales?'

Alyce shook her head. 'None of those.'

'We had such hopes when we sent you to Lady Faulconer. Not only that you would learn the seemly behaviour we were unable to teach you.' Alyce leant forward to protest, but her father held up his hand. 'We hoped you would find a husband there.'

Alyce scoffed, 'My lady was very old, as were most of her household, and visitors were rare. Besides, who of those rare fine visitors would have considered a plain serving maid?'

'Serving maid?' Her father sat back, surprised. 'You were to be a waiting woman.'

'I have been these last few years, but for the first five or so I was no better than a serving maid.'

'We assumed you were content. You should have come home.'

Alyce raised her chin. 'I thought I was not welcome. Can you imagine how I felt? They hanged Grandmother's friend as a witch a month before Grandmother died.' She closed her eyes tight at the memory of the old woman's jerking dance, the excited, flushed faces of the crowd. She had not wanted to watch the hanging, but her grandmother, unable to go herself, had begged Alyce, saying it would comfort Bridget if she chanced to see one face in the crowd that she knew would be praying for her.

'Bridget Mason was a good woman. She would not have killed a child to spite its parents.' She sighed and opened her eyes. 'Yet they hanged her. Then the talk began that Grandmother was a witch too. I was terrified for her.' Alyce looked down to the floor, her mouth tight. 'I should have been relieved that she died peacefully. Right or wrong, I loved her above all others. She never judged me and found me wanting. I know I behaved unacceptably after her funeral but I was beyond myself with grief. Then to have Mother beat me within an inch of my life, was that not punishment enough?'

'Alyce.' Her father's shoulders fell. 'I would not have… Your mother was so shamed…'

'You sent me away.' She took a deep breath. 'I was certain you had chosen Dalstead as an especially fitting place of punishment.'

'You said nothing in your letters.'

'How could I? My lady read any letter sent by a servant. I

could not have written—*For the sin of pride I was locked in my room yesterday, on bread and water, instructed to remain on my knees praying to be granted the humility fitting to one of my age and station.* Or perhaps—*Last week I was beaten with a rod by my lady's most senior woman for stealing food.*'

'You did not have enough to eat?'

'I did, but...' Alyce's voice wavered as she pressed on, 'I had hidden one of the barn kittens in the bedchamber I shared with the other maids and was keeping morsels from my plate to feed it. When her woman discovered it, my lady said I was only entitled to the food that went into my body. To take more than I needed was to steal.'

'Oh, Alyce,' he groaned.

'Had you visited me, I would have told you what I dared not write. Could you not have visited me once in all the years I was away?'

'I... I...' He opened and shut his mouth.

'But I am not a fool.' Alyce stared straight ahead, afraid that if she were to see pity in her father's face, she would be lost in the misery of that lonely girl of sixteen. 'I learnt quickly how to live there. How to be silent and obedient and not draw attention to myself.'

'I am sorry,' he said quietly. 'What do you want to do now?'

'To find a position in an agreeable household.' She forced herself to smile. 'Ay, a household where there is singing and dancing, where the seasons are celebrated with gaiety. And no more than half a day's ride from a sizeable town. A household where I will be a waiting woman—an attendant and companion —not a maid.'

'I will do better than that. I will find you a husband.'

Alyce blinked.

'Do not look surprised. It is what every woman wants: husband, children, a household of her own.'

'I think the time for that has passed.'

'Do not be foolish, Alyce. How old are you? Twenty-eight? Many women marry at your age and older.'

'Where will you find this husband? I see no line of suitors at the door.'

'A sizeable dowry will bring them.'

'I am surprised you did not think to offer such a price those years ago.' Alyce wondered for a moment what manner of man her father would have chosen. Life with Lady Faulconer might not have been the worst that could have happened to her.

'God's teeth!' Her father pushed his chair back from the desk. 'What's done is done. We tried our best. We failed. I have said sorry. You would not have contemplated a marriage at that stage.'

Alyce shrugged.

He inhaled loudly. 'I will have a care to see any husband is worthy of you.'

'And will I have any say in the matter?'

'Master Reynes, the curate at St Peter Mancroft, would not countenance an unwilling bride. But it will not help if you are over-particular.'

'You should advise me of what you consider reasonable grounds for refusing a suitor: hunchback, missing limbs, foul breath, drunkenness, papistry?'

Her father burst out laughing. 'Alyce, you have not changed. Your tongue is as sharp as it ever was.'

He came around the desk and took Alyce's hands in his. 'We will take our time and make a wise choice. I'll offer a dowry large enough to make it worth a man of high standing, but not so high to attract adventurers. And I promise you, you will have the final say, yea or nay.'

'Well, I had better fall in with your wishes,' Alyce said, unsmiling. This time she would make sure she had a say.

2

Isabel Sutton glanced across the table at Alyce. And to think she had spent hours dressing, afraid her sister, newly returned from life in a noble household, would outshine her. Still, it was an opportunity to wear her new gown of cherry-coloured wool. The embroiderer Lettys had recommended had done a fine job of the rosebuds stitched across the forepart.

Will had been right to remind her that time could not improve beauty that had never been there. But Will did not understand that rich clothing could almost make up for its lack. Isabel's gaze drifted to her sister, deep in conversation with their mother. The ruffs and sleeves she wore belonged to Mother. And why had Alyce dressed her hair so severely, pulling it tightly back into a beaded caul? Her hair had been beautiful when they were younger, thick and wavy—the one thing Isabel had been jealous of.

It was easy to see why Alyce had not made the advantageous match her parents had hoped would come of her time with old Lady Faulconer. She wondered what the whole tale was. She had managed only a brief whispered conversation with Mother when she and Will arrived. Alyce was not likely to tell her much, although she seemed not as ready to take offence at every word as she had been years ago. And she was getting on well with Mother, discussing a recipe of some sort, as if she were an ordinary housewife. Perhaps she had changed.

Isabel strained to hear what they were saying above the chatter of the journeymen and apprentices farther along the table. They should eat in silence as her mother-in-law, Dame Katharine, demanded. No doubt they appreciated Mother's efforts with the meal. Mutton stuffed with garlic and capon boiled with leeks was far beyond anything a servant or apprentices should expect to eat. Mother treated the apprentices as if they were family, especially the younger boys. Dame Katharine served them plainer fare, eaten with the servants after the family had dined. It was much more fitting.

'When I have tried anything elaborate, even small fruits, they fall apart,' Mother said.

'A smooth sugar paste, finely ground, worked to the right consistency, will stick hard enough once it sets. I can show you how to do it.'

'You sound quite skilled, Alyce,' Isabel called to her.

'My lady's one weakness was a sweet tooth.' Although Alyce smiled, there seemed no happiness in the memory. 'And she liked to set an elaborate table when her nephew visited.'

'You can show me too. I have little to do this afternoon.'

'I will, but another day perhaps,' Alyce said politely. 'I am visiting the de Jongs this afternoon.'

'Marieke married an English weaver, not another Stranger,' Isabel sniffed. And had effortlessly produced a tribe of children.

'George Thompson,' Father put in. 'He'll be as skilled at cloth-making as Peter de Jong. De Jong deserves the success that has come his way. He has tried to do what was for the best, not like some of them who keep only to themselves.'

'And Grietje can still be talked into making the most exquisite lace.' Isabel touched her hand to her ruff, edged with fine cut-work lace. 'She does it for me because I am your sister.'

Alyce stared at Isabel, her green eyes icy.

Those eyes. The same as their grandmother's. No wonder people had thought Grandmother was a witch.

'She is the best lacemaker…' Isabel opened her mouth to justify herself but stopped, her words lost in the clatter and scraping of stools as the apprentices and journeymen rose from the table.

Mother spoke above the noise. 'Do you still play the lute, Alyce?'

'Music was one talent Lady Faulconer did appreciate in me.'

'We should sing a few rounds together.' She glanced around at her family. 'A pleasant end to the meal.'

They moved into the parlour, and Mother brought the lute to Alyce.

'You kept my lute?'

'Why would we not? I knew you would come home one day.'

Alyce's fingers played across the strings. 'It is in tune.'

'Wat sometimes plays it in the evening.'

'A lad of many talents,' Father laughed.

Isabel pressed her lips together. Mother was almost fawning over Alyce. She was certain her mother had been glad Alyce had left, rarely mentioning her since. Why was she now acting as if she was delighted to have her back?

Isabel walked over to her husband and linked her arm through his. 'Will, let us sing, "Come Away, Sweet Love".'

Will smiled at Isabel with the hint of a wink and Isabel's heart fluttered. He was the most handsome man in Norwich: tall and slender; with golden hair, moustache and pointed beard; his eyes a matchless blue. Those half-heard whispers about him were simply the spite of jealous women wishing they stood in Isabel's shoes.

They turned to each other as they sang, Will staring deep into Isabel's eyes. If only they had been alone, she would have melted into his arms.

Father followed with a martial ballad, his voice deep and rich, and finally they all joined together in a series of catches.

The rounds finished, Isabel watched as her father and Will drifted to the settle by the hearth. With their goblets of wine, they continued their intense dinner conversation concerning the capture of those Catholic plotters and what it might mean for the fate of the Scottish queen. She wished they did not talk of such things; it was too worrying.

Alyce sat, her head bowed, picking out a tune on the lute.

Isabel carefully arranged her skirts as she seated herself beside her. 'You must be glad to be home.'

Alyce continued her playing but looked up at Isabel. 'Ay, I am.'

'I would die if I were exiled in the country.'

Irritation flickered in Alyce's face. She stopped her playing. 'If all thought that way, who would grow the food that graces city tables?'

Isabel rolled her eyes. 'You are right.' Alyce had always been right. 'But it is not the life for everyone. I need to sing and dance, visit friends, linger at the booths on market day.' Before

Alyce could say country people did the same, as she was sure to, Isabel said brightly, 'So Father is seeking a match for you.' Money aside, she wondered what manner of man would be interested in Alyce. An older man perhaps, widowed, wanting someone to care for his children.

Alyce sat silent, her fingers resting on the soundboard of the lute.

'He will offer a substantial dowry. Mother said—' She gasped. 'Have you not been told?'

'Told Father is going to market to buy me a husband? Ay, he informed me a mere two hours ago. I am surprised he made you privy to the details before he had even discussed it with me.'

'No, no,' Isabel said quickly, 'Mother told me just before dinner.' Why did Alyce do this, turning what should have been a pleasant conversation into a marsh with traps at every turn?

Isabel took a deep breath. 'But what could be better? You would have your own home. And Mother said it would be someone who met with your approval. You would not be forced.'

'I should be grateful for that. And when they were considering marriage for you, did you need to be assured that you would not be forced?'

'Nay, but I—' She stopped. However she tried to say it, Alyce would find a way to take offence. Of course she had not needed that assurance. So many men had courted her; she had been the one to do the choosing.

Isabel stared at Alyce, her brow creased. 'Alyce, I do not understand you.' She rose from her seat and moved across the room towards her husband. Alyce had not changed; she was still a waspish piece of work. Mother would learn that soon enough.

~

Sunlight danced on the bright awnings of the market stalls and the produce on display; apprentices called their master's wares; shoppers haggled and chatted. And again, Alyce felt a stirring of excitement. Away from her parents' house, when she was young, she had felt the world was as full of possibilities as a shopper carrying a purse heavy with coin. Today, despite knowing life offered her few choices, Alyce felt that same sense of freedom and hopefulness.

The de Jongs lived in Colegate on the other side of the river Wensum. Here the streets were as busy as any other part of Norwich, the muffled thud of looms in the background and sounds that brought back Alyce's childhood vividly— conversations in French, and Dutch and in gentle, accented English.

A row of windows ran along the upper storey of the de Jongs' house. Alyce stood on the well-scrubbed doorstep and knocked at the door. It was opened almost immediately by a maid in a white apron and coif.

'I am looking for *Mevrouw* de Jong,' Alyce said.

'*Wie is het?*'

Tears welled in Alyce's eyes at the sound of the voice.

'*Een dame,*' the maid called back into the house.

A young matron, a toddling child's hand in hers, came up behind the maid. 'Alyce,' she cried. 'Come in.' She called over her shoulder, '*Moeder, het is Elsje, Elsje Bradley.*'

As Alyce stepped through the doorway, the young woman grasped Alyce's hand and kissed her on the cheek.

Alyce struggled against her tears. 'Marieke, it is good to see you.'

Marieke moved back and her mother threw plump arms around Alyce. '*Elsje, lieveling.*' She pulled Alyce's head down to kiss her.

'Good day, *Mevrouw* de Jong.'

'I am an Englishwoman now.' Grietje de Jong brushed a tear from Alyce's cheek. 'Everyone calls me *Mistress* de Jong.' She smiled at Alyce, her own eyes glistening. '*Mijn verloren dochter is teruggekeerd.*'

Alyce looked at her, puzzled.

'*Elsje,*' she chided, 'you have forgotten your Dutch.'

'I was never very good, and it has been so long.'

'*Ja,* far too long. Now into the parlour with you.'

'Katrien. Cake and beer for our guest,' she called to the maid. '*De taart die ik vanochtend gemaakt heb.*'

Ushered into the neat parlour with its scrubbed floor and sparse but solid furniture, Alyce was hardly seated when Grietje began, 'What have you been doing, *Elsje*? 'Tis ten years since we saw you last.'

'Twelve years, *Moeder*.' Marieke lowered herself into her chair and pulled the child onto her lap.

Alyce reached over and shook the child's fingers. She had the same rich blond hair and golden complexion as her mother.

She smiled shyly at Alyce and buried her face against Marieke's shoulder.

'What is her name?'

'Elisabeth, and she is nearly two. Then there's Margriet who is four and Robert is five.'

'Robert?' Alyce raised her eyebrows.

'It is my husband's father's name. Do you remember George Thompson? He was an apprentice weaver then.'

Alyce shook her head.

'I thought I never stopped talking about him.' Her cheek dimpled as she smiled at Alyce. 'Well, I married him.'

The maid came in with a tray, and Grietje took over, setting out the plates and beakers. She cut a large slice of cake and placed it in front of Alyce. 'Eat up, I'll wager you've not tasted anything as good since you were last here.'

'For certain.' Alyce smiled.

'And who did you marry?' Grietje sat herself opposite Alyce.

'I did not marry.'

Marieke said, 'Alyce went to serve a great lady.'

'That's right.' Grietje nodded. 'But there was that apprentice of your father's, Robin something? He had his eyes on you.'

'You noticed that?'

'*Moeder* notices the smallest thing if there is the chance of a marriage.'

'Is he married?' Grietje asked.

'If he were the last man on earth, I would not consider him.'

'I remember now.' The older woman's eyes twinkled. 'You could not abide him.'

'Who is this?' A tall man with a square ruddy face and thinning blond hair poked his head around the door.

'*Elsje* Bradley.' Pieter de Jong smiled. 'It is a delight to see you.'

Alyce made to stand but he said, 'Do not get up.' He bent down, kissing Alyce on the cheek.

'And how many do you have?' he asked as he ruffled the hair of the child on Marieke's knee.

'I am not married, Master de Jong.'

'What a waste. A fine woman like you should be married.' He raised a sandy eyebrow. 'You want a husband? We have a nephew. He is around thirty, sober, hardworking, a printer.'

Alyce smiled. Here in this house, she did not mind what was said. The de Jongs had treated Alyce as if she were their own daughter, never finding any lack in her.

He cut himself a slice of cake. 'I'll leave you ladies to your talk.' He smiled again at Alyce as he left the room.

'*Elsje* could be the godmother,' Grietje said. '*Ja?*'

'Ay.' Marieke spread her hands over the swelling obvious through the folds of her loose gown. 'Would you be this one's godmother, Alyce?'

'It would please me greatly.' Alyce smiled as an unexpected surge of happiness swept through her. 'When is it due?'

'Early in November.'

'Not so far away.'

'Nay,' Marieke said.

The soft thud of the looms filled the silence in the room.

'And what was life like with this great lady?' Marieke asked.

Alyce took a deep breath. 'Not very different from life here. Sewing, candle and soap-making, brewing, cheese-making. The seasons brought different tasks.' She picked up her beaker and sipped, unwilling to meet Marieke's discerning gaze. 'More sewing in winter, storing the harvest at the end of summer, salting the meat, preserving fruit. It was a large manor in the middle of the countryside, more than halfway from Lincoln to York. There was reading from godly books and prayer and sermons. And, on occasions, music.'

'Little time for your own concerns,' Marieke shook her head. 'And we imagined you had gone off to a life of singing and dancing, banquets and fine gowns.'

Alyce gave a bitter laugh. 'It was a sober household.'

'And the lady herself?'

'Lady Faulconer was a very learned old woman and could discourse on many subjects. She was a fine distiller too. I learnt much from her.'

'But what of the young men?' Grietje grinned. 'Every girl needs young men to court her.'

'There was no one young in the household except for the housemaids and, occasionally, Lady Faulconer's nephew. Every summer he would arrive with a small retinue and brought her news of the Queen and the court.'

'Was he handsome? Did he pay you *court*? Or any of his men?'

Alyce frowned down at her hands. Marieke placed her hand over Alyce's. '*Moeder*, you are such a matchmaker.'

'But you want to marry, *Elsje*? You could be as happy as Marieke here,' Grietje threw her arms open, 'or even me. You want me to ask this nephew of mine?'

'You… you should speak to Father first. He too thinks I should be married.'

Marieke rolled her eyes. 'I warn you Alyce, you will be married by Christmas if *Moeder* takes on the role of matchmaker.'

3

Alyce surveyed the stillroom, satisfied with yesterday's work. She had dusted away cobwebs, scrubbed down the benches and the table at the centre of the room, sorted through old jars of crumbling salves and boxes of well-desiccated herbs, discarding what was beyond use. She had washed the collection of bottles, pots and bowls as well as the mortars and pestles and the two stills, carefully drying and reconnecting them when she was finished. As she worked, Alyce had allowed her mind to touch on the idea of marriage. By eighteen, she had concluded it was a path she would never have the chance to follow, yet another punishment that came with her banishment to Dalstead. But now, considering the prospect coolly, she recognised its benefits—with the right husband, she would have some say in her life and a real purpose. It would, no doubt, take time for anyone to show an interest, but while she waited, she could keep busy at the activities she enjoyed best.

And now she would give in to the temptation she had been resisting since her return—she would go into her father's shop. There would be tasks with which she could assist without offending her father's sense of his daughter's proper role in life.

The shop was busy. At one end of the room, an apprentice weighed silken thread for a well-dressed woman accompanied by a female attendant nearly as fashionably dressed as her mistress. Another woman, her hat bedecked with dyed feathers, marched up to Robert Chapman. The feathers bobbed as she launched into a complaint. Her serving man dumped a bundle of heavy cloth onto the counter in front of Chapman. At the other table, Wat carefully cut cloth under the watchful eye of another journeyman.

Alyce's father walked back from the door, having bade farewell to his customer. 'And how may I help you, Mistress? Cloth for another gown, perhaps?'

'Thank you, Father, but I am more than satisfied with what I have.' Alyce glanced around the shop. 'Had I been born Alan, not Alyce, I would have been apprenticed and by now would be expanding your business here or in some other town.'

'I have no doubt you would, but you were born a girl.'

'Girls sometimes are apprenticed.'

'The Guild would not have countenanced it. And even if it had, it was not the path for any daughter of mine.'

'All this work,' she gestured towards the room, 'and in the end it will come to naught.'

'I hope for grandsons. And seeing Isabel has not obliged, you can do your part.'

'So these marriage plans, they are for your benefit?'

Her father opened his mouth and stammered, for once lost for words.

Alyce grinned at him. 'Robert needs your help over there.'

The woman in the feathered hat had taken several pieces of cloth from the bundle and laid them on the table. She stabbed her finger at various places on the cloth where she perceived flaws in the weave. Chapman glanced over towards Alyce's father.

Her father shook his head as he moved off. 'Not Alan, I would never call a son Alan.'

A tall gentleman strode in through the door from the street. Alyce, with the eyes of a mercer's daughter, took in the brocade of his doublet, the bright silk showing through his slashed sleeves, the ruff edged with fine gold-threaded lace, the paned trunk hose, the leather boots. He was the sort of customer her father courted. With his dark face and crooked nose, it was clear the rapier at his side was no affectation.

Alyce looked towards the apprentices, the journeymen, her father—all were still busy with customers. She stepped towards him. 'Sir, may I assist you?'

'Ay, I am here to see Hugh Bradley.' Although he was not discourteous, it was clear he took Alyce to be a servant.

'If you will wait a moment, I will let him know. He is with another customer at present.'

But her father had seen his visitor, and, after directing Chapman to replace the woman's cloth, he excused himself and came over. The men greeted each other warmly.

Her father beckoned Alyce forward. 'Master Granville, may I introduce my daughter? Alyce was a waiting woman to the late Lady Faulconer at Dalstead.'

'Mistress Bradley?' Granville looked to Alyce and bowed. 'Forgive me, I did not recognise you.' He smiled. 'You were little more than a girl when I met you last.'

Alyce curtsied and gave a weak smile in acknowledgment. As the men walked away through the shop to the stairs leading to her father's office, she frowned, irritated by the unaccountable flush spreading up her face.

Thomas Granville. She remembered who he was—unjustly called a pirate by some, he was a privateer sailing under letters of marque, authorised by the Queen to attack England's enemies. He had been younger when she had last seen him and far more handsome. But her strongest memory was of his graciousness. On the few occasions he had visited her father those years ago, he had always greeted her, and Grandmother too. And he had paid Grandmother the courtesy that was her due, unlike many in the merchant community. Grandmother may have been beneath their notice but their wives and daughters had come, as had so many others, to the garden gate and, with whisperings and lowered heads, had explained their woes to her. No one left without comfort of some sort, even if it was nothing more than soothing words or a bowl of soup to warm an empty stomach.

Alyce stared around her. Her father was right: even had he been willing to allow her a place in his business, the Mercers' Guild would have had something to say about it. As she turned to leave, a woman approached her not only wanting help with choosing cloth but advice on how to cut it to achieve the effect she wanted. When Alyce had finished with her, another woman stood waiting, although both Chapman and Wat were free. Alyce wondered if her father would permit her to work in the shop if she did no selling, but only offered advice on trimmings, and cutting and sewing.

Chapman strolled over as her customer left. 'It seems I have competition.'

'What do you mean?' Alyce snapped.

'The man with your father.'

Alyce stared at him. This was the first time Robert Chapman had spoken to her since her return, yet he acted as if he were continuing a conversation from yesterday. That yesterday, twelve years ago, he had pressed her against the storeroom wall and tried to kiss her, murmuring lewd suggestions of what he *knew* she wanted from him.

'Do you not have work to do? If there are no customers, there is always plenty that needs to be done in the storeroom.'

'Only if you intend to assist me,' he said, the hint of a smile on his lips.

Alyce had seen her mother do it—straight back, tall neck, staring along her nose as if she had before her some miserable form of creeping life.

'Do not give yourself airs, Alyce,' he laughed. 'You are not your mother.'

Alyce stiffened at the presumption in his use of her Christian name.

'I hear your father is casting about for a husband for you, but plenty remember your vicious tongue. Few will be as willing as I am to overlook it. I may be the only one to offer.'

Alyce gasped. If he were the last man on earth... No! Marriage to Robert Chapman would be her worst nightmare.

'There is much to recommend me—I know your father's business well, and we are related.'

She found her voice. 'So distant it counts for naught.'

'It will count,' he smirked, 'when he begs me to take you off his hands.'

'I would drown myself in the Wensum first.'

A cough, or a stifled laugh, brought their dispute to an end. A wiry man in his mid-twenties stood not more than a yard from them. By the glitter of his eyes, he had heard most of the exchange.

'May I assist you, sir?' Alyce asked, relieved to turn away from Chapman.

'I seek Master Thomas Granville.' He bowed. 'Kit Watkins, his man.'

'He is with my father. You may wait...' Laughter carried

from the rear of the shop. 'Ah, here they are now.'

Chapman walked away to the street door to greet Goodwife Hall. He guided her in and gave her his full attention as she fussed over a length of dark brocade.

Granville bowed to Alyce as he passed, his eyes flickering over her. 'Good morrow, Mistress Bradley.'

'Good morrow, sir.' She inclined her head in answer.

Her father watched Granville leave and crossed his arms, a satisfied gleam in his eyes. 'Thomas Granville commented you had grown to be a fine woman.'

'Did he? And what did he mean by that?'

'Take a compliment for what it is.'

'But things are rarely as they seem.'

~

The goblet of sack stood untouched in front of Thomas Granville as he waited for William Sutton the elder, knight and master grocer of Norwich, to get to his point.

Sutton sat at the other side of the desk, the image of a toad who had swallowed its hoard of gold.

'From what I heard, this last venture of Sir Francis Drake's paid very well. And there is a fortune out there to be made from Spain.'

So that was it. 'There is far more to it than plunder,' Granville replied. 'What we do is to England's glory, to remind the King of Spain that we are an enemy to be feared.'

'Ay, ay,' Sutton said, impatient. 'I hear you are preparing for another voyage yourself.'

'Where did you hear that?' Granville fought down his rising irritation.

'I have ears.' Sutton smirked. 'The word was everywhere— you were no sooner on dry land than you were scurrying about seeking investors for your new venture.'

Granville watched Sutton, noting the man was rushing, not choosing his words with care. He continued to sit, silent.

Sutton cleared his throat. 'I am offering to finance this privateering venture for you.'

Granville leant back in his chair. 'I have all the investors I need.'

'But think, anything I supply is something you do not have to provide for yourself.'

'You forget a goodly portion of any prize is due to the Crown.'

'Bah! There is plenty to go around.'

'There is an element of chance—not all ventures pay.'

Sir William laughed, his heavy gold chain catching the light with the movement of his well-padded chest. 'When have any of your undertakings not turned a profit?'

Granville clenched his jaw.

'If you are not interested this time,' Sir William continued, 'I can obtain letters of marque for the next. No need to scratch around for an excuse to make it legal. And you would have control of the enterprise.'

Granville continued to stare at Sutton. It would be as well to offer the man a few crumbs. 'If, as you say, you have letters of marque and are willing to fully back a venture, I can suggest the names of a couple of captains who might be interested.'

Colour flooded Sutton's face. 'No. I want you.'

Twenty years ago, he would have been across the desk and had the cur by the throat. Age and experience had its benefits. Granville slowly rose from his seat. 'I am not for sale.'

Sutton slammed his fist down on his desk. 'You owe me this.'

Granville's eyes travelled slowly from Sutton's clenched fist to his florid face. 'I owe you nothing.'

'You damn well do, man.' Sutton pushed himself away from his desk. He glared up at Granville. 'You take me in, and I will consider the account between us settled, else I will see you hanged for piracy.'

'You have tried already, Sutton. And failed.'

'It was piracy.'

'I sailed with the *Watergeuzen* under Willem van der Marck and fought at the Battle on the Zuiderzee against the forces of Spain. When I came home, I found that, rather than being praised for fighting England's enemies, I faced charges of piracy brought by someone who had been sitting in comfort, growing fat counting his coins.'

'Sea Beggars seized a ship carrying a cargo of sugar of mine worth thousands of pounds.'

'I was not a captain with my own ship, but a mere fighting man and I was only ever involved in the capture of Spanish ships. For me to have had anything to do with the capture of a ship carrying your cargo, you must have been trading with our enemies.'

'Do not be ridiculous,' Sutton blustered. 'There were Water... Waterger... Sea Beggars, who were nothing but pirates, you cannot deny that.'

'A handful, perhaps, in the same way not all grocers are honest men.'

Sutton glared at Granville and said through gritted teeth, 'I know it was you.'

'You do not. You had no proof. And, fortunately for me, the courts require proof, not mere accusation.' Granville walked to the door.

He turned back to face Sutton. 'It is clear you have not forgotten, *Sir* William,' he placed sneering emphasis on the title, 'and neither have I.'

Sutton's face mottled purple. 'You will find it difficult to trade in this town.'

'I do not trade, merely dispose. And Norwich is not the centre of the world.'

'I have a far reach,' Sutton spat, the venom almost frothing from his lips.

'Do you?' Granville lifted an eyebrow. The man was an overweening cur. 'I will bid you good day, *Sir* William.'

He strode out through the shop, the sound of a slamming door echoing through the building behind him.

~

Alyce's father returned to his office without a backwards look, so Alyce lingered, exchanging pleasantries with customers, helping to select cloth from the fustians and damasks, silks, taffetas and brocades. Chapman glanced at her occasionally, his eyes narrowed, but for the most part he kept his attention on his customer, an imperious lady ordering cloth for her daughter's wedding. Wat grinned at Alyce as he carried over yet another bolt of cloth for Chapman's customer.

As the crush eased, Alyce knew it was time to go back to the parlour and return to her own sewing. She wandered into the storeroom for one last look around that treasure house of colour and texture.

She sighed with a contentment she had not felt in years. Despite her father's plans, she had, in the few days she had been home, begun a pattern of life doing those things she enjoyed best—working in the stillroom, ordering the medicinal garden, reading, playing her lute and working with beautiful cloth. And, in that moment of hopefulness, she thought that perhaps her father would find her a husband who would value her for what she was.

'Have you given further thought to my suggestion?'

Alyce started at the voice behind her. She turned and, straightening her shoulders, tried to step around Robert Chapman.

He blocked her way, leaning his arm against the stacked bolts of fabric.

'What suggestion was that?'

'That I ask your father for your hand.' He smiled.

Panic churned in her stomach. 'You jest, Robert Chapman.' She had refused, from the time he had arrived as an apprentice, to use his familiar name, Robin.

She tried to move her way past him, but again he blocked her.

'I am serious.' His good humour faded.

'I will not consider it. Go back into the shop—there may be customers waiting.'

'I have more important business here, Alyce.'

'You forget your position. I am Mistress Bradley to you.'

'You are no better than I am, *Mistress*,' he hissed the word. 'Your father will get no better offer. You are no young maid,' he sneered, 'and you have a reputation.'

'A reputation for what?'

'Witchcraft.' His eyes narrowed. 'Like your grandmother.'

'She was no witch, you fool, just an old woman who dealt in minor ailments.'

'Plenty remember her as one who made potions and spells to cast out babies and to make men quick with desire. No doubt she taught you her tricks.'

'Your mind is a cesspit.'

Chapman backed Alyce against stacked bolts of cloth. 'You have not changed.' He pressed himself against her, his breath hot on her face. 'Why else were you loitering in the shop, playing at a man's job, if not to lure me in here?'

She struggled as he gripped her arms, his fingers pressing into her flesh.

'Your behaviour is a scandal.' Alyce's voice was shrill with rising panic.

'Do not play the innocent with me—pretending reluctance to mask your lust.'

'You disgust me.' She feigned an authority she did not feel. 'Let. Me. Go.'

Chapman clamped his lips on hers; his tongue battered against her gritted teeth.

Drawing on all her strength, Alyce stretched her head back from Chapman and brought her knee up hard against his thigh. Surprised, he loosened his grip, and Alyce twisted away from him.

She fled up the stairs into the house, past her mother. She called to Alyce, surprise in her voice, but Alyce rushed on.

She sagged heavily on the end of her bed, breathing fast, as her dreams crashed around her. She could not go back into the shop. Her presence would only encourage Chapman's fantasies. She knew there was no point in telling her parents. It was her word against his—the well-mannered, godly, diligent journeyman against the plain, graceless girl with the unruly tongue. And worse, her father was sure to see it as some form of love play just like Chapman did—the only possible reason she could have for entering the shop was to attract Robert Chapman's attention.

Angrily, she willed herself not to cry. Had she not learnt that it was foolish to harbour dreams?

4

Thomas Granville sat at the head of the table next to Alyce's father. Isabel, who had called in to see their mother, had stayed for dinner and appeared to be enthralled by Granville's tales of the strange places he had visited. He had been away thirteen months, sailing with Sir Francis Drake on his Great Expedition to the Americas.

Instead of the rapt attention Alyce normally gave to such tales, she was barely listening, sick at the thought of Robert Chapman's plans. She dared not look along to where Chapman sat with the apprentices and household servants. Watkins, Granville's man, was among them, jesting and leading the cheerful conversation at that end of the table.

When the meal finished, the family moved into the parlour.

'Would you like to hear my daughters sing, Master Granville?' Alyce's mother asked.

'I am sure Master Granville has business he would rather discuss with Father,' Alyce said.

Granville smiled politely. 'That would be delightful, Mistress Bradley. There will be time enough for business later.'

Alyce glanced at him. He was as well-mannered as she remembered. She lifted the lute from the settle beneath the window and began to tune it.

Isabel came and stood beside her. 'Play "The Lowest Trees". You remember it?'

'Ay,' Alyce said, 'I remember the tune, but not the words.'

Alyce played while Isabel sang. She kept her sight on her lute, letting the music fill her mind, pushing all else away.

The firmest faith is found in fewest words;
The turtles cannot sing, and yet they love.

Alyce looked up from her instrument straight into Granville's eyes. Her breathing paused. Her skilful fingers plucked a discordant note. She forced her attention back to her lute, fighting the heat rising in her face.

True hearts have ears and eyes, no tongues to speak;
They hear and see, and sigh, and then they break.

Isabel basked in the polite clapping and took her leave of her father and Granville. She linked arms with Alyce as the women left the room together.

She grinned. 'He was watching you.'

'Ay, he was.' Their mother smiled. 'You should return to the parlour, Alyce.'

'I have some distilling to do, Mother.'

'If you must.' Her mother frowned, exasperated. 'But go and take your leave of Master Granville.'

Granville and her father were deep in conversation and did not notice Alyce's return. Her curiosity stirred by Granville's topic, she slipped onto a stool by the fireplace. The distilling could wait a while.

'Ay, we called in at Sir Walter Raleigh's colony on Roanoke, an island off the coast of the Americas. Their food supplies were running low, and although Sir Francis offered to replenish them, most of the men preferred to return with us to England. We brought back plants from there not seen before in England, among them a roundish root that boiled makes good meat called *potato* and a medicinal herb the Spanish call *tobacco*. Dried, it can be swallowed as smoke and is reputed to preserve the health.'

Her father stood to refill their goblets of wine and frowned. 'I did not see you return, Alyce.'

What had they been discussing before that he should frown at her presence? Ignoring her father's obvious displeasure, she asked Granville, 'Were there other plants with medicinal uses?'

'I am afraid, Mistress, I did not take much notice of these things. I did hear speak of a sweet-smelling wood called *sassafras* that is reputed to cure many diseases.'

'I would there was something for those who leave seeking a cure until it is almost too late.' Alyce sighed. 'I helped Lady Faulconer tend her husbandmen and tenants. Some would leave wounds, even cuts from scythes and pitchforks, until they had begun to putrefy, injuries that new made would have been easy to heal. Left so long, they were often fatal.'

Granville nodded. 'My mother found the same. She would

treat tenants when they needed it. The worst were those who resorted first to some aged woman who applied skin of toad or gave them a potion to be drunk only at the full moon or some such nonsense. By the time they came to her, the injury was beyond help.'

'Some old women are greatly skilled at healing, far better than doctors. And apothecaries will tell you certain herbs are best harvested at the full moon.'

'I have heard such but find it hard to credit.' He regarded Alyce, a crease of concentration between his brows. 'But I do know men can behave their worst when the moon is full. There may be truth in it.'

Aware of her father's deepening scowl, Alyce rose from her stool. 'If you will excuse me, sir, I must go—the stillroom calls.'

Granville stood. 'You are skilled at distilling mistress?'

'Only the simples, syrups and waters used in every household. I learnt a great deal both from Lady Faulconer and from my grandmother.'

'I remember your grandmother, a most gentle person.'

Alyce's face softened at the memory, and she smiled openly. 'That she was.'

Granville bowed to her. 'Mistress Bradley, it has been most pleasant to meet you again.'

Alyce smiled politely as she curtsied to him. She turned away, aware that his gaze followed her as she crossed the room.

~

Whistling cheerfully, Robin Chapman strode along the darkening lane to a row of narrow houses. The smell of cooking wafted past him as he pushed open the door of the end house. His mother, hovering at the fire, looked up as he came in.

'Ah, Robin, supper will not be long. I have pie for you tonight.'

Robin undid his cloak and threw it over the back of a chair. He sat, stretching his legs out beneath the table. The room was pleasingly warm after the brisk chill of the evening.

'A mug of beer before you eat?'

'I'll get it,' he said.

He returned from the larder with a jug and poured himself a

full beaker.

'You appear well-pleased with something. Has Hugh Bradley finally asked you to act as his agent in Italy?'

'Nay, Mother.' He fought down a flicker of irritation. 'Not yet—perhaps in time.'

His mother carried the tray to the table and left the pie to cool. 'What, then? I know you have a secret.'

'It is too early to say, but if things fall out as I plan, you will be assured of comfort in your old age.'

Understanding lit in his mother's sharp eyes. 'I believe you are the husband that one needs.' She carefully lifted the pie from the tray onto a wooden plate. 'And that business of right should come to you—the life, the work you have given to it. A son could not have done more.'

Robin took a long draught from his beaker and leant back in his chair, his thoughts returning to the storeroom and the fire in Alyce Bradley's eyes. Why did she play these games? It had been the same twelve years ago—pretending she was interested in cloth, lurking in the storeroom, feigning disgust and defiance when he pushed her against the wall. Had he persisted, she would have given in to him, and there would have been no sin if they were immediately betrothed. But she had left suddenly and he had lost his chance. He had worked hard for Bradley, and he knew he was valued. For certain, Bradley would not object to an offer for his daughter.

He muttered a swift grace to himself when his mother placed the plate in front of him and set to the pie with relish.

'I was right, was I not?' She nodded. 'There was no profit in getting too involved with that maid of Maude Middleton's.'

Robin tried to answer, spluttering, his mouth full of food. 'Ay, Mother.' He supposed she was right. But Susan had never feigned disgust, and her eyes had lit up whenever she had seen him. But her father was not a wealthy mercer, and that had set his mother against her from the start.

~

Granville stared through the open shutters into the yard below. The sun was not long risen, dew glistening on clumps of grass against the stable wall, yet the inn yard was a hive of activity:

barrels rolled out from the shed, horses on the move, two maids on their way from the brewhouse, the smell of baking bread on the air.

Behind Granville, Watkins moved around the room packing their saddlebags. Granville turned from the window. 'A fruitful evening, Watkins?'

'Ay, sir. The fellows in the taproom at the White Swan tattle like old women, especially after a drink or two.'

Granville leant back against the windowsill, his arms crossed.

'It seems young Master Sutton is keen to be involved in any moneymaking scheme.'

'I doubt that would please his father.'

'A few expenses his father may not know of—ladies to keep in trinkets, a wife to keep happy when he is otherwise pleasurably engaged.'

'Not unlike his father.' Granville's lip curled with distaste. 'Although, it sounds as if the son relies on charm for his seductions rather than the force preferred by the father.'

'The elder Sutton has gone from strength to strength since he was knighted a couple of years back. Recently, a ship carrying a cargo he had invested in was lost in bad weather. To hear him tell it, they say, the storm was conjured by the Spanish. Very keen to strike a patriotic blow.'

'Which, no doubt, would make good his losses. And what of Bradley?'

'No talk of any difficulties, business expanding. His daughter is home not much more than a week and already he is looking for a husband for her. Large dowry offered. Most think that journeyman of his, Chapman, is a likely chance. Chapman appears to think so himself, though I doubt Mistress Bradley would want the match.'

Granville raised an eyebrow.

'He was trying some love play in the shop. You should have heard her take her tongue to him. She has plenty of spirit.'

Granville frowned. 'Alyce Bradley had the reputation for a waspish tongue. Glad to hear it was not beaten out of her by old Lady Faulconer.'

He turned away and stared back into the yard. 'Is his main

concern to find a son-in-law to carry on the business or a husband for his daughter?' he murmured. The woman he had met yesterday appeared sober, intelligent, hardworking and deliberately unassuming. Not the sort to sit in idleness and allow her head to be turned by a handsome face whispering sugared words into her ear. But beneath the modest exterior, he sensed there was much more. And, of course, there was the dowry.

'Watkins, we will stay a day or two longer.'

5

Alyce walked into the parlour, surprised to see Isabel sitting by the window, staring down into the garden.

She turned in her seat, smiling happily. 'Good morrow, Alyce. Mother asked me to help with cutting out your new gowns.' She ran her eye over Alyce's gown. 'That gown is pretty, but Mother said—'

'I came back with next to naught,' Alyce finished for her. She brushed her hand down the moss green worsted of the skirt. 'Mother had it put away. I did not take it with me to Dalstead.' She took a bolt of cloth from the chest in the corner of the parlour and spread it on the table. 'It fits well enough, though it is a mite too short, but I am not going anywhere today.'

Isabel took out the sewing box their mother had stored in the chest. 'Mother should get a tailor to do this for you. You do not want to spend your whole time sewing.'

'I like to be busy.' Alyce straightened the cloth and took the measuring stick from the box.

'Did you know,' Isabel handed Alyce a piece of chalk to mark the cloth, 'old Sir Henry Crabbe is looking for a new wife?'

'Sir Henry Crabbe,' Alyce's eyes widened in horror, 'but he must be ninety at least.'

'Seventy-five. And he has buried three wives.'

'But he is old and fat and bald and…' she shuddered, '… and hideous.'

Isabel giggled. 'He is indeed.'

'Father would not…?' Alyce stood rigid, the chalk crumbling in her hand. 'I would rather die.'

'Of course they would not. Mother and Father do want someone you can be content with.' She smiled brightly. 'Would Thomas Granville do?'

There was something about Granville. Perhaps it was that he was courteous and one of the few men she had met who listened when she spoke.

'He was definitely watching you yesterday, and it was more than that he was entranced by your lute playing.'

'I think it was more the discordant notes I plucked,' Alyce lied. He had been watching her, but she doubted it was as simple as Isabel imagined.

'He is old and not so pretty any longer. And there are the numerous women he has debauched. Hundreds, if the stories are all true.'

Alyce did not want to believe that of him. 'Not all stories are true, Isabel.'

'Perhaps not all.' Isabel shrugged. 'But tales always begin with some grain of truth.' She frowned, her eyelashes fluttering with thought. 'Well, what about Robin Chapman?'

Alyce groaned.

'He is rather handsome. I wonder why he is not married. He has only kept company with one girl for any length of time, Maude Middleton's maid, Susan, and that ended a few months ago.' Her eyes twinkled. 'Perhaps he's been keeping himself for you.'

Alyce glared at her. 'You do realise Chapman believes he will be the only one to offer for my hand?' She blinked against threatening tears. 'He said I would get no better offer.'

'He what?' Isabel gaped. 'The presumption of him! The only person to benefit would be Robin himself.' Colour flooded her face. 'Be assured, no matter what Father might think, Mother would not stand for it. Nor would I. I will have something to say to Father, and Robin Chapman too, if such a ridiculous proposal is taken seriously.'

Isabel put her arms around Alyce, pulling her close. 'It was a foolish jest on my part.'

Alyce gave herself up to comfort and laid her head on her sister's shoulder.

'You are worthy of a man of far higher standing than Robin. And remember, Father said you would decide.'

Alyce moved away from her and dropped into a chair. 'Service in a pleasant household would be easier.'

'But you must want to marry—all women do.'

'I do not know that I do. When I was young, I supposed I

would. Now I no longer care.'

'Well,' Isabel screwed up her face, 'let us pretend. If we lived in a perfect world, what would the husband of your dreams be?'

'I abandoned foolish dreams a long time ago.'

'I do not believe you.' Isabel pulled out a chair at the side of the table. 'We all dream of something. I dream of children. Alyce,' she lowered her voice, 'I have a secret. I will tell you if you promise not to tell a single soul, not even Mother.'

'I promise,' Alyce said warily.

'I think I am with child. Every morning I awaken feeling queasy.' Her face glowed with happiness. 'I have been married nearly three years, and it has never been like this before. I have hoped I was with child many times but always, whether it is a few days or a week later, the bleeding comes.' Her lashes glistened. 'But now it has been two whole months and you are here.'

'What difference do I make?'

'You have Grandmother's gifts.'

'Isabel,' Alyce spoke slowly, 'Grandmother had no special gifts. She knew much of herbs and healing. The help she offered was no different from the apothecary or a housewife tending to the physic of her family.'

'That is not what most people say.'

A shiver ran down Alyce's back. 'Most people are wrong.' The sight of her grandmother's friend dancing on the gallows was one that would never leave her. No doubt some had thought Bridget Mason had special gifts too.

Isabel closed her eyes and sobbed. 'You'll not help me?'

Alyce sprang up and folded Isabel into her arms. 'I will do all I can to help you but I have no knowledge of births and babies, and no special gifts. I follow recipes that anyone can.'

Isabel's sobs slowly subsided, but she continued to sniffle.

Alyce stared at her. She had not considered the lack of children or what that meant to Isabel. She hardly dared ask, 'Is Will unkind?'

'Not at all.' Isabel smiled and blinked to clear her tears. 'Will is wonderful, but what is the point of a woman's life without children? Now I will no longer be useless. And Sir William will be delighted. He wants grandsons, many of them.' She stood up and kissed Alyce on the cheek. 'And with you by my side, I have nothing to worry me. Now let us cut out these gowns.'

As she stepped away, she looked Alyce up and down. 'Please do not be offended, but if you took a little trouble, you would look pleasing. Throw away that coif and show your hair, paint your face. You are not willowy, but many men like buxom women.'

'Janet Wilson!' they laughed together.

'You should see her now. And her husband is thin as a stick. I wonder how...' Isabel giggled. 'I cannot discuss that with you, being a maid. See, if you were married, we would have much more to talk about.' She grinned at the look Alyce gave her.

'Isabel!' Alyce shook her head, amused, hoping this was a new beginning.

~

The afternoon was quiet, as if the town were slumbering in the summer sun. A basket of lavender lay on the path behind Alyce. She had stopped her harvesting and knelt to uproot a patch of weeds she had missed when she put the garden in order earlier in the week. She drew satisfaction from the pattern of the plants, the feel of the rich earth between her fingers. With the buzzing of a bee over the lavender blooms, the warmth of the sun, the cooing of pigeons on the garden wall, Alyce drifted into a thoughtless reverie as she weeded. She looked up with a start as the hair on the back of her neck rose.

Robert Chapman stood not a foot from her.

'Ah, Alyce, on your knees before me—will you now beg me to marry you?' He gazed around him. 'This garden makes a pretty setting for a proposal.'

She got up, brushing the dirt from her hands, and stepped away from him. 'Why do you persist with this nonsense?'

'Love makes us all speak nonsense, does it not?' He smiled as his dark eyes slowly travelled up towards her face. 'I have raised the matter with your father this afternoon. He sees great advantage in your marriage to me.'

Alyce stood rigid, panic sparking through her.

'The business will continue beyond his lifetime and remain

within the family.'

She squared her shoulders. 'I will never agree, and Father says nothing will be done without my consent.'

Chapman moved closer and caught her hand in his. 'Put off this pretended coyness—even your father sees through it.' He pulled her to him. 'It is time we behaved like true lovers.'

'No!' Alyce wrenched her hand free, jerking away from him. Cold sweat trickled between her shoulder blades. 'If you force me to be your wife, your life will be a misery. You will fear I have poisoned every mouthful you swallow.' Her voice rose, edged with panic. 'You will not know a moment's peace from the moment you bind me to you. If you even think of touching me, your manhood will wither.'

Chapman's face contorted. He drew his hand back and struck her hard. 'You foul witch.'

Alyce reeled and stumbled backwards onto the garden bed.

Chapman strode towards the house, pushing past Eliza, Alyce's mother's maid, who stood open-mouthed at the door.

Eliza ran to Alyce. 'Mistress, are you hurt?'

Alyce was on her feet, dusting leaves and broken twigs from her skirt. 'Look, a branch is broken from the rosemary.'

'He struck you. I'll get the Mistress.'

Alyce grabbed Eliza by the wrist. 'No. Please,' she pleaded. 'There is no need.'

Eliza pressed her lips together.

'Dust down my skirt for me, will you?' Alyce's voice quavered.

From behind Alyce, Eliza said, 'I do not know what is between you and Robin Chapman but this is not proper. You should tell your mother.'

'It was an accident. I tripped and fell.'

'There is a great red mark on your cheek. You are lucky he did not hit your nose.'

'It happened when I fell. I do not want you spreading fanciful tales.'

'I know what I saw.' Eliza shook her head, frowning. 'But, unlike some, I do know my place.'

'I feel ill, Eliza. Fetch me a drink, please.'

Alyce collapsed onto the stone bench beneath the pear tree and put her head in her hands. Her heart still pounding, she fought to keep her breathing even. What had she done? Had she cursed him? A curse was an evil thing. She had meant every word as she had said it, but surely, of themselves, words had no power except to frighten. All she had wanted was to frighten Robert Chapman away. But would he be frightened? Or would it only make him more determined to have her? And would her father take any notice of her wishes? Alyce bent forward and prayed for a way out of this mire.

6

A s Alyce rose from the table following the evening meal in
the hall, her father said, 'Come, sit with me.'

She followed him to the settle at the fireside and sat staring
into the flames of the small fire crackling against the chill of the
evening.

'I said last week I would seek marriage offers for you.'

'No!' Alyce sprang up from the seat, her voice carrying
across the room.

The servants clearing the table paused and watched.

'If I am of no use in this household, I will find a place
elsewhere.'

'What ails you, girl?' her father said, impatient. 'All women
want marriage.'

'I will not marry Robert Chapman.' Her worst days with
Lady Faulconer would be as nothing compared to life with
Chapman.

'Pah!' He scowled at her. 'You would do well to learn
humility—good women are led by their parents.'

She stared back at him—he did regard Chapman's offer as
worthy of consideration.

'You said I would have the final say.' Alyce's voice creaked. 'I
would rather die than marry him.' What evil had she done in life
to earn such a living hell?

'His is not the only offer.' He patted the seat beside him. 'Sit
down.'

Alyce gripped her hands tight in her lap, her knuckles white.
Who did he have in mind? Some aged man with grown children
who would despise her?

'Thomas Granville is interested too.'

She let go her breath. 'Ah, his interest would be the dowry.'

'He does want a wife. He needs someone to help his sister—
her health is failing. From what I know of him, I doubt he
would marry for money alone. And remember, all good

marriages involve property and all parties try to make the best they can of it. Granville insists you agree to this marriage.'

'How kind—a willing lamb to the slaughter.' Alyce knew she was being unfair to Granville. Many men would not care. And, she suspected, he was a far better man than common rumour suggested.

'And Robert does not care whether I am willing or not.'

'Robin has much to recommend him. He is diligent and hardworking and knows the business well.'

'And, in expectation of inheriting your business, the dowry would be much lower. Does the fact I despise him count for anything?'

'Solid marriages can be built from inauspicious beginnings.' Her father frowned. 'What do you want, a love match?'

'I am not a fool, Father,' Alyce said bitterly. 'I would like honour and respect. Even a mutual liking. And the freedom to make my own choice.'

'Such freedom would be fine if you had plenty to choose from.'

Alyce drew a sharp breath. It was hardly her fault she had spent her most marriageable years in what amounted to exile.

'Look,' his voice softened. 'Who has freedom in this life? Most of us do what we must. Love is no basis for marriage. Hard decisions need to be made. View marriage as a business decision—weigh the pros and cons. Love can grow later.'

'So it must be Thomas Granville? He is charming, but word is he has debauched hundreds of women. The wife of such a man would have no peace of mind.'

'God-a-mercy, girl. It is idle chatter. He is unmarried—you cannot expect a man to live like a monk.'

'Women are expected to.' All went to church. All heard the exhortations to continence. Nowhere did it say that these applied only to women. 'St Paul said—'

'I do not want to hear what St Paul said,' her father raised his voice over hers. 'We live in the world as it is where it is an entirely different matter for women, as you well know.'

'And if I do not accept his offer?'

'What future is there for you? In service for the rest of your days, a dependant in someone else's household. When your mother and I are gone, where would your home be then?'

'I could stay here…' She knew she could make a useful place for herself if only given the chance.

'Alyce. Have sense. As a single woman, even with wealth, you would be prey to every foul-tongued rumour-monger. They would have you a witch, a whore or worse.' He leant forward, his palms spread on his thighs. 'You must want a home of your own, children, a husband to keep you safe.'

'In a perfect world—'

'The present world is all we have. You have no choice but to consider these offers and decide on one.'

'Can we not wait? You said we would take our time.'

'And risk no one else offering?'

'You think so little of me?'

He jerked his head. 'If what is offered is good enough, grasp it. If you wait, hoping for a green girl's dream, you will end up with nothing.'

Alyce, her lips pressed tight, rose from the bench.

'Think on it tonight and tell me your decision on the morrow.'

'My decision? It appears you have made it for me,' Alyce said as she moved towards the stairs.

She slammed the door to the bedchamber and walked across the unlit room to the window. Her arms crossed tight, she watched as night claimed the garden. It was happening again— her father making fine assurances that meant nothing. He had told her, those years ago, it was her decision whether she serve in Lady Faulconer's household, yet, in the end, it had been made plain she had no other choice. It was no different now. When her father had said they would take their time and find someone who suited her, Alyce had not thought it meant she would be forced to accept the first man to offer. She had imagined she would be allowed time to determine whether he was someone she felt she could respect and live comfortably with. She understood her father considering Thomas Granville, a wealthy man with influential connections. But Robert Chapman? As Isabel had said, who would benefit from such a marriage other than Chapman? Her father would only consider him if he viewed Alyce as a burden to be disposed of as quickly as possible.

She slouched onto the stool beside the window. She had never understood Chapman's interest nor his persistence despite her protests. She had barely noticed him until the day he had pushed her against the storeroom wall, whispering that he knew she wanted him. Her rejection he had taken as encouragement, pressing against her and murmuring lewd comments whenever he caught her alone. She had confided in her grandmother, who had spoken to her father. He had laughed, saying it was the lad's way of showing his interest; in time he'd learn a courtlier approach. Her father had held Chapman in high regard, and she was the plain, disobedient girl with the unruly tongue. Had she not left when she did, she was certain Chapman would have forced himself on her and her father quickly organised their marriage. And now it was beginning again.

Alyce sighed heavily. She would have to accept Granville. She did not know what manner of man he was but hoped the courtesy he had shown her grandmother was a measure of his character. Granville's manor was in Northamptonshire, two counties away; marriage to him would take her far from Chapman.

A single tear rolled down her cheek. Despite what she had said to Isabel, she did have dreams. Barely formed dreams not of hair or eye colour, height or shoulder breadth, but of a man who would see her as a true helpmeet, a mercer who would recognise the skills she had with cloth and would welcome her as a blessing to his business. If such a man existed, he was worth the wait. And while she waited, she could make a useful place for herself in her father's business.

A green girl's foolish dreams.

~

Alyce paused at the head of the stairs and tugged at her new square-necked doublet. She brushed her hands across her partlet, borrowed from Isabel and of delicate embroidered lawn. Squaring her shoulders, she followed her mother down to the hall.

She was aware of Granville's scrutiny as soon as she entered the room. He watched her walk towards him. She could read nothing in his face and hoped her own face was as guarded.

He bowed courteously. 'Mistress Bradley, Alyce.'

Both women curtsied.

Her father stood beside Granville, looking exceedingly pleased with himself. 'Alyce, Master Granville wishes to speak with you.'

As her parents moved to the other end of the hall, Alyce said, 'Master Granville, please sit.' She indicated the settle beneath the window overlooking the street. She sat, ensuring a distance between them, and tried to ignore her parents pretending an intense conversation at the other end of the room.

'Alyce.' He paused.

For a ridiculous moment, Alyce thought that he was as uneasy as she was.

'As you are aware, your father has suggested that you would make a suitable wife. I am—'

Alyce's eyebrows shot up. 'My father suggested it?'

'Perhaps not so directly. He made me aware that he was seeking a husband for you. And I know that it is beyond time that I married. It seems to me, from our recent acquaintance, that we might make a reasonable match.'

It was not the most elegant, nor courtly, of proposals but Alyce knew that she would have despised him if he had claimed he was suddenly smitten with her.

As she sat in silence, Granville continued on, describing his manor and the household there.

Alyce lowered her eyes to her hands in her lap. So close, she found herself acutely aware of him as a man. Beneath the brocade doublet, pinked to show the bright silk lining, she could sense the strength of his broad shoulders, his muscular arms. Her downward gaze took in his strong hands crossed with scars, his broad wrists. She forced herself to look towards his face. He looked to be around forty. His eyes were grey, deep creases at the corners. Ruddy, weathered skin, dark close-cropped hair. His lips were firm, not fleshy, above his neatly trimmed beard. His nose was crooked; broken how many times? The flaws in his once-handsome face somehow made him more appealing.

Silence stretched out between them.

Granville was staring at her, an eyebrow raised. 'Do you consider your skills are sufficient to the task?' He spoke with the patience of someone repeating an obvious question, which no doubt he was.

'Skills?' Better to have him think she had misunderstood than that she had not been listening.

'The skills you learnt from the late Lady Faulconer in the management of a large manor.'

'I have never managed a manor.'

'But you learnt the necessary skills when you were with her.'

Alyce paused, blinking quickly. She supposed she had. 'Ay, though Lady Faulconer was always at my shoulder. Hers was an elderly household. When servants died, she had no wish to employ and train younger people to her ways, so over time many tasks fell to me.'

'You can cast accounts?'

'I can. My ledgers always balanced.'

'Ledgers can be made to balance even by those with poor arithmetic. Say you were to add one hundred and ninety-three to two hundred and fifteen?'

'The answer would be four hundred and eight.'

'And divide it by three.'

Alyce paused. 'One hundred and thirty-six.'

'Double it.'

'Two hundred and seventy-two.'

'Subtract ninety-seven.'

Alyce frowned with concentration. 'One hundred and seventy-five. Is that correct?'

'I have no idea,' Granville laughed, 'I gave up at the addition.'

Alyce grinned. In that moment the thought of a life spent in this man's company seemed a not unpleasant prospect.

'Were you involved with any aspects of the management of Lady Faulconer's manor lands?'

'Not to any great degree. My skills are in household management including ensuring meat was cured or salted for the winter, stores got in. I oversaw the dairy and cheesemaking. I can card and spin wool as well.'

'And you have your skills in physic. You would understand the workings of the body and the balancing of the humours.'

Alyce shook her head. 'My lady would not permit me to read any of her texts concerning that, nor would she explain it to me. She said it would be beyond my understanding. I use those remedies I know will work.'

'I will not stand in your way of reading whatever you wish, short of seditious tracts.'

'I would not know where to find such things.'

'It is safest not to know,' he said. 'Up until now, my manor and household have been managed by my sister, Cecily, but she is ailing and in need of care herself. My sister is very dear to me, and I would expect my wife to treat her as a sister.'

Alyce nodded, wondering what this sister was like, what she would be taking on beyond a husband she barely knew.

'We are agreed.'

Alyce said nothing in reply—he was not asking, merely stating an accepted fact.

Granville frowned. 'The proposition displeases you?'

'Nay, but marriage is a serious step. I have been given less than a day in which to make up my mind. I know nothing of you.'

'You are right. We both know each other only by repute. Would you like longer to consider the matter?'

It was not Granville's fault she was being hurried into marriage by her father. 'Nay, I believe even if we waited half a year, my decision would be the same.'

He stood. 'Your father and I will now beat out the details of the dowry and jointure. Once the documents are ready for signing, we can plight our troth.'

As Granville walked across the room towards her parents, Alyce thought they might as well have been discussing the sale of livestock. It would not have surprised her had he asked to examine her teeth and run his hands down her legs. But she supposed she had been measuring the flesh too—he was pleasingly tall, and although no longer truly handsome, she found him disconcertingly masculine. No matter how appealing he was to her eye, she knew little of his character. Alyce hoped the man she had agreed to marry would respect her and regard her as a helpmeet.

7

She is a dutiful woman,' Hugh Bradley said.
'I do not doubt it,' Granville replied. Bradley had said it several times during their negotiations over the past few days. It strengthened Granville's suspicion that Bradley had in some way pressed Alyce to agree to the marriage. As Alyce said it was her decision, he must take her at her word. All women wanted marriage, and she would benefit from marriage to him—it would make her a gentlewoman, a rise from the position of a merchant's daughter, no matter how wealthy. And he suspected she would have more freedom to order life to her pleasing than she did here or, most certainly, had during her years with Lady Faulconer. A woman who could last so long in that household was clearly not one given to lightness of morals.

'Ah, here they are.' Bradley walked across the room to the women—Alyce and her mother and sister. He took Alyce's hand and led her towards Granville.

Her face was unreadable. Granville could not tell how she felt, though, for certain, she was not filled with joy. Why should he expect it? He supposed it was his own vanity that wanted more from her.

He took her hand. It was warm and firm, not roughened, the fingernails neatly trimmed—the hand of a woman used to work but who cared for her appearance.

He whispered, 'You are sure of this?'

She nodded, but still he had the sense that she was not quite as willing as she claimed. Truth was it was too late to withdraw. He needed the dowry.

He walked with her to the table where the contract setting out the marriage settlement lay. He signed first, Alyce after him. She did not pause, but signed with a clear, steady hand.

They stood side by side and Granville spoke his promises to marry Alyce at a future time meet and convenient, to keep faithful to her, with her parents, her sister and Watkins the only witnesses. He doubted even Bradley's workers in the shop below knew what was happening. This was in every way unlike the last time he was betrothed. That had been witnessed by dozens of guests and followed by a feast with music and dancing. And he had been so besotted with the woman that his judgement had failed him. This was a sensible beginning to a marriage, no emotion to cloud his judgement. He would love Alyce as duty demanded, respect her and keep her safe.

Alyce repeated the promises Granville had made, clearly and without hesitation. She must have memorised and practised them.

He slid the ring onto the third finger of her right hand. The gold patterned band was the work of Middleton, the goldsmith whose shop faced the market square. Fine enough, but he would give Alyce something better once he knew her tastes.

He bent forward and kissed her, brushing his lips against her closed mouth. As formal and sober a kiss as the ceremony and the woman he had promised to marry. Close, she smelt of lavender and a hint of a richer spice, a suggestion that there was more to Alyce Bradley than first impressions gave.

Wine was passed around and their future together toasted. Alyce's parents and her sister were effusive in the good wishes they offered to Granville.

Alyce stood alone in the middle of the room, as if she were incidental to the celebration.

Before Granville could move towards her, Watkins strolled over from his position by the door. He bowed to Alyce. 'My blessings, Mistress. I am delighted you will be our lady at Ash-thorpe.'

Alyce's face relaxed as she smiled at him. 'I look forward to going there.'

'It is a beautiful place. They will all be pleased to see you too. I know I'm speaking out of turn but the Master could not have made a better choice than you.'

Alyce's eyelashes fluttered in surprise, colour rising up her cheeks. 'Thank you, Watkins.'

Grinning, he bowed again and moved away.

Granville came to her side and grasped her hand, squeezing

it. 'All will be well, Alyce,' he murmured.

She smiled at him, still wary, but hope shone in her clear green eyes.

All would be well; he would make sure of it. Their marriage may not be a grand affair of the heart but it would be solid and comfortable—the sort of marriage recommended by all, the sort of marriage that lasted well.

~

The crowd spilled out of the church of St. Peter Mancroft and drifted along the street into the marketplace, the best part of their duty done for another week. Isabel joined a group of women chatting near the market cross.

'Isabel, is it true? Your sister is betrothed to Thomas Granville?' Martha Powell asked. She held the hand of a girl, a smaller version of herself.

'Ay,' Isabel replied.

'Come Isabel, there is more to tell than that,' persisted Lettys Rowe. 'Why so reticent?'

Isabel glanced over her shoulder. 'My father-in-law is exceedingly angry.'

'He is not here, so tell us.'

'It was yesterday, at my parents' house. Granville left for London straight after.'

'There was no grand celebration? Are they in a hurry?' Lettys asked.

Martha bent down and whispered in her daughter's ear. The girl smiled at her mother and skipped off to join a group of children swinging on the pillars of the market cross.

Isabel watched her go. Would her child be a pretty, obedient girl like Martha's? She turned to Lettys and pulled a face. 'I know what you are suggesting, Lettys. No.'

'When will the wedding be?' Martha asked.

'Within twelve months, I imagine.'

'It does not matter when.' Lettys smirked. 'The betrothal is firm should passion overcome them.'

'Lettys, you have just come from church,' Martha gasped.

'We all know what human nature is.' Lettys raised a finely plucked eyebrow.

Isabel laughed. 'Not with Alyce.'

Lettys's eyes widened. 'She is not willing?'

'She agreed to the marriage. But when they spoke their promises it was as if they were reciting an oath in court.' Alyce claimed to be content with the match, yet Isabel had sensed some understandable discontent. It was a pity Granville was so much older and would no doubt be faithless, but he was wealthy enough. And Alyce would get no better offer, however long she waited. 'And the kiss,' Isabel laughed. 'I kiss my mother-in-law with more passion.'

'Thomas Granville too?'

Isabel raised her eyebrows and nodded. 'Every bit as wooden.'

'Ladies.' Her husband bowed, the sun shining on his golden hair. 'Whose character are we destroying today?'

'Will!' Isabel tried not to smile.

'Isabel was sharing Alyce's good fortune with us,' Martha said.

'If you can call it that.'

'You do not approve, Master Sutton?' Lettys smiled falsely at him.

'I see little to be gained by either Isabel's sister or her father.'

Puzzled, Martha said, 'But Master Granville is held in high regard by many.'

'His reputation is such I would not allow my sister even to contemplate marriage to him.'

'Ay, he is said to be a notorious seducer of women,' Lettys said, a hard glint in her eyes. 'It is interesting, is it not, what we see as a vice in one we dislike, we will regard as a mere peccadillo in someone closer to home?'

Will scowled at her. 'If you will excuse us.' He took Isabel's elbow and propelled her away from the women. 'You should have little to do with tale carriers such as Lettys Rowe. Spend more time in the company of my mother, or at least your own.'

Several months ago, such an outburst from Will would have had Isabel in tears, lamenting that she had time for such chatter—it was not her fault her days were not busy with children. Instead she smiled happily and slid her arm through his. 'Lettys is no worse than anyone else—our talk is harmless: births, marriages, love, little scandals.'

'I fear she plays with the truth when it suits her.'

'As we all do.' Isabel dimpled. 'And you enjoy these tales too.' She leant in close. 'I have something to tell you, but you must wait until we get home. A habit Martha's husband brought back with him from Italy! And poor innocent Martha cannot work out how he has come by it.'

'I am agog.'

'Are you sure you want to know?' Isabel fluttered her eyelashes. 'It is not the sort of story I would ever hear in your mother's company.'

He rolled his eyes and grinned. 'You win, Isabel—I admit my life would be duller without your friends' doubtful tales.'

~

Robin Chapman walked beside his mother out into the church-yard of All Saints after the Sunday service. His mother joined a knot of women eagerly exchanging news. Robin stood alone, listening to the snatches of conversation around him. His face rigid, he strode away, ignoring those who greeted him.

How could he not have known? He had heard nothing of it. In truth, his mind had been occupied with rehearsing the words he would say to Alyce when he had the chance. He knew he should not have struck her. He had been a fool in his anger, remembering later the words of a journeyman who had worked at Bradley's when he was an apprentice—*The more they insult you, the hotter they are for you. Especially the plainer ones.*

It made sense now. Granville's visits these last few days, Alyce keeping her distance—she no longer came to the shop, left the hall as soon as dinner was over, had not looked his way once. He had assumed she was feeling guilty at her dishonest game of playing hot and cold.

His mother, puffing, caught up with him, but Robin did not slow his pace.

'They are saying,' she gasped, 'Alyce Bradley is betrothed to that pirate, Thomas Granville.'

'Ay, I heard. Hugh Bradley played me false. Encouraged me to offer my hand, then she refused me in the vilest terms. And all the time they were entertaining Granville.' He scowled. 'I do not know what game Bradley is playing.'

'She must be worse than I thought to choose a villain like Granville over you.'

Robin was silent. If he opened his mouth now, the fury would spill out. Alyce Bradley had once again toyed with his hopes of a better future—dangled them enticingly in front of him then snatched them away, trampling them underfoot.

8

September 1586

Alyce glanced up from the pan sitting over the coals of the chafing dish as the cook thumped her dough down at the other end of the table. A skilled woman of middling age, she came in daily to assist Alyce's mother with preparation of the main meals. Clearly unimpressed at Alyce and Eliza's invasion of her domain, she was punishing her dough and barking orders at the scullery maid cleaning pots in the trough.

Alyce dipped a ladle into the bowl beside her and poured a small amount of melted sugar onto the fennel seeds in the heated pan. She swiftly rolled the seeds into the sugar with her fingers. Eliza, sitting opposite, sliced oranges, her knife hitting the board with regular thuds.

Isabel swept in with a rustle of skirts and stood beside Alyce, her eyes on the movement of Alyce's fingers. 'You said you would show me how to do this.'

Alyce looked at Isabel's new gown of willow green. 'I'm sure Eliza can find you an apron.'

'I need to see Mother first.' She picked up a single finished comfit from the plate in the centre of the table, popped it into her mouth and smiled with the guiltiness of a small child as she left the room.

Alyce and Eliza went on with their work in companionable silence, ignoring the thumping of dough and the clatter of pots.

Alyce stopped her rolling, frowning as she strained to hear a faint wailing noise.

She rose from her chair and walked through the pantry and the stillroom and stood at the foot of the stairs. The noise was louder, a shrill keening sound coming from the hall above. Gripping her skirts, Alyce took the stairs two at a time.

Isabel had sunk onto the floor of the hall, her arms wrapped tight around herself, rocking to and fro. Her mother, on her knees beside her, looked up at Alyce. 'I found her like this.'

Alyce knelt and took Isabel's face between her hands. 'Isabel.

Look at me. Open your eyes,' she said sternly. 'Tell me what is wrong.'

Isabel slowly opened her eyes. 'Help me, Alyce,' she whispered. 'I am bleeding.'

'Oh Isabel.' Alyce rocked her gently. 'Is it heavy?'

'A few drops. But that is always the start,' she whimpered. 'I thought with you here, it would not fail.'

Alyce met her mother's troubled eyes over the top of Isabel's head. 'We should take Isabel to my room and let her rest there.'

~

Alyce stared around the stillroom at the array of bottles, jars and vials and neatly labelled boxes. She pulled the printed herbal across the table towards her. It was a surprising gift from her mother, a tacit acknowledgement both of Alyce's skills and of her mother's trust in her. Alyce flicked through the pages, stopping every so often to read a few lines before moving on, her lips compressed with concentration. She must find a way to help Isabel, but if she did the wrong thing?

'Lord guide me,' she whispered.

She measured a few drops of syrup of poppies into a posset cup and went into the kitchen, adding a measure of small beer and swirling the two together. She spoke quietly to Eliza and sent her with a note to the apothecary and climbed the stairs to her bedchamber.

Isabel lay against the pillows on Alyce's bed, a blanket spread over her. She opened her eyes as Alyce came into the room.

'This will help calm you.' Alyce went over and placed her arm around Isabel's shoulders, holding the spout of the cup to her lips.

Isabel screwed up her face and swallowed. 'That must be good.' She shuddered. 'It tasted foul.'

'It is a few drops of poppy in small beer.' Alyce placed the cup on the chest at the end of the bed. 'I have sent Eliza to the apothecary for some tansy. I'll make a poultice when she comes back. The herbal says when applied to the navel, it stays miscarriage.'

'If you had not been here...' Isabel shuddered and lay back against the pillows.

'I cannot say it will work, but it will do no harm.' She pulled the blanket around her sister's shoulders. 'You need to rest now.'

'Stay with me, Alyce. I am afraid.'

Alyce sat on the stool beside the window and picked up her Psalter. Prayer would help Isabel too.

As Isabel drifted towards sleep, their mother tiptoed in.

'Will she lose the child?' she whispered.

'I have no idea.' Alyce shrugged. 'The best we can do now is pray.'

'It barely seems enough when a child is so wanted.'

'We do not always get what we want,' Alyce said flatly.

~

Will sat on the edge of the bed, Isabel's hand tight in his. 'Why did you not tell me?'

'I was too afraid. I thought if I said a word, I would lose the baby.' She closed her eyes a moment, shuddering at the thought.

Isabel stared into her husband's troubled eyes and forced herself to smile. 'Alyce was sent home for a reason—this child of ours is meant to be. She gave me a potion, and when I woke, the bleeding had stopped. If Alyce had not been here, the child would have been lost.'

Will's brow furrowed. 'That is a large claim to make. Bleeding can stop of its own accord I believe.'

'Are you not glad Alyce saved our child?'

'Of course I am, but we still have a long road ahead of us.' He rubbed the bridge of his nose. 'I am afraid to hope.'

'Alyce should come and live with us.' Isabel blinked, thoughtful. 'Perhaps I nearly lost this child because there is too much work managing our household.'

'We could employ an extra maid, two even. Or Frances could come and help you.'

'But your sister is only a girl. I will have to teach her.'

'Mother has schooled her well, and Father is considering prospective suitors for her. Besides, I doubt Granville will take kindly to Alyce living with us. You know how things stand between him and my father.'

Of what importance was any of that compared to her baby?

She hunched forward, her body racked with sobs. 'I need Alyce with me.' Tears spilled over her lashes. 'If she is not with me, I will lose my baby.'

Will pulled Isabel against him, holding her tight. 'If you need her, she must come.'

'Oh, Will. I do love you.' Isabel smiled through her tears, feeling the weight of the baby in her arms.

~

Alyce sat by the window of Isabel's parlour frowning intensely, a book open on her lap. She did not understand what she had been reading.

She gazed out the window, not seeing the activities in the street. She needed someone to explain it to her. She had thought, to begin with, that the book on bodily humours she had found in the bookseller's shop had almost been waiting just for her. But there had been problems at every step. At first, the bookseller had refused to sell it to her, saying it was not suitable for an unmarried woman. She had told him it was a gift for a married gentlewoman she knew, well-versed in physic, who had her husband's permission to read such books. So many little duplicities—it was a gift to herself, who would, once she was married, be considered a gentlewoman, and Master Granville had said she could read anything except seditious tracts. She had not realised that she could so bend the truth when she wanted something badly.

The illustrations of the body in the book were clear and understandable but she was struggling to grasp the balancing of the humours and the way their upset caused particular diseases. She could not go to Master Booth, the apothecary, with her book and ask for an explanation; he would most likely have the same objections as the bookseller or else consider that she was trying to encroach on his territory. Perhaps if she could fashion a question to get her answer and present it to him, telling him that she needed to understand to ensure she did not make mistakes in following his instructions. Master Booth liked to display his knowledge and provided she paid for his potions, she was sure she could get him talking.

'Alyce!' Isabel's shrill voice broke through her musing. 'You do not have time to be sitting here dreaming. The plate needs to be polished. And have you managed to get that stain from my embroidered partlet?'

Alyce continued to stare out the window, her lips pressed tight together. Each day since she had come to live with Isabel, Isabel's demands had increased. At times she felt she was nothing more than a serving maid.

Alyce forced down the surging irritation and turned to Isabel. 'No, I did not manage to get it out. As I told you, it is an old stain and has been washed a number of times since. It is set. You could perhaps dye it, but there might still be a difference in the colour.' She took a deep breath. 'And as for the plate, it did not occur to me that you were ordering me to do it. You have already given me a long list of tasks. Do you want me to sweep the ash from the hearths and set the fires each morning as well?'

'There is no need to be nasty,' Isabel snapped. 'I am in no condition to do everything myself.' Tears glittered on her lashes. 'This is very important to me. Will has finally become a freeman of the city and I want to celebrate it with the feast he deserves, but I must be careful. This child...' She spread her hands protectively over her gently swelling belly.

Alyce knew it did not pay to argue and upset Isabel. She set her book aside and rose from her seat. 'Perhaps you should ask Mother to lend you one of her maids to help with all the preparations.'

'That is a good idea. And one more thing.'

Alyce turned back from the door.

'Can you prepare one of those dishes with a lark within a capon within a goose?'

'I cannot, and even if I did, your cook does not have the skill to bake it properly. Better to bake the birds separately.'

She hurried away before Isabel could think of anything more to load on her.

9

Isabel stepped the length of the room at walking pace, her hand resting on Sir William's as they led a stately pavane, the one dance she still dared now.

As they turned to face each other, Sir William winked at her. While Isabel doubted that even his mother could have thought him handsome, he exuded power, a power it did not pay to resist.

Isabel smiled and fluttered her eyelashes at him. Since she had revealed her pregnancy, he had lavished attention on her in a way he had not done since she had first married Will. No terse greetings, no tales of the pointlessness of barren wives or what he called the sensible practices of those in distant lands who could take second or even third and fourth wives to get as many sons as they needed. For once, Dame Katharine had been angry with him but, Isabel supposed, it was more that he was praising non-Christians than concern at the cruelty of his words.

The dance ended, and Isabel curtsied.

Sir William leant forward, tapped a finger against one of Isabel's earrings, setting it swaying. The gold earrings with small pearl drops were a gift given for no reason other than she was with child.

'It is a pleasure to give pretty trinkets to so comely a woman.'

Isabel dimpled. 'It is a pleasure to wear your generous gifts.' They had been few and far between since the first year of her marriage. Would he withhold his generosity again if the child she carried was a girl?

As Sir William strolled away in search of another dancing partner, Isabel glanced around the room at her friends and family. This feast had surpassed her expectations. Compliments flowed, particularly for the gingerbreads, comfits and fruits moulded from sugar that finished the meal. Truth be told, they should be praising Alyce, but Isabel had planned each course and directed Alyce as well as assisting her in moulding the marchpane subtlety in the shape of a turreted castle. Even Sir William had been impressed with that—it was not often he complimented women's skills. It did not hurt to have her friends imagine she had been hiding her culinary skills under a bushel.

Isabel caught sight of her mother-in-law beckoning to her.

Dame Katharine smiled as Isabel gave her a shallow curtsy, brushing her plump hand against Isabel's cheek. 'Daughter, you are radiant. I see all is well with you.'

Isabel carefully arranged her skirts as she eased herself down beside Dame Katharine.

'Ay, it is, and I owe it to my sister, Alyce. Without her physic, I fear I would have lost the child.'

Dame Katharine's pale eyebrows shot up in surprise. 'Physic?'

'Alyce brewed me a potion that stopped both the bleeding and my queasiness. She takes such care of me I need trouble myself about nothing.'

Dame Katharine put her hand on Isabel's wrist. 'Isabel, I would like to talk with your sister.'

~

Alyce stood with her father watching the dancers, her mother among them alongside Sir William. Her mother had always been as much in demand as a dancing partner as any of the younger women.

'Would you care to dance?' her father asked.

'Thank you, Father, I would.'

Before they could move into position, Will came up and, ignoring Alyce, said to her father, 'Come and talk to Mark Powell. He has just returned from London—orders have gone out for men from the counties to be ready to march on London to protect the Queen.'

Her father shrugged an apology to Alyce.

'If the Scottish queen could be dealt with as those papist plotters were last month, that should be the end of such treasons.' He scowled. 'And the end of Spanish designs on England.'

Alyce shuddered and walked away, pushing it from her mind.

Isabel waved to her from her seat beside Lady Sutton.

Alyce curtsied to Lady Sutton, who shuffled along to make room for Alyce, her bodice creaking beneath the heavy brocade of her gown. 'Sit here, Alyce.'

'Isabel is full of praise for your care of her.'

'I am glad to be of help.'

'And Alyce will be with me until the baby comes,' said Isabel happily.

'But when is your wedding to be?' Lady Sutton asked.

Alyce would not say she had no idea when the *time meet and convenient* would be other than some time in the coming year. Her betrothal to Thomas Granville was a transaction between her father and Granville in which she was more like a parcel of goods transferred than a participant. While he had been courteous, Granville had in no sense wooed her. It had felt more like a hiring arrangement made at Michaelmas where she would take on the position of *wife*. This position, though, was not one she could walk away from after a year if it was not to her liking, and far more would be expected of her than of any waiting woman.

'The date is not yet firm,' Alyce answered.

'Well after the baby is born.' Isabel was emphatic.

'Will you invite your betrothed to share the Christmas season with you?'

Alyce wondered why Lady Sutton asked, knowing Sir William's attitude to Thomas Granville. And if he did come, what sort of welcome would he find in the house of William Sutton the younger? It occurred to Alyce, not for the first time, that there was a seam of malice beneath Lady Sutton's pious exterior.

'Master Granville is busy with preparations for his next venture, Lady Sutton.'

'Indeed. Now tell me of your time at Dalstead.' Lady Sutton frowned. 'I hear there is much papistry in those parts.'

'I saw nothing of it.'

'One must be careful. Was it a godly household?'

Alyce answered with what she knew Lady Sutton wished to hear, though it was no lie. 'Prayer and instruction were regular. We attended service on both Sunday morning and evening, with a sermon in the hall in the afternoon.'

Lady Sutton nodded, clearly pleased.

'There was much work to do, but there was music and reading too. Lady Faulconer had travelled far in her youth. She was interested in physic and knew numerous remedies from distant lands.'

Lady Sutton's pale eyelashes fluttered. 'It is not fitting we dabble in the corrupt practices of the heathen.'

'Surely all knowledge comes from the Almighty. Much of what we know today, in remedies and in other fields of learning, comes from the writings of men who were not Christians. The use of herbs and poultices to heal the sick cannot be corrupt.'

'But I would beware—'

'Did not the Lord enjoin us to minister unto the sick?'

'But... but...' Lady Sutton spluttered.

'Then what is ungodly in it?'

Lady Sutton took a deep breath. 'Some remedies involve ungodly practices. You are too innocent to see the evil in what you do. The soul can be corrupted by stealth.'

'I have done nothing evil.' Alyce fought down her rising anger.

Lady Sutton touched Alyce's hand. 'Alyce, Alyce, I was not saying you have done evil. I meant in your desire to do good you may not recognise that you are using evil practices.'

'I have never used, nor seen used, any remedy involving anything evil.'

'But you do have pride. It is wrong to set yourself up as a doctor. You are a clever girl and I do not have the wit to argue with you, but you must speak with Master Reynes. He is a learned and godly man, the best minister we have had at St Peter's for many years.'

'Lady Sutton, I have not set myself up as a doctor. Here in the town you have doctors and apothecaries nearby if you have no inclination toward physic, but in the countryside a housewife must tend to these things herself.'

'You may be right, but I have never found the need to meddle in physic, and while you are here, I would recommend you resort to my brother, Master Booth the apothecary.'

Isabel touched Alyce on the arm. 'I think Father wants you.' 'I must go.' Alyce rose, grateful for Isabel's small lie. 'If you will excuse me, Lady Sutton.'

Alyce had barely turned her back when Lady Sutton began. 'Isabel, your sister worries me.'

Alyce was certain the woman had raised her voice.

'She is stiff-necked and full of her own opinions. And remember what she was like as a girl—disobedient, disrespectful and, under your grandmother's influence, only a step from witchcraft.'

Alyce walked away, her mouth shut tight. It was Lady Sutton's stupid prattle that had upset Alyce so much at her grandmother's funeral. It would not do to turn and tell her what a vicious, hypocritical fool she was. Last time she had done that she had been banished to the emptiness that was Dalstead.

~

The candles were already lit in the de Jongs' parlour as the day was overcast. Grietje de Jong was asleep in a chair beside the fire. Marieke's two elder children played quietly with wooden animals near the window. Alyce, seated farther back from the fire, held Elisabeth, Marieke's youngest, nestled on her lap.

Marieke sipped from a goblet of warm spiced wine. 'Life has not turned out as you imagined when you returned here?'

'Nay.' Alyce stared at the logs glowing in the fireplace. She had expected a cooler welcome and thought only to stay as long as it took to find another position. The first month after her return was possibly the easiest of her life. The days had fallen into a pattern of Alyce's choosing—time spent in the garden and the stillroom, playing the lute and reading, shopping and sewing companionably with her mother and, every few days, visiting Marieke. And she had come to accept most marriages were made the way hers was. She even allowed herself to indulge barely formed dreams of a life where she was her own mistress. But now she was living with Isabel, she had little time for herself, and her fantasies had faded. The sole blessing was she rarely caught sight of Robert Chapman.

'And how is life with Isabel?'

Alyce raised her eyebrows. 'How do you imagine?'

'Do you argue much?'

'I know how to hold my tongue now.' She exhaled heavily. 'I am supposed to be Isabel's companion, but I am acting more as her maid and housekeeper.' She laughed bitterly. 'And I thought Lady Faulconer a hard mistress.'

Marieke pressed her lips together, fighting a smile.

'Isabel has a constant stream of visitors. Her friends seem to have nothing better to do than spend hours pulling apart the lives of others—even Isabel's, in her own house, once she leaves the room. Though they do not say it outright, they hint that Will is not faithful to her.'

'There has always been talk about Will Sutton. While he has never flaunted his mistresses, he could be more discreet.'

'Are no men faithful?'

'Some are—the best sort. They expect nothing of their wives they would not expect of themselves. Do you expect Thomas to be faithful?'

Alyce blinked at Marieke's easy use of Granville's Christian name. Even in her thoughts he was Master Granville. He had not suggested she call him otherwise.

'I do not know him well enough to say.' Alyce thought of marriage as a solemn promise, a promise she would keep no matter how Granville behaved, a promise he would regard as binding on her. She had no idea if he viewed it as binding on himself.

Marieke leant over and placed her goblet on the table. 'How is the sewing for your wedding progressing?'

'We had barely started when I went to Isabel's and nothing has been done since. It will have to wait until after her baby is born.'

Marieke rested her hands on her belly. 'I should be churched a week or two before Christmas so I can help you once the Christmas season is over. And I am sure *Moeder* would love to as well.'

'Oh, Marieke, that would be wonderful.' But what would be more wonderful, Alyce thought, would be not to feel she was a servant again, to truly feel she was betrothed and to be happy like other women contemplating marriage seemed to be.

Part 2
৵৵

They that marry for love, shall lead their life in sorrow.
The Instruction of a Christian Woman
Juan Luis Vives

10

November 1586

Alyce pushed the casement open, thrilled by the clamour of the dozens of bells ringing out across Norwich.

'Shut that window,' Isabel whined. 'Cold air is dangerous for me.'

With a final glance at the high, light clouds, Alyce pulled the window closed.

Isabel lay back against a mound of soft pillows, her arms crossed tight against her bosom. Her eyes were red and her face blotched. 'He hates me.' She pouted. 'He does everything he can to make my life miserable. He refuses to understand, insisting it's wrong for you to be here—another man's betrothed keeping house for him.'

Alyce tried to interrupt but Isabel was in full flight. 'Will wants Frances to take your place, but she is just a girl and knows nothing.' She took a deep breath and rushed on, 'I do not believe this but Will says he heard you have been spreading abroad details of what goes on in this house—our finances and more private matters.'

Yesterday Alyce had caught sight of Will in the street, deep in conversation with Jane Bedford, the haberdasher's new wife, a buxom young woman barely older than Bedford's daughter. They had stood close, not quite touching, an air of shared secrets. Will had glanced up and seen Alyce. He had smirked, no doubt at the shock in her face, knowing that she would not upset her sister over something she had no power to change.

'I have no time for idle chatter,' Alyce said.

'But you will be careful what you say?'

'When do I do otherwise?' There were a dozen times each day when Alyce bit back her words. Irritated, her restraint slipped. 'I am not here for my own pleasure. I can return to Father's house if my living here causes too many problems.'

'Why is everyone spiteful?' Isabel's face crumpled. 'I imagined being with child would make life perfect, but it is dreadful. I look hideous, Will does not love me, and now you are being cruel.'

'I will stay as long as you want and Will is willing to tolerate me.' She could answer no other way, although life would be easier if she were still at her parents' house. Alyce felt a growing unease at Isabel's often-stated belief that Alyce was crucial to the safe delivery of her child.

She picked up a plate from the tray she had earlier placed on the chest at the end of the bed. 'Here, you must eat.'

Isabel took a piece of the bread and cheese and nibbled.

'Dry your tears. Mother will be here soon. It is Accession Day, and even the weather has decided to celebrate. Listen...' Alyce paused. 'You can hear the church bells ringing even though the window is closed. I have not been to a real celebration of the Queen's accession since I left here. There were prayers and sermons at Dalstead, but nothing else.' She frowned. 'If we hurry, we will be in time for the prayers of thanksgiving at St Peter's.'

'No. If we go to the church, I will also have to stand listening to an endless sermon at the market cross afterwards. I will be tired enough visiting all the stalls at the market—there will be merchants and pedlars from out of town today. Now what will I wear?' Isabel moved to the edge of the bed and slid her feet to the floor. 'Get the yellow damask for me.'

Alyce took the gown from the press in the corner of the room and laid it on the bed.

'Alyce,' Isabel said slowly, 'do you know how to make a potion to keep a man constant?'

Alyce breathed through her nose. 'God—' She stopped herself, horrified at her uncharacteristic use of the Lord's name. 'Isabel. I know physic. Not magic.'

'I do not understand it. Both you and Will quote the scriptures, yet you take the Lord's name lightly,' Isabel sniffed.

Alyce opened her eyes wide. 'Will quotes scripture?'

'Ay, great tracts of it when the fancy takes him. His mother saw to that.'

Alyce shook her head, puzzled at the contradictions others' lives presented.

~

Weighed down with packages, Alyce and the two maids, Eliza and Julia, trudged behind her mother and Isabel through the press of people celebrating the Queen's accession. Avoiding the usual stalls of the butchers, poulterers, fishmongers and wool merchants, they had visited most of the brightly decorated booths set up around the market square. They had looked at trinkets, ribbons, gloves, all manner of gewgaws as Isabel picked and chose and haggled for whatever took her fancy.

'Would you get me some gingerbread, Alyce?' Isabel called over her shoulder. 'I am worn-out. I'll be sitting outside the Angel Inn.'

Alyce passed her packages to Julia. 'Would you two like some too?'

Both Eliza and Julia nodded. 'Thank you, Mistress.'

Alyce bought the gingerbread from a lanky boy carrying a tray, shouting his master's wares. She wound her way through the crowd to the Angel on the western side of the market square, but neither Isabel, her mother nor the maids were anywhere in sight. A surge of resentment swept through her. She had spent the morning traipsing after Isabel, yet she could not be bothered waiting.

Alyce noticed a grubby-faced urchin staring longingly at the gingerbread. She bent down to him. 'Would you like one?'

The boy nodded, mumbling something about his sister.

'Here, give her some too.' Alyce passed him the gingerbread. He took it, muttered a thanks and disappeared into the crowd as if fearful this sudden bounty would be withdrawn.

Alyce pulled a handkerchief from her purse, wiped her hands and pulled on her gloves. Around her pedlars and local tradesmen called their wares, shoppers haggled at the stalls, men and women stood in knots chatting. At one side, a group watched tumblers in particoloured clothes clambering over each other performing amazing feats of balance. A stilt walker, ribbons fluttering from his clothing, stalked through the throng, like a great wading bird. Music carried from outside the Guildhall where the musicians of the town waits played.

Alyce caught sight of Robert Chapman striding in her

direction. She turned and pushed into the crowd to get away. She was jostled by a group of apprentices smelling of ale and bumped into a broad-bosomed brew-wife who swore at her. People were close around her, hemming her in. Alyce fought down panic as memories of another crowd twelve years earlier swept over her: the noise, the smells, the flushed laughing faces were no different. All that was lacking was the pent-up excitement and the sight of her grandmother's friend as she was hauled aloft on the gallows.

Alyce's heart thumped. Her breath came in shallow bursts. She clamped her mouth shut against a scream. Head down, she forced her way through the press of bodies, not seeing where she was going, and collided with a tall, broad-shouldered man.

He put his arm out to steady her.

Alyce stared up into Thomas Granville's surprised face.

'Alyce? What is wrong?'

Alyce took a slow shuddering breath. 'I found the crowd too close.'

He frowned. 'You are out alone?'

'Nay, Isabel and Mother are here somewhere.' She shook her head to clear it. 'We will be going home soon—Isabel is tired.'

Annoyance flickered in his face. 'Celebrations of this sort are never over until the sun is well set. Do you wish to stay?'

With Granville's protective arm around her, Alyce's panic drained away. 'I do, Master Granville, but I should find Mother and Isabel.'

'Let them find you.' He smiled, his eyes intent on hers. 'Alyce, you must call me Thomas.'

'Thomas.' She felt a startling swell of happiness as she tried the name.

Thomas linked her hand through his arm, and together they wandered through the crowd like any other couple. A space had been cleared for a sword swallower dressed in gaudy satin, gold earrings dancing in the light. Awed, Alyce gaped at the spectacle of the sword disappearing down his throat. They stopped to watch the card games, the cup and balls trick. Thomas seemed to know every fairground secret. He whispered to Alyce to watch the crowd to see who was most intently watching the trick then look at who was behind him. A lean youth, his cap pulled low, stood close to the portly apothecary, Booth, whose narrowed eyes were on the trickster's hands.

Alyce glanced at Thomas and whispered, 'The lad, there?' She inclined her head towards him.

'Ay,' Thomas nodded.

The youth looked across at Alyce and, in the instant that she blinked, disappeared.

'A cutpurse,' Thomas said. 'In league with the rogue playing the cup and balls.'

Alyce shuddered. Here in the daylight, in familiar Norwich, not even someone as puffed-up and smug as Master Booth was safe.

'Alyce. Alyce.'

Alyce turned to face her mother.

'Where have you been?' she snapped. 'I have been searching for you everywhere. Isabel wants to go home, and Goody Hall said you were flinging your arms around a strange man.'

Alyce braced herself. Even now her mother's anger was quick to spark at any behaviour that brought the slightest hint of public discredit.

Her mother's gaze flickered to Alyce's hand resting on Thomas's forearm.

Alyce moved to slide her hand free, but Thomas placed his hand on top of hers. His touch burnt through her glove. She stood, her eyes on her mother, aware of nothing but Thomas so close beside her.

'Good day, Mistress Bradley,' Thomas greeted her.

'Master Granville.' Her mother's eyelashes fluttered in surprise. 'I did not realise you were here.' Her anger was swiftly set aside and replaced with a genial smile. 'We were worried what had become of Alyce.'

'She is safe here with me, Mistress Bradley.' He pressed Alyce's hand before removing his.

Her mother nodded, a hint of strain in her face. 'We should leave now, Alyce. Isabel is keen to go home.'

Alyce found her voice. 'I wish to keep Thomas company a while longer, Mother.'

'Isabel…'

'I wish it, Mistress.' His voice was firm. 'I assure you I will see Alyce safely home.'

'Of course, Master Granville.' She nodded, flustered. 'I must get back to Isabel.'

As her mother disappeared into the crowd, Thomas said, 'The whole world now dances to Isabel Sutton's tune?'

'Isabel is with child.'

'I see no star rising in the east.'

'Not yet, but it may when the child is born,' Alyce laughed. 'It appeared Isabel might lose the babe at one point but now all seems well.'

'And your sister is not one to forego the opportunity to play the queen.'

Alyce raised her eyebrows. She should defend Isabel, but knew Thomas was right.

'Alyce,' Thomas gazed into her eyes, 'I want us to be wed in January.'

Unsettled by the intimacy of his gaze, Alyce looked away. 'So soon? I assumed it would not be until later in the year. Isabel is counting on me to be with her until her baby is born in April.'

'She will have to count on some other.'

They stopped near a pair of jugglers tossing balls into the air. 'Why so soon?'

'I need to sail by early March and do a deal of rewarding hurt to Spain before we are called on to fight in earnest.'

'It will come to that?' Alyce groaned.

'Ay. Talk is the King of Spain is exceedingly angry at the damage we did on Sir Francis Drake's Great Expedition.'

'I thought sailing in winter was dangerous.'

'We will be moving towards spring by then, and the weather should be better farther south.' He watched the jugglers. 'I do not know how long this journey will take, but I wish to wed and spend time with my bride before I leave.'

Alyce kept her eyes on the spinning balls as a flush spread up from her neck. Thoughts jostled. He needed the dowry to finance this venture. And there was the fuss, the prying interest she would have to endure in the weeks ahead.

'I suppose the sooner it is done…' What had possessed her to speak so ungraciously?

'You sound reluctant.'

'Nay,' she said, calmer now, 'but I detest putting myself on display for others to whisper at. I wish I did not have to go through the whole public spectacle.'

He raised an eyebrow. 'You would come to me without the rite?'

'There is no need to misunderstand me.'

Thomas's mouth twitched as if fighting back a smile.

Alyce glowered at him, aware of the increasing heat in her face. 'Scripture exhorts us all to be continent.' He seemed to consider it a jest. 'Why is it few consider chastity to be required of men?'

'There are good reasons why it is required of women,' Thomas answered evenly. 'A man needs to be sure the children he raises are his own.'

'I am not arguing women be as profligate as many men seem to be. To my mind a vow is a vow—binding husband and wife equally.'

'A notion that would trouble a great many men,' Thomas replied.

Alyce held her tongue. Most women accepted that this was the way life was, and she supposed she would have to as well.

They continued on their way around the market.

'What do you think these others are whispering?'

Alyce did not answer.

'Have you thought you might be the object of some envy too?'

'Envy,' she laughed. 'You do consider yourself highly.'

'My sister makes the same accusation.' He stopped at a booth and picked up a length of scarlet ribbon embroidered with silver. 'Do you like this?'

Alyce brushed her fingers against it. 'It is pretty. Isabel bought a length earlier.'

He dropped the ribbon. 'I care little for whisperings and empty prattle. You should do the same. Treat the prattlers with contempt.'

'But such whisperings can destroy lives.' She thought of her grandmother's friend, Bridget.

'Only the lives of the powerless. I am neither powerless nor friendless, and with me neither will you be.'

Alyce's heart lurched—if only that were true.

Thomas glanced towards the Angel Inn and said, 'Are you hungry?'

He led Alyce to an empty table and ordered pie and ale.

Alyce looked towards the square. 'I have not been to a fair like this since I was last in Norwich.'

'I imagine there was little festivity associated with Lady Faulconer's household. Did you celebrate Christmas?'

'Of course we did—with prayer and hymn singing, good food and gifts.'

'I'll wager she gave you pious tracts and prayer books.'

'She did give me a Psalter three years ago,' Alyce laughed, 'but last New Year I received an embroidered kerchief. By then, Lady Faulconer had satisfied herself I did not embody all the vices she suspected youth possessed.'

'In my experience, age keeps company with vice more often than youth. And the greatest place of all for vice, and for the magnificence of its festivals, is Venice. The Carnevale is almost indescribable.'

'You have been to Venice?' Alyce asked, enthralled. 'It seems an almost magical place with its canals and piazzas and domed cathedrals.'

Thomas took a mouthful of ale and leant back in his seat. 'I remember the first time I met you. You were twelve or so, your head buried in a book, sitting at the window in your father's office. You did not notice us enter, or even your father's request that you leave.'

Alyce gave a sheepish smile. 'I would hide there when I wanted to read undisturbed. Mother considered reading a waste of time.'

'When you realised we were there, you fled the room, leaving your book behind. What surprised me was your taste in reading—travellers' tales, not the love stories favoured by most girls.'

'I imagined a world of adventure lay beyond the walls of Norwich.'

'You have changed your mind?'

'It may for men, rarely for women.' She looked across the table at him, seeing him for the first time as more than the man she would have to learn to live with. He had seen so much of the world and it would be an unlooked-for gift if he would tell her of the places he had visited. 'Venice,' she sighed. 'Describe it to me.'

'Venice is a city of immense beauty—bathed in crystal light, it appears to float upon the water. There you can see people from every compass point on earth...'

Alyce drew from Thomas tales of places she had only visited in her imagination and, for those moments, regained her youthful belief that the world was full of possibilities.

As the shadows lengthened, Thomas said, 'Unfortunately, it is time to take you home.'

Alyce smiled. 'It has been a delightful day.'

A gust of chilly wind tugged at Alyce's skirts as they left the Angel. Thomas linked Alyce's arm through his and drew her close. 'You have no cloak.'

'The day started out warm for November, and I did not think I would be out so late.'

'It is not far to your father's house.'

Alyce glanced up at Thomas and said, 'I am staying with Isabel at present.'

'Why?'

Although the dusk shadowed Thomas's face, Alyce was certain he scowled.

'I have been caring for her since she nearly miscarried two months ago.'

'As her companion, I hope.'

'Yes and no. I do help her with her housekeeping.'

'I will not have my wife playing housemaid in another man's house.'

'I am not your wife yet.'

'You are as good as.' He placed his free hand over hers and pressed it tight. 'I will call on your father tomorrow. You are to return to his house.'

'But Isabel is my sister, she needs—'

'The Suttons can meet your sister's needs.'

Alyce opened her mouth to argue but thought better of it.

'We will be married in less than two months. You will need that time to prepare yourself.'

'I suppose you are right.'

They walked on in silence towards Isabel's house. The house stood in darkness, not a light flickering in any window.

In the doorway, Thomas wrapped his arms around Alyce. So close she felt the warmth of his body, the strength beneath the padded doublet, the scent of cloves and leather and something more, an essence that was Thomas alone. His moustache prickled as he brushed his lips gently against hers. Alyce's lips parted in wonder at the melting delight that washed through her, taking her breath with it. She clung to him as the kiss lengthened and he held her tighter. He slowly moved his lips away and pressed them to her forehead. Safe within his embrace, Alyce listened to the thudding of his heart and wanted him to kiss her again.

Thomas released her. 'Till tomorrow, Alyce.' He disappeared into the night, and Alyce made her way into the unlit house, feeling for the first time since she had exchanged promises with Thomas Granville that she was indeed betrothed.

11

Isabel laid the tiny smock she was embroidering in her lap and adjusted the cushion at her back, her narrowed eyes intent on Alyce. She had come in late last night and had not bothered to check on Isabel after spending most of yesterday with that man, unaccompanied. When she had brought Isabel her breakfast and Isabel had tried to warn her of his reputation, as any good sister would, Alyce had immediately begun to talk of returning to their father's house. Isabel stared down at her hands, twisting her rings. Alyce knew how much she needed her, how such talk distressed her. To protect her own peace of mind, Isabel had ordered Alyce from the room.

Now here she was, sitting bent over her stitching, humming to herself, as if she had never uttered a malicious word in her life. And it was malice to threaten to leave when Isabel needed her so sorely.

Isabel smiled as her parents came into the parlour, surprised by this early visit.

Barely greeting Isabel, Father turned to Alyce. 'Thomas Granville arrived almost at cockcrow and says he wants the marriage to take place in January.'

'What?' Isabel shrieked. 'That is ridiculous.' Alyce could not leave her.

Mother drew her chair alongside Isabel's and grasped her hand.

Father scowled. 'Hush Isabel.' He turned back to Alyce. 'He said you are agreeable.'

'I am.'

Isabel glared at Alyce. 'You promised you would stay with me.' If Alyce did not stay, her baby would die.

'We both assumed I would stay here until your baby's birth,' Alyce said calmly, as if this were not a matter of life and death, 'but I made no promises. Thomas wishes to marry soon and I see no reason to delay.'

Isabel mouthed the name *Thomas*. So Granville had worked his charms on Alyce. What had made her so besotted that she would forget she had given her word and go chasing after him? It would be no surprise to hear they had slipped away and spent the day in his chamber at whatever inn he was staying.

'I wish Master Granville was more understanding,' Mother said. 'I doubt everything will be ready in time. And a wedding in spring or summer would be much prettier.'

'We will manage.' Father was dismissive. 'Another thing, Alyce, with your marriage close, you should be at home with us.'

'Who will take care of me?' Isabel wailed.

'Dame Katharine and young Frances can help as easily as Alyce,' he said.

Isabel glared at Alyce. 'You knew,' she gasped, her heart racing. 'He told you yesterday and you said nothing.'

'I tried, but you ordered me from the room before I had a chance to explain.'

Isabel could not breathe. She must do something. She hurled her cushion at Alyce, who dodged it. Trembling, she screamed her fear, throwing cushions and upturning chairs. Alyce must stay.

Alyce turned away and walked out of the parlour as if Isabel's distress was of no account.

Father followed her.

Mother pulled Isabel into a tight embrace. 'You must calm yourself. Think of the baby.'

'I am thinking of the baby,' Isabel sobbed. She laid her head against her mother's shoulder. 'I need her with me until the baby is born.'

'It is not Alyce's decision. Master Granville has the right to call the marriage at a time convenient to him.' She stroked Isabel's hair.

Her mother's touch was calming. Isabel turned her head, gazing at her. 'But I do need her.'

Mother tucked a loose strand of hair behind Isabel's ear. 'There is nothing Alyce can do we cannot.' She moved away from Isabel and sat down. 'Alyce is a maid with no knowledge of childbirth. She will be of no use to you in the birthing chamber.'

Isabel lowered herself onto the chair beside her mother and spread her hands protectively across her belly. 'But I need her beside me. If she had not been here two months ago, I would have lost this baby. And if it happens again, and Alyce is not here…' She had to stop saying it. It was like a spell—say it often enough and it would happen. 'And Alyce has Grandmother's gifts.'

It was only now she could appreciate their grandmother. She had felt a degree of shame at her grandmother's lack of interest in attire and her strange notions that all should be treated with the same courtesy regardless of wealth and position. Ay, a silly old woman more interested in plants and brewing potions and giving soup to the beggars who called by the back gate. It was only since her marriage and her own sorrow that Isabel understood the tales of her grandmother's skills and potions.

The colour had drained from Mother's face. 'Your grandmother had no gifts.' She rubbed her fingers hard between her eyebrows. 'Many saw my mother as a foolish old woman meddling with physic beyond her abilities, but a few saw her as more than that, even though she did not give incantations with her herbs. It helped she never said a bad word against anyone. After they hanged her friend, talk started that my mother was a witch too. I do not know what would have happened had she not died when she did.' She shivered. 'And Alyce was close to her. It would not have taken much for Alyce to be drawn into it all. It was one of the reasons we sent her so far away.'

Isabel did not care. 'Alyce is a faithless trull.'

'Isabel, have you no idea?' Her mother's voice quavered. 'Many believe witchcraft is passed through the blood from mother to daughter. That is why I tried so hard to teach both you and Alyce seemly behaviour. I wanted no breath of scandal near us.' She stared downward, worrying at the corner of her thumbnail. 'People have long memories. We will all be tainted by your talk of special gifts. Alyce only knows the physic and herbs any good wife uses. Everything you need...' She stopped.

Isabel looked up. Alyce stood inside the doorway.

'Isabel, I will take my leave of you now.'

Isabel turned away and stared out the window, her lips pressed tight together. If anything happened to her baby, it would be Alyce's fault. Promises did not need to be spoken.

~

Thomas opened the door to the parlour of the Bradleys' house where Alyce was laying cut pieces of cloth in piles along the table—brocade and silk and fine wool, though none in particularly bright colours or, Thomas thought, as pretty as what she was wearing. Alyce's skirt was of marigold brocade; her embroidered doublet was unbuttoned at the neck and without its heavy sleeves. She wore, as she did most of the time, a coif covering her hair. She was singing softly to herself.

Alyce turned at the sound of the door and stopped singing. Her smile lit her eyes at the sight of him.

'You have a sweet singing voice, Alyce.'

Although she still smiled, the light faded in her eyes, replaced by wariness. 'Good morrow, Thomas.'

Thomas came over and caught her by the hand. 'Good morrow, Alyce.' He brushed his lips against her fingers. She lowered her eyes, a flush spreading up her face. He drew her to the settle beneath the window. 'We have some matters to discuss.' He let Alyce sit before seating himself close, her hand still caught in his.

'First, do you have a waiting woman of your own?'

'Nay,' Alyce laughed as if the idea was preposterous, 'but I suppose I should find one.'

'My sister Cecily has said, if you wish, you may have one of her women, Marian Haines. She is the wife of my steward. She will help you settle in at Ashthorpe.'

'That is kind of her.'

'I'll bring her when I return for the wedding. As soon as the wedding festivities are over, I will be leaving for London as I sail in early March.'

Alyce's mood altered in an instant. 'I am to go through this fuss to be left behind, nothing changed?' She slid her fingers from his and clasped her hands in her lap.

'I did not say that,' Thomas snapped back. 'All I meant was we cannot linger after the days of feasting your mother has no doubt planned.' He shrugged. 'It is your decision—you may stay here if that is your wish, you may go straight to Ashthorpe, or you may come with me to London. The decision is entirely yours.'

'I have a say?'

'Have you not had a say in this all along?' She had insisted that she had not been forced. He had heard she could be sharp-tongued but had not thought Alyce to be ill-humoured. He did not want a future where he had to tiptoe around in fear of a woman's moods. 'If you wish it, we can break this arrangement by mutual consent.'

'Is that what you want?'

'No,' he looked into her clear green eyes, 'but I have no wish to marry you if this is not what *you* want, if your father has forced you to this.'

'No one has forced me, Thomas.' She took a long slow breath. 'Forgive me. I am tired. I was indulging ill temper.'

He pulled her close. 'You have worked hard for your sister and now,' he nodded towards the small piles of cloth, 'all this is ahead of you.'

'It will not be so bad. Mother is employing a couple of needlewomen to help.'

He rested his fingers under her chin and turned her face up to his. 'Alyce, I believe we can build a good marriage—respect and kindness are a solid basis. Who knows what may grow from that?'

Alyce's eyes widened, hope clear in them.

He loosened his hold but continued to stare at her. 'There is something about you today. Your style of dress, the pretty colours, they suit you.'

'For heaven's sake.' Alyce stiffened. 'I am in my shirt sleeves, in no state to see visitors.' She waved towards the table. 'I was about to start work on these gowns.'

Thomas watched Alyce—she was not one to receive compliments easily. It was a pity he had so little time; she needed to be wooed slowly, by actions rather than words.

'Take off your coif,' he said.

'Why?'

'Because I hate coifs,' he grinned, 'and I want to see your hair. It is unusual for an unmarried woman to keep her hair covered in the way you do. You are not bald, perhaps?'

'I am not.' She lifted her chin and said, 'It is the way a woman with work to do keeps her hair clean.'

She snatched off her coif and pulled the pins from her hair, letting it cascade down her back. She shook it around her shoulders, the faint scent of lavender mixed with a hint of spice drifting on the air. It shone a deep brown in the light from the window.

Thomas reached out and touched a lock, rubbing it between his fingers. 'You should not hide it.' He brushed his fingers down her cheek, and slid his hand around behind her neck, drawing her into a kiss. Her lips were soft; her breath tasted faintly of the anise she used to clean her teeth. As the kiss lengthened, she trembled, leaning in against him, her kisses growing in confidence. Thomas grazed his lips along the line of her jaw, breathing softly on her neck, 'Are you coming with me to London?'

'Ay,' Alyce murmured.

Footsteps echoed in the hall. Thomas sat upright, pulling Alyce with him. He stood to greet her parents as they entered the parlour. Alyce rose more slowly, the heat fading from her face. Thomas glanced back at her—ay, she would make a more than satisfactory wife.

~

Marieke cradled her newborn daughter to her breast as the child sucked steadily. 'Who knows, by Christmas next year you could have a child of your own?'

'Perhaps,' Alyce said without conviction. There were moments still when she found it hard to believe she was on the brink of marriage and family; by the time she was not much more than eighteen she had put aside such ordinary dreams.

Marieke held her daughter against her shoulder, gently rubbing the baby's back as her head lolled sleepily.

'Here,' she placed the baby in Alyce's arms, 'time for you to hold your goddaughter.'

Alyce gazed at the baby, Grace. So tiny and fragile, looking almost like an old woman, yet her translucent skin, long dark lashes and light downy hair hinted at what she would become. 'She is beautiful,' Alyce said, surprised by what she could see in the small face.

'All babies are beautiful,' Marieke smiled, 'especially your own.'

Alyce relaxed back in her chair, carefully rocking the child.

Marieke walked to her chair opposite Alyce at the small fireplace in her bedchamber. She stared at the glowing logs and said, 'Has the day been decided?'

'Ay, the third day of January. You will both come?'

'Most certainly. And how do you feel about it all?'

'I suppose,' Alyce said slowly, 'I am pleased to be marrying and finally to have a proper place in the world. I like the idea of children too. But Thomas...' She paused, her brow furrowed. 'He seems a good man, and charming, but I do not know him well enough to judge his character. And I have no idea what he feels for me.' She liked his company and wished she could be with him more. For the few days he had been in Norwich, Thomas had courted her, and she did not understand why. Without doubt, the main attraction of their marriage was the dowry. She suspected that his courtship was a strategy, that he wanted a wife whose love was more than duty. She should be glad of that, for it showed he did value the marriage of itself. But if she were not careful, she would feel more for him than the temperate love that was the basis of a good marriage. That would be the certain road to unhappiness if he did not care as much for her.

Marieke took the baby from Alyce, placing her in the cradle beside her own chair. 'You would know if he had no liking for you and were marrying you solely for your dowry.'

Alyce nodded, hoping Marieke was right, but was it her own wishful thinking, or perhaps Thomas's skill at acting, that made her believe that he wanted more than money from the marriage? She wished she knew how to read him.

Marieke rocked the cradle with her foot as Grace whimpered in her sleep. 'Six weeks is not much time to prepare for the wedding.'

'Nay.' Alyce shrugged. 'Mother has hired two needlewomen to help with the sewing. They started this morning in the old workroom behind Father's office.'

A door banged at the front of the house followed by a creaking on the stairs and Grietje de Jong bustled in. 'How is *mijn lieve kleindochter?*' She bent over the cradle.

'*Sttt, Moeder*, she has just fallen asleep.'

Grietje turned and said, her eyes twinkling, '*Elsje*, I saw you with your young man last week.'

Alyce doubted Grietje was much more than ten years older than Thomas. 'I did not see you.' She smiled at Grietje. 'I would have introduced you.'

'You looked so happy strolling together, stopping now and then to gaze into each other's eyes. I did not want to interrupt.'

Marieke raised her eyebrows at Alyce. 'You did not tell me this.'

'We were not gazing into each other's eyes.' Alyce flushed. 'Thomas was telling me of his plans.'

'He is a fine-looking man.' Grietje grinned. 'Nice strong legs—that is a good sign in a husband.'

'*Moeder,*' Marieke said sharply, only half disapproving.

'You will come to my wedding, Mistress de Jong?'

'I would not miss it for the world. It will feel like I have married off the last of my children.' She nodded happily. 'And very well too.'

Alyce acknowledged that, in the eyes of the world, it was a good marriage. And if she and Thomas could treat each other with respect and kindness, as he suggested, she would have more than many women.

12

December 1586

Alyce gazed at the images in the glass panels of the great east window of the Church of St Peter Mancroft. Her attention wavered as the minister, William Reynes, set out the true foundation of the Church in Christ himself and expounded on the errors of the papists and their furtive support of rebellion against both Queen and country. Her thoughts drifted to Accession Day and she felt again Thomas's arms around her. For all her attempts to think coolly of the marriage, the first thought of him always brought his physical presence to her so vividly her resolve was in danger of being swept away.

Master Reynes boomed out, 'I publish the banns of marriage between Alyce Bradley of the parish of St Peter Mancroft in Norwich and Thomas Granville of Ashthorpe in the county of Northamptonshire. If any one of you persons should know cause, or just impediment, why these two persons should not be joined together in holy matrimony, you are to declare it. This is the first time of asking.'

The silence after the calling stretched on. Then, in a rush, the service was over and the knot in Alyce's chest began to unravel. Well-wishers surrounded her outside the church including Isabel's friends Martha Powell and Lettys Rowe and young Frances Sutton, a touch defiant in her good wishes. Some who did not belong to the parish were there, including Agnes Hall, who, although she repeated the customary words, did not look as if she meant them. Some smiled with genuine delight; others were merely curious. And one or two stood back, their wishes withheld, Lady Sutton, with Isabel beside her, the most obvious.

As those around her drifted away, Alyce hurried to find her parents who were somewhere amongst those standing chatting along the street leading to the market. She heard Agnes Hall's shrill voice as she approached the market.

'Will you look at that, Maude? Bedford the haberdasher is talking to the wife of that tailor that lives along from the

Bradleys. I wonder what is going on there.'

'They would be simply passing the time of day,' Maude Middleton answered.

'And Alyce Bradly is to be married in three weeks—any idea why the marriage is so rushed?'

Alyce paused.

The women stood with their backs to her.

'I believe Master Granville is sailing soon and may be away six months or more,' Maude answered. 'If not now, they would have to wait until this time next year.'

'More likely a little Granville will appear in a few months,' Hall scoffed.

Alyce took a deep breath. She would not permit a creature like Agnes Hall to defame her. She was a woman who revelled in rumour, not only talking to anyone who would listen of what she had heard of others' lives but hunting out secrets and, when that failed, spreading malicious lies of her own invention.

Alyce marched towards the women, her heart thumping.

'I am certain you are mistaken, Agnes,' Maude said. 'Alyce Bradley is a sober, godly woman. She travelled with us from Lincoln and I have formed a good opinion of her.'

Maude turned, a blush spreading over her face when she saw Alyce standing beside them.

Hall still looked away, her eyes darting from churchgoer to churchgoer as they moved off towards their homes. 'And did you get a good look at Alyce Bradley's ring?' She laughed unpleasantly. 'You would think with all his pirate plunder, Granville could have given her something better, rubies or diamonds perhaps.'

'It is very fine workmanship, Goodwife Hall,' Alyce said as calmly as she could. 'Would you like a closer look?' She gripped her cloak closed and made no attempt to remove her glove.

Hall started at the sound of Alyce's voice. She turned, no hint of shame in her face. 'I do not think so, I saw it before—it is just a plain gold band.'

'It is not!' Maude glared at Hall. 'It is fine goldsmith's work with great detail in the pattern. Jack made it and is rightly proud of it.' She smiled at Alyce, the colour still high in her face. 'No one else will have a ring like you have, Alyce.'

'No, they will not, Mistress Middleton.' She pulled her cloak tight around her. 'If you will excuse me.' Ignoring Agnes Hall, she nodded to Maude and walked off in the direction of her parents' house, wondering if anything short of a ride in the scold-cart would silence Agnes Hall.

~

Thomas stretched his feet towards the hearth. Beside him, his dog raised its head, alert to the sound of faltering steps on the hall dais beyond the parlour door. Thomas rose, ready to help as his sister, Cecily, assisted by her women Marian and Judith, struggled to the chair opposite.

Stifling a groan, Cecily eased herself down and laid her head against the chair's padded back. Her women seated themselves farther back from the fire and waited, quiet and forgotten, until they were needed again.

'You are in much pain tonight?' Thomas dropped his hand to the dog's head and scratched behind its ears, the dog closed its eyes and murmured with contentment.

'No more than usual.' She rubbed one hand across the swollen joints of the other. 'The end of the day, and the beginning, are the worst.'

He glanced across, noting the tiredness in her smallpox-ravaged face. 'You need not have stayed up late for my benefit.'

'I do relish any time spent with you as you are away so often.' She broke into a smile. 'The banns were called today for the first time—your wedding is less than three weeks away.'

Thomas's gaze drifted to the tapestry of a hunting scene hanging on the wall behind Cecily.

'Thomas?' Cecily raised her voice.

Frowning slightly, he brought his attention back to her.

'Is there a problem?'

He shook his head. 'I have much on my mind at present.'

'Perhaps you should postpone your wedding until you return.'

'It has to be now. I need the dowry as one of the investors has withdrawn.'

Cecily nodded, thoughtful. 'Will Alyce come here straight

after the wedding?'

'She is coming with me to London. We will stay at Anthony's.'

'Our brother Anthony?'

'Do not look surprised—our relations have been civil for some time. Not so civil we would share a house,' he laughed. 'He is leaving in January as part of an embassy to the French court led by the Queen's agent, William Waad. And he has invested in this venture. I have done nothing to discomfit him in over fifteen years.'

'Will he be present at your wedding?'

Thomas shook his head. 'He did not offer, but he has given me his blessing—not that I sought it.'

'I am pleased you and Alyce will spend some time together.' Cecily stared into the fire. After a few moments she took a deep breath and said, 'And how is Beth Marston, still as welcoming?'

Thomas scowled. 'Beth Marston is none of your concern.'

Cecily looked down at her knotted hands resting in her lap. 'All who live at Ashthorpe are my concern be they labourers, tenants or, as in the case of the Marstons, yeomen.'

Thomas crossed his arms and sat back in his chair.

'I thought you had finished with her.'

'Cecily, why do you persist?'

Cecily furrowed her brow and watched the flames. 'Because I do not understand. It does not fit with what I know of your sense of honour. You value Peter Marston, yet you cuckold him.'

'Do I?' Thomas spoke softly.

Cecily rushed on, 'Beth has, with hints and barely veiled suggestions, kept alive the rumour she is your woman.'

Thomas glowered, his mouth a grim line. Even here, in his own home, the worst was thought of him.

'Tom,' she said with care, 'no bride would welcome the knowledge her groom comes warm from another woman's bed.'

'You think me depraved?' he snarled as he flung himself from his chair. He stood, his hand against the mantel, glaring into the fire.

'We thought Marston would never marry and were surprised

90

to have him return from London after collecting his uncle's legacy without most of the money but with a bride. And then to have her suggest...'

Thomas bent down and poked the glowing logs, sending a spray of sparks up the chimney. He replaced the poker with a clatter and straightened, facing Cecily. 'Beth was no common whore. It was not long after I broke that betrothal.' He jerked his head and faced the fire. He still could not bring himself to say her name. He had been a fool, besotted with her, all judgement fled. Ay, as the common wisdom suggested, marrying for love brought a world of sorrow. Better to coolly choose a woman for her virtue.

'Common or uncommon, a whore is a whore.'

Thomas continued to stare into the crackling flames. Was Cecily speaking of his former betrothed or Beth?

'By coming here, Beth hoped to continue whatever it was between you.' Cecily shifted in her chair and groaned. 'Enough of Beth, you have told me next to nothing of Alyce Bradley. I know the most intricate details of the contract, the dowry and the jointure, but nothing of the girl herself. You do realise a young maid enamoured of the idea of being the lady of the manor will not take kindly to an ailing resident sister-in-law?'

Thomas almost laughed. He supposed his sister knew him well. Cecily knew how far to push, how to make sure she had her say, then changed the subject. He turned to her. 'You know I would be careful to choose someone who would care for you. I made that clear to Alyce.'

'How delightful for her,' Cecily said tartly.

He returned to his chair. 'You are in a most contrary mood this evening. I thought you wanted me to marry—you have nagged me for years.'

'I do, but I want you to have a happy marriage. Tell me, what is it about Alyce Bradley that made you settle on her?'

'The dowry—I would not marry her without it but I believe she will make a good wife whom I can respect.'

'And your feelings for her?'

'It is a man's duty to love his wife.'

'Oh, Thomas,' Cecily said, exasperated. 'That tells me

nothing. What does Alyce look like?'

Thomas laid his head back against the chair and stared at the ceiling. 'Alyce is tall enough to stand face to face with many men. She would be called buxom if she did not dress so soberly. Clear skin, no blemishes. She uses no tricks or artifice, nor wears much adornment.' But, he was sure, with a little help she would be more than pleasing to the eye. 'She has an open face and the bloom of health. Thick dark hair. She is nearing thirty but I would say she still has many breeding years ahead.' He gave a bark of laughter. 'It sounds like I am measuring horse flesh.'

'Indeed,' Cecily said. 'And the colour of her eyes?'

Thomas's face relaxed, remembering the last time he was with Alyce, the softness of her skin and her intriguing scent of spiced lavender. Perhaps his judgement was not as cool as he imagined. He already felt a growing affection for Alyce—a good basis for a satisfactory marriage.

'The purest peridot,' he said.

Cecily nodded. 'A pleasing answer.'

~

Her embroidery abandoned in her lap, Alyce gazed out the parlour window at the darkening garden.

She had expected Thomas a few days ahead of the wedding hoping that he would celebrate some of the Christmas season with her, but he had not yet returned to Norwich. She would not leave the house tomorrow unless she was certain he had come. She refused to face the shame of arriving at the church with no bridegroom to greet her.

Eliza moved quietly around the room lighting candles.

Alyce looked away from the window and could not help the smile that spread across her face as Thomas walked into the parlour. In his presence, all her doubts melted away.

He caught her hands in his and kissed her formally, a dry brush of his cold lips against hers.

Alyce's heart skipped a beat.

Her mother had followed him in as well as a cheerful dark-haired woman of around forty. Thomas beckoned the woman forward. 'Alyce, this is Marian Haines, your waiting woman.'

Marian curtsied. 'Good even, Mistress, I am glad to meet you at last.'

'Thank you, Marian. I am pleased you are here.'

Before Alyce could say more, her mother said, 'Marian, I will show you your room—you will be with Alyce and Eliza.'

Beyond hospitality, Alyce was certain her mother intended to politely question Marian about the household at Ashthorpe.

'If you will excuse me, Mistress.' Marian curtsied again to Alyce.

Thomas rose and picked up a small wooden casket he had placed on the cabinet beside the door as he entered the room. 'This is a gift from my sister, Cecily.'

Alyce opened the casket. The light from the candles danced on the facets of the diamonds, caressed the heavy pearls of an ornate carcanet and earrings.

'Oooh,' she breathed, struck by both the beauty and the workmanship.

She picked up one of the earrings, a large pear-shaped pearl suspended from a gold ring.

'Those I had made for you. I noticed that you have taken to the new fashion of bedecking your ears with jewellery.' He brushed his finger against her earlobe. The small golden ball hanging there swayed gently.

Alyce closed her eyes. She could not think with Thomas's fingers on her skin.

He watched her but continued sensibly, 'The carcanet was a wedding gift from my father to my mother. Cecily wore it on her wedding day and sends you her greetings and her wish that you wear it too.'

Alyce's eyes glistened. 'I am honoured. I have never…'

She did not finish. Isabel sailed in followed by Frances Sutton, her young sister-in-law.

'Where is Mother?'

'Upstairs, I doubt she will be long.'

'We have been to the old workroom, Alyce.' Isabel glanced at the casket on Alyce's lap and moved closer. 'The style of those gowns is out of date and I see you still have a liking for the dullest of colours.'

Alyce kept her mouth shut, heat rising up her face.

'I like them all,' Frances said with a defiant glance at Isabel. 'The kirtle of figured silk is beautiful.'

Isabel peered into the casket. 'What is this?'

'A gift from Thomas's sister.'

'Diamonds do flatter sallow skin,' Isabel sniffed as she turned away. 'I do not have time to waste here.' She swept from the room, Frances rushing to keep up.

Thomas stared after her. 'Your sister—'

'Isabel is Isabel,' Alyce interrupted. 'She still has not forgiven me for *deserting* her. And to think when you said I could choose what to do after the wedding, I was tempted to stay here with Isabel.'

'Tempted?' Thomas raised an eyebrow. 'Temptation usually involves some prospect of delight.'

'Perhaps more the thought crossed my mind. My duty lies with you.'

'Duty need only be the beginning of the journey.' He looked deep into her eyes and leant forward, his fingers tracing her hand.

Alyce held her breath, waiting for the touch of his lips on hers, but he looked away and rose from the seat beside her.

Her father strolled into the room. 'Ah, Thomas, you have arrived at last.' He clasped his hand. 'You must be cold after your journey. Will you take a glass of claret with me—a taste of what we will serve tomorrow?'

'That would be most welcome.' Thomas turned to Alyce. 'Will you join us?'

'Thank you, no. I will find Marian. We should work out what can be packed now for the journey to London.'

'And how many extra packhorses should I arrange?'

'Oh, I was thinking more a large dray pulled by a team of oxen,' Alyce laughed.

She smiled as she climbed the stairs to her room. She had agreed to marry Thomas because she felt she had no other choice, but his courtesy and light-hearted humour made the prospect not unwelcome.

13

January 1587

Alyce lay open-eyed, staring at the tester above her bed. The tread of feet on floorboards, the murmur of cheerful conversation, the scrape of furniture being rearranged carried from the floor below.

Today she would give herself into the care of a stranger who would own her completely. She hoped he truly was as good-humoured and courteous as he had shown himself so far. If he were, she had nothing to fear of the life she would have with him. She told herself whatever her life with Thomas came to be, it was better than anything she could expect in Norwich. But she must keep in mind that he was marrying her not because of affection, but because she was the price of the generous dowry her father had offered. To yearn for more than kindness and respect would only bring her unhappiness. Then there was tonight, the matter her mind slid away from. She knew many men, and women, sought it out, licit and illicitly, but there were women who regarded it as a burden for whom the only joy it brought was children.

She started as the door to the bedchamber slammed.

Her mother bustled in and pulled the bed curtains open. 'Time to wake up, Alyce.' She hurried her out of bed. 'Come along, everything is ready in my room.'

Her parents' bedchamber was pleasantly warm with braziers burning in two corners. A new tapestry hung on the wall, the bed curtains had been changed, the bedding folded back to show fine linen with an embroidered edge.

With a jolt, Alyce realised it was here she and Thomas would sleep tonight in the best bed in the house, the bed her parents gave up for honoured guests.

Eliza poured steaming water from a jug into a basin set on a cabinet near the braziers. She finished by sprinkling the water with scented oil.

Once Alyce had washed and pulled on a smock of cambric,

she sat on a stool as Marian dampened her hair with a sprinkling of lavender water and combed it out. Alyce closed her eyes and tried to empty her mind, passively accepting Marian's attentions.

Too soon Marian gently touched her shoulder and said, 'Time to dress, Mistress.'

Alyce opened her eyes and shivered, although the room was not cold.

The women helped her dress, layer by layer: silk stockings and garters; shoes of tawny dyed leather; petticoat of yellow buffin with a stiffened bodice; farthingale; kirtle of primrose taffeta, the forepart embroidered with glass beads; gown of marigold damask lined with satin; ruffs edged with fine silver-threaded lace made by Grietje de Jong.

Marian dressed Alyce's hair, plaiting and twisting it into a silken caul with spangles stitched across it.

Her mother watched and said, 'I do wish this wedding was in spring and we could have more than rosemary and lavender in your bridal garland. And the lavender is not even fresh.'

'They are the best for a marriage, Mother—rosemary for constancy and lavender for devotion.'

'You are right,' she sighed, 'but rosebuds are very pretty.'

Her mother applied a light dusting of powder to Alyce's face, a touch of paint to her mouth.

'Now for the final touch.' She hooked the pearl earrings into Alyce's ears and clasped the carcanet around her neck. The gems sparkled in the morning light. 'This is worth a small fortune.'

Alyce arched an eyebrow. 'Perhaps it is pirate booty.'

'He said it belonged to his mother.'

'Perhaps they have always been pirates.'

Her mother shot a quick look at Marian whose eyes glittered with amusement, and stepped back from Alyce. 'You do us credit.'

Alyce could read her mother's mind. Finally, she was someone she could boast of: well-dressed, well-married, well-connected.

Her mother leant forward and brushed her lips against Alyce's cheek. 'Well, Daughter, marriage is as hard a road as anything else in this life, but much contentment can be gained from it. I wish you every happiness.'

Alyce's eyes prickled at the earnest blessing.

~

The household, heavy cloaks drawn tight over their finery, set out together in the bright but icy morning. Alyce, carrying her bridal garland, walked with her father; two pages were ahead of them; three bridesmaids, the daughters of her father's friends, beside Alyce carrying beribboned bouquets of rosemary and lavender. Her mother, Marian and the rest of the household followed. Behind them musicians played as they walked. Well-wishers stood in their doorways, waved and called greetings, some joining in the short walk to the church. Half of the town appeared to have turned out, crowding around the front of the church. Master Reynes and Thomas waited at the porch beneath the bell-tower but moved back into the church as Alyce arrived.

The crowd parted to let the bride's party through. In the porch, the eldest bridesmaid took the garland and placed it on Alyce's head.

Alyce stepped through the doorway into the church and walked beside her father to Thomas standing with the minister at the chancel steps.

Master Reynes raised his voice, 'Dearly beloved friends...'

The shuffling and murmuring of the crowd stilled.

Alyce stood beside Thomas, her mind empty of all except the sound of his voice as he said his vows. Her right hand in his, she repeated the vow, 'I, Alyce, take thee, Thomas, to my wedded husband, to have and to hold from this day forward...' She spoke clearly, without wavering, aware of the solemnity of the promises.

Thomas placed the ring Alyce had worn on her right hand, the betrothal ring, on the fourth finger of her left hand and said, 'With this ring, I thee wed: with my body, I thee worship: and with all my worldly goods, I thee endow.'

With the minister's final blessing, Alyce was joined for the rest of her days to a man she barely knew.

They came out through the great doors together and stood at the front of the porch. Thomas turned to Alyce and kissed her to the cheering of the crowd. And to Alyce it was nothing more than the touching of lips. The delight of yesterday had fled, replaced by a heavy solemnity.

The sun broke through the leaden clouds, light dancing on rooftops and trees lightly dusted with overnight snow. Alyce's heart lifted as a robin settled onto a branch in the closest tree. All would be well once she and Thomas were alone, away from the watching eyes of the whole town.

Women crowded around offering their good wishes. Grietje de Jong pushed through and flung her arms around Alyce. '*Elsje*, I wish you joy and many children.'

Behind Grietje, Marieke smiled happily at Alyce.

'Thomas,' Alyce introduced them, 'this is Mistress de Jong and her daughter, Marieke Thompson. Marieke is my dearest friend.'

Marieke kissed Alyce and linked her arms with her. 'I am happy for you, Alyce. And,' she whispered, '*Moeder* was right, he is a fine-looking man.'

Grietje smiled at Thomas. 'Sir, you have managed to catch yourself the best of wives.'

'*Dank u, Mevrouw,*' Thomas answered.

There followed a swift exchange between them in Dutch. Grietje smiled and tossed her head, almost as if she were flirting with Thomas. And whatever it was she was saying, it appeared to amuse him.

As Grietje and Marieke began to move away, Alyce said, 'I will see you at the feast.'

'Not until tomorrow, *lieveling*,' Grietje answered, 'but we look forward to it.'

Alyce watched them go, saddened that although her mother knew how much the de Jongs meant to her, she had not thought them important enough to invite to dine on the first day of the festivities.

'What did Mistress de Jong say to you?'

'She was telling me how to take care of you, said she will have the severest words with me if you are not the happiest of women the next time she sees you.' He grinned, still amused. 'And a few suggestions on how to win your heart.'

Alyce gasped. 'I am sorry.'

'At least someone read me the lecture.' His lips twitched into a smile. 'A new husband expects it.'

Servants wove among the crowd handing out drink—wine rather than the usual ale. Thomas took a goblet from one of the passing servants and passed it to Alyce.

Alyce sipped the wine, shuddering as she swallowed. It was worse than vinegar.

Thomas reclaimed the goblet and drained it. 'It is not that bad.' He placed it on the tray of a serving man and took Alyce in his arms. As he kissed her, the crowd around them cheered again. Alyce felt the heat of his kiss but could not answer it. The thought of what lay ahead tonight and in her uncharted future pressed down on her.

~

Robin Chapman stood at the back of the crowd where he had a clear view of Alyce, if not her new husband. Barely recognisable in her finery, she was every inch a gentleman's wife—marriage to a journeyman mercer would have been a step down for such a woman.

His anger had solidified into something cold and hard in the months since Alyce's foul-mouthed rejection of his proposal. She had dismissed him like some worthless creature and had refused to acknowledge his existence since. She rarely passed through the shop, and then only in the company of her mother or her sister. They greeted him, but Alyce continued on her way. On the rare occasions they came face to face, she stared through him as if he were invisible.

He had blamed Bradley at first, thought he was playing some sort of game, using Robin's interest in Alyce to reduce the dowry to Granville perhaps. Robin had contemplated finding another position but that would have meant leaving Norwich. A week after the betrothal, Bradley had come to him and expressed his regret Alyce had not chosen him, said he would have welcomed Robin as a son-in-law, but the decision was Alyce's alone—it was the only way he could get Alyce's consent to any marriage. He clearly valued Robin's goodwill to offer any explanation.

The crowd cheered as Granville kissed his bride.

That was the end of Robin's hopes. Alyce's sudden return had stirred up his youthful dreams. As a girl, she had been a strange one, living in another world, head in a book or making potions with her grandmother or wandering abroad with that Stranger friend of hers. She had ignored him then too, unless he forced her to pay attention to him. And she had pretended his interest was a surprise and unwanted. The older apprentices had egged him on, saying she was playing coy, girls did that. If she were truly unwilling, she would have told her father to put an end to it. Bradley's journeyman, a plain man himself who claimed a vast experience of women, had been free with advice: *You're on to something there, lad. The plainer ones always pretend they're not interested to hide their eagerness.* So Robin had persisted, understanding the more Alyce reviled him the deeper her desire for him. Had she stayed in Norwich, she would have been his.

His mother had encouraged him too, saying Alyce Bradley was the sort of bride she wanted for him, one who would improve the family's position. Edith's sharp voice echoed in his head. *A bride's unruly tongue and wayward manner are no obstacles if she is heir to a thriving business. They are easily corrected. A bride who brings nothing but herself is a burden.* He stopped a sigh as he thought of Susan Graham, a kind and uncomplicated girl. Hardworking too, she would have been a true helpmeet not a burden. But his mother had made her contempt plain. Life would have been a misery trying to live with both of them.

Robin pushed into the crowd and grabbed a goblet of wine from a passing servant—he was as good as any of them. He glared towards Alyce and Granville surrounded by their well-wishers. Good riddance! They deserved each other.

14

Musicians played at one end of the hall in the Bradleys' house. Servants moved among the guests with platters of meats and pastries. Wine and ale flowed. Thomas and Alyce seated in the position of honour, ate from the same plate, drank from the same cup. Thomas's hand rested on Alyce's as he spoke to Sir Robert Southwell, one of the leading gentlemen of the county and Vice-Admiral of Norfolk, Thomas's witness and his only guest.

A man in his early twenties, Sir Robert was well regarded in the highest circles. Favoured by the Queen herself, he had been knighted the year before. He had told Alyce, laughing, he had been invited to be Thomas's witness yesterday. He was lucky to find him in Norwich as he usually spent the Christmas season at court.

Alyce stared down at Thomas's hand—the darkened skin, crossed with scars, the muscular strength. And she felt nothing. She could have been holding her own hand. Even yesterday, when his fingers had brushed hers, his touch had thrilled her. She wanted to be married to no one else but instead of the growing delight she had felt whenever she was with him, all she felt now was a chilling anxiety.

The main feasting over, the tables were cleared away and dancing began. Thomas led Alyce onto the floor in a formal pavane—together they were the image of elegance. As the music progressed to a livelier gavotte, other couples joined them. Thomas and Alyce were swept apart as guests pressed them to dance. Men who had never given Alyce a single glance sought her out, treating her with a newfound respect. The compliments flowed too, as if she were a fresh-faced sixteen-year-old. And beneath the light banter were thinly veiled references to what would follow later. Her unease deepened—so private a matter should not be the topic of common conversation.

Will Sutton claimed her as a dancing partner. His eyes never left her as they slip-stepped forward hand in hand. They faced each other and turned about, Will now intent on the movement of Alyce's breasts beneath the fine lawn of her partlet. Alyce stared straight ahead. She wished she could hide away in a corner out of sight.

Finally, the almaine ended and Alyce curtsied to him.

'You surprise me, Alyce,' Will said, smirking. 'You certainly have been hiding yourself beneath your coifs and aprons.'

'I wear what becomes the situation. A coif and apron would be out of place here.' Although she knew her gown was beautiful, there was safety in a coif and apron. Wearing them, few of the men present today would have given her a second look.

'I am certain Granville is well pleased with the bargain he has made. Or, as will soon be the case, *unmaid*.' He laughed loudly at his own jest.

Alyce quickly moved towards the safety of the older women who were sitting at one side chatting, but before she could reach them, she felt a hand upon her sleeve.

'May I have this dance, Mistress?'

Thomas caught her hand and drew her into the line of couples stepping down the hall. Turning, they moved away from each other, turned again and glided back. As Thomas skipped around Alyce, he watched her. There was a question, an invitation in his eyes that Alyce was afraid to answer. She concentrated on her steps as she skipped around him. The pairs of dancers bent towards each other, kissing lightly, bringing the courante to an end. Instead of stepping away, Thomas drew Alyce closer, his breath against her ear, 'Would we be missed if we slipped away?'

Alyce's eyes widened. 'It is still afternoon.'

'You think the sun must be set for a man to take pleasure in his wife?' he laughed, a low rumble.

Alyce stuttered, not knowing how to answer.

'I see I have much to teach you, Wife.' Thomas brushed his lips, tantalising, against hers.

Alyce closed her eyes, wishing she felt as she had yesterday. She opened them to see, across Thomas's shoulder, Isabel seated amid her court of young matrons, her eyes on Alyce.

Thomas turned, following Alyce's gaze. 'Ah, the sweet-natured Mistress Sutton.'

Alyce said nothing.

'I have little time for vain idle women who have nothing better to do than to sit around and destroy the character of any hapless soul who wanders into their gaze.'

'And what of vain idle men?'

'I despise pampered fools, be they male or female.'

'You sound the sterner sort of Christian.'

Thomas gave a short bark of laughter. 'I have been called many things in my life but not that.'

Before Alyce could reply, they were surrounded by a group of young men eager to draw Thomas into the parlour, where games of cards and dice and tables were underway. Alyce watched Thomas disappear into the crowd.

'Lovesick already, Alyce?'

'It is a delight to see you too, Isabel.'

'Do you know how he spent last night?' Isabel did not wait for an answer. 'He had two trollops in his chamber at the Maid's Head.'

'Only two?' Alyce raised her eyebrows. It was so ridiculous, she wanted to laugh. 'Are you certain it was not three? Or four? Why not six? It makes a more amusing story.'

'How can you bear it?' Isabel glared at her. 'Every night from now, will you not wonder, with every new love trick he tries, who taught him this, who else likes this done?'

Despite her shock at Isabel's venom, Alyce saw the pain in her sister's eyes. Was she talking as much of herself? She reached out and touched Isabel's arm. 'Isabel, let us put our animosities aside for one day.'

'Daughters.' Their father's voice cut across them. 'Surely you are not arguing on a day like this.'

'Isabel is wishing me well,' Alyce said with forced brightness.

He smiled indulgently at his younger daughter.

Isabel pressed her cheek against Alyce's and muttered through her teeth, 'I wish you all that you truly deserve.'

'And I hope life grants you what you desire, Isabel.' As Alyce said the words, she knew she meant them.

Alyce turned to her father, 'Father, you have not yet danced with me.'

'It is remiss of me.' He bowed formally to Alyce and led her onto the floor.

~

By the time the sun set, the guests had begun to tire, but the Bradleys' hospitality continued with wine and sugared delicacies. The musicians still played, and rather than dance, many joined together singing, though some were quite drunk and the songs became increasingly bawdy.

Thomas stood with his arm around Alyce as a final toast was drunk and the throng called their wishes for the couple.

While the men took Thomas to what had been Alyce's room to change from his wedding finery, Alyce, accompanied by the women, went to her parents' bedchamber. Piece by piece, her gown, sleeves, petticoats, bodice and smock were unpinned, unlaced and carefully laid aside and Alyce dressed in a bed-smock of lawn embroidered at the neck and wrists.

As Marian stood behind her, combing out her dark, glossy hair, Alyce stared at the dried rose petals strewn on the bed and shivered despite the warmth from the braziers.

Her mother patted Alyce's hand. 'There is no need to be fearful, dear.'

Lady Sutton, who had spent most of the day sitting with her husband watching and judging, not joining in, spoke up. 'Even though it is unpleasant, Alyce, it is not unbearable.' Alyce's mother and Marian glanced at each other. 'You will become used to it and if you are truly fortunate, children will come quickly and you can put it behind you.'

'It is better than that.' Her mother glared at Lady Sutton. 'And I am sure Thomas Granville is a man who knows how to please a woman.'

'Mother!' Alyce shut her eyes.

'And who knows what tricks he has learnt of late?'

The women, save Lady Sutton, gasped at Isabel's sneering remark.

Alyce wanted to scream. This was worse than anything that

could possibly happen later. She immediately regretted the thought with the noise of the men outside the door.

Thomas's voice rose above the others. 'Gentlemen, I am not so drunk I need to be carried.'

'I'll wager you desire to be carried by your new wife.' The men laughed raucously.

If only she could cover her ears, shut her eyes and find, when she opened them, they were gone and the worst over. Alyce stared straight ahead, meeting no one's eye as the men tumbled into the room.

Master Reynes stood in front of the crowd and said sternly, 'It is time for the blessing.'

Thomas, dressed in a nightgown, knelt beside the bed. Alyce joined him, her back to the crowd. As the minister prayed for their marriage and their fecundity, some struggled to remain serious.

Finished, Reynes said, 'We will now leave the man and his wife to perform their duty.'

'The bride's stockings,' a slurred voice called. Alyce continued to kneel, her head bowed.

'It will not take long, Alyce,' Thomas said quietly. He helped Alyce onto the bed and blocked view of her from the crowd. He deftly removed her stockings and tossed them out, amid shrieks and whoops, to the men at the back.

Her father called above the hubbub, 'There is food and drink below for those who need refreshment before they retire.'

'But we have not completely undressed the groom.'

'He may need to be helped into bed.'

'I can manage, gentlemen.'

'And if not, your bride can climb the mainmast for you,' came the slurred voice again.

Alyce sat at the edge of the bed, her head lowered.

Thomas raised his voice, 'It is time to leave.'

~

The room cleared and the door bolted, Thomas came over to Alyce. 'They are drunken fools. Forget them.'

He placed his hands on her shoulders and kissed her. Her lips were soft, but she barely reacted to him. He eased the smock from her shoulders, his lips travelling down her throat. Alyce sat motionless. Thomas looked up and grazed his fingers over her forehead, tracing them down her cheek, over her lips.

'There is nothing to fear.'

'I am not afraid,' she said, stoic, 'just tired.'

'I know a fine prelude to sleep.' Thomas got off the bed, dropped his nightgown to the floor and stood naked, his desire obvious. Alyce looked straight ahead, embarrassment flaming in her face.

Thomas climbed into bed and drew Alyce down beside him, aware he must hold back and approach her slowly. He was willing to take as much time as was needed. He kissed her, stroking her back and shoulders but she lay stiff beside him. 'You seem unwilling. This can wait.'

'I am not unwilling,' her voice wavered. 'I will do my duty.'

He breathed on her neck. 'I want more than duty.' She did not move, even away from him.

He let her go and lay back against the pillows, his hands behind his head. 'You can put out the candles.'

Alyce pulled her bed-smock back over her shoulders as she slid to the edge of the bed.

'Leave off the gown.' He might as well have the satisfaction of seeing her as she truly was.

'No.' Alyce turned her back to him and tied the smock at the neck. She blew out the candle on her side of the bed as well as the candle on the cabinet by the door. The remaining light burned beside Thomas.

'You could blow the last one out,' Alyce said from the darkness near the door.

'I want you to do it for me.'

She squared her shoulders and walked around the bed. Thomas watched the movement of her body beneath the flimsy covering of her bed-smock, her female curves unrestrained by rigid bodices and yards of cloth. Her hair fell to her waist, shimmering red-brown in the remaining light. She bent and blew out the last candle. As she moved away, Thomas reached over and caught her hand.

'It is dark now. Take off the gown.'

As the cloth slithered to the floor, he caught her around the waist and pulled her into the bed with him.

He held her tight, kissing her deeply. He had wanted this marriage for a number of reasons unrelated to the woman in his arms, but at this moment he wanted Alyce herself. She did not fight him but lay like a wooden doll. In the silence, he could feel the thudding of her heart.

'A pity,' he murmured as he released her. Alyce lay still beside him. He reached down and pulled the covers over them both.

'Tomorrow morning, when you are rested.' He buried his face against her shoulder, moving with small kisses towards her ear. 'Then you will see,' he murmured. And he would ensure she did—he wanted a wife who was bound to him by far more than duty.

~

Alyce lay against the pillows, letting Thomas's voice wash over her as, beyond the bedcurtains, he talked with Watkins while he dressed.

Somehow sleep had washed away her fears. She had woken with Thomas lying close. They had lain together talking of mundane things, the rumble of his voice caressing her as his fingers played upon her skin until there was no longer need for words and Alyce had followed naturally where Thomas led. The hurt she had expected barely mattered as she was overwhelmed by what passed between them.

Thomas opened the curtains, leant in and kissed Alyce—a long, slow kiss.

She sighed as he drew away.

'Nay, Wife.' He grinned. 'We must face the throng your mother has assembled below.' As he stepped away and let the curtains drop, he called, 'I will send Marian to help you dress.'

Alyce stared into the crack of light falling through the bed curtains and smiled.

15

A lyce walked around the tailor's dressing room, watching the cloth of her newly finished gown catch the light from the window.

'Mistress,' Marian said, 'that gown suits you well.'

Alyce brushed her hand against the cloth of the skirt. 'It is a lovely gown.' Wearing it, she would not look out of place beside the highborn ladies who would be at Lord Reading's. She should accept Thomas knew more of the ways of London than she did.

She had been both angry and shamed when Thomas had insisted she accompany him to Cheapside to arrange a new gown for her to wear to a feast held by one of his acquaintants, Lord Reading. Thomas had chosen the cloth, figured damask of a deep green, discussed the cut of the gown with the tailor and one of the needlewomen, the trimmings, the embroidery on the stomacher, the depth of the bodice, the design of the sleeves. It was to have a farthingale and a large open ruff. He went on to suggest the style of gown that could be made with several other bolts of bright fabric he selected.

Alyce had kept her tongue in check until they were in the street.

She had not been able to stop herself. 'You think me incapable of dressing myself in a way that does not shame you?'

'It is not that. You are new to London, and we need to make an impression. Lord Reading—'

She had spoken over him. 'You are treating me like a kept woman, to be dressed and displayed at your whim.'

'Alyce...' He had stopped, as if he did not know where to begin. 'I have no time for this. I have pressing matters to see to at the docks.'

He had stridden off through the crowd and come home late that night. He was gone before she woke and from then he had taken to sleeping in the room adjoining hers. Last night he had not come home at all.

And Alyce missed him. She liked his company—he was charming and amusing, and she was coming to trust his behaviour towards her was the result not only of respect, but perhaps, of a growing fondness. Clearly, she had been mistaken.

Without Thomas, her days were quiet, spent mostly in the company of Lucy, the garrulous wife of James Foster, the captain of Thomas's second ship. The Fosters were also staying at Anthony Granville's house.

As Alyce stepped out of the tailor's shop followed by Marian, two grooms from Ashthorpe, who had been lounging outside the door, fell in step with them. Stokes, a burly man of around forty, the elder of the two, walked behind Alyce, the other groom ahead, pushing a way through the throng. When they had arrived in London, Thomas had been emphatic that Alyce was not to venture out without an escort. Alyce had shrugged, thinking the notion ridiculous, but had accepted it, sensing this was an argument she had no hope of winning.

Alyce and Marian wandered through the Cheapside crowds, past the impressive shops of the mercers and goldsmiths. In the short time she had been here, Alyce had come to love London —a place full of life, teeming with people from many corners of the world, of sights, sounds and movement, alive with possibilities.

In their first week here, Thomas had shown her the city in its variety and glory: the majesty of St Paul's with its ornate tombs, its preachers at the stone pulpit outside and its row of booksellers; the imposing Royal Exchange with its merchandise from many nations; the streets crowded with shops, great and small, selling everything imaginable; the mansions of the nobility with gardens sweeping down to the river; the exotic animals in the menagerie at the Tower. And, stretching east of London's incomparable bridge, moored ships with their forest of masts and rigging, overshadowed by busy cranes on the docks.

They had dined with Thomas's wide circle of acquaintances, among them men he had sailed with and fought beside, like the seamen Christopher Carleil and Edward Winter. She had glimpsed men and women she knew only by repute—Sir Christopher Hatton, the Lord Chancellor and the Queen's favourite; the stunningly beautiful Lady Rich; the dashing Earl of Essex. Among these well-dressed, well-connected men and women there was respect for Thomas. To Alyce they were courteous, but she was not especially drawn to anyone. She had learnt the hard lesson of speaking only when spoken to at Dalstead and now could not easily initiate and maintain the flirtatious and frivolous talk that was the common language of these assured and elegant strangers. Only once, when Alyce had met Sir Walter Raleigh, had conversation come naturally. Though some years younger, he was as imposing and forceful a man as Thomas, bursting with enthusiasm for his newest colony in the Americas. Alyce had been more than simply an audience for him. He had answered her questions carefully, detailing the perils and the pains faced by the small group of men and women who would set out from Plymouth a few months hence.

Marian stopped suddenly, turning to Stokes. 'Who is that?'

Stokes's hand slid to the dagger at his waist.

'A cut-purse?' Stokes asked, frowning. 'Where?'

Alyce looked over at the Great Conduit to where Marian and Stokes were staring. She could see nothing but two well-dressed merchants deep in conversation and beside them an elegant blond gentleman, one side of his cloak tossed over his shoulder, displaying the lining of bright blue silk. He stared about as if he were waiting for someone.

'Nay, the one with the blue-lined cloak,' Marian said. 'I have seen him three times today and twice last week. I am certain he is following us.'

'Oh, Marian,' Alyce laughed. 'I doubt we have anything to fear from a gentleman.'

Marian pressed her lips together and did not reply. Alyce sensed that, perhaps, Marian did not have as high a regard for gentlemen.

~

A week later Lucy Foster fussed, supervising Marian's efforts with Alyce's hair.

'You should have tried the dye I offered you.' Lucy patted her own unnaturally red hair.

Marian pushed two decorated pins into Alyce's artfully coiled hair and stood back. 'Well Mistress. I am finished.'

'Stand up and let us look at you.' Lucy brushed her fingers over the ropes of pearls hanging over Alyce's stomacher, the pattern of the cloth picked out in beads. 'Ooh, you are lovely, Alyce.'

She stopped, her head cocked like a spaniel. 'That must be the men home. I'll go down and greet my husband.' She almost skipped from the room.

Alyce had not seen Thomas for days, and when he put his head around the door, she was shocked by the fatigue in his face, the dark smudges under his eyes.

'Good, you are ready. I'll not be long.' He shut the door again.

Alyce sat on a stool beside the window, her skirts spread around her. She ruffled through the pages of a book on navigation by the stars she had found in Sir Anthony's library.

'Mistress, are you sure you do not want me to attend you? Most other—'

'Nay, Marian,' Alyce snapped. 'It will not be necessary.' She understood Marian's unspoken criticism but as she would be with Thomas, she saw no need for an attendant. She had spent too many years as an attendant herself, the unregarded observer, to be unaware of their presence. Attendants knew their masters and mistresses better even than family—every move, every word spoken, every slight change of mood was seen and judged.

Alyce had reread the same page four times when Thomas came back in, his face fresher now.

'What are you reading?' He took the book from her, flicking through the pages. 'If you are interested, there are several books on astronomy at Ashthorpe.' He put the book on the windowsill.

'Wear these.' He held out a pair of earrings, emerald with a heavy irregular pearl drop.

'They are beautiful.' She unhooked her plain gold earrings and slid them in.

'Booty from my last voyage.' Thomas grinned. 'I hope to bring home richer pickings this time.' He drew Alyce to him, kissing her gently.

She fought a sigh, relieved he had forgotten their argument at the tailor, surprised he seemed pleased to be with her.

~

The garden of Lord Reading's grand three-storeyed house stretched down to the river. A few hardy couples strolled along the gravelled walks winding through clipped arbours devoid of blooms, or sat on carved stone seats set into recesses in the hedges as music carried on the chill air. Within the house, the walls of the vast rooms were hung with large tapestries glowing with colour and gold Venice thread. The furniture was heavily carved; the chairs cushioned with padded velvet; cabinets displayed gold and silver plate, exotic glassware and marble carvings.

Guests stood in knots talking or promenaded in twos and threes, displaying their presence and their finery—men and women dressed in deep reds and mauves, bright yellows and oranges, vivid blues and greens in damasks, velvets and brocades with snowy ruffs, jewels glittering from heads and breasts and sleeves. Their attendants were well dressed too, if not so brightly or so richly.

With the music and the noise of the conversations around them, Alyce could only exchange the briefest greetings. She sat content beside Thomas and watched as, between the varied courses, musicians played and actors danced and sang. A masque began as subtleties were served—some of the guests dressed as maids and men declaiming poetry, singing and dancing. Thomas, his lips at her ear, whispered occasionally, telling Alyce who the players were, how related—an intricate network of cousins, husbands, wives, in-laws and paramours. Some names she knew by reputation; others she had met as they had explored London in their first week.

The players drew the audience away to dance. Thomas rose and guided Alyce towards the door but they were stopped by an elegant woman of an age with Thomas. Diamonds sparkled in her hair and on her sleeves, and the bodice of her gown of white brocade was picked out with silver thread.

Thomas bowed deeply. 'My lady.'

Delight was plain in the woman's eyes as they travelled over his face.

She stepped close to him, kissing him on the mouth. Longer, Alyce thought, than a mere greeting kiss required.

Thomas half-turned and said, 'My lady, may I present my wife, Alyce.'

As Alyce curtsied, she felt not only the usual scrutiny but calculation in My Lady's violet eyes.

'Alyce, we meet at last.' My Lady's smile reached no further than her mouth. 'Tom has been so preoccupied with you he has not visited his old friends.'

Alyce opened her mouth to speak, but My Lady continued. 'You will not mind if I take him from you for a short while.' It was not a request. She linked arms with Thomas and steered him away.

Thomas turned and shrugged in mute apology.

Alyce watched as My Lady, with a slow smile, spoke to him. When Thomas replied, My Lady laughed and laid the palm of her hand against his cheek. Thomas did not flinch or pull away but returned her smile.

An ache gripped Alyce's throat. She took a goblet from a passing tray and sipped at it.

'Drinking alone, Mistress?' a handsome man not much older than Alyce asked. 'Surely you would rather dance.'

'I am happy here,' Alyce said. 'I am waiting for my husband to return.'

'I am certain he would not mind if you whiled away the time dancing.'

'I am happy here,' Alyce repeated. There was something familiar, and unsettling, about him but she was certain she had not met him before.

'That I do not believe.' He took her goblet, thrust it into the hands of a surprised woman standing behind them and grasped Alyce's hand tightly, pulling her towards the door to the adjoining room, where the dancing progressed in a sea of swirling colour.

Not wishing to draw attention to herself, Alyce thought it better not to resist. Once the dance was over, she could return to the other room and wait for Thomas.

The gentleman released her hand and bowed ostentatiously, light glistening on his curling blond hair and the silver embroidery of his doublet of popinjay taffeta. 'Giles Clifton, at your service, Mistress.'

Alyce curtsied. 'Alyce Granville.'

'Ah, the pirate's bride.'

Alyce stiffened. 'My husband is not a pirate.'

'Forgive me, Mistress, it was a clumsy jest.'

His apology seemed honest, so Alyce let him take her hand as they joined in with the dancing couples progressing the length of the room.

'Has Tom told you of his adventures on the Narrow Seas? They make an entertaining story.'

'You are a friend of my husband?' Alyce asked as she stepped around him.

He gave the slightest of smiles. 'I have known Thomas Granville for many years.'

They skipped away from each other and back in again. 'And what of lovely Julyan's renewed interest in our Tom?' He caught Alyce's hand.

'Julyan?'

'The alluring Lady Reading.' He smirked. 'You should ask your husband to tell you of his adventures there too.'

Alyce flung Clifton's hand away and left the dancing crowd but was soon sought out by other men, young and not so young, to dance. She caught glimpses of Thomas now and then as she danced around the room. He stood beyond the door, deep in conversation with two serious men. Lady Reading moved closer to him and whispered in his ear. When Alyce looked again the serious men remained but Thomas and Lady Reading had disappeared. Alyce danced on—she would not think, she would not care.

Clifton found his way to Alyce's side as she watched a group of couples dancing an energetic galliard.

He leant in close and said, 'Tom kept you well-hidden. Were you betrothed long?'

'Four months,' she answered curtly.

'So short a time. Was he afraid someone would snatch you

away?'

'That I doubt,' Alyce laughed without real humour.

The tempo of the music increased. Some dancers moved away to watch; others threw themselves into the spectacle that was *la volta*.

Clifton grasped Alyce's hand. 'Come, let us enjoy ourselves.'

'No. No.' She tried to twist free, but Clifton strengthened his hold and pulled her, stumbling, after him into the middle of the room. Every set of eyes was on her. If she were to struggle away from Clifton now, she would draw even more attention. It was easiest to let the dance run its course. She stared ahead, her jaw set as he caught her tight and with one hand gripped the lower end of the busk stiffening her bodice. He slid his other hand around her waist. Alyce rested her hand on his shoulder. They turned together in small springing steps. On their second step, Clifton lifted her into the air, his thigh under hers. Alyce forced her eyes wide open, willing away hot tears of helplessness and shame. The dance was an intimate embrace, unwanted and unpleasant. It felt as if he were publicly forcing her to unfaith-fulness.

Clifton seemed to be dancing out of step with the rest, pulling Alyce tighter, whirling faster, lifting her higher. Her head began to spin.

At last, the music ceased. Clifton did not stop but, with a flourish, brought Alyce to the ground and let her go. Unbalanced, she stumbled, the room swaying around her.

Afraid she would be sick, Alyce staggered from the room and found her way out into the darkened garden. The freezing air was like a slap to the face. Her hand clamped over her mouth, breathing deeply through her nose, she made her way carefully to a seat just beyond the pool of light spilling through the windows. She waited for her head to right itself, her nausea to ease.

'A drink for you, Mistress.'

Clifton stood in front of her holding two goblets of wine. Where had he come from? Alyce had not sensed him following her.

'I have drunk more than enough.'

'One single drink will not hurt.' He passed her the cup.

Alyce held it but did not sip.

Clifton watched her over the rim of his goblet. 'Alyce,' he purred her name.

'Hush.' She set her goblet on the seat beside her. 'Listen.'

The sound of a single treble voice, accompanied by a lute, drifted from the room. All other noise ceased, the crowd stilled. The voice was clear and pure.

> *Orpheus with his lute made trees,*
> *And the mountain tops that freeze,*
> *Bow themselves when he did sing.*

Alyce closed her eyes, her mind empty of all but the pure notes: crystal, cool, the tongue of angels.

> *In sweet music is such art,*
> *Killing care and grief of heart.*

All thought, all discontent washed away, she slowly opened her eyes.

Her husband glared down at her.

Clifton smirked. 'Well Granville, you cannot begrudge a man paying a woman the court she deserves when her husband is pleasurably engaged elsewhere.'

Alyce caught at her skirt as she rose, her fingers brushing Clifton's hand resting there, inches from her heavily swathed legs.

She recoiled as if she had been burnt. Behind her the goblet clattered to the ground, splattering wine.

Clifton stood slowly and faced Thomas. Although not as tall, he had the same muscular strength beneath the silk and taffeta. They eyed each other with the wariness of two circling mastiffs.

Clifton bowed to Alyce. 'Good night sweet Alyce. Until we meet again.' He blew her a kiss and strolled back into the house.

Thomas's face was a mask. 'It is time you went home.'

With a rush of irritation, Alyce said, 'And if I have no wish to go?'

'If you do not walk out with me now, I will carry you.'

Stunned by the restrained fury in Thomas's voice, Alyce walked away towards the house.

~

Thomas did not speak or even glance at Alyce all the way home, his face rigid with self-control. She kept quiet, disturbed by the depth of his anger. He escorted her to the door of her chamber.

As he turned to leave, she said, 'So you are off back to Lady Reading?'

He opened the door and propelled Alyce inside. 'What sort of man do you think I am?' he snarled. 'You believe I would debauch a man's wife at the same time I was taking his money? Lord Reading, her husband, is helping to finance this venture.'

'I did not know. I am your wife yet—'

'Yes. You are my wife,' he cut her off, 'and as my wife I expect you to behave in a way that brings me credit not scandal.'

'Scandal! What did I do that was unseemly? I could not avoid dancing—'

He raised his voice over hers. 'Indeed you danced, showing preference for one man only—Giles Clifton. Then you slipped out into the dark with him. It would be inexcusable in a maid, much worse in a married woman.' Thomas's face was inches from Alyce's. 'I will not be made a cuckold.'

'Why would I do that?' She shrank back, tears pricking at her eyes. 'It is not an activity to be undertaken merely for amusement.' But she knew many men—and women—did just that. She turned away from Thomas, her hand over her mouth stifling a swelling sob. When he had first lain with her, her soul had bound itself to him, and each time since those bonds had tightened. There would never be another man.

The door slammed behind her.

Alyce threw herself onto the bed. She knew Thomas had not married out of any special liking for her, that his courtesy and attentions had been to ensure he stood first in her affections, as should be the case in a marriage. Yet she had no power over the intemperate emotion she felt for him and, fool that she was, wanted him to feel the same for her. And now, having failed to behave with the dignity he expected of a wife, she had lost not only his affection but, more importantly, his respect.

16

Lucy Foster paced the parlour. 'I am tired of sewing and endless games of tables and cards. We could go to the Royal Exchange. I heard they had...?' She stopped beside Alyce, staring down at Alyce's sewing. 'Will you have that finished in time?'

'I believe so.' Alyce kept her head bowed to her sewing. 'The jerkin pattern is plain and Marian is working on the lining. We will pad it with wool.'

'It is not something I have ever made.'

'We made everything we could at Dalstead. I am certain Lady Faulconer would have had us make shoes too, if she thought we had the slightest skill.'

Lucy sat and took up the linen shirt she had been embroidering earlier. 'Even when I get James's shirts made, I like to put the finishing touches. This pattern...'

Alyce concentrated on her stitching, carefully sliding the needle into the spot where the previous stitch ended.

Lucy raised her voice. 'Did Thomas tell you of their latest problem?'

Alyce looked up, frowning. She had not been listening. 'Problem? Nay.'

'Well,' Lucy settled herself comfortably in her chair, 'they have had difficulty getting enough shot for the cannons with all these worries about Spain. Thomas was hoping to speak with Lord Reading last night, to see if he can use his influence.'

So that was it, Alyce thought. Thomas was beset by problems and she had imagined the worst of him. Just as he had thought the worst of her.

'There is a new crisis every other day. Longstanding orders for provisions have been cancelled. James said it seems someone has been pretending to be Thomas's agent. Then yesterday, they found half the flour they had bought was infested... Oh, who is this?'

Lucy dimpled at Giles Clifton, who was standing in the doorway.

'You move quietly, sir. We did not hear the door open.'

'Ladies.' He bowed deeply. 'I did not wish to disturb such an assembly of beauties in their natural state.'

Alyce rose from her stool, unsmiling, her sewing sliding to the floor.

Clifton walked over to her and kissed her on her tightly closed mouth.

'Allow me, Mistress Granville.' He picked up her sewing and handed it to her. 'But, Alyce, who has died? You are dressed in mourning.'

Lucy laughed. 'Alyce is dressed to suit her sombre mood.'

Clifton bowed to Lucy. 'Mistress, Giles Clifton, at your service.'

Alyce rubbed the back of her hand across her mouth and sat. She took up her needle and, frowning, peered at it as she rethreaded it.

'I am Lucy Foster,' Lucy smiled at Clifton, 'wife to Master James Foster, the captain of Master Granville's second ship.'

'Good day to you, sweet Lucy.' He inclined his head. 'I may call you Lucy?'

'Of course, Giles.' Lucy fluttered her eyelashes.

Clifton dragged a chair beside Lucy. 'And, Lucy, do you live here in London?'

'No, we live in Hampshire, but I always spend the final weeks before an expedition with my husband. I do like best when he sails from London—there is much to see and do here.'

Alyce closed her ears to the conversation and continued her swift stitching. She stopped and compared the length she had just sewn to the one she had done earlier—the cloth was puckered, the stitching uneven.

'Would a visit to the playhouse lighten Alyce's dark mood?'

'Oh yes!' Lucy clapped her hands together.

'You will need to dress her, though. We cannot have those we meet assume she is a widow.'

Alyce glared at them, seated side by side with the air of two conspirators.

'I do not think that would be at all suitable.'

'Alyce, Alyce.' Clifton's lips twitched as if he were amused by her objections. 'What harm can come to you? You will be in company of Lucy, a respectable matron like yourself. And your woman, sitting there glaring at me like an angry terrier, will doubtless guard you further.'

'Please Alyce,' Lucy said. 'It would be delightful—we have been shut away here for days.'

Alyce did not have the strength to fight them.

~

Alyce watched the mock swordfight in the courtyard of the inn that also served as a playhouse.

'Alyce.' Clifton touched her hand. 'You were such a vision of loveliness last night. And today, now you have cast aside the widow's weeds.'

Alyce pulled her hand away. 'Master Clifton, I am not swayed by hollow compliments.'

Clifton gazed at Alyce. His long-lashed eyes were a guileless blue. 'There is nothing hollow in my praise of you. Last night you were gay and full of life. What has happened?'

'I am ashamed to say what you saw was the result of too much wine.' Alyce stared down to her lap and resisted the urge to twist her ring.

'You behaved no differently from anyone else there. Had you hidden in a corner like a pious mouse, you would have attracted more attention than had you danced in nothing but your smock.'

'While I was not dressed in a smock, my dancing attracted attention,' she said bitterly. 'It was not courteous of you to force me into that lewd dance.'

'Alyce,' he drawled her name. 'How can a dance loved by our Queen be lewd? It is clear you spend too much time out of company. What is your husband thinking, locking you away?'

'I am not locked away.' She looked down to the activity on the stage. 'We should watch the play.'

Below them, the young woman beloved of the duke, the hero of the play, resolved to test his fidelity by disguising herself as a serving man in order to watch his every move.

The scene ended and tumblers frolicked. 'May I speak now, Mistress?'

'Provided you cease as soon as the players return.'

'Is this your first marriage?'

'Ay.' She concentrated on the antics of the tumblers.

'You had no desire to marry before you met Tom?'

'I was twelve years in service to Lady Faulconer at Dalstead. It is not the best place to meet prospective husbands.'

'Ay,' Clifton paused, 'it is, to my mind, the remotest corner of the kingdom.'

Alyce turned to him, surprised. 'You know the place?'

'I do. I served Lady Faulconer's nephew for a short time. Around that long ago.'

She stared at Clifton. 'I do not remember you at all.'

'You break my heart.' He rubbed his thumb against the tuft of beard beneath his lip. 'I thought every young maid had her heart set on me.'

'There were not many of us and we would not have dared notice anyone in Sir Christopher's retinue. Besides being far too busy, my lady would have beaten anyone who even glanced at a young man. She was a godly woman.'

'She was a pompous old trout.'

Alyce smiled weakly. 'She was a stern woman, very much concerned with proper behaviour. She took a long time to decide whether a person was worthy of trust.'

Clifton took Alyce's hand. 'Poor, poor Alyce.'

Alyce withdrew her hand, aware that even accompanied by Lucy and Marian, this visit to the playhouse was a mistake.

~

The play over, Clifton arranged for the group to dine at the inn, privately, then escorted them home.

Later, as Marian helped Alyce prepare for bed, she said, 'Mistress, the Master would be unhappy you are spending time with Giles Clifton.'

Irritated, Alyce said, 'This is none of your concern.'

Marian gulped a large breath. 'But there is ill feeling between him and the Master.'

'Why did you not tell me?' Alyce closed her eyes, her fingers spread over her mouth. 'I would never…'

'I thought you knew.'

'If I knew, why would I do that?' Alyce groaned.

'Perhaps… to…' she blurted it out, 'to make the Master pay attention to you.'

'No, Marian, never.' She rubbed her fingers between her eyebrows. No matter what she did, it was wrong.

~

Alyce pulled her cloak tight. Although the surrounding buildings and the press of the crowd protected her from the wind, the air was icy. The preacher in the pulpit of St Paul's Cross expounded on the topic of rebellion, drawing on examples from the Bible of those who had rebelled against the authority of God and their rulers, and their fitting fates.

Marian, standing close to Alyce, fidgeting and stamping her feet against the cold, was clearly not listening to the sermon. Turning from side to side, watching the faces in the crowd, she seemed uneasy without Stokes's protection. Alyce knew she should have brought him but it felt as if he were guarding her like a prisoner rather than keeping her safe. Of course, Thomas was probably right that this was no time for a woman to be abroad alone. Despite the bonfires and pealing bells that had greeted news of the execution of the Scottish queen, frightening rumours still swirled that Spain had landed soldiers in Wales and that London was on fire. The last was clearly untrue but it would only need a single angry papist to set alight a city made of wooden houses.

The preacher prayed for the deliverance of the Queen from her enemies both within and without the realm. Alyce shivered. Proving the danger of these times, Sir Philip Sidney, the most valorous of knights, was to be buried this week at St Paul's. He had taken wounds at Zutphen last year, fighting against Spain. The same enemy Thomas would face on the seas.

The sermon ended, Alyce and Marian struggled through the mass of churchgoers eager to get home, out of the cold and to their dinners. Here and there Alyce recognised faces, some nodded in greeting but none stopped to speak.

She turned to Marian. 'Did you enjoy the sermon?'

'It was a bit hard to follow. I am content with one sermon on Sunday and the shorter the better.'

'The preachers here are interesting. At every sermon, I have learnt something new. And last week the sermon answered the arguments of the preacher of the week before. Even learned, godly men argue over the meaning of scripture. It makes me wonder how we can ever—'

'Alyce, what a delight.' Giles Clifton swept his hat from his head and bowed to them. He searched the faces around them. 'You are unescorted. Again.'

As Clifton stepped close to kiss her.

Alyce moved away, her mouth clamped shut.

'Why so unfriendly today?'

'Master Clifton, you are not my friend.'

'Surely,' he arched an eyebrow, 'I have been more than that.'

Passers-by stared.

'Never. And I insist you call me Mistress Granville. Such familiarity is uncalled for when I have met you only twice.'

'You deny our former friendship?' He smirked. 'At Dalstead.'

'I did not know you at Dalstead.'

He came closer, his breath in her ear. 'Playing coy?'

As he stepped back, he stared at her, his courtly mask set aside for a brief moment. Alyce could see cruelty in his piercing eyes. He hated her.

Alyce shuddered. 'Leave us.'

He blew her a kiss and melted into the crowd.

They pushed out into Cornhill, Marian looking as worried as her mistress. 'Did you know him at Dalstead?'

'Nay. I do not remember him, but he says he came to Dalstead with Sir Christopher, Lady Faulconer's nephew.'

'You must speak to the Master. Tell him Clifton has been bothering you. He is a dangerous man.'

Alyce shivered as an icy blast gusted around them.

17

Thomas opened the door to the bedchamber. How could a woman be so deceptive? Sitting there beside the window reading a book, no one would dream of describing Alyce as wanton.

She looked up, startled by the slamming door.

He moved to the centre of the room and stood, his legs apart, fists planted on his hips. 'Perhaps, Mistress, you would care to explain why you have been consorting with Giles Clifton against my wishes.'

Alyce rose and placed the book in the cabinet behind her chair. 'I have not deliberately sought his company.' She clasped her hands together. 'But it seemed churlish to decline his invitation to the playhouse. I was not alone—Lucy and our women accompanied me.'

'My anger at finding you with him the other night meant nothing?'

'I saw no reason for that anger.'

'No reason!' His face contorted. 'The fact he is my enemy is not a reason?'

Alyce blinked and whispered, 'Enemy? I did not know.'

He grasped at the thought that no one had told her, that she had not chosen the surest way to injure him. But even if she did not know, her behaviour had been unseemly. 'You accompany him to the playhouse, sit hand in hand deep in whispered conversation, dine with him hidden away behind a partition. Then you meet again yesterday at St Paul's, like secret lovers, ensuring the man I set to protect you was left at home. Why would you take such a risk in times like these if not for dishonest purposes?' He held his right hand out at his side, slowly opening and closing it. 'St Paul's is such a convenient place for illicit lovers to meet, imagining they are invisible in the crowd. Who knows how many other encounters you have had that I know nothing of?'

'None.' Alyce stood rigid. 'I did not know he would be at St Paul's. I have been to hear the sermons there with Marian for the last three weeks. I do not see why I cannot go anywhere without Stokes behind me. Master Clifton came upon us as we were leaving. I told him to leave me be. Marian will tell you.'

'How do you think it appears for my wife to be wandering about either unattended or in close company with Clifton?' Thomas slammed his fist into his hand.

Alyce jumped, fear in her eyes.

'All know how things stand between Clifton and me.'

'I did not.' Alyce held herself upright. 'If you had told me, I would have known how to refuse him.'

'Alyce,' his voice grated, 'he claims you and he were lovers at Dalstead.'

She paled and sat heavily in the chair. 'Are you so desperate to believe ill of me that you will seize on any baseless tale?'

'You swear you have never lain with him?' He came two steps closer then stopped himself. He had learnt to use his anger coldly; this time control was slipping away. He forced a deep slow breath and clenched his jaw.

'Never,' Alyce whispered.

Thomas continued to glower. He would have sworn she had no experience of men, that she was a virgin. Unless she had tried a whore's tricks to fool him. He shook his head to clear the thought. Why was he thinking this of her?

'He has put about that the young women at Dalstead were most accommodating to any man in Sir Christopher's retinue.' He watched Alyce closely.

'He is lying. It was a strict household. The year I arrived a maid was caught with one of Sir Christopher's men. Lady Faulconer had her thrashed and then dismissed her.'

Thomas sat on the chest at the end of the bed and crossed his arms. 'It could be this he was referring to.'

'Yet you choose to believe it was me.'

'He implied it was you.'

'You think me licentious?'

Was the pain in her eyes feigned? 'I do find it hard to credit,' he said, his voice harsh, 'but I found you in the dark with him holding hands.' Even if she had not lain with Clifton, she had allowed him liberties.

'I was not holding hands with him. Neither were we in the dark.'

He grasped the edge of the chest, his head spinning. A vein pounded at his temple. 'You are playing lawyer's tricks,' he said through gritted teeth. 'I saw it with my own eyes.'

'Your eyes deceived you. I was not holding his hand. Our fingers brushed as I stood up. I was not aware his hand was close.'

Thomas stared past Alyce. When he had stepped out into the garden and seen her sitting there with Clifton, it had been like the blow of a mailed fist to his chest. He had imagined the worst. Yet she had not acted like a woman caught with her lover. She had not moved as he walked towards them. Her eyes had been shut and, yes, her hands were resting in her lap. She had seemed unaware of anything but the music. He could imagine Clifton creeping his fingers across the cloth of her skirt.

'How do I prove my innocence?'

Thomas rested his hands upon his thighs and stared at the floor. Why was he willing to believe the stories Clifton had set slithering abroad? Clifton was untrustworthy. If he had seduced Alyce, he would have been dripping poison in her ear and her attitude to him would have altered.

Alyce shivered. 'Thomas, for better or for worse, we are married. As your wife, my only wish is to please you, yet every step I take angers you. Despite my flaws, I have been faithful.' She was emphatic. 'I have kept my vows.'

She stood and walked away to the window. A robin hopped along the windowsill, its cheerful whistling breaking the silence in the room.

Thomas rose slowly from the chest. Clifton only ever resorted to lies and slander when a direct approach failed. Relief washed through him. Clifton had not seduced Alyce. But if he undermined Thomas's trust in her, he would achieve his aim.

'Alyce.'

She turned and faced him.

'Did you encourage Clifton in any way?'

'No.' Her composure cracked. 'I vowed before God to have no one but you. Why would I then seek the attention of other men?' Her eyes brimmed. 'I have never, I will not ever, betray you.'

Thomas pulled Alyce to him and held her, his lips against her forehead. He had so nearly been seduced by Clifton's words as easily as a faithless woman.

~

Thomas stood at the hearth staring into the fire as the table was cleared after a sombre evening meal where even Lucy Foster had been silent.

Alyce went and stood beside him. 'I am retiring early. My head aches. I can barely hold it up.'

She noticed his haggard face and supposed that, unwittingly, her behaviour had added to his cares.

'Tomorrow morning a limner is coming to paint you in miniature.'

Alyce blinked, surprised.

'I have assumed that you did not have one done for me.'

'It did not occur to me you would want one.'

'Alyce...' He shook his head. 'Betrothed couples do usually exchange such portraits.'

'You did not have one done either.'

'I did, and I intended to give it to you as a New Year's gift, but I forgot—too caught up in the wedding and its festivities.'

Alyce thought of the pair of gloves she had for Thomas but had not given him for the same reason. A gift she could have given to anyone with nothing of herself in it. She should, at least, have thought to embroider them. 'I am sorry.'

He brushed aside a strand of hair that had slipped from her caul. 'Go to bed, Alyce. You are worn-out.' His fingers trailed down her cheek, and he smiled at her for the first time in days. 'I will be up soon.'

~

Thomas woke with the first light and slowly extricated himself from Alyce's sleeping embrace. He watched her as he hastily dressed. She lay tangled in the bedclothes, her thick dark hair spread across the pillow. He looked down on her face. The stern and wary mask she sometimes still wore was cast aside in sleep. On that first day, when he had spoken of her grandmother, the mask had slipped, and he had glimpsed warmth and kindness beneath. The thought struck him that he cared as much for Alyce as anyone in his life, even Cecily. She was his in a way no one else ever had been. Perhaps the vows did make a difference. He did not want their remaining days to pass quickly, but he would not be happy until she was safe at Ashthorpe.

He carefully arranged the blankets around Alyce's shoulders and quietly left the room.

~

James Foster and Thomas pored over a map spread on the parlour table while they waited for supper to be served in the hall. Lucy sat opposite them, listening intently to their conversation, her adoring eyes on her husband. Seated by the fire, Alyce looked away from them and watched the dancing flames, no longer hearing their words only the sound and rhythm of Thomas's voice.

Married love should be temperate yet what Alyce felt for Thomas was in no way measured. In his presence, she had no doubts or fears; when he was away, she longed for him. While common sense told her what she felt was the result of his seduction of her, mind and body, she had neither strength nor will to fight it. Even the fact he had so readily thought the worst of her mattered little when he was with her. He had offered no explanation for it, nor why he had as quickly cast his doubts aside. Thomas now had a wife whose love was more than duty. He filled every corner of her heart and mind but she knew she took only a portion of his. There may be nothing between Lady Reading and Thomas in the present, but they clearly had more than friendship in their past. There would be other women like her, beautiful and accomplished, temptations it was ridiculous of Alyce to expect he would resist. There was little censure for a man who forgot his marriage vows. Alyce wanted happiness, wanted to be glad in what she had, and to do that she had to push aside all thought of what Thomas did when he was away from her. She would not be like her sister, pretending her husband adored her; she would be content with that part of

Thomas's life that he shared with her, ignoring the rest.

The door creaked open, and a woman's voice cut through the murmur of conversation. 'Thomas.'

There was such pleasure in the voice that Alyce's heart sank—another of Thomas's former loves? She must harden herself. The present was all that mattered.

Alyce turned to see a stout woman nearing sixty, nothing like Lady Reading.

Thomas greeted the woman with a kiss. 'Lady Rossiter.'

He held out his hand to Alyce and said, 'May I present my wife, Alyce.'

Before Alyce could curtsy, Lady Rossiter had thrown her arms around her and kissed her.

'I am delighted to meet you, Alyce.' Lady Rossiter's face creased into a broad smile. 'We did not even know Tom was to marry until the banns were called. Cecily could tell me little. She knows little enough herself.' She barely drew breath. 'We would have come to your wedding had we been invited in time.' She gave Thomas a mock frown. 'Tom knows how much I enjoy a wedding. We are in London at present because my niece was married last week.'

A florid white-haired man had followed Lady Rossiter in. Blue eyes sparkled in a face as creased with laughter as his wife's. 'Ah, this is the bride.' He gave Alyce a smacking kiss. 'You have done well here, Tom.'

Alyce blushed.

'You have not told Alyce who we are, have you?'

'I have not been given the chance.' He grinned at Lady Rossiter. 'This is Sir Philip and Lady Rossiter, our nearest neighbours at Ashthorpe. They are good friends. You are travelling back to Ashthorpe with them.'

'This is the first you have heard of this?' Lady Rossiter asked. 'He did not even tell you he had invited us to sup with you tonight?'

Smiling, Alyce shook her head.

'I'll wager he tells you little.' She pulled a face at Thomas. 'Well then, I'll have to take you under my wing, advise you how to keep this one in hand.'

'Heaven forfend,' said Thomas, 'and have Alyce leading me the merry dance you lead Sir Philip.'

'It makes for an interesting life,' Sir Philip said. 'When do you sail?'

'First light a week from Friday.'

Alyce's smile faded. They would have been married two months exactly.

Lady Rossiter put her arm around her. 'Never mind, dear, I'll make sure your mind is well-occupied on the journey home.'

It was the most pleasant evening Alyce had spent since they arrived in London. The meal was informal with everyone at ease. Lady Rossiter easily drew Lucy and her husband into the conversation but ensured Lucy did not dominate. In the company of the Rossiters, Thomas seemed unguarded, the weight of his worries put aside. Alyce wished she had met Lady Rossiter three weeks ago; she would have had no time to spend in the company of Giles Clifton. And she was certain, if she asked, Lady Rossiter would explain why there was animosity between him and Thomas. But now it did not matter—Clifton belonged to the past.

18

Isabel's bed-smock twisted tight around her as she tossed and turned, unable to lie comfortably.

Will, his eyes squeezed shut, groaned and flung himself to the far side of the bed. 'God's foot, Isabel. Will you lie still? How do you expect me to sleep with you threshing about?'

'It is well for you—you can lie down and sleep. Every part of my body is swollen with *your* child. But do you care?' She gave him no time to answer. 'No. I must lie here in agony, forbidden to move for fear of disturbing you.' She reached over and prodded him. 'You are not even listening to me.'

'Isabel,' he groaned.

'You made me like this. You wanted a son,' Isabel's voice caught. 'I could die. Women die in childbirth—Lettys Rowe's cousin in Ipswich last month. Within a year, you'll have married again—some other poor woman to get more sons on. All men think of is sons and their own pleasure.'

'As I remember you took your share of pleasure.'

'You wretch,' Isabel screamed, 'I hate you.'

Will's shoulders sank. 'I am going to sleep downstairs.' He eased himself off the bed.

'Off to lie with one of the maids?'

'Do not be ridiculous,' he snapped. 'As if I would bring that sort of discord on my own house.'

'So you would not care if it were someone else's maid?'

Will slammed the door behind him.

'Knave!' she shrieked after him, then fell back, sobbing, onto the bed.

Life was unfair. She knew her face was puffy and pallid, her breasts and belly swollen. It was no wonder there were so many whispers of Will and other women. But he wanted this baby. His father too, on and on, talking of his need for a grandson. And now she was doing what they wanted, they despised her. She could tell Sir William, despite his talk of foreigners and their numerous wives, had liked what he saw when he looked her way. Now he scarcely glanced at her.

And all her visitors brought were dire tales of childbirth and death and monstrous babies. Alyce had promised she would stay but she had skipped away, without a backward look, off into the arms of that pirate. No one cared whether Isabel lived or died.

Worn-out with misery, she lay still, her hands spread over her belly, watching the gentle movements as the baby stirred. 'I have waited long for you my little one,' she murmured as she drifted into an uneasy sleep.

~

Julia clattered into the chamber and set a tray with bread, cheese and small beer on the chest at the foot of the bed.

As she tugged open the bed curtains, Isabel pulled herself up against the pillows. She glanced at the breakfast tray. 'Get rid of that. I am not hungry.'

She dragged herself to the edge of the bed and swung her feet down. She ached with tiredness. Pain nagged low in her back.

Will walked in, his face fresh from seven hours of unbroken sleep. He placed his hand on Isabel's shoulder. 'Another couple of months and it will be over.'

'That is fine for you to say.' She winced, the pain in her back twisting sharply.

'What is wrong?'

'What do you think? I am heavy with child. I am shut away at home. An ordeal lies ahead of me.'

Will put his arms around her, holding her to his chest. 'Oh, Isabel. There is no need to worry.' He tightened his grip on her. 'I must go but I will hold you in my thoughts throughout the day.' He brushed his lips against hers and breathed, 'Remember that I love you.'

Before Isabel could plead with him, he was gone.

As she slid off the bed, warm liquid trickled down her legs. 'Julia!' she screamed and collapsed back against the bed.

Julia rushed back in, the worry on her face easing at the sight of the puddle of clear water on the floor. 'It's the baby coming, Mistress, that is all.'

'But it's too early,' Isabel wailed.

'Babies come in their own time. I'll clean this up, then go for the midwife.'

Isabel took a shuddering breath. 'Do not leave me.' She would die if she were left by herself. Alyce should be here.

'I'll go to the door and call Mistress Frances. She will stay with you while I run for the midwife and your mother.'

'Mother,' Isabel whimpered, 'I want Mother.'

~

To Isabel it was an eternity, but within the hour her mother, her mother-in-law and the midwife Goodwife Godfrey had arrived and, not long after, her friends Lettys and Martha. Curtains were hung across the shuttered window, candles lit and the fire stoked. Julia rushed in and out bringing food and drinks, fetching and carrying whatever the women needed.

There was little time for friendly gossip as the pain came in slowly building waves. The lulls between them brought no relief as the ache in Isabel's back was unremitting.

Isabel lay on the pallet beside the bed as Goodwife Godfrey lifted her gown and examined her. 'All is well, Mistress, but the baby is not quite ready yet.'

'But why does it hurt so much?'

'It is your body preparing the way, opening up for the baby.'

Isabel moaned as Godfrey helped her sit up.

'You may find ease if you move around.'

Isabel staggered back and forth across the room, Lettys and Martha at her side, holding her as the pain gripped her. The world contracted to this one room, to her place in it. She struggled up great mountains of pain, slid into shallow valleys of fear-filled respite. Hour after hour, no end in sight.

~

Isabel lay on the birthing chair, gripped by the pain. Beside her Dame Katharine knelt, praying.

'Out of the deep have I called unto thee, O Lord: Lord hear my voice.'

Isabel whimpered. She did not have the energy to cry out. With each clenching, the pain enlarged, swelling to be her whole existence.

At the edge of her consciousness, she heard the whispers. 'How much longer?'

The midwife answered, 'The babe is not full-grown. It should come easily.' A pause. 'Sometimes, in these cases, the mother's pain is greater.'

'Will it survive?'

'I fear not, and Mistress Sutton is losing strength.'

'Do what you can for Isabel.' Her mother's voice was hoarse. 'Save her.'

Isabel lay against the chair, her body filmed with sweat. If her baby died, it did not matter what became of her.

Her mother brought her a drink, held it to her lips but Isabel could only sip.

'Alyce,' Isabel whispered.

Her mother bent in close to her.

'This is Alyce's fault.' Isabel's voice rose with her distress. 'If she had stayed the baby would not be coming early.'

Dame Katharine hauled herself to her feet. 'Ay, your sister cursed you.'

'Do not be so stupid,' Mother raised her voice.

'She cursed Isabel at her wedding—Isabel told me. Alyce said Isabel would get what she deserved.'

'How is that a curse, you foolish woman?'

'Ladies.' Goodwife Godfrey pushed herself between them.

'Your other daughter said the words, and this is what happened?'

'What Isabel deserves is a healthy baby,' Mother said.

'Ladies!' The midwife raised her voice. 'Have a thought for Mistress Sutton.'

Isabel groaned. It was she who had said she hoped Alyce got what she deserved. Alyce had not cursed her but she had broken her word.

Mother knelt beside her. 'Alyce wants what is best for you. We all do.'

'If she did, she would be here,' Isabel gasped. 'She could make the pain go, make my baby safe.'

'I wish Goody Williams had not left town for her grand-daughter's lying-in,' Dame Katharine complained. 'She prays while she works—if you did the same, Godfrey, this birth would be easier for Isabel.'

'Katharine Sutton,' Mother said, exasperated, 'be quiet.'

Offended, Dame Katharine took herself to a chair beside the door.

'My first duty is to aid the mother,' Godfrey said. 'But, Lady Sutton, perhaps you can pray on my behalf.'

Dame Katharine began her recitations again, one prayer tumbling into another in an incessant, irritating drone.

Martha, sitting close beside Isabel, brushed the hair away from her brow. 'Think Isabel,' she said gently, 'with every pain, you are closer to holding the baby in your arms.'

Pain gripped Isabel again. 'I am going to die,' she sobbed.

'You are not,' the women all said together.

'Hold onto this.' The midwife placed an eagle-stone in Isabel's hand. 'It will help ease the pain.'

Isabel clenched the stone, her knuckles white. The smaller stone contained within the larger rattled as pain crashed down on her.

~

Dawn crept through the shutters, leaking around the curtained window.

Isabel pressed back against the birthing chair, pain overwhelming her. Goodwife Godfrey rubbed her hand against Isabel's bare thigh. 'Not much longer now, my dear,' she exhaled. 'I can see the baby's head.'

Isabel moaned. If Godfrey could see the baby, she should lift him out. Isabel had no will, no fight left to push or strain.

Dame Katharine's prayers became shriller.

'For heaven's sake, Katharine, pray quietly,' Mother snapped.

Dame Katharine's voice rose, '*Comfort the soul of thy servant. We would all do well to pray, we can do nothing without the Lord. For unto thee, O Lord, do I lift up my soul.*' She droned on and on, barely pausing for breath.

Isabel turned to her mother. 'I want Will,' she sobbed.

'William cannot come.' Dame Katharine's voice was harsh. 'This is no place for a man.'

'I cannot bear it, Mother.'

Mother bent towards her and placed her lips against Isabel's hair.

The pain swept on, and in a welter of blood and sweat the baby was born. Its first cry was no stronger than the mewling of a kitten.

The women crowded around it. 'You have a son, Isabel.'

'Let me see him.' Isabel stretched out her arms, and Mother placed the baby on her chest. She caressed the tiny head. Her own sweet boy at last. 'He is so small.' The baby lay quiet—pale, blood smeared, a scrap of precious life.

The women surrounding her were silent, strain on their faces.

'What is wrong with him?' Panic swelled within her.

'He is very tired,' Mother said.

'He needs to be cleaned and swaddled,' Godfrey bent down to take the baby, 'and the wet nurse is here for him.'

Isabel touched his tiny fist. His fingers uncurled. She held them, rubbing them gently between her own. Flesh of her flesh. Between the fingers, up to the lowest joint was a thin web of skin.

'He is deformed,' she screamed. 'His hands are webbed.' She struggled to sit upright, the baby rolling off her chest.

Martha snatched him up and handed him to Godfrey.

'These things happen all the time. They mean nothing.' Goodwife Godfrey carried the baby to the wet nurse who had been dozing by the hearth since the previous evening.

Dame Katharine rose from her chair and hurried over, horror and excitement glittering in her pale eyes. 'He is cursed,' she screeched. 'Alyce cursed him too.'

'Ignore her, Isabel.' Mother grabbed Isabel around the shoulders. 'Listen to what Goody Godfrey says, it means nothing.'

Isabel strained to see what was happening. They were not behaving as if it meant nothing.

The wet nurse beckoned Godfrey. She held the baby close, brushing her nipple against his lips. 'He will not suck.' He lay still in her arms, his breathing shallow.

'Try a little longer,' Godfrey said. 'He is tired—it was a hard journey for so small a mite. If all else fails, squeeze out a few drops and drip them into his mouth. It might get him started.'

Isabel knew he would die. She began to keen, the desolate sound of her grief filling every corner of the room.

Dame Katharine's voice rose above the sound. *There is no health in my flesh through thy displeasure; neither is there any rest in my bones by reason of my sin.'*

~

Robin stood at the doorway of the shop. Behind him, the apprentices tidied away unsold cloth and locked the cabinet where the more expensive buttons, laces and threads were kept. The street outside was empty as other shopkeepers put up their shutters, the working day over. Farther along the street a knot of women stood talking excitedly, his mother among them.

Agnes Hall looked over and saw him before he could step back into the shop.

'Robin,' she yelled. The woman had the voice of a pedlar. 'Robin Chapman.' She waved. 'Come over here.'

He straightened his doublet and walked towards them. 'Good even, ladies.'

Maude Middleton was with them and two other women he barely knew.

'Robin,' Hall gasped, 'have you heard about Isabel Sutton?' She did not pause for an answer. 'Poor Isabel was brought to bed of a son this morning, but the baby drew breath for no more than an hour.'

That would explain Bradley's absence from the shop today and why neither he nor Joan Bradley had joined them for dinner.

'Poor, poor Isabel.' Mistress Middleton frowned, concern in her eyes. 'That babe has come far too early—few survive such a birth.'

'My daughter, Lettys, says Isabel is inconsolable,' Hall said. 'She has longed for a child since she married nearly four years ago. Lettys had two children by this time.'

'The ways of the Almighty are beyond understanding,' Mistress Middleton sighed.

'The Almighty had little to do with it.' His mother's voice

was harsh. 'Malice was involved.' Robin watched his mother—it was not sympathy she was feeling. 'I saw Dame Katharine on my way here. The poor woman is exhausted with sorrow and helping Isabel in her travail. She says Alyce cursed Isabel and gave her potions to blight the child in her womb.' She looked around the group of women. 'The child was monstrous, deformed beyond recognition.'

The women all gasped, staring at her, their mouths open.

Robin stood silent. Best to say nothing. Whatever he said would be trumpeted abroad by Agnes Hall.

His mother rushed on, 'She said Alyce fed poor Isabel potions that she thought were tonics to strengthen her and then, at her wedding two months ago, she cursed Isabel.'

'The Lord preserve us,' the women said together.

Robin drew a sharp breath. Why, instead of being happy at her marriage, would Alyce turn and curse her sister? For that matter, why would she answer an offer of marriage with threats? Her behaviour was unnatural.

'Ay, she said Isabel would get what she deserved,' his mother continued.

'If that is a curse,' one of the other women scoffed, 'I curse my children every day.'

'It is not a curse at all,' Mistress Middleton snapped. 'If anything, Alyce would be hoping Isabel got what she wanted most—a child.'

Robin's mother glared at the other two. 'She was not saying it the way we would. She was saying Isabel would get what she thought Isabel deserved and that was the death of her baby.'

'You cannot know what she was thinking, nor can Dame Katharine.' Mistress Middleton glared back at her. 'Alyce Bradley may have behaved oddly at times but she was never bad.'

'Never bad.' His mother's lip curled. 'Would a good woman break an understanding with a decent, hardworking man like my son to run off with a pirate like that Granville?'

They all turned to Robin, their eyes boring into him. He kept his mouth shut, his anger rising as his mother continued.

'Ay, she rejected him in the vilest language. She said—'

'Mother. Enough.' He would not have these women using his shameful treatment as entertainment. His mother glanced quickly at him and stopped. 'It does not bear repeating.'

Robin turned away and marched back to the shop. Alyce Bradley was an unnatural woman answering kindness with vicious threats and curses and, like her grandmother, was little better than a witch.

~

'Mistress.' Marian passed Alyce a small cloth-wrapped parcel. 'This was just delivered.'

'It must be the portrait.' Alyce tugged at the wrapping and moved towards the window, away from the trunk standing near the door leading from her chamber to Thomas's.

The miniature was set in a dark frame and bordered with gold and blue. It was flattering—the lines were softer, the face prettier. It was someone who looked like Alyce yet was not her.

Thomas walked in and stood close to her. 'It has finally arrived.'

He took the miniature from Alyce and frowned. 'Hmmm. It has your features, but it lacks your spirit.' He wrapped the miniature in its cloth and placed it in his satchel. 'But it is enough to remind me of you.'

It was as if her breath had stopped. Thomas wanted to remember her while he was away? She had thought the miniature a formality, something that he thought should be done. She could not think how this sat with the notion she had assumed he had, that a man could forget his wife when he was away from her and do as he pleased.

'I thought you would be here until tomorrow,' she said, her voice small.

'We sail at first light. I need to be on board tonight.'

Alyce drew a quick breath. 'I have a gift for you.' She picked up a folded garment lying at the end of her bed. 'I should have given you this sooner, before you packed.'

Thomas took it from Alyce and held out the padded jerkin of dark chamlet embroidered with silver thread and finished with a row of silver buttons.

'You made this for me?'

'With Marian's help, otherwise I would not have had it ready in time.'

He put it on over his doublet, moving his shoulders as he measured the fit of it. 'It will certainly keep me warm.' He looked up and smiled. 'I will wear it every day and think of you.'

He turned away and walked out the door.

Alyce watched him leave, aching with longing at the impersonal leave-taking—no embrace, no kiss to remember him by. She turned to the window, staring out at the wheeling gulls.

'I almost forgot.' Thomas was beside her. He handed her a miniature set in a jewelled frame.

She glanced from Thomas to the painting and back again, a crease between her eyebrows. The features and colouring were Thomas as she saw him, but there too was the dry humour, a hint of the ruthlessness, the strength lying beneath the surface.

'The skill of the painter makes a great difference,' Thomas said. 'Mine was done by Master Hilliard. When we are next in London, I will arrange for him to paint you.' He took the miniature back and laid it on the bed. 'Now, Wife, I must leave.' He wrapped her in his arms.

Alyce slid her arms around his waist beneath the jerkin, holding tight to the solid strength beneath his padded clothing. She gazed up into his face, in a single moment memorising every feature, every breath, every sense of him, fearing that as soon as he was out of sight she would forget.

She closed her eyes as his lips touched hers, holding on to the moment of his kiss, forcing away all thought of the empty months ahead.

Part 3

೦‌‌

True hearts have ears and eyes, not tongues to speak;
They hear and see, and sigh, and then they break.

'The Lowest Trees'
Sir Edward Dyer

19

May 1587

Thomas's sister, Cecily, pushed the heavy leather-bound ledger across the table to Alyce. 'I want you to go through this with Haines this afternoon.'

'Will you be present?'

'Nay. It is time for you to do this alone,' Cecily said patiently. 'Allow Haines to explain, question anything you do not understand, and say yea or nay depending on what you think is best. After all these years I know we can trust Haines—his whole life is here.'

'Very well,' Alyce said without enthusiasm.

'It would be good if you would sit at the manor court at Midsummer as well—oversee any payments due from the tenants, settle disputes and any other matters that arise. Haines will be at your side to guide you.'

Alyce stared at the papers on the table in front of them. There were moments when she felt she would never master all that was required of her in managing Thomas's manor. She also knew that some of the household held that view more firmly than she did herself.

Yesterday she had overheard Marian talking with Cecily's woman, Judith. Alyce had only caught the end of the conversation, but Judith's judgement must have been harsh, for Marian had rebuked her. 'She is a good, kind woman, and I'll not hear a word against her. Would you rather she had come here playing the great lady, ordering us around?'

Judith had muttered a reply that Alyce had not stayed to hear.

'We will do this differently today,' Cecily said. 'I want you to explain to me what is in this ledger.'

Alyce forced herself to concentrate and read down the entries listing monies spent, wool and livestock sold, payments to workmen. She paused, pointing to the final entry. 'Is this correct? It is a lot to pay for restocking the fishpond.'

'It is indeed,' Cecily said. 'I must have accidentally added an extra nought or two.'

Alyce looked at her. 'Ay, I can see now that you have squeezed it in deliberately.'

'I wanted to prove to you that you know what you are doing.'

'Perhaps I do.' Alyce was not fully convinced. 'It helps that I am feeling so much…' She trailed off at the gleam in Cecily's eyes.

'You have been unwell?'

Alyce looked away to the windows of the hall where they sat. She sighed as if she had been holding her breath. 'Nay, but I have felt queasy now and again. Not all the time, not every day.'

Cecily's eyes narrowed. 'And how many months have you missed?'

'Three.'

'Three! Why have you left it so long?'

'I was not sure.' She had nursed her secret, barely allowed herself to hope, each day expecting to discover that her hope was without foundation.

'How can you say that?' Cecily's voice was harsh. 'One missed month, two at most, but three. You know for certain.'

'I thought you could not be certain until the baby quickens. Besides, when I first went to Dalstead I missed two months.'

'Two not three, and you were a maid.' Her frown deepened. 'This is Thomas's child you are carrying. It is your duty to keep it safe. And you have been out racing on that horse.'

'It was a gentle trot.'

'Alyce,' Cecily leant forward in her chair, 'Thomas is far from us. I do not want to think it, but he may not return. This child you carry may be all we have of him. It is more precious than anything in the world, so you must take no more risks.'

Alyce closed her eyes, her hand held to her mouth as the thought of its loss washed through her. Her eyelashes glistened as she opened them. 'I did not think of it as a risk. I will stop riding. I will do whatever is needed to keep the child safe.'

'A gentle trot along the lanes will do no harm, but no racing to the top of the hill.' She grasped Alyce's hand and drew her closer, kissing her on the cheek. 'A son for Tom,' she said, smiling. 'I have dreamt of this day.'

Alyce let out her breath and smiled. It was a dream that until now she had not permitted herself.

~

Alyce rose from her seat at the table on the dais at the end of the hall and turned to Haines. 'I think that went well enough.'

Haines continued to gather together the ledgers and rolls spread across the table. 'It went very well, Mistress. I doubt you will need me with you at Michaelmas.'

'No matter how much I learn in the next three months, Haines, it will not come near to your knowledge of Ashthorpe and its customs.'

He bowed his head. 'Thank you, Mistress.'

Alyce stepped down from the dais and walked across the near-empty hall. The day had gone far better than she had hoped. It was the first time she had truly acted as Thomas's lady. Cecily had prepared her well, and in truth, her time with Lady Faulconer had been an apprenticeship for this.

She had sat beside Haines and greeted tenants as they came forward to pay rents due and listened as some made their cases for changes to their tenure or pleas for deferments or per-mission to sub-let their land. Later, with a jury of the more prosperous tenants, they had heard disputes including a dung heap placed too near a neighbour's house and a case of brawling between two women. Alyce knew she could not have managed the day without Haines at her side. He had, with lowered voice, drawn on his knowledge of the people concerned and explained each incident, leading her to the outcome he preferred, though she had been the one to deliver any judgement. Haines had been quick to sharply reprimand anyone he thought was not showing the deference due to Alyce as the wife and representative of Thomas Granville. Only in the case of the brawling women were they not of one mind. Haines would have fined them both, but Alyce told them to make their peace between now and Michaelmas, saying that if they had not, she would not be so lenient at that time.

A few tenants and their wives still lingered in the courtyard chatting, some greeting her as she stepped out into the bright afternoon light. A group of women standing not far from the door fell silent as Alyce came down the steps. She wondered if they had been discussing her. Although they all knew who she was, few had seen her close. With time, their interest in her would fade. She was striving to remember the names of those she met, hoping that by the end of the year she would have learnt not only the name, but the nature of each person who lived at Ashthorpe.

'Oh, Mistress.' One of the women stammered, clearly discomforted to see Alyce so close to them. She bobbed a quick curtsy. 'I... I... heard that you are good at making salves and liniments. My son George has a cough that will not go.'

'The poor boy,' Alyce said. 'Come with me to the stillroom, and I'll see what I can find.'

The other women quickly curtsied and moved off in silence. One remained where she was, her eyes on Alyce, no deference in her manner. She was beautiful, with thick dark hair; her bodice was tightly laced, accentuating the swell of her breasts, the modest kerchief worn around the shoulders by most other women at Ashthorpe absent. She looked Alyce up and down, her gaze lingering on Alyce's thickened waist and, with a smirk, turned and swayed away.

Alyce looked back to the woman beside her. 'How long has your son had this cough, Goodwife... Collins?'

'Joyce Collins, Mistress. My husband is the blacksmith here. George has had the cough a good month or more. It does not seem to be getting any better.'

'Perhaps you should bring him to see me.' They walked together back into the house, Alyce wondering who the woman in the courtyard was.

~

Alyce stood at the window of the parlour gazing out over the formal walled garden to the ash tree-lined river, a broad thread of silver winding past the manor house and its orchards, and on through the village. From every aspect, Ashthorpe filled her with joy. It was not only the beauty of the house and its surroundings but the people who lived here. It was such a household as this Alyce had hoped for service in when she had returned to Norwich. Instead, she was its lady, and in the seven months she had been here, she had come to feel that she was truly part of this place. Beyond her duties running the busy household and, with Haines's help, managing the wider manor lands, Alyce had been able to put to use the other skills learnt at Dalstead, from the creation of comfits and gingerbreads to the preparation of medicinal salves and cosmetic waters, distilling oils and tending the sick and injured of the household and the village. And now summer was over, the harvest was in, food-stuffs were preserved and stored against winter, and she had played no small part in it all.

Alyce turned away from the window and glanced at Cecily, asleep by the fire. Already she loved her better than a sister. It was clear she had been a beauty in her youth, but the smallpox that had nearly taken the Queen twenty-five years ago had taken Cecily's husband and child and left her face heavily scarred. For the last ten years her life had been increasingly restricted by the arthritis in her hands and feet.

Alyce lowered herself carefully into the chair opposite Cecily and rubbed her hand against her large belly.

Cecily opened her eyes and shifted in her chair. 'The baby moves strongly today?'

'Ay.' Alyce smiled.

'What a surprise we will have for Tom when he returns.'

Alyce stared towards the fire, wondering where Thomas was at this moment. She knew little of his life at sea other than he was out in the middle of the ocean facing danger not only from the Spanish but the fickle elements. Her longing for him was constant, filling her waking hours.

She looked over at Cecily. 'I hoped he would be home by this.'

'He was away over a year when he sailed with Sir Francis Drake.' Cecily looked down at her knotted hands and said, not meeting Alyce's gaze, 'I am certain he will return home.'

It was what Alyce wanted to hear but Cecily added, 'God willing.'

Silence hung over the room, the two women lost in their own memories of Thomas. They turned at the clatter at the door as Marian ushered in a messenger.

He had his satchel open and brought out a thick letter. Bowing, he said, 'Mistress Beaumont.'

Cecily nodded and took the letter from him. 'You are?'

'Peter Clynton, Mistress.'

Alyce stared at the letter lying unopened in Cecily's lap.

'Where have you come from, Clynton?'

'From London, Mistress. Master Granville said I should speed the letter to you as he cannot come home at present.'

'What has happened?' Alyce gripped the arm of her chair and hauled herself up.

'There are rumours of war, Mistress. Despite Sir Francis Drake's efforts five months ago at Cadiz—singeing the King of Spain's beard, they call it—the Spanish are still massing a great fleet to send against England. The trained bands in London have begun drilling with muskets as well as pikes and halberds.'

Cecily picked up the letter and broke the seal. 'Thank you Clynton. Go with Marian—she will get you food and drink.'

Alyce sat back in her chair as Marion led the messenger from the room.

Cecily's eyes moved rapidly across the page. Her face changed from guarded to concern to outright distress.

'May I read it?'

'I… I am not sure.'

'I am neither a child nor a weak-minded fool to have secrets kept from me.'

Cecily passed the letter to Alyce.

She read quickly. After the greeting, *Commend me to my wife, Alyce,* came a brief explanation of Thomas's absence: *I had hoped to be home ere this, but it is beyond my power. We must prepare for attack by Spain. It is better that we meet them on the seas than on England's soil.* Then advice on management of the manor, details of a ram to be bought, a horse to be sold.

'Thomas does not mean to return home for some time?'

'He has always been like this, telling us what to do, in case,' Cecily said.

Alyce spread a hand across her belly as she read of the death of Isabel's baby. And finally, the heart of Cecily's concern.

The wife of William Sutton the elder has alighted on the preposterous suggestion that curses were involved. And the source of these lie in Alyce, my wife. These accusations are denied by the midwife who attended Isabel Sutton and are believed only by the willing gulls of Norwich. The Bradleys, for fear of offending said William Sutton, have been weak in defence of their daughter.

Alyce threw her head back and groaned, 'Why would they think I would harm Isabel?' She straightened her shoulders and looked over at Cecily. 'Some people are such fools. Nothing happens by fate or ill luck or even the will of God—any ill that befalls them and theirs must be by design or malice.' Her eyes glistening, she leant over and grasped Cecily's hand. 'Every day I thank God Thomas married me and that this is my home and you are my family.'

20

November 1587

Alyce's breath came in small misty puffs as she stood in the doorway and watched the comings and goings in the courtyard: a cart trundled in laden with wood; a couple of women, their arms folded across their bosoms, ran from the brewhouse towards the manor house itself, skipping around the wind-ruffled puddles; Bart, the stable-boy, led Haines's saddled horse into the yard and, stamping his feet for warmth, waited for Haines to come out.

With a heavy sigh, Alyce turned back into the house and made her way through the hall to the parlour.

Cecily glanced at Alyce's face and frowned. 'You have been outside.'

'I stood on the steps and breathed in the fresh air.'

'Alyce!' She gave an exasperated jerk of her head.

'It is unsafe,' Eloise Wyard said. 'Cold air endangers the baby.' Eloise was a neighbour—a cheerful talkative woman of an age with Alyce, already the mother of three sons. 'And it looks as if it is due any moment.'

Alyce lowered herself into a chair by the fire but rose almost at once and paced the parlour. 'If I stay locked in any longer, I shall go mad.'

'Elizabeth Jefferies and Lady Rossiter will be here soon,' Cecily said.

Alyce stared past her to the tapestry hanging above the virginals, a deer fleeing the hunters.

'I have a tale that will take your mind off everything else,' Eloise said. 'My mother-in-law's latest campaign to win back my brother-in-law Edmund's affections.'

'This will be interesting,' Cecily laughed.

'But how did she lose his affections?' Alyce frowned, puzzled. 'Should a son not...?'

'We are required to honour our parents, but I do not know about being affectionate—not a word I'd use regarding Dame

Margaret. Have I not told you the story? It will keep you entertained all afternoon.'

Alyce gasped, her eyes wide open. She pressed her hands against her belly and waited for the spasm to pass. 'I think it has begun.'

~

The windows were covered in Alyce's chamber and the fire stoked. Elizabeth Jefferies arrived with Lady Rossiter. The wife of Ashthorpe's rector, she was a well-regarded midwife.

'On the bed, dear. Let's see how you are.' She lifted Alyce's smock. 'That's right, legs apart.' She patted Alyce's knee and pulled the smock down. 'A while yet, but the baby is on its way.'

The women sat around the fire chatting, sharing the news of their many friends and relations. It was easy for Alyce to sit and listen, to join in only when she felt inclined, pausing every few minutes with the clenching pain.

As the pains slowly strengthened, she found it hard to concentrate on anything else happening in the room.

Elizabeth took up her Psalter and began to read. *'I will lift up mine eyes unto the hills: from whence cometh my help.'*

Cecily joined in the recitation with Elizabeth. In moments of respite, Alyce added her voice. She need not think, only say the well-worn words.

'The Lord shall preserve thee from all evil: yea, it is even he that shall keep thy soul.'

The familiar words were a balm.

Lady Rossiter and Eloise walked with Alyce, their arms around her waist, holding her when the pain gripped her. Alyce moaned with shame as warm liquid flooded down her legs.

'Come dear, we will clean you up.' Lady Rossiter rubbed Alyce's back. 'It is the water the baby swims in. And it is good and clear. Not too long now.'

Inch by inch the pain possessed her. When her legs could no longer hold her up, Alyce sat on the birthing stool, writhing, groaning with each spasm, in a timeless place where nothing but pain and pressure existed, the insistent voices of the other women all that tied her to the present.

Marian offered her a drink. 'You need to drink it, Mistress, even a sip at a time. It is mother's caudle—it will sustain you.'

Although she did not want it, it was easier not to argue, so Alyce obediently sipped the pleasantly spiced wine.

She strangled back her cries each time the pain overtook her, tried to hold on to the restraint that had borne her through the difficult years. But it was more than she could bear and something in her broke open. Screaming, Alyce gave herself wholly to the struggle to bring her child into the world.

Elizabeth Jefferies cried, 'I can see the baby's head.'

Voices crowded in on Alyce. 'Hold on.' 'Now push.'

She grabbed someone's hand, gripped it like iron.

'Easy, easy. Again. Push.'

With a cry of delight from the women, the baby slipped into Elizabeth's waiting hands.

Its bawling filled the room, echoing out through the house, to be greeted by muffled cheering from the household on the floor below.

'Alyce, you have a beautiful, healthy daughter,' Eloise said.

Alyce held her arms out for the dark-haired, blood-smeared infant.

As Elizabeth settled the baby on Alyce's chest, Cecily sniffed, 'The child should be swaddled immediately.'

Elizabeth was unconcerned. 'A few moments unswaddled never hurt any baby I have delivered.'

Alyce lay against the chair, cradling the baby, tears welling in her eyes as she was overwhelmed with a love stronger even, at that moment, than her love for Thomas.

The child had a will of her own. Her eyes unseeing, she found Alyce's uncovered breast.

'It is best I take her now,' Elizabeth said. 'The wet nurse is here.'

'No,' Alyce raised her voice. 'I will nurse her myself.'

'Alyce,' Cecily was sharp, 'this is most improper.'

'There is nothing more proper than a mother should nurse her child,' Elizabeth said.

'For heaven's sake, Elizabeth,' Cecily said, exasperated.

'Many learned and godly men recommend it. It is the way ordained by God—the good Lord himself was nursed by his own mother.'

'Do not worry, Cecily,' Lady Rossiter said. 'My mother was an earl's daughter and nursed her own children and still managed to produce a baby every second year.'

'Oh Margaret,' Cecily said, exasperated. 'That was years ago.'

'No harm will come of it.'

Eloise reached over and gently lifted the baby from Alyce. 'This little one needs to be cleaned and swaddled.' She smiled at the child, wistful. 'Such a pretty girl.'

Alyce groaned as her body convulsed with a sudden rush of blood.

Elizabeth knelt beside her. 'Nothing to worry about, dear.' She stood up, examining the bloody lump in her hands. 'The afterbirth has come away clean—everything is as it should be.'

~

The only sound in the bedchamber was the crackle of the fire blazing brightly in the hearth. Washed and in fresh linen, Alyce lay in her bed gazing at her daughter asleep in the crook of her arm.

'My beautiful, beautiful girl, what shall we call you?' She brushed her lips against the infant's head.

Marian tiptoed into the room. 'I thought you might be asleep.'

'I am too happy for sleep.'

Marian lifted the child from Alyce. 'It will come on you quickly, so I'll put her in her cradle. My eldest, Sarah, will sleep by you and bring the baby to you when she needs nursing.' She looked into the sleeping infant's face. 'Such a sweet child.' She glanced at Alyce. 'You do not mind she is not a son?'

'She is perfect as she is. My sons will come later,' Alyce said, surprised at her own certainty.

After Marian had settled the baby in her cradle and left the room, Alyce lay back against the pillows. She could hear the noise of life around her, the murmur of conversation, the clatter of dishes from the hall below, the whinny of a horse from the stables, the hoot of an owl on the night air. Alyce's breath drifted into the rhythm of sleep, contentment washing through her.

~

Within a fortnight of her birth, Alyce's daughter was presented by her godparents Lady Rossiter, Eloise Wyard and Lord Reading by proxy at the Ashthorpe parish church, before the congregation of villagers and invited guests and was christened Elinor. The guests then made their way back to a feast at the manor. And Elinor received gifts: silver spoons and mugs, and a finely wrought covered cup from Lord Reading. These were displayed on a sideboard in the hall where the festivities were underway.

Wrapped in her scarlet bearing cloth, Elinor was carried back to Alyce. The women guests visited Alyce, still confined to her bedchamber, admiring Elinor lying in the cradle beside the bed. She was a contented infant, happy to be held, happy to be surrounded by the murmur of women's voices.

Lady Rossiter sat herself beside Alyce. 'You should be well pleased—a baby not much more than ten months after your wedding is a very good sign. When Thomas returns, we will expect a son as swiftly.'

Alyce forced herself to smile.

Lady Rossiter, as if reading Alyce's mind, put her arm around her shoulder. 'He would be back by now, dear, if it were not for those godless Spaniards.'

~

The days of Alyce's confinement lingered. Within three days of the birth she had been able to rise from her bed and receive the visitors who came and went in a constant stream to sit and chat, and share the news of the neighbourhood. And, most of all, to see the baby. Alyce learnt more of the life of the county in these weeks locked away than she had in the months leading to the birth. She watched the movement in the courtyard, yearned to be busy, but bowed her head to custom and counted the days.

Six weeks after the birth of her daughter, dressed in a gown of peach-coloured taffeta with a veil covering her hair, Alyce went with the women, Cecily included, to the parish church. She gave thanks to God for her safe deliverance in the great danger of childbirth. Alyce knew she had survived an ordeal as surely as if she had been forced to do battle and her thanks was genuine and heartfelt, a thanks made with joy for her daughter.

Communion followed the churching service, and Alyce made her offering to the Church and returned the chrisom cloth that had been placed on her daughter's head at her baptism. Finally, she walked back down the aisle ready to enter fully into the life of the manor. She caught the sullen gaze of the woman she had noticed in the courtyard at Midsummer. Since arriving at Ashthorpe, Alyce had become used to the gaze of others—all they saw was the lady of the manor. But this was personal, a look of contempt.

On their way back to the manor house, Alyce walked beside Cecily's litter. 'Who was the woman in the church? Comely, dark hair, russet gown?'

Marian and Judith exchanged a quick glance.

'That was Beth, wife of Peter Marston, a farmer here,' Cecily said. 'I am sure you have seen her before this.'

'Is there something I should know about Beth Marston?' Even as she spoke, Alyce knew she did not want an answer.

'Of course not,' they answered together.

Another love of Thomas's, as beautiful and alluring as Lady Reading and by comparison Alyce felt as drab and insignificant as a sparrow.

~

Bart, the stable-boy, poked his head around the stable gate at the sound of hooves. He yelled to Perry, the stablemaster, as Thomas Granville, Kit Watkins and their grooms rode into the deserted courtyard. Before Thomas could dismount, Bart darted out to take the reins.

Thomas gazed up at the silent house. 'Where is everyone, lad?'

'At church, Master.'

Thomas shook his head not quite believing what he was hearing. 'On a weekday?'

Servants filled the yard and began unloading the packhorses, dogs danced around their legs, barking. Thomas slung his satchel over his shoulder and turned towards the gatehouse, surprised by the sight of a litter being carried into the courtyard, surrounded by a knot of women. And there was Alyce among them. She wore a pretty peach-coloured gown beneath her cloak; tendrils of hair had escaped her caul and fluttered in the gusty wind. There was a softness about her face, so unlike the stiff guarded woman he had plighted his troth to last year. As he strode towards her, Alyce did not take her shining eyes from his face, her lips parted as if her breath had caught. He dropped his bag on the cobblestones when he reached her and folded his arms tight around her, kissing her full on the mouth. Her warm body pliant against his, the hint of her spiced lavender scent melted him and the tamped-down desire of the past ten months flooded through him. He was home.

'Alyce,' he breathed. He could think of nothing else to say.

'Thomas,' Alyce sighed.

Then the others surrounded them. Thomas stood with his arm around Alyce, answering the greetings. 'Welcome home, Master.' 'Welcome back, sir.' 'It is good to see you home.'

Cecily, still in her litter, held out her arms, and Thomas bent into her embrace, kissing her. Her face fuller, she appeared in better health than when he had left.

'Welcome home, Brother,' she said, smiling at him. 'We have been waiting so long.'

'It is good, at last, to be home.' He stared around at the women with Alyce and Cecily. 'But what is happening here?'

'We have been to church.'

'On a weekday? Do not tell me you have become a pious congregation and I'll be forced to church each day and twice on Sundays,' he laughed.

'Alyce has just been churched. A little later than is usual, as both Margaret Rossiter and Eloise Wyard were away and Alyce would not have it without them.'

Thomas was barely listening. Churched? A child? He was a father? He turned to Alyce, a slow smile spreading across his face. 'We have a child?'

'A daughter. We have called her Elinor.'

'My mother's name,' he murmured. He had been back in England near three months. Had he been told, he would have found a way to come home sooner. 'And no one thought to let me know?'

'I did not know where to send a message,' Alyce said.

He frowned. Cecily should have had more idea.

'Tom, when do we ever know what your movements are?' Cecily chided. 'Your letter did not mention where you were.'

'She has been christened, no doubt. Who were the godparents?'

'Of course, she has been christened,' Cecily answered. 'Lord Reading, and Margaret and Eloise are the godparents. I am surprised Lord Reading did not mention it to you.'

'I have not seen him since September.' Thomas scowled at her implied criticism. 'I have not been sitting idle in London.'

'What's done is done,' Cecily dismissed his complaint.

Alyce touched Thomas's arm. 'Will you come and see Elinor?'

All his irritation evaporated as he gazed at Alyce. 'Of course.' He smiled, watching a flush spread up from her neck.

They walked into the house together, close but not touching. At the top of the stairs, Thomas pulled Alyce to him and kissed her. 'It seems I have chosen the right time to return.' As he brushed his lips against her neck, she gasped and clung to him more tightly.

It was good to be home.

~

In the nursery, Elinor was awake and crying. Sarah, her nursemaid, rocked her as she paced the room.

'I am glad you're back, Mistress. She is hungry.'

Alyce sat beside the cradle and undid her bodice. She took the baby from Sarah, grinning into Elinor's face. 'You are indeed, my sweeting.'

'*You* are nursing her?' Thomas asked. He watched as the baby sucked hungrily.

'It is best for a baby,' Alyce said brightly. 'Besides, I did not know when you would return.' She turned towards Sarah. 'Let Mistress Beaumont know we will be down as soon as Elinor is fed.'

Once Sarah had left, Thomas said, 'Are you afraid Cecily will assume we are already attempting to produce a brother for Elinor?'

'Nay.' Alyce blushed, her eyes on the baby. But if he had wanted, if she had not had to nurse Elinor, she would have willingly. When he had kissed her in the courtyard, desire more intense than anything she had ever felt had leapt through her.

'Will this interfere with our relations as man and wife?'

Alyce kept her head down. 'I know some think it is not fitting, but Elizabeth Jefferies said it is the usual way of things the world over.'

'Did you have much of an argument with Cecily?'

Alyce blinked, surprised.

'I know my sister,' he answered her unspoken question.

'Lady Rossiter's mother nursed her own children and she said there was no problem either. And Elizabeth said it was ordained by God.'

'Even Cecily could not argue with that.' Thomas reached out a finger and brushed the child's downy head.

'Do you mind she is a daughter?'

'Nay, her brothers will come later.' His grey eyes were gentle, wonder on his face as he gazed down at Elinor, lolling content in Alyce's arms.

Sarah bustled back into the room and took Elinor. 'Mistress Beaumont wants me to bring Elinor down to the hall.'

'I think that means we should join her too,' Thomas laughed.

'Cecily has missed you a great deal.'

'And what of you Mistress Granville?'

Alyce lowered her eyes, afraid they would betray the depth of her longing for him. 'Of course I have.'

21

Thomas stretched his legs towards the parlour fire. Beside his chair, the oldest of the dogs lay sleeping, its head on its paws. Cecily, at the other side of the hearth, stared into the flames.

Alyce came in, unnoticed, and sat on a padded stool to one side where she had a clear view of Thomas. Her years with Lady Faulconer had taught her to move unobtrusively. She did not begrudge that the celebration of her churching had become a welcoming feast for Thomas. The women had flocked around him, fluttering in his presence, even devout Elizabeth Jefferies. And he had played to them, the consummate charmer. Eloise Wyard appeared to be as artful at flirtation as Thomas, and had Alyce not known how much Eloise was taken with her own husband, she would have felt more than a twinge of jealousy.

'So, Tom.' Cecily continued to stare into the flames. 'This venture went well?'

'Far beyond expectations. We brought home two pinnaces, all manner of costly cloth, gemstones and pearls, one hundred tuns of excellent wines, porcelain and,' he grinned, 'even elephants' teeth.'

'I imagine you are already planning another voyage.'

'Not for a while yet. I want to expand my interests on land— another manor or perhaps a mine. It is best not to have everything in one place.'

The conversation lapsed again into silence.

Alyce, although interested in Thomas's plans, felt there was nothing she could add.

Cecily stirred in her chair. 'And how do you feel about Alyce nursing Elinor herself?'

Thomas shrugged. 'I see no harm.'

'I think it most improper,' Cecily snapped. 'I have tried to reason with her, but I have never met with such stubbornness. Alyce is usually so sensible.'

'It does not surprise me,' Thomas said, a hint of softness in his voice.

Alyce sat still. She wanted no part in this conversation.

'And after all this time away, you will restrain yourself?' Cecily asked acidly.

'I believe Elizabeth Jefferies sees no problem.'

'She may not, but I have heard say it harms the milk.'

'Elizabeth has far more knowledge than either of us of birth and babies. Lady Rossiter was free with advice too.'

'Margaret is deliberately contrary at times.' Cecily shrugged.

'If it is what Alyce wants, I will not interfere. They both say the baby takes on the character of the one who gives it suck. It is fitting, then, it should be the baby's mother.'

'Either way, I imagine it does not matter to you. There is always Beth Marston.'

Alyce bowed her head, wishing herself elsewhere.

'This is none of your concern, Cecily,' Thomas snarled as he jerked upright in his chair.

Cecily shot him a quick look and changed the subject. 'How long will you be home?'

He frowned but answered evenly. 'I have to be gone by February.'

Alyce's whimper of disappointment was masked by Cecily's much louder groan.

'The danger has not passed? I hoped, seeing you had come home...' Cecily's voice trailed away.

Thomas leant over and scratched the dog behind the ears. It raised its head against his hand, its eyes shut. 'It is only a matter of time. Drake's sally against Spain six months ago only delayed the inevitable. Veterans are being brought back from the Low Countries. Men from the maritime counties have been ordered home from London to see to their defences. I have begun refitting my ships so we are ready when the time comes.'

'I do not understand why.'

'The help we give the Dutch against the Spanish, punishment for execution of the Scottish queen, Spanish anger at the damage we have done to them in the Americas, plain greed.'

'The times we live in,' Cecily sighed. 'I remember the tales of the massacre of Huguenots in Paris on St Bartholomew's Eve. And the Spanish are worse than the French.'

'I saw the Spanish influence as a lad. The stench of roasting flesh from Smithfield has never left me.'

'It cannot come to this.'

'It will not as long as there are true Englishmen to draw breath. Even our raw levies are a force to be reckoned with. Under Lord Leicester, they did not give way to Spanish veterans in the mud by the Meuse last year. It will be the same here—the Spanish will pay dearly for every inch of English earth.' Thomas stared hard into the fire.

The silence was broken only by the gentle snores of the dog and the soft hiss of the logs settling in the fire.

Cecily finally spoke. 'Have you visited Norwich of late?'

'Ay. The *delightful* Isabel Sutton is with child again.'

Alyce gasped.

Thomas twisted in his chair. 'Alyce, I did not know you were there.'

'I have just come in.' She flattened her skirt over her knees. 'Isabel is with child?' She forced herself to speak brightly.

'The baby is due in early spring.'

'She is well?'

'Your mother assured me she is in good health.'

'And what of these foolish accusations against Alyce?' Cecily asked.

'It has blown over. Most understood your sister's grief was fanned by the malice of Sutton the elder and his wife. Your mother and father send their greetings, but they did not mention that you were with child. I would have come home then, had they told me.'

'They knew—I wrote to tell them. Perhaps Mother feared, if she said anything, she would have to explain why she had not answered my invitation to the lying-in.'

Thomas shook his head as if to clear it. 'Sometimes it is best to forget them all.' He rose from his chair, and as he passed by Alyce, he gently rested his hand on her shoulder. The old dog padded behind him as he left the room.

'Such a strange dog,' Cecily said. 'He will not enter the house when Tom is away but barely leaves his side when he is home.' She glanced at Alyce. 'What ails you, Alyce? You seem sad.'

Was she sad? Alyce was afraid to put into words what she felt.

Cecily watched her, waiting for an answer. 'Alyce?'

'I am tired, Cecily,' Alyce's voice caught, 'it has been a long, busy day.'

'Time for bed, then.'

As Alyce stood to leave, Thomas returned, a bundle of cloth in his arms.

'Sister, I have a gift for you.' He held out a length of tasselled cloth woven in a brightly coloured pattern.

Cecily rubbed the soft woollen cloth between her fingers. 'It is beautiful.'

'It is a garment from the Indies, called a *shawl*, I believe. I'll warrant you are the only woman in England with one of these.'

'Tom, your gifts are such a delight.'

'I am forgiven for my tardiness?'

'Indeed,' Cecily sighed happily. 'But it is Alyce you need to ask the greatest forgiveness of.'

They turned towards her, but Alyce had slipped from the room.

~

Alyce lay on her side, her eyes used to the dimness, watching the sleeping infant in the cradle beside her bed. On the other side of the cradle, Sarah snored softly on her pallet. Alyce was drifting towards sleep when Thomas came in and began to undress. He pulled the bed curtains closed and climbed in beside her. He drew her wordlessly into a brief and urgent union. His arms still tight around her, he murmured her name and within a few short minutes was soundly asleep.

Alyce lay awake, fighting the thoughts crowding her mind. In the courtyard, in those first few moments, she had been certain of Thomas's feelings for her. Yet, other than for the short time in the nursery, he had kept his distance from her, his attention elsewhere. It was a dance where Thomas chose the steps and Alyce could only follow when he invited her. Thomas had not married her out of liking, yet he treated her with kindness. And he had kept those promises he had made to love, comfort, honour and keep Alyce in the ways expected of any man. She had nothing to complain of—it was her unruly heart that yearned for more.

~

Sarah woke Alyce with the first light, bringing Elinor to her to be fed. As the child suckled at her breast, Alyce watched Thomas sleeping. She fought the urge to reach out and trace his face with its broken nose, strong dark eyebrows and firm lips. It struck her that once you knew someone well, their appearance mattered little; it was a cipher for the person who was beneath. And this weathered face she loved as much as the perfect face of her child.

After Sarah had taken Elinor to the nursery, Alyce made to rise from the bed but Thomas caught her by the wrist.

'Stay a while longer.'

'I thought you were asleep.'

'It is hard to sleep when one is watched so closely.' He reached over and unbound Alyce's long dark hair. With a drawn-out sigh, he wrapped his arms around her.

Alyce closed her eyes as his fingers slid across her skin, every fibre thrilling, eager to welcome him.

~

Christmas was almost upon them, and Alyce was determined this, her first at Ashthorpe, would be a feast all would remember. While Thomas rode out with Haines, surveying the dormant fields and taking stock, Alyce threw herself into the Christmas preparations, making up for the time lost during the period of her lying-in. Ivy and holly needed to be collected to festoon the hall. When Haines returned with Thomas, she would speak to him about that, the selection of the Yule tree and where the remains of last year's log were stored. And there was the baking, pies and tarts and wafers. She needed to prepare enough comfits not only for their guests, but to give to the village children following the Christmas service in the local church. She could not do it alone—Marian would help her with the comfits and Judith, Cecily's woman, efficient and a touch overbearing when the mood took her, would make sure the hall was decorated in style.

There would be a stream of guests over the twelve days of festivities—Sir Philip and Lady Rossiter and the Jefferies on St Stephen's Day, and the Wyards and their children the following day along with Lionel Metcalfe, another neighbour, whose wife had died in childbed six months earlier. Alyce did not want his daughters sitting grim at home when other children were playing happily.

The morning had been busy. She had discussed the amount of grain to be milled with the baker, planned the festive meals with the cook and sent for the butcher to arrange for the slaughter of a cow and a pig.

In the early afternoon, wearing a coif and a clean apron over her gown, Alyce saw those tenants and husbandmen who had ailments she could attend: coughs and minor aches, treated with the simples and remedies she was skilled at distilling; grazes and scratches, spread with salves and dressed.

Peter Marston, a farmer whose family had held land by copyhold at Ashthorpe for generations, came through the door. Alyce had met him this morning, on his way to speak to Thomas, and ordered him to come so she could tend a deep reddened scratch down the side of his face. Marston was hardworking and decent, a broad, solid man, not given much to talk.

As Alyce washed the scratch, she noticed smaller shallower scratches to either side, as if the wound had been made by the claws of an animal. When asked, Marston had muttered something about a cat. Alyce did not press him, fearing this cat walked upon two legs. She smeared the scratches with a salve of comfrey, explaining to Marston that it would aid healing and keep pus at bay.

After Marston left, Alyce went to the workbench and stared out into the courtyard. There her husband stood talking to Marston's wife, Beth. Thomas's head was bent towards her as she spoke. Beth gazed up at him, her body angled to give Thomas a good view of her ample charms. She tossed her head, the winter sunlight glittering on her bright earrings. Beth seemed to train her attention on Thomas, a slow seductive smile spreading over her face, a smile that to Alyce was false and calculating. Were men such blind fools?

Alyce turned back to the room as Toby Gerrard, one of the husbandmen, shuffled in. He had regularly made his way to Alyce's room in the months leading up to her lying-in, complaining of all manner of minor ailments. A weather-beaten man, past his prime, he doffed his cap, screwing it around in his hands like a nervous boy.

'What's the matter this time, Gerrard?'

'I got this sore here, Mistress.' With a grimy finger, he pointed to the back of his neck.

'Sit here. I'll see what I can do.' She indicated the stool beside the workbench where the light fell clear and bright from the window. Alyce unwrapped the grubby cloth from around his neck.

'You have a nasty boil that needs lancing.'

'Will it hurt?' he whimpered.

'No more than it does now.'

Alyce walked to the small stove at one end of the room and poured a decoction of lady's mantle simmering there into a bowl, adding a measure of cool water to it. Gerrard sat tense as she washed the area around the boil. As soon as Alyce touched the blade to his skin, Gerrard screamed.

The knife trembled in Alyce's hand. 'For heaven's sake, Gerrard, I have scarcely touched you.'

Watkins poked his head around the door. 'Do you need help, Mistress?'

'Ay,' Alyce nodded, 'find Marian and ask her for a measure of aqua vitae.'

Watkins brought back the aqua vitae and drew a stool alongside Gerrard. 'Drink up. This will take the edge off the pain while the Mistress lances your boil.'

Gerrard gulped the liquid down. He exhaled, satisfied, and wiped the back of his hand across his mouth.

Alyce glanced at Watkins, who was fighting a grin.

'Now Gerrard,' she said, businesslike, 'bite on this.' She passed him a tightly folded wad of towel.

Watkins spoke to him, his voice a reassuring drone as Alyce

set to work. It was quickly done. She dressed the wound with a poultice of dittany, binding it with clean cloths.

'Mistress,' Watkins said, 'you'd make a good barber surgeon, better than many I've seen.'

Alyce grimaced and wiped her hands on her apron.

Thomas stood in the doorway. 'I wondered who was being murdered.'

'I was lancing Gerrard's boil,' Alyce said. She turned to the husbandman. 'Come back tomorrow and I will check all is well.'

Gerrard bobbed his head to her and gave a toothless grin. 'Thank you, Mistress.'

When Gerrard and Watkins had gone, Alyce said, 'He is surprisingly sensitive for such a tough-looking old man.'

Thomas raised an eyebrow. 'I would say his pain has more to do with the promise of aqua vitae than any hurt.'

Alyce rolled her eyes. 'I am a fool. I will have to find something else to ease his pain.'

'I fear you'll lose a regular patient.'

As Alyce began to clean away her instruments, Thomas picked up a jar from the shelf, unstoppered it and sniffed. He glanced across at Alyce. 'Your perfume?'

'Sandalwood. I add a grain or two to the lavender water.'

She took the jar from him and stoppered it.

'Why was Peter Marston here?'

'A nasty scratch,' Alyce answered, not meeting his eyes, 'said it was done by a cat.' She could not help herself. 'I suspect it may be a term he uses to describe his wife.'

'Her temper can be something to behold.'

Alyce returned to the workbench.

'You know?'

Alyce gazed out the window. 'As Cecily often says, there are few secrets on a manor of this size.'

'She is right.'

Alyce gripped the bench with both hands. 'If it is in the past, then I believe it is not my business.' She stared at the place where earlier she had seen Thomas talking to Beth Marston. 'It is only the present that concerns me. Still, I do not see why a man who would die rather than break his word to another man would see no evil in breaking the word given to a woman, a solemn word given in the sight of God.'

Thomas did not reply.

Alyce straightened her shoulders, forcing Beth Marston from her mind. She turned to face him.

He strolled around the room, looking at the array of jars and vials, the herbs hanging to dry. 'My mother treated the tenants in here. She also visited the infirm in their cottages.'

'I intended to do the same but Cecily thought it best to leave it once I found I was with child.'

'A sensible idea.' He walked back to her and slid an arm around her waist. He plucked the coif off her head. 'I hate these things.'

Alyce raised her eyebrows. 'You would rather I ended up with muck and pus, like that from Gerrard's boil, in my hair?'

'Heaven forfend.' Thomas pretended a shudder. 'Wear them, but only when you must.' He smiled at Alyce, his eyes warm, and she could not help but smile back at him.

22

January 1588

The Christmas season over, life fell into a routine. Alyce rode with her husband, sat with him as reckoning was made by the steward, sat at his right hand at mealtime, sang and danced with him in the evening, knelt beside him as he led the household prayers at the end of each day, slept in his arms at night and hoped this was the pattern of their future. Each day that passed strengthened what she felt for him, but, as she had so little experience of matters of the heart, she could not gauge what Thomas truly felt for her. His actions she took to be a measure of the love he owed her as a duty, the love spoken of in their marriage vows encompassing kindness and courtesy, respect and protection. She told herself that it was enough— wishing for what could not be would only taint the good in her life.

Over these days hung the growing threat of war. Alyce knew that each passing day brought closer the moment when Thomas would leave to take his part in the battle that was sure to come. She turned away when she saw Thomas and Watkins drilling those men in service at Ashthorpe in the use of musket and pike. She closed her ears to the sounds from the courtyard, the clash of metal on metal as they practised a ferocious swordplay each afternoon.

The crying of her baby could be heard through the house, drowning out the courtyard noise. Alyce hurried up to the nursery where Sarah paced, rocking Elinor in her arms.

Alyce sat and unfastened the front of her gown, pushing down her loosely laced bodice and her shift. She bent her head and kissed the child once Sarah had placed Elinor in her arms.

'Leave if you have something else to do, Sarah. I will put Elinor to bed.'

Alyce cradled Elinor's head, her free hand stroking the dark silky curls, as the baby sucked hungrily.

Elinor, having taken all she could, wriggled in her swaddling bands and squalled.

'You hungry little ladybird,' Alyce murmured as she moved Elinor to the other side where she began again. Alyce's mind drifted, peaceful. When she looked down, Elinor had fallen asleep, a smear of milk dribbling from her mouth.

Alyce sighed. Despite the fear of war and the corners of her life that would never be as she wished, she was content. She glanced up to see Thomas standing at the door and smiled at him.

He did not return her smile. 'I need to speak with you.'

She gently laid Elinor in her cradle and turned away to redo her bodice.

Thomas walked over and stared down into the cot.

'Thomas, what is wrong?'

'Nothing.' Frowning, he moved back to the door.

A leaden weight in the pit of her stomach, Alyce followed him up the staircase tower.

~

Thomas rested his hands on the battlements at the top of the tower and gazed out at the hills, the strips, the hedged fields, the orchards, the village, all dusted with snow.

'This is our land as far as you can see. Parcels of land were sold or lost to neighbours by my grandfather. When my mother came here, it was half the size. I have, in the fourteen years I have owned it, reclaimed all that was once ours. It is no longer a rotting farm, but a thriving manor.'

He still remembered what it was like to be nineteen and penniless. 'This is the first place I can truly call my own. It is not easy for a younger son. We either have to accept whatever largesse our elder brother is willing to bestow or we have to fight for ourselves.'

Alyce, standing at his side, looked out across the view. 'I cannot imagine a better place to live.'

Thomas placed his arm around her waist and pulled her close. It had struck him forcibly this last month that she was the most important part of Ashthorpe now. She made it home.

'It is time for me to leave.'

Alyce straightened her shoulders and continued to stare out

over the fields.

'I'll not see the Spanish take what is mine. They will never do to us what they have done in the Low Countries.' He tightened his grip on her. 'Sir Philip is directing the militia. Watkins and I have organised our men, and Haines is to see they keep to their musket practice. It is of more use than archery these days. By the time we face Spain, our men will be a fearsome enemy.

'And here, I want you to have this.' He unhooked a small dagger from his belt and handed it to Alyce.

She took it and withdrew it an inch or so from its scabbard. The winter sunlight glinted on the razor-sharp blade.

'Keep it on you at all times. If I had any sense, I would have taught you to use a wheel-lock pistol but, foolishly, I hoped word would come the Spanish had broken up their fleet.' He grimaced. 'I pray you never need to use it.'

She continued to stare at the knife, blinking rapidly.

He reached over and gently brushed the tears away. He blinked himself. Never before had a woman been brought to tears by thought of his departure. 'I promise you...' He fought to control his voice. 'I promise you when this is over, I will be home more often. I have been fighting more than half my life, and adventure has lost its glamour. While I am not ready to don a long gown and sit by the fire, I want to enjoy what I have here—my wife, my family, my friends.'

'When do you leave?' Her voice was barely above a whisper.

'Tomorrow.'

Alyce kept her eyes on the horizon. 'God bless you and keep you, Thomas. I will pray without ceasing the whole time you are away.'

He held her closer. 'There is no doubt, then, I will return.'

~

Isabel arranged the daffodils in the vase on the parlour window-sill. The sight of them filled her with hope. Spring was nearly here, and with it her baby would arrive. She brushed her hand over her belly as she felt the gentle movements of the child.

Will had given her the daffodils. He said he had found them growing beneath a tree near St Giles churchyard. She had wondered what he was doing over there but did not ask. She took comfort in the thought that wherever he had been, he was thinking of her and was willing to risk the laughter of other men by carrying a bunch of daffodils through the street to give to her. She closed her eyes. She must not give in to suspicion. She had confided in Dame Katharine, told her of the hints dropped by Lettys Rowe, the whispers she had tried not to hear. Dame Katharine had been stern, saying that entertaining such thoughts was as great an infidelity as lying with a man not your husband.

Isabel wished she did not care so much, wished when Lettys Rowe made sly comments she could react as Alyce had to Isabel's suggestion that Thomas Granville had spent the night before his wedding with two trollops. Alyce had treated it as a jest, and Isabel would have laughed had she not been so angry with Alyce. She should not have made up the story, but Alyce had been standing there smug and arrogant in her wedding finery. When Isabel thought back on it, she felt a tremor of shame—what woman was not entitled to look as well as Alyce had on her wedding day. But Isabel had been angry at Alyce's desertion when she needed her so much. And look what had happened because Alyce had not been at her side.

Isabel forced her eyes wide open. She would not cry. Remembering served no purpose. Her hand slipped down again to her well-rounded belly. She stared out the window and up at the sky. The clouds had broken apart and a brilliant ray of golden light shone through. Another sign of hope.

'Isabel.'

She turned to find her mother standing close beside her.

'Mother, I did not hear you come in.'

'You were lost in thought.' Mother moved closer, kissing Isabel on the cheek.

'I was,' she sighed. She watched her mother. She seemed uneasy. Isabel hoped she did not have bad news—she could not face another's troubles at this moment. 'Look at the daffodils Will brought me.' She touched a finger gently to the yellow trumpets.

'They are pretty,' Mother said, frowning. She took a deep breath. 'I have had a letter from Alyce.'

'She is well?' Isabel asked, looking past her mother, not

meeting her eyes. She did not truly blame Alyce. She could not have foreseen what would happen. But if Alyce had been here to make a potion for her, perhaps she could have held the babe within her until the right time. She was nowhere near as bad as Dame Katharine insisted.

'Alyce has had a child,' Mother said into the silence of the room.

Isabel turned to her, her eyes prickling. 'A boy?'

'Nay, a daughter. Born last November.'

Isabel let out a slow breath. It did not cause her pain. 'She has taken her time telling you. Did she let you know she was with child?'

'Ay, she did.'

'And you did not go to her lying-in?'

Mother shook her head. 'My place was here with you. You needed me.'

Isabel wrapped her arms around her mother and laid her head on her shoulder. She knew Mother cared for her best. She should never have doubted it.

'I am happy for her,' Isabel murmured. She straightened up. 'Granville must be disappointed.'

'No doubt,' Mother said. 'It is strange he did not mention that Alyce was with child when he was here last year. I expected him to and was ready with my excuses for not being able to go to the lying-in, but he said nothing.'

'That tells us much.' Isabel smiled.

~

Isabel eased herself back against the freshly plumped pillows. Although she felt weak and tired, she could not stop smiling, the pain and struggle of the last day already a fading memory.

A wet nurse sat at the bedside, suckling Isabel's newborn son as Isabel's mother and Dame Katharine watched, proud grandmothers. Isabel's friends Lettys and Martha chatted on the other side of the bed.

Sir William strode in, Will behind him.

'Well done, Isabel.' Sir William stared down at the child at the nurse's breast.

The nurse glanced shyly at Sir William. 'I think he is finished, sir.'

Sir William gently scooped up the baby and carried him into the clear light from the window. 'So tiny,' he breathed. 'You were once as small, Will.'

Isabel blinked back tears at the tenderness in Sir William's voice.

As the baby started squalling, Sir William grinned. 'Such a healthy child! The plans I have for you, my boy.'

The wet nurse rose from her chair. 'I'll put young William in his cradle now. He needs to sleep.'

It was accepted without discussion the child would be named for his grandfather.

Will took young William from his father and carried him to the nurse, rocking him in his arms, reluctant to hand the baby over.

'Now the christening.' Sir William glanced at his wife, who was staring wistfully into the cradle. 'Dame Katharine thinks Thursday will do. It is time enough to organise the godparents. They have all been approached—Sir Christopher Layer, the former mayor, and his lady, and William Oates, the London grocer. They should stand William in good stead for the future.'

Isabel knew Sir William saw his grandson as the next link in a long chain of William Suttons stretching into a prosperous future. But what mattered most was that Isabel now had what she had longed for—a healthy boy.

Will sat in the chair beside the bed. 'He is beautiful.'

'Oh, Will, he is. You cannot know how happy I am.'

'I can Isabel, I can.' His eyes glistening, he leant across and kissed her.

23

July 1588

A cart carrying stores from London brought news of bands of apprentices training in the streets and of merchants preparing for battle. The carter said that in every village he had passed through, men and women stood ready for what may come when the great Spanish fleet, outnumbering the English two to one, finally attacked.

Alyce began each day with a prayer and ended it with the same prayer: for Thomas and for all those on the sea and on land defending their country. She knew she should accept God's will, whatever it may be, but she could not. Instead, she prayed, fervent and unceasing, for her husband's return—safe and whole.

As she rode past the village green where Haines oversaw the drilling of the husbandmen and farmers of Ashthorpe, she thought of Norwich's Strangers who had arrived from the Low Countries when she was a girl and their tales of slaughter and brutality at the hands of the Spanish. She barely comprehended the barbarities they had suffered. Her hand slid to the dagger hanging from her girdle, hidden in the folds of her skirt, and prayed she would never need it.

July drew towards its close and the able-bodied men of the manor, together with those of Sir Philip's, set out for London to join the army of the Earl of Leicester at Tilbury. They were men Alyce knew by name, men whose families were part of the daily round at Ashthorpe. The minds and hearts of every person left behind stretched after them in fervent prayer.

Then, as July became August, winds and storms raged on the sea and the great fleet of the King of Spain, the greatest ever assembled, was defeated by the English naval forces, and the Protestant wind sent by God blew the ships away. They were saved. All across England bells rang out, bonfires crackled and fireworks flared.

By the end of August, the men had returned safe, not a shot

fired. They told how they had seen the Queen, a goddess in silver and white riding her magnificent white horse. She had spoken to them, words meant for each and every one, a memory to stay with them all their days. They had seen London, marched through its streets cheered by its masses. In the village decked out with pennants, it was no different. They crowded into the Ashthorpe's church and thanked God for their deliverance. The bells pealed, the men come home let off their muskets in salute, the music played and there was dancing and celebration.

~

Alyce took the casting bottle from her cabinet and sprinkled lavender water on her wrists, rubbing them together. She traced her finger over the engraved pattern on the silver mounting of the bottle of yellow-green glass and thought of Thomas. He had given her the bottle when he had arrived home last December. She placed it back on the cabinet, picked up his miniature lying there and went to the window, where the light was brighter. She had thought it the very image of him when she first had seen it, but now it seemed to be nothing more than paint marks on a board. She closed her eyes and saw his smile, remembered how his eyes lit up and recognised that, in that moment, all he had been thinking of was of her. When he returned, she would be bold and tell him what she felt for him. Not that she loved him, that would be too much, but she would tell him how content she was with the life he had given her, the pleasure it was to be his wife. In less than two years, she had gone from being a woman with no position to a wife and mother and lady of the manor. And just over a month ago, after the men returned to Ashthorpe, Thomas had written from Portsmouth. His letter was full of their victory and directions for management of the manor. And it was addressed to Alyce, not Cecily. He had said he would be home as soon as he could, but the weeks dragged on and still he had not come.

Alyce's heart skipped a beat as she looked out through the window to a group of eight horsemen riding towards the house.

She sped down the stairs to the parlour, where Cecily sat wrapped in her bright *shawl,* listening to Marian read.

Breathless, Alyce said, 'There's a party of horsemen on their way.'

'Go out to them, Alyce.' Cecily caught her excitement. 'Welcome them home.'

Alyce waited on the steps as they rode in through the gatehouse, puzzled. They were brightly dressed, men and a couple of women, not stained and weary travellers. Among them was Sir Philip and Lady Rossiter's youngest son, eighteen-year-old Geoffrey. He dismounted clumsily and came over to her.

'Mistress Granville,' he said, bowing courteously, 'we were passing and thought we would call upon you.'

'You are most welcome, Master Rossiter.'

'Ay Mistress,' drawled a voice from behind him, 'we hope to provide you with a pleasant morning's company, exiled as you now are in the country.'

Giles Clifton. What was he doing here? Alyce inclined her head, acknowledging him. 'I have spent near half my life in the country, Master Clifton, and find much to recommend it.'

He smirked. 'Ah, the country pleasures of Dalstead.'

Geoffrey looked from one to the other. 'You have met?'

'I met Master Clifton in London last year.'

'Oh, we go back farther than that.'

'You are mistaken,' Alyce snapped. She turned to Geoffrey. 'Mistress Beaumont will be eager to see you and hear news of your parents.' She led the way to the parlour, the others following. Close up, she smelt the reek of wine.

Cecily shifted in her chair and, smiling, greeted Geoffrey. 'You and your guests are welcome, Geoffrey.'

He bowed to her, not quite steady on his feet.

'As it is nearing dinnertime, I hope you will dine with us.'

'Most certainly, Mistress.'

'Marian, will you arrange refreshment for our guests while we wait for dinner?'

'I will do it,' Alyce said. 'I need to speak to the cook.'

She was out the door before Cecily could protest. Lifting her skirts, she took the stairs two at a time and ran to the nursery, where Sarah sat with Elinor on her knee, spooning pottage into her as the child waved her own spoon in the air.

At the sight of her mother, Elinor dropped her spoon and held out her arms, babbling, 'Mamma, mamma.'

'Oh, sweeting,' Alyce groaned. 'Not now.' She turned to Sarah. 'On your life, do not bring Elinor downstairs. You are to bolt the door after me and open it only to me or to your mother,' she said her voice sharp with panic.

'But…'

'I will explain later.' Alyce bent and kissed Elinor and was gone.

~

The household ate their meal in wary silence. The guests, rather than sit in their appointed places, congregated at the other end of the table. Their manners deserted them—bread was thrown, wine spilt and bawdy stories told as they ate.

'Who is that man?' Cecily asked. 'The blond one, in the blue and silver? He is not as drunk as the others. I am sure he is urging them on.'

'That is Giles Clifton.'

Cecily drew a hissing breath. 'You should have ordered him from the house.'

Although out of earshot, Clifton seemed to be aware he was being spoken of and swept his hat off to Cecily.

'Would he have gone?' Alyce toyed with her food. 'I fear he has come here deliberately.'

'You know the man is dangerous?'

'I do.'

'Look at Geoffrey,' Cecily sniffed. 'He can hardly stand. Margaret will roast him alive when she hears of this.' She glared along the table. 'And the woman with Geoffrey, in the tawny dress, is she wearing the latest in London fashion?'

'Only in the Southwark stews, I would say.'

Cecily breathed through her nose, her lips pressed together. 'That does not surprise me. They are behaving as if this were a low tavern.'

Before the meal had finished, Clifton and another guest rose and went into the parlour. Clifton returned with Alyce's lute and settled himself back with his companions. Stretching back on his seat, he rested his feet on the table and plucked out a tune, his eyes on Alyce. He called to the man in the parlour, 'Morton! Play us a dancing tune.'

Morton pounded on the virginals.

The two women in the group rose, pulling Geoffrey and another of the guests into a graceless galliard.

Clifton put the lute aside and strolled towards Alyce. He gave an ostentatious bow and said, 'Mistress, I beg you, join me in this dance.'

'Master Clifton, I have no wish to dance.'

'Do not play coy, Alyce.' He gripped her wrist and pulled her from her chair.

If she called on Haines, he and the grooms could remove these varlets. But Alyce noticed, although they had set aside their rapiers, they all wore poniards. In any struggle, her men were certain to be harmed. The safest course would be to dance with Clifton and then convince Geoffrey to be on his way.

Scowling, Alyce fell in step with him. At each turn he spoke. 'So that is the sainted Cecily Beaumont. Is she a hard mistress?'

'I am mistress here.'

He smirked as she skipped around him. 'I have news that might interest you of your husband's doings in the fleshpots of London.'

They stepped between the other dancers. 'I am not interested in your lies.'

'But there is always a kernel of truth in what I say.'

Alyce glared at him and, following the flow of the dance, skipped away.

As she stepped back again, Clifton pulled her to him. 'Alyce,' he purred her name, 'since you cruelly spurned my friendship last year, you have never been far from my thoughts.'

She jerked away from him, pushing past Geoffrey Rossiter who had his arms around the young woman in the low-bodiced tawny gown, using her more as a prop than a dancing partner.

Most of the servants stood near Cecily, unsure how to begin clearing away the remains of the meal with their guests clearly intent on prolonging it.

Alyce lowered her voice. 'Go about your other duties, leave this until after our *guests* have gone.'

Cecily frowned as two of the party carried a small barrel into the hall, dumped it on the table and roughly breached it. Wine dripped onto the floor, seeping into the rush matting.

'I doubt they are in any mood to leave,' Cecily said.

'I want them gone.' Alyce rubbed her fingers across her furrowed brow. 'I will send Stokes for Sir Philip.'

Alyce and Judith helped Cecily from her chair and walked with her towards the door.

Clifton, sprawled farther down the table, called to her, 'Alyce, will you not stay with us and, for once, enjoy the company of the young and lusty?' He picked up the lute and sang,

'Alyce come kiss me now,
Kiss me once again, my love.'

Cheers and laughter greeted his song as his companions joined in,

'Alyce come kiss me now.'

The song followed Alyce as she helped Cecily to the stairs.

'Alyce lie with me now,
Lie with me once again, my love.'

'He is nothing but a varlet,' she muttered between her teeth.

'I know that well,' Cecily said.

Behind them the company roared their laughter as the song descended into crudity.

~

Alyce stepped into the hall, Haines at her side, and surveyed the chaos of chairs and upturned stools, the mess of plates and beakers and food strewn over the floor and the table.

Geoffrey Rossiter sat at the end of the table, his head in his hands. He looked up, his eyes unfocused. 'Here wench, bring me more wine.'

'You have had more than enough to drink,' Alyce answered.

'Who are you to say what is enough?'

'Your behaviour, Master Rossiter, is a disgrace,' she said icily. 'I have sent for your father to come and collect you and your *guests.*'

Geoffrey blinked hard. Recognising where he was, he drooped in the chair and groaned. 'Oh Mistress, what have I done?'

'A word of advice, Master Rossiter: eschew the company of the likes of Giles Clifton if you would be a quarter the man your father is.'

Geoffrey stumbled to his feet and shook the shoulder of a young man asleep at the table, his head resting on his arms 'Get up, Dawes, we are leaving. You do not want to face my father.'

Clifton leant against the parlour doorpost. 'An entertaining little speech, Alyce,' he said, clapping slowly, 'but who are you to lecture your betters on their behaviour—you, a shopkeeper's daughter?'

'It is time you left, Master Clifton.' Alyce walked away, her back rigid.

24

Alyce sat by the nursery window feeding Elinor, finally at ease. The rest of the household was at work below, sweeping, scrubbing and polishing away any trace of their *guests*.

Sir Philip and half a dozen grooms had arrived as his son and his friends were leaving. The others had galloped away, but Sir Philip had forced Geoffrey to stay as the cost of his visit was measured—the broken furniture, the soiled tapestries, the virginals with keys sticky with spilt wine, the mess and the waste. They had left together, Geoffrey chastened and queasy, Sir Philip mortified his son could so shame him. Sir Philip had assured Alyce he would pay the price of the damage and inflict a fitting punishment on his son.

And Clifton would be well away by now. At the thought of him, Alyce held Elinor tighter. The child whimpered, wriggling in Alyce's arms. Alyce took a slow, deep breath, and Elinor settled again, drifting to sleep.

Alyce rose and carefully placed her in the cot. She gazed, wistful, at the sturdy child. Elinor was growing and too soon these quiet times would be a thing of the past.

'A pretty sight.'

Alyce's head shot up at the sound of Clifton's voice.

He stood at the door, his eyes on Alyce's exposed breast.

She fumbled to pull up her bodice and tighten the laces.

'Leave it. It is most becoming.'

Her stomach lurched as Clifton shut the door and shot the bolt into place. He walked to the cot and stared down at the sleeping baby. 'Ah, this is the spawn. A pity it is not a son. It would be so easy…'

Alyce saw the pale network of veins beneath the translucent skin at her daughter's temples, the dark lashes resting on plump cheeks, the lips parted in innocent sleep, the fragility of her life.

Her heart thumped. 'You leave her alone.'

'Or what?'

'I will kill you.' Her words were a vow.

Clifton smirked. 'A most Christian sentiment, my little hypocrite.' He came around the cot, backing Alyce against the wall, and placed his hand above her shoulder, his face no more than an inch from hers, his breath hot on her skin.

She turned her head to the side, but Clifton grasped her chin and pulled her face towards him, his mouth covering hers.

Alyce stood immobile, her mouth clamped shut, her arms rigid at her side. Clifton stopped and drew his head back, his eyes intent on her. 'Alyce, why are you so unfriendly?' He pressed himself against her.

She could smell his musky scent, see the network of lines around his eyes, a patch of rough skin near his hairline. Close, there was a sense of brittleness and decay.

'We could surprise your husband,' he said, his voice deepening with the movement of his body against hers. 'Take for yourself the son he cannot give you. He will be home soon enough for you to cover the deed.'

She could push him away, try to grab Elinor from the cot and run for the door but she knew he would be on her before she was halfway.

'Elinor could cry at any time. It will bring the maids running.'

'You had better hope she does not cry.' His eyes glittered, hard and soulless.

'God help me,' Alyce whispered. If it would save Elinor, she would submit to what he wanted. She stretched her fingers, bracing against the thought, and felt the stiletto beneath her hand, hidden in the folds of her skirt.

'God has turned his face from you,' Clifton laughed. 'He has no wish to watch our sport.'

The muffled sound of a maidservant singing while she worked drifted from the hall below.

Elinor whimpered in her sleep.

Clifton moved away from Alyce towards the cot.

She knew he would kill Elinor first, make her watch her daughter die. Her hand closed around the handle of the knife. Her heart raced, blood pounding in her ears. She would not let him touch her child. She reached out with her left hand and grabbed his arm, pulling him back.

'Ah, Alyce, I always knew you were a slut at heart.' He moved closer, his codpiece undone. 'From this day on, every time your husband touches you, whether here...' He grabbed her head and pressed his mouth on hers, forcing her lips apart. 'Or here...' He tugged at her bodice, exposing both her breasts, squeezing them to the point of pain. 'Or here...' He thrust his hand between her legs. 'You will remember that I have been there too.'

He grinned, his teeth bared. 'The spawn will have to wait.' He tugged her skirts upwards, his eyes on Alyce's.

She saw no spark of pity there, only all-consuming hate. If she could injure him, there was a chance she could get Elinor away.

She jerked the knife upwards as he pressed against her, felt it slice into his groin.

Clifton opened his mouth and groaned, shock and pain in his eyes. He grabbed her hand, trying to wrench it back but searing anger drove Alyce on, twisting the blade, tearing, ripping at the flesh.

'You bitch,' he gasped, clawing at her bloodied skirt, dragging Alyce towards the floor with him.

He writhed, moaning, his eyelids fluttering as he gasped for breath. His blood flooded out with each beat of his failing heart, soaking through Alyce's skirt and petticoats to her skin.

She clenched her mouth shut against a scream as he opened his eyes wide, fixing his gaze on her. She dared not look away.

He seemed to take an age to die. But she supposed it was not long—the maidservant had only just finished her song as the shadow passed across his face.

Alyce stayed on her knees beside him, frozen, afraid that if she moved he would spring back to life. One thought filled her mind, blocking out all else—Elinor was safe. It did not matter what came after this, Elinor was safe.

She struggled up and stood in the middle of the nursery. Silence hung over the whole house. Clifton lay on the floor, his face peaceful as he stared at the patterned ceiling, his blood pooled around him, a deep red that drained all colour from the room. Starlings chattered on the windowsill, careless. Elinor slept on undisturbed.

~

Thomas strolled in past the screens at the end of the hall, whistling. He stopped and scowled around at the broken chairs and soiled matting stacked against the wall, the mound of food scraps and shattered beakers and plates the maidservant had swept into the middle of the room.

'What has happened here?'

'There... there were guests, sir,' the girl stuttered.

He doubted he would get much sense from her. 'Where is the Mistress?'

'Mistress Beaumont is in the parlour.' She glanced up towards the dais as she dipped a curtsy.

'Mistress Granville?'

The girl bobbed her head. 'She is in the nursery, sir.'

He took the stairs two at a time and strode along the gallery to the nursery. He was home at last with no intention of going anywhere until after Christmas. He had so much to tell Alyce, so many plans. He pushed at the nursery door, but it did not move. The nursery was never locked. A chill crawled down his back. He pushed hard against the door. It was bolted. He rattled the latch.

'Alyce, are you there?'

There was no sound in the room. Outside, birds squabbled on the nursery windowsill.

Footsteps padded across the floor, the bolt groaned as it was pulled back and the door flung open. Alyce stood on the threshold, her bodice undone, blood smeared over her face and drenching her skirt. Behind her, a body lay between the chair and the cot.

'Thomas,' she sobbed.

'My God! Alyce.' Words failed him.

'I killed him.'

Thomas stared at the corpse. Clifton. Alyce could hang for this. He saw the misery, the horror in her eyes, and knew she needed to be held, to be comforted, but there was no time for that—yet.

'Wait here.'

He shut the door and was halfway down the stairs when Watkins, saddlebag slung over his shoulder, came in through the door. Thomas beckoned to him to follow, signalling him to be quiet. He ushered Watkins into the nursery and bolted the door behind them.

Thomas glanced into the cot where his daughter slept, undisturbed by whatever had happened. 'Amazing child,' he murmured, 'she would sleep through the final seven trumpets.'

Watkins squatted by the corpse and brushed his fingers over the eyes, closing them. 'A well-judged strike. I could not have done better myself.'

'Alyce, who knows Clifton is here?' Thomas asked.

Her eyes were unfocused, her arms held tight across her chest. She rubbed a hand back and forth over her mouth. 'I do not know. No one?'

He looked to Watkins. 'We will move him into the armoury for now and dispose of him tonight.' His voice was harsh. 'No one is to know of this, understand?' There was no need to say it; he could trust Watkins with his life. 'You'll need to find his horse and get rid of that too. It will not be far.'

Watkins nodded, grim-faced.

'Step out of your skirt, Alyce. We'll wrap him in that. We want no trail in the gallery.'

Alyce sat in her petticoats, her bodice roughly laced, as Thomas and Watkins carried the swathed body, sagging between them, from the room.

Thomas bolted the door when he returned and leant against it, his arms crossed. 'What happened?'

Alyce shivered, her arms wrapped around herself, rocking. 'I killed him,' she said wearily.

Thomas sidestepped the blood pooled on the floor and knelt beside her. He crushed her against him, feeling the trembling of her body. 'What happened, Alyce?' he asked again.

Alyce took a ragged breath, her face buried against his chest. 'He came with Geoffrey Rossiter. They were unruly and would not leave.' Her words spilled out, tumbling over each other. 'I was afraid.' She looked up at him, fighting back a sob. 'We sent

for Sir Philip. They left when he came. He will make good... I thought it was over, but he came back.' She looked up at Thomas, her eyes wide with uncomprehending horror. 'He said he would ... kill Elinor,' she gulped, 'if I did not...'

He asked as gently as he could, 'Did he rape you?' If Clifton were not already dead, he would kill the accursed cur.

'He...' Her voice failed. She shook her head and looked straight into Thomas's eyes, her own desolate and empty. 'I killed him first.'

Thomas stood slowly. 'I'll take Elinor down to Cecily.' He picked up the baby, kissing her on the forehead as she whimpered. 'Go to my chamber. I will not be long.'

~

Alyce huddled in the corner of Thomas's chamber, her head on her knees. She could not remember walking there. She shut her eyes and saw Clifton's face as he lay on the floor—the face a mother would weep for.

She heard Thomas come in, heard the sloshing of a pail, the splash of water into a bowl. She did not want to look at him, see the reproach in his eyes. He would blame her, say she had encouraged Clifton to visit.

'Alyce.' Thomas drew Alyce up by the hand. 'You need to wash.' He gently stripped off her petticoats and smock, rolled down her stockings, helped her out of her blood-soaked shoes.

He handed her the washcloth, but Alyce stood staring at it. There was so much blood on her hands. One little cloth would never wipe it all away.

Thomas took it from her and washed away the blood from her face and the places where it has seeped through her clothing onto her skin, rinsing the cloth often. He had her dip her feet in the pail and, last of all, placed her hands in the bowl. Rubbing her hands and forearms with his, he lathered them with soap. When he had rinsed off the soap and dried her hands, she felt cleaner.

He helped her into a fresh bed-smock and lifted off her coif. 'As much as I hate these things, it has served its purpose today.' He pressed his lips against her hair, breathing in her scent. 'Your hair is clean.'

Her hair combed out and inexpertly plaited, Alyce followed Thomas through to her own chamber.

She could still smell Clifton's scent, taste his putrid mouth. She took the casting bottle from the cabinet beside the door, unscrewed the lid and took a swig of lavender water, washed it around her mouth and spat into the close stool. She splashed the water on her hands, rubbing it across her mouth, and scrubbing at her hands. Would she never be rid of the stench of him?

Thomas clenched his jaw, his eyes blazing over glistening lashes. He took the flask as Alyce lifted it to take another mouthful. 'Enough.' He brushed his fingers across her lips, removing the moisture there. 'I'll get you a tonic.'

He helped Alyce into bed and pulled the curtains around.

'Do not leave me,' she whispered.

He dragged the curtain open and sat on the bed beside her. 'I will be gone only a few moments.'

Alyce was afraid to close her eyes, fearful she would see again Clifton's cold blue eyes. His malicious laugh echoed in her ears. *God has turned his face from you.* She felt his bruising fingers, his hot breath on her skin, the sickening realisation he would harm Elinor. The raging fury, the pressure of the blade driving, twisting into his flesh. The weight of him gripping her skirt as he crumpled to the floor. The blood, pools of it, spreading across the floor. And his eyes fixed steady on her, glazing over as life left him.

Alyce threw herself to the side of the bed and vomited, her body racked with great spasms.

The door creaked open. Thomas was beside her. He helped her up and wiped her face with a cloth. He held a flask to her lips. 'It is aqua vitae. Drink it down, as much as you can.'

She placed her hand over his and tipped the flask up. She swallowed and shuddered. It burnt her mouth removing all taste. Fire spread from her throat, through her body, traced down her arms and legs. She collapsed against the pillows, trembling, her eyes closed.

Thomas squatted beside the bed, cleaning the mess.

'Why did you take so long to come home?'

He paused his cleaning. 'We were kept at our posts even after the danger had passed—many of those who had survived the Spanish attack died of fever and hunger while we waited.' He stood up. 'And payment did not come for the men. In the end, I paid my men off myself, as the other greater captains did.'

He went to the cabinet and washed his hands in the basin.

Alyce began to weep. Thomas climbed onto the bed beside her and held her.

'It is over Alyce. You have nothing more to fear.'

'He kissed me. He said he would...' She did not want to say the words.

'It does not matter.'

'I would have done anything he asked,' she sobbed.

'Shhh.' Thomas placed his fingers on Alyce's lips. 'But you did not. And no matter what, a woman cannot be blamed when her child is threatened.'

'I killed him,' she groaned. 'I took his life.'

'You protected our daughter. Your choice was Clifton or Elinor. Who would you rather were dead?'

'Clifton,' Alyce whispered.

'And no one will judge you for that.'

'God will judge me.'

'He will judge you free of any stain.' Thomas sighed heavily. 'You need to sleep now.'

They lay together on the bed. Thomas stroked her back, his lips against her forehead as she drifted into sleep.

25

Faces pressed close to her—malevolent, contorted, jeering, spitting, screaming. 'Whore, witch, murderer.' She was pushed hard from behind and fell onto damp cobblestones. Her gown was ragged and filthy, the skirt soaked in blood. She struggled to her feet and looked up to the scaffold silhouetted against a grey, icy sky. The hangman beckoned to her. He pulled off his hood and Alyce stared into the pitiless eyes of Giles Clifton. She opened her mouth to scream but nothing came.

Her eyes snapped open. She could see into every corner of her dimly lit bedchamber. Thomas dozed in a high-backed chair by the fire. She tried to move, tried to call out to him, but she was paralysed. She could not move, pinioned to the bed by a great weight on her chest. Although she could not see it, she knew the shape of the presence. Its hot breath was on her skin, rank with the smell of death. Her heart raced as she strained to move even a little finger. She tried again to scream out to Thomas, but he slept on unaware.

Her throat was raw from voiceless screams.

She was awake, Thomas shaking her, his voice urgent. 'Alyce, Alyce wake up.'

She shuddered, sobbing. Free to move at last, the terror lingered in her racing heart. Thomas held her tight, crushed in his arms. She rubbed her face against his doublet, her fear fading as she breathed in the scent of him.

He brushed her hair back from her forehead. 'You are safe, Alyce. It was only a dream.'

'Only a dream,' she murmured. Yet it had felt more real than here and now.

Panic crashed down on her again. 'Where is Elinor?'

'She is sleeping with Sarah in the nursery.'

'But I need to feed her.' Her fingers trembled with the lacing on her bed-smock. 'I want her here, safe with me.' Her breasts ached beneath tight bindings. Alyce closed her eyes as tears spilled through the lashes.

Thomas put his arms around her, rocking her as she wept. 'Elinor is strong,' he said, soothing. 'She is eating other foods. And Maggie Pye, the young widow, came from the village this morning. She will stay as long as Elinor needs her. She is a healthy woman with plenty to spare—her son is not much younger than Elinor.'

She looked at him, a crease between her brows. 'This morning?'

'Ay, you have slept for more than a day. We did not know how you would be when you woke.'

He turned her face up to his, and she saw in his tired grey eyes the pity she had never wanted from anyone.

She stared past him into the darkness. 'I have committed murder,' she said, her voice almost lost in the silence of the room.

'Does a soldier commit murder when he kills the enemy?'

Alyce shook her head.

'Then neither have you. You performed a soldier's task— killed in defence of your child and your own honour. As long as Clifton drew breath, he was a mortal threat to us all.'

'I did not think what I was doing. He pushed me against the wall and,' she closed her eyes, screwing up her face at the memory, 'he kissed me. I knew no matter what I did, he would harm Elinor. I thought if I could injure him, it would give us time to get away. He did not expect it.' She swallowed and straightened her shoulders, her face rigid. 'That knife, it was sharp as a razor. I twisted it hard.' Alyce dropped her head. 'I hated him.'

'Such a killing blow takes skill.' Thomas raised her chin. 'Perhaps God guided your hand and you fulfilled his will in what you did?'

The strain lessened in Alyce's face. 'How long did it take you to think of that argument?'

Thomas raised an eyebrow. 'It came to me now—it may be divine inspiration.'

Alyce sighed and lay against the pillows. 'Why did he hate you?'

'It is a long story.' Thomas rolled back beside her. 'Clifton had a sister, Kate, about eight years older than he was. He adored her. Their father, Sir Richard, brought Kate to London hoping to place her at court as a waiting woman to one of the Queen's ladies. She was seventeen, beautiful and alluring, but wilful and empty-headed. She got with child and was sent home in disgrace. She named me as the father.'

'Were you?' Alyce held her breath.

'I could not have been. She was pregnant even before I arrived in London. I may have been an eager lad, but I was no fool. From the start, it was clear she had no moral sense at all. I did no more than courteously rebuff her advances several times. I have no idea why she named me.' He gave a bitter laugh. 'Father had not long died, and my brother, Anthony, took great pride in his new position as head of the family. When Sir Richard demanded I marry his daughter, I was dragged in and told of my fate. I denied having anything to do with Kate, said while I liked my women willing, I drew the line at common whores. I am not sure who was angrier, Sir Richard or Anthony. The two of them, ignoring my protest, organised the wedding. The day before the marriage, I slipped out of London on a ship bound for Le Havre to join our army supporting the Huguenots. In the eyes of my brother and the Cliftons, I jilted poor pregnant Kate at the altar. So at nineteen I started my roving.' Thomas stared bitterly into the past. 'The last few years though, Anthony has started to thaw. I have my uses now.'

'And Kate?'

'Poor Kate. She died in childbed, the baby with her.'

'Oh, Thomas,' Alyce moaned.

'About ten years later Clifton approached me to sail on one of my ventures. I turned him away. He was a green boy with no skill beyond the fencing schools, taken with the idea of easy treasure, more used to giving orders than following them. I did not know who he was and was none too gentle with him. He then challenged me to a duel. He had barely drawn his sword before I disarmed him. I saw no point in killing him—he was not worth the trouble I would earn for that. To Clifton that was just another display of contempt for him and for his family. Not only had I seduced his virgin sister, enticed her into whoredom, got her with child and deserted her, but I had refused him the place on my vessel he considered his due, and I had spat into his face by not killing him, as I would a worthy opponent.'

'Did no one point out to him you could not be the father?'

'It made no difference. He wanted someone to blame.'

Alyce moved closer to Thomas. As she laid her head against his chest, he wound his arm around her.

'He has made it his business since to try to ruin everything I touch. For a while, he presented himself as my agent, entering into victualling arrangements that I had difficulty cancelling. Most know now that I will only honour agreements I have entered into personally. This last time he cancelled orders for salted beef and arranged delivery of barrels of rancid meat bought cheap. And—' Thomas stopped, scowling into the past.

Alyce thought he would not go on, but he clenched his jaw and said bitterly, 'And the year before I sailed with Drake, he ruined the marriage I had planned. He seduced the woman I was betrothed to, dripped poison in her ear. She wanted nothing to do with me by the time he was finished.'

Alyce closed her eyes and groaned, understanding now the reason for Thomas's anger at her association with Clifton in London. If only he had told her then. She imagined this woman too—beautiful, witty, well-connected—someone whose loss still caused Thomas pain these years on.

Thomas wrapped both arms tight around Alyce. 'When I saw you with him at Lord Reading's, it was my worst fear. He can—' he corrected himself, 'he could be charming.'

'A charm no deeper than his skin.' Alyce shuddered. 'What has been done with …?'

'The less you know the better, but it will be a long, long time before anyone discovers the body, months before anyone even notices he is missing. He lived a vagabond life, had few real friends.'

'And no one knows but Watkins?'

'And Cecily.'

'What did you tell her?' Her voice was muffled, her face buried against his chest again.

'The truth—he threatened Elinor, and you stabbed him with the stiletto I had given you. The household has been told that you took a sudden fever, that I found you collapsed in the nursery. You will have to stay in bed a few days more to maintain the fiction.'

'I am glad he's gone.'

Thomas nodded. 'We must not speak of him again. If this were known, you could be charged with murder, even though you were defending yourself. Or else some would imagine I killed him because of the ill will between us. Either or both of us could stand trial.'

Alyce refused to think where that would lead.

'We should give thanks. The threat that was Giles Clifton is gone. With God's help, we have defeated the Spanish. The sky ahead is clear.'

Warm and safe in Thomas's arms, Alyce shivered.

26

December 1588

The hall, festooned with ivy and box and sprigs of holly, thronged with the villagers of Ashthorpe in their Sunday clothes, well-fed and in a festive mood. A troupe of players had entertained them with a tale of mistaken identity where all had turned out well in the end, tumblers and a saucy fool providing amusement in the intervals between the acts.

Thomas watched his wife from the other side of the room as she wandered through the hall, doing her best to smile as she greeted the wives of tenants and villagers. She gave her full attention to those who stopped her, most often seeking her advice about the salves and simples she dispensed, helpful in treating day-to-day ailments. She was all that could be wanted in a wife—dignified, intelligent, industrious and kind. Thomas knew the manor was in competent hands when he was away. Since Clifton, although she attended to her duties with her usual care, she seemed to take little pleasure in life. She no longer played her lute or the virginals. He had not heard her sing while she worked. Light shone in her eyes only when she was with Elinor. Would another child bring her back to herself? But even that was difficult. The few times he had lain with her, she had been distant, not with him at all. He would not press her, no matter how much he wanted her. It was better to wait until she was ready to welcome him.

'Tom.'

He turned toward the speaker, who had placed a hand on his arm.

'That play was a delight.' Beth Marsden gazed up at Thomas, a dimple in her cheek.

He looked away, hoping her husband was standing nearby so that he could draw him into the conversation. There was a space around them; most had turned their backs as if to afford them privacy but there would be covert glances and straining ears.

'I thought it a fitting celebration not only of the season but of our victory over the Spanish,' he said.

'It was as good as anything you would see in London.'

'They are London players. I managed to persuade them to travel into the countryside in winter—there is much work for them in London this time of year.'

'London,' Beth sighed. 'You must miss it. I know I do—the high-born ladies in their silks and damasks, the latest fashions. Here women still dress like they did when I was a child.'

Thomas's eyes drifted down to Beth's painted lips and her bodice, cut lower than any other woman present, her kerchief accentuating rather than masking her charms. It was not a style of dress favoured by the women of Ashthorpe.

'I keep asking Peter to take me back, only for a short visit, but he says he is too busy, even in winter.'

'There is always work on a farm,' Thomas answered.

'Speaking of London, an old friend visited me a couple of months back. He said he had called on you, but you were not at home.'

'An old friend?' Thomas said, wary.

'Giles Clifton.'

'Clifton—' He stopped himself. He had almost said *was*. 'Clifton is a friend of yours?'

'Ay,' she smiled, her eyelashes lowered. 'He was a very good friend.' She slowly raised her eyes to his. 'Until I met you. Giles pointed you out, said you were in need of distraction.' She arched an eyebrow. 'And that worked out well, did it not?'

Thomas stared at her, his jaw clenched. Beth had been a comfort when he needed it, and while no money had changed hands, there had been commerce in their relationship—gifts given, bills paid, clothing bought. She had prevented him from wallowing in his misery. For that, he felt a debt that meant he had ignored rather than curtly dismissed her less than subtle attempts to insinuate herself back into his bed. What game had Clifton been playing? He swallowed. It made him sick to think she was Clifton's leavings.

'And your husband, did Clifton send you to him?'

'I met Peter by chance. He was besotted the moment he set eyes on me.' She tossed her head, the light catching on gold earrings far beyond the means of Peter Marsden. 'And it was time I lived a more settled life. He was so generous with his gifts I assumed he owned a grand manor. Still, it was pleasing to find Peter lived close to you.' She fluttered her eyelashes again. 'Giles said I should let him know, now and again, how you fared.'

He stretched his fingers. 'And have you?'

'Only once or twice. You were married before I could get word to him and he was sore disappointed at that but I told him of your daughter's birth.'

Thomas wanted to blame her, but she had been no more than a willing dupe. He breathed heavily through his nose. 'And when do you expect to see him again?'

She shrugged. 'He said he might travel abroad, perhaps to Venice, after he had dealt with some unfinished business.'

Thomas knew what that business was—and it was finished now. He looked up, across the room, straight into Alyce's pain-filled eyes.

He turned away from Beth, but she caught him by the wrist. He shook her off angrily.

'Goodwife Marsden, I suggest you set aside any dreams of London. You are married to an honest man who has provided you with a good home and a decent life. If you are to have any contentment from this life, look to him and give him the care he deserves.'

He strode away, past the enquiring faces, towards the screen at the end of the hall.

~

Out in the courtyard Alyce stopped and hugged her arms tight, shivering. She had rushed out without a cloak. She could not stand around moping in the snow, but neither did she want to go back into the hall to watch her husband make assignations with that... that woman.

Alyce hurried to the stables and pushed open the creaking door. It was warmer inside and sharp-smelling, a not unpleasant mixture of hay and manure. Horses snorted softly as she moved past their stalls. Gleda hung her head over the gate and snickered. Alyce rubbed her hand against the horse's warm face.

She opened the gate and went into the stall. The horse

nuzzled at Alyce's hands. 'I am sorry. I do not have anything for you.'

She laid her head against the palfrey's neck. 'It is a pity it is so cold, else we could go out riding.'

She saw again her husband standing close, his head bent towards Beth Marston. Pain gripped her throat. Her worst fear. She had known it would happen, but not here, not in front of her.

'Gleda, what am I to do?'

She wished she did not care. There had been warmth in his eyes twelve months ago, but that was gone. He was courteous and kind, but distant. She knew any feeling he had towards her now was duty.

Then there was Clifton. She did not regret killing him, was glad he was gone, but still she felt guilt. He stood, often, at her shoulder whispering every criticism she had made of herself, telling her that a man like Thomas could never love a woman not of gentle birth, lacking both wit and beauty, a woman he had married only for the money her father had promised.

Never in her life had any wrongdoing gone unpunished. She feared punishment was still waiting, hanging over her, and at some future point would be exacted. Worse, the punishment could be that ill would befall someone she loved, Thomas or Elinor. And it would be her fault.

She lifted the blanket off the horse's back and took the brush from the shelf beside the gate. 'What advice would you give me?'

The horse blinked its large dark eyes.

'Alyce.' Thomas stood at the gate to the stall. 'I wondered where you were.' He smiled at her, his usual courteous smile.

Alyce stopped her brushing. 'It was too warm in the hall. I needed some air.' She could not look at him, her mind full of the Marston woman.

'What is the matter?'

'Nothing.' She shivered. 'I should go back. I have not given out the comfits to the children.'

'I hope you have plenty to spare. For certain, Sir Philip will be disappointed if there are none when he comes tomorrow.'

He helped Alyce put the blanket back on Gleda. 'If it starts to snow heavily, we may have to quarter them for the night.'

How convenient, Alyce thought. 'Not a few of the household would be most put out by that.'

He held the gate open for her. 'Who is coming tomorrow?'

'The Rossiters and the Wyards, and the Jefferies again.'

'It is a great deal of work for you.'

'There are many to help here.'

He looked into her face, and Alyce forced herself to meet his gaze. He rested a hand on her shoulder but kept his body stiffly apart from hers as he pressed his lips chastely to her forehead. Thomas only held her now when she woke from her hag-ridden dreams, calming her and whispering that it was only a dream. Otherwise, even though they still shared a bed, he slept well away from her. Often as not, she woke to find pillows between them or Thomas so entangled in his blankets it was not possible for him to come close to her in sleep.

Alyce melted at the touch of his lips on her skin but gave no outward sign. She supposed this was a token of his care. He kissed his sister thus, but Alyce was not his sister, she was his wife.

~

Alyce walked into the hall beside Thomas, her head held high. They stood together, surrounded by their guests, as Alyce gave out the small sugared packages to the eager children.

Thomas watched Alyce's face soften with a fleeting happiness, as it no longer did when she looked towards him.

This was his fault. Had he not married her, she would never have become Clifton's target. Among other reasons, he had married Alyce for her virtue, yet without that virtue she would have succumbed to Clifton's blandishments, and that would have satisfied the varlet—she would have been safe.

He knew her problem—she had been forced to a soldier's task. Had she been a lad, he and Watkins would have sat down with her, got her drunk and let her talk, let her listen to their tales of skirmishes and near misses. She would have been one of that band of brothers. But she was a woman, his wife, and he did not know how to begin to mend her hurt.

27

May 1589

Alyce walked along the gravel path of the formal garden. She should be proud of last year's work—the bushes she had planted of lavender, rosemary, hyssop, marjoram and winter savory now formed intricate patterns of colour and varied leaves. The arbours were heavy with honeysuckle and budding roses. Within the month, the garden would be filled with their scent mingling with that of the lavender, and the pinks planted around the knots. Here and there she could see straggling weeds. Last year she would have uprooted them as soon as they dared show a shoot but now even the thought of finding the gardener was too difficult. Next year her lack of effort would show.

At the far end of the garden, Cecily sat against the wall, her eyes shut against the bright sunlight. She should go and sit beside her, close her eyes, drink in the warmth and think of nothing at all. Perhaps when she opened them, her cares would have washed away.

Alyce turned at the crunch of footsteps on the gravel behind her.

Thomas strode towards her, his face unreadable as ever. The sight of him filled her with yearning—his long, muscled legs, the strength of his arms, the stern set of his face contained everything she wanted.

He stopped beside her.

She wanted to reach out, take his hand, kiss the tip of each finger. Instead she remained where she was, two steps apart from him.

He was watching her. Alyce wondered what his first thought was whenever he saw her, what he was thinking now.

'Alyce, when I go to London next month…'

She frowned. Did she know this?

'Did I not tell you?'

Alyce shook her head. 'You probably did, and I have

forgotten.' She sighed. 'I forget so much these days.' She looked towards the garden. A blackbird was scratching beneath a lavender bush. 'How long will you be gone?'

'A month, maybe two. It depends how things fall out.'

'We should expect you home by Michaelmas?'

Thomas laughed. 'You know me well.' He touched Alyce's arm. 'Do you want to visit your parents while I am away?'

Alyce continued to stare down the garden. Away from Ashthorpe, could she throw off her burdens? 'Ay, I do, but Cecily is not as well as she was.'

'It need only be a short stay. Leave Marian to help if you are concerned about Cecily.'

'Mother has written, Isabel too. I believe they will welcome me.' She was arguing with herself. 'And I do want to see them.'

'We can travel together as far as Norwich, then I will go on to London. You will need to make your own way back, but I will leave Stokes and at least two other men with you.'

The thought of returning to Norwich, her husband beside her, pleased Alyce, no matter what the problems beneath the surface.

Thomas walked away towards the stables, and Alyce moved down the garden to Cecily.

Cecily lifted her hand to shade her eyes as Alyce sat beside her.

'Have you decided whether you will have Amy Metcalfe here to learn her place? It would be better if she were a year or two older, but with Lionel marrying again in November, she is unlikely to take much notice of a new stepmother.'

Alyce thought of the thin girl with her large hungry eyes, so clearly missing her mother. 'I'm not sure I am the best person...' Her voice trailed off.

'You do not value yourself highly enough, Alyce. You run this household well. And the girl has a liking for you. She was watching you with adoration Christmas last.'

Perhaps it would help to have someone to teach. It would leave less time for her censorious thoughts. 'I suppose I should. I will speak to Lionel when I return from Norwich.'

Cecily winced as she turned towards Alyce. 'Norwich?'

'Thomas suggested I visit my parents while he is away.'

'Are you sure you will be welcome?'

'All that trouble is forgotten but I will send them a message to warn them of my visit.'

Cecily placed her hand on Alyce's. 'It will not be the same without you here.'

Alyce blinked back tears. 'I will be back before you are used to the idea that I have gone.' She reached over and broke off a head of lavender and began to shred it.

'I do think it will be good for you to be away from here for a while, but I would be happier if you were going to London with Tom rather than to Norwich.'

Alyce dropped the broken lavender blooms, one by one, and watched them fall.

When she did not speak, Cecily said, 'We will keep you constant in our prayers.'

Alyce brushed her hands clean of the remaining blooms and kissed Cecily's cheek, struck by the thought that even though she wanted to visit Norwich, she would miss Ashthorpe more.

~

The travellers dismounted outside Hugh Bradley's shop in the early afternoon. Alyce gazed around her. Norwich did not change, ever a noisy, bustling place.

Thomas accompanied Alyce through the shop and up to the hall. Jane, a maidservant who had come in place of Marian, trailed behind them while Watkins, Stokes and the grooms saw to the horses.

Thomas was welcomed formally, but Alyce was embraced by her parents.

Her mother stepped back after kissing her, admiring her appearance. Alyce blushed at the unexpected compliments, surprised they gave her no satisfaction.

She barely recognised her old room. The bed hangings and coverings were of heavy brocade, a padded chair was set near the window, and a carved chest stood in place of the plain one that had been part of the furniture all the years of Alyce's childhood. A tapestry, not a painted cloth, hung on the wall. It was a room decorated for valued guests—Thomas Granville and his wife.

Thomas went down to speak with Alyce's father after quickly washing and changing from his travel-stained clothing. With help from Jane, Alyce put on a gown and sleeves of tawny damask. As a final touch, Jane offered a pair of heavy earrings of gold and topaz, Thomas's New Year's gift.

'Did Marian instruct you on how I was to be dressed?'

Jane flushed and lowered her head. 'She told me which sleeves, kirtles and gowns were best together and which jewels.' Jane's brow puckered with worry. 'Have I done something wrong?'

'Nay.' Alyce caught Jane's hand and squeezed it. 'I am glad Marian has explained it all to you. She has a far better idea of what I should wear than I do myself.'

~

Isabel and her mother rose from the bench beneath the old pear tree as Alyce approached them. For certain, Alyce looked a wealthy gentleman's wife in her gown of damask and her partlet embroidered with tiny beads—not at all what you would expect a woman buried in the countryside to wear. And the Granvilles certainly had ideas about themselves considering the army of attendants they had ridden in with.

Isabel held out her hands to Alyce and drew her into an embrace. Alyce was still using that strange-smelling lavender water—some things did not change.

It did not matter. Isabel's news was better than any gaudily decorated gown.

'I have just told Mother,' Isabel said. 'I am with child again.' She could scarcely contain her happiness. 'I visited an astrologer to confirm it and he assures me it will be another boy, with many more to follow.'

'I am delighted for you,' Alyce said, smiling as if she meant it, 'but an astrologer?'

Why did Alyce never fail to find something to criticise?

'My friends all consult him. It is a way of being certain and putting worries to rest.' Isabel's eyes strayed to Alyce's earrings. 'I have not told Dame Katharine. She says it is unchristian to seek to know the future, akin to witchcraft.'

Alyce said nothing, but Isabel knew she was itching to say she agreed with Isabel's mother-in-law.

'Alyce has left Elinor at home,' Mother said.

'She is too young to travel far.'

'That is disappointing.' Isabel linked her fingers together in her lap and forced herself to look away from the pirate booty hanging from Alyce's ears. 'What is she like?'

'An angel and an imp in one,' Alyce said. 'Chubby with dark curling hair, grey eyes. She runs rather than walks and chatters all the time. She takes after her father.'

'She has a beard?' Isabel jested.

'Oh, she has his will,' Alyce laughed.

Now what did that mean? Isabel wondered what hope she had of prying the story of Alyce's marriage from her.

~

Alyce woke with the dawn light slipping through the bed hangings. Thomas lay on his back at the other side of the bed, the blankets tight around him, snoring lightly. She eased herself out of bed and tiptoed to the window, careful not to disturb Jane, who was asleep on a pallet beside the bed.

Lifting the latch slowly, Alyce pushed the window open. The light of the rising sun bathed the sky a soft pink. The view, with its glimpse of the road leading towards St Stephen's Gate, had once led her to imagine that a vast world of possibilities lay beyond Norwich. She knew now that although the world was narrower than she had imagined, what she had found there was far broader than the life she would have lived in Norwich. And, with the cool breeze on her face, dormant hope stirred.

Alyce returned to bed and carefully lay alongside Thomas. She stretched out her hand and gently rested it on his chest, outside the blankets, and drifted to sleep.

She woke to the sun streaming through the openings of the bed curtains and knew Thomas was gone from the room.

She sprang out of bed and looked around—his saddlebag was missing. He had left.

She pulled her velvet nightgown over her smock and grabbed her coif, bundling her hair into it.

Alyce ran barefoot into the hall as Thomas came up from the

shop below.

'I feared you had left,' she gasped.

'Not without saying goodbye.' He walked over to her and brushed her forehead with the briefest of dry-lipped kisses.

'Keep safe, Thomas,' she whispered.

'And you, Alyce.'

He moved off towards the stairs but turned back and caught Alyce into a crushing embrace.

She wrapped her arms tight around him and, fighting down a sob, kissed him hungrily.

Thomas looked down into her face, surprise in his sad grey eyes. 'I will be home,' he breathed, 'as soon as I can.'

Alyce watched him walk away, her eyes swimming with tears, overcome with an aching loneliness.

Isabel stood in the doorway to the parlour, Robert Chapman at the head of the stairs, a pile of ledgers in his arms. They both stared at her.

Aware of her undress and the judgement sure to be in their faces, Alyce fled back up the stairs to her room.

28

June 1589

Isabel had invited Alyce and her parents to dine at her house along with a number of other guests. Following the meal, she linked her arm through Alyce's and strolled with her around the room, talking of her family's rising fortunes.

'Things have gone well for us since you were last here: business is thriving, we have young Willkyn and now another coming. Sir William is certain he will be made mayor next year, and Frances is betrothed—to Sir Oliver Squires, a cousin of the late Earl of Leicester.'

'A cousin as close to the earl as Robert Chapman is to us,' Alyce said, laughing.

'Do not be so grudging, Alyce.' Isabel was unamused. 'He was a relation.'

'Frances is content?'

'She should be more than that married to a titled man with connections at court.'

Alyce thought better than to argue there was more to marital happiness. She glanced around. 'Frances is not here?'

'She is in London, staying with an aunt.' Isabel grinned. 'Supposedly to give her the opportunity to get to know her future husband, but it is more Dame Katharine found, since the betrothal, Frances has not been meek and obedient, and Sir William could not stand the constant bickering.'

A smile twitched at the corners of Alyce's mouth. 'Do pass on my good wishes to her.'

They sat with Isabel's friend Martha. Alyce commented on Lettys's absence.

'She is due to be delivered in a week or two. It is best to keep close to home near the end,' Martha said.

Alyce murmured her agreement.

'Lettys never has any problems.' Isabel said it like a judgement. Her face softened with happiness as she caught sight of her son walking into the room at his nurse's side.

Isabel held out her arms and the nursemaid let go of his hand, allowing the small boy to run unsteadily the short distance to his mother. Isabel caught him up. 'Sweeting, you can sit on your Aunt Alyce's lap.'

Without a murmur, Willkyn nestled against Alyce, a thumb in his mouth.

Alyce gazed at the delicate face, as finely drawn as his parents', and was overcome with a burning longing for her own sturdy child.

'He has the face of an angel, Isabel.'

'That he does,' Isabel smiled. 'He is forward too. At two weeks, he was already smiling. He cut his first tooth at three months.'

'Poor nurse.' Alyce looked at the nursemaid, a slight, mousy girl no older than Jane.

'Milly is Willkyn's nursemaid, not his wet nurse.'

Will Sutton appeared at Isabel's side and said, 'My turn now.' Isabel rolled her eyes.

Will lifted the child from Alyce and set him on his hip, talking to Willkyn as he walked across the room.

Isabel pulled a face, as much embarrassed as amused. 'Will dotes on him.'

Will stopped at a large tapestry to explain its story to the child, who was more interested in tugging Will's ears and sticking his fingers in his mouth. Will seemed a different man from the peacock Alyce remembered.

'And Alyce,' Isabel said, 'Willkyn walked at eleven months. It would have been earlier if he had had his way. We could not keep him swaddled—he kicked his way out of his bands. When did your Elinor walk?'

'She was completely unswaddled by ten months but did not walk freely until twelve. It was then she cut her first tooth too.'

Isabel's eyes widened. 'That is very slow.'

'She is more than making up for it now,' Alyce said evenly, 'hurtling everywhere.' She would not give in to the rising irritation she felt. 'Besides, our neighbour Lady Rossiter says by two years they are all the same. Her view is the longer teeth stay in the gum, the less chance they have to rot.'

'For certain, it shows the child's intelligence and strength of will. Willkyn is sure to be as full of vigour as his Grandfather Sutton.'

'I am sure he will be.' The undercurrent of competition was there, and if Alyce were not careful, she knew she would be swept into it.

Isabel beckoned to Milly and sent her off to collect the little boy. After they had left the room, Isabel continued tallying Willkyn's abilities. To hear her talk, he was the most wondrous child to exist upon the earth in the last millennium and a half.

A consort of recorder, lute and cittern had been playing softly as Isabel's guests talked. They struck up dancing music, and with the table now moved back, guests formed along the centre of the room.

Alyce walked over to her father who was sitting at one side, watching. She followed his line of sight. 'Isabel and Will dance well together.'

'Indeed,' he said without warmth, his eyes on Will. He turned to Alyce. 'You wish to dance?'

'I am content to sit and talk.'

An elderly man hobbled over to them, leaning heavily on a stick. Alyce's father rose and greeted him, 'Master Harrison, this is my elder daughter, Alyce Granville.'

With some effort, Harrison bowed to Alyce. 'Thomas Granville's wife, eh? How fares your husband?'

'He was well when I saw him last and still is, God willing.'

'He is at sea again?'

'He has gone to London,' Alyce said.

Harrison eased himself onto the settle beside Alyce. 'And what is he planning now?' he asked bluntly. 'Another strike against Spain I hope.'

'In truth, I do not know.' And had she known, she would not have discussed it.

'The world is your husband's sphere and yours the home,' said Harrison with the satisfaction of one seeing a world ordered to his liking.

'The Ashthorpe manor is as big a venture as any to manage when my husband is away.'

'But your husband would have a good steward—no need for you to trouble yourself about it.'

'A steward is a hired man,' Alyce countered. 'Many wives manage their husband's interests better than any steward, not just on manors but in businesses in the towns.'

He smiled at her indulgently, as if she were an oddity like a bear trained to dance on two legs. 'If I remember right, Mistress Granville, you were always reading when you were young—traveller's tales. I used to tell your father you would beggar him with your appetite for books.' He laughed. 'No doubt your husband has tales to tell, cheaper than buying you books.'

'I read still—most recently a book my husband bought me on the stars.'

He blinked, shock in his face. 'Divination?'

'Nay, Master Harrison,' Alyce said quickly. 'Astronomy, the way the sky is ordered.'

'Ah.' Harrison relaxed. 'As a lad, on my first journey beyond the sight of land, it seemed like magic that with a cross-staff, a sandglass and a knotted rope a man could use the stars to tell where he was on the endless sea and how far he had travelled.'

Will Sutton strolled over. 'Excuse me sirs, my wife has sent me to rescue Mistress Granville.'

Harrison said, 'There is not much pleasure for a young woman in the company of old men.'

'Good conversation is always a pleasure.' Alyce smiled.

Will bowed to Alyce. 'Isabel has ordered me to dance with you.' He steered Alyce towards the dancers. As they took their place, he gazed at her as if she were the only woman in the room, and although Alyce knew it was play-acting, she understood how a susceptible woman could be seduced by his charms. He was like Clifton without the malice. She pushed the thought away.

As they stepped together along the line of dancers, Will said, with the slightest rise of an eyebrow, 'Marriage suits you, Alyce.'

Alyce ignored his hint—he was the same man, his delight in his son a new facet to his character.

'I hear your husband is often away from home. Do you miss him?'

'Ay,' Alyce said. 'I do.' Despite their troubles, Alyce knew she was happiest when Thomas was near.

'I have no doubt he is missing you.' His eyes slowly travelled over her.

She felt naked before his lingering gaze and, blushing, looked away.

Will stood as Alyce skipped around him, his eyes glittering. 'I see our minds travel similar paths.'

Alyce blinked fast, seeking a safe reply. 'Isabel seems very content.'

'That she is. All she needed was a child.' He smiled slowly. 'I am surprised you are not with child again.'

Alyce stepped back to her place, and the music stopped. Relieved, she curtsied to him.

Will caught her hand and traced his thumb from her wrist across her palm before he raised it to his lips.

Alyce pulled her hand back and, forcing an uncomfortably bright smile, walked quickly to where Isabel and Martha sat.

Martha shifted aside to make space for her.

'You enjoyed the dance?' Isabel's stiff smile did not touch her eyes.

'I did, but I fear I am not so light a step as you. You and Will make a pretty pair together.'

'Ay, we do.' She peered around the room, her eyes narrowed, until she found Will.

Struck by the sudden melancholy in Isabel's face, Alyce said, 'What is the matter, Isabel? Is something wrong?'

'What could possibly be wrong?' Isabel glared at Alyce. 'I have everything a woman could want: wealth, position, a handsome husband who adores me and a son.' She emphasised the final word.

Alyce shut her mouth. Life was much easier at Ashthorpe.

29

A lyce stood face to face with Stokes in the middle of the hall. 'Did the Master give you a direct order?'

'Nay. But I know he wanted you well protected.'

'This is not London, Stokes. There you were told you must accompany me whenever I went out, were you not?' She did not give him time to answer. 'If the Master had wanted you to guard me as closely, he would have given you exactly the same orders. As he did not, he saw no threat here.'

'But, Mistress,' Stokes pleaded, 'if anything should happen to you...'

'Nothing will.'

'But it does not look good,' he blurted out, 'a lady wandering around unattended.'

He was right. All manner of assumptions would be made if the wife of a gentleman went abroad without the attendants due her position. 'I am taking Jane with me.'

'She is just a little maid. Will you at least let young Price go with you too?'

Alyce frowned, her lips compressed. He was simply doing his job. 'Very well,' she relented, 'but only so I do get to leave the house today and not spend the entire afternoon arguing with you.'

'Thank you, Mistress,' he said, visibly relieved. 'I'll go and hurry Price along.'

Later than she had hoped, accompanied by Jane and another Ashthorpe groom, Nick Price, Alyce made her way through the market, past the Guildhall and through the streets she had walked so often as a girl. They crossed the newly rebuilt Blackfriars Bridge and walked on to the de Jongs' house in Colegate.

Grietje opened the door and threw her arms around Alyce, kissing her. *'Elsje, lieveling.'*

Tears pricked at Alyce's eyes. 'I was heartsore to hear of

Master de Jong's death.'

Grietje's lashes were wet. 'It is near a year now, but every day I miss him. I will miss him until the day I die.' She squeezed Alyce's hand tight. 'Come in.' She beckoned Jane and Price, still standing in the street. 'You two, come in.' She called into the house, 'Anna, Anna.'

A plump young woman in an apron came running, tendrils of dark hair escaping from beneath her coif, a smear of flour on her cheek.

'Anna, see Mistress Granville's servants to the kitchen and give them something to eat and drink.'

Alyce nodded at Jane and Price, but Price seemed reluctant to follow the maid. 'You too, Price. Despite the orders you have from Stokes, I am as safe in this house as I am at Ashthorpe.' She dismissed the half-formed thought—safer even.

Grietje ushered Alyce into the parlour, where Marieke sat with her feet on a stool. Marieke struggled to sit up, smiling tiredly at Alyce.

'Stay where you are, Marieke.' Alyce drew a stool alongside her. 'It looks as if this one is due any moment.'

Marieke spread her hands over her swollen belly. 'Not for weeks yet. *Moeder* thinks I am carrying twins.' She sighed loudly. 'I'll be glad when he, she or they are delivered. I get so tired that I have to sit, but if I sit too long I end up with pain in my back and down my leg.'

'I am told it is harder each time.'

'I have not found that, but this time is different.'

Grietje shot her daughter a sharp look from where she sat beside the window, the light falling onto intricately embroidered cloth as she carefully cut between the stitches, making the fine cut-work lace she was known for.

Marieke smiled at Alyce. 'And you have a child of your own too.'

'Elinor. She is over a year and a half now.'

'You remember, just before you married, I said in a year you might be holding your own in your arms. No sign of another yet?' Alyce shook her head. 'And how are you finding married life?'

'I am content—more than I could have imagined.' Alyce tried to sound her brightest, aware of Grietje's sharp-eyed interest.

'I told you all would be well,' Marieke said, accepting her at her word. 'Did Thomas come with you?'

'Ay, but he has gone on to London. I have been here over a month and would have visited you sooner, but Isabel comes every day and it is hard to get away.'

'Isabel,' Marieke laughed. 'Are things better between you?'

'Ay, but I would not want to contradict her. And she likes to compare our children—when they first walked, cut their teeth, said *Mamma*.'

'I believe sisters are sometimes like that, but I had brothers.'

Grietje rose from her seat and stood behind Marieke. She placed her hands on her daughter's shoulders, kissing her on the top of her head.

'*Elsje*, do you want to see your goddaughter?'

Marieke caught Alyce's hand. 'If you do not mind, I will stay here. After, I'll tell you of *Moeder's* matchmaking efforts—poor Cousin Hans.' She saw the puzzlement on Alyce's face. 'You remember, the printer *Moeder* offered you? Hans is thinking of leaving Norwich to avoid the girls *Moeder* keeps throwing at him.'

'That boy is too fussy,' Grietje tutted irritably, 'he'll end his days a dried-up old bachelor.'

As Alyce followed Grietje towards the back of the house, she could hear the high-pitched squeals of children in the yard, the deeper sound of Price's laughter underneath.

'I'll wager Anna is out there too. That one has an eye for the boys.' She grinned. 'She is a good girl, knows how to flirt without giving anything away.'

Alyce raised her eyebrows, surprised by Grietje's indulgence.

'She is a good girl,' Grietje said emphatically. 'I will help her find a good husband.'

'Would she do for Hans?'

'The silly boy will not even consider her, but she will make someone a very happy wife.'

They stepped into the yard. On the paved space between the

house and the kitchen garden, Price was piggybacking two-year-old Grace across the yard. Her sisters, Elisabeth and Margriet, were bouncing up and down squealing for another turn. Anna was there too, the flour wiped from her pretty face and her coif set aside, laughing with the girls.

Beside the door, Jane stood with her arms folded, her lips tight with disapproval. She came and took her place at Alyce's side.

Six-year-old Margriet ran over and caught her grandmother's hand. '*Oma*, Nick offered Anna a ride too. Make her, please.' Her eyes sparkled with excitement. 'It is such fun.'

Grietje gave Alyce a wink and said, 'Oh, Anna is too old for that and she has work to do.' She beckoned to Anna. 'Take some cake and beer into the parlour.'

Anna bobbed a curtsy and, with a glance over her shoulder towards Price, walked back into the house, pulling on her coif as she went.

'Grace, come here,' Grietje called to the youngest girl, who clambered down from Price's back. She ran to her grandmother, her golden curls bobbing in the sunlight, her sister Elisabeth following. 'This is your godmother, Mistress Granville.'

The small girl gave an unsteady curtsy, smiling shyly at Alyce.

Elisabeth slid her hand into Alyce's and said, 'I remember you.'

'But Elisabeth,' Alyce paused, 'you were barely two.'

'I remember your lovely eyes.'

Alyce's heart swelled towards these delightful children. She must find a way to reach out to Thomas. Beyond what she wanted for herself, she wanted more children, dark-haired angels who would make Ashthorpe ring with squeals and laughter like this house did.

She smiled at Grietje, aware that she had been watching her, a crease between her brows.

'Before we go back to the parlour,' Grietje said, 'I'd like your advice on a cordial I am having difficulty distilling.'

'How is Marieke truly?' Alyce asked as she followed her back into the house.

'I am sure she is carrying twins, so she has a greater travail ahead. My poor girl is afraid but she would not admit it.' Grietje held the door to the stillroom open. 'If anything should happen to her, I will have the sternest of words with the Almighty.'

Alyce glanced around the well-stocked room with its neatly labelled jars and boxes, its herbs hanging to dry. 'What is this cordial?'

'Do not worry about that, *lieveling*.' Grietje gestured towards the chair. 'Sit and tell me what is wrong.'

Alyce pressed her lips together. 'Nothing is wrong.'

'I am not a fool, *Elsje*. Is he cruel to you?'

'Thomas?' she gasped. 'No, no. He is the best of men.'

'Then why are you unhappy?'

'I am not unhappy.' Alyce's chin quivered like a mutinous child, her eyes brimming. She had not realised her hurt lay so near the surface.

'I know you better than your mother,' Grietje said gently. She cradled Alyce's head against her broad bosom.

Alyce wrapped her arms around Grietje's waist and gave a drawn-out, shuddering sigh. And the barriers gave way and all Alyce had held back came spilling out: every fear and hurt, the aching loneliness, the humiliations—at Dalstead, in London, at Ashthorpe.

Grietje paced the room, her hands forming angry fists. 'If I could get my hands on that man, I would kill him again. *Ik zou zijn keel doorsnijden*.' She paused, her eyes blazing. '*Nee*, a poker, a heated poker. I would...' She stared at Alyce, admiration in her steely eyes. 'You did good.'

'But you must tell no one,' Alyce said hoarsely. 'I could be hanged, or Thomas for getting rid of the body.' She twisted her damp handkerchief.

'It was justice. That wicked man deserved it. I would never say a word—you are one of my own.' She pulled a stool over and sat facing Alyce. 'Thomas must be proud of you.'

'It was a relief to him but nothing has been the same since. He keeps his distance.' She closed her eyes, heat flooding her face. 'He... he no longer lies with me. I knew there would be other women, but I did not think I would know of it, nor did I think—'

'Other women?' Grietje cut her off. 'Mistresses? He flaunts his whores in front of you?'

'Nay, but I have seen these women and know they have been something to him in the past. I have seen the way they look at him. They are beautiful.' She paused. 'The opposite of me.'

'*Elsje*,' Grietje rolled her eyes, 'if you were my child, you would not think this nonsense. You have your own beauty. And how dare you compare yourself to them—they are whores.' Her cheeks were flushed an angry red. 'And did he take one of these to be his wife? *Nee!* He chose you. And I tell you, the day you were married he was happy to stand with his arm around you.'

Alyce raised her chin and stared straight ahead. 'That is not the case now.'

Grietje frowned. 'And this coldness only started after the evil man came.'

'It is not even coldness. He talks to me—we discuss the business of the manor. He is kind and gentle but he keeps a space between us.'

Grietje took Alyce's hands in hers. 'And when you approach him, lay your hand on him, try to kiss him, what does he do then?'

Alyce stared straight ahead. 'I have not done that. I could not bear to have him turn away from me.'

'I am sure I have not misjudged your Thomas.' Grietje's brow furrowed. 'I would say he is afraid for you, afraid even to speak of what happened in case he brings your memories of it to life. He is waiting for you to share your burdens with him.' She stared deep into Alyce's eyes, her own grey-blue eyes earnest. 'I want you to promise me that when you next see him, you will not wait for him, you will smile at him, put your arms around him, kiss him and see what happens.'

Alyce thought of their parting embrace. 'Perhaps.'

'No perhaps, you will do it. And when you are expecting your next child, you will invite me to your lying-in.'

'I will, I promise you.' Alyce smiled at the idea of Grietje de Jong and Margaret Rossiter together—they could make the unlikeliest of friendships.

30

Robin Chapman glanced up from the woollen kersey he was cutting under the suspicious eye of his elderly customer.

Alyce strolled into the shop with her father. Bradley sent the apprentice, Simpson, to the storeroom for the newest of his stock. There was a light-hearted exchange between Alyce and Simpson as he spread a length of watered chamlet on the table for her to examine.

His mind only half on his customer, Chapman slowed his careful cutting.

'Young man, are you paying attention to what you are doing?' the old woman snapped.

Robin wondered if her face would crack if forced to smile. 'I am, Mistress. You would not want me to rush and give you short measure?'

She grumbled under her breath and stood silent, her hands clasped together at her substantial waist.

Robin overheard Alyce say the cloth was for a gown for her daughter. The tone she used with Simpson was little different from other boastful gentlewomen, talking of husbands and children, buying expensive cloth to make out they were more highly placed in the world than they were.

He walked his customer to the door and held it open as she swept through, a galleon in full sail.

Alyce now treated him as if he were just another servant. She was polite, greeting him as she did the other men whenever she passed through, no acknowledgement there had ever been anything between them. When she had returned three years ago, he could see the girl she had been beneath the studied composure. That girl was gone. It was more than the fine clothing. She carried herself as if she were of importance.

And here was he, his life unchanged. Still Bradley's journeyman, selling cloth like an apprentice, still a labourer in someone else's field. He had nearly enough put by to pay to become a freeman of the city. As a freeman, he could set up on his own and take on apprentices, but a man needed even more money for that. Had Alyce married him, he would not have needed to count his pennies so carefully. He would have had his own business.

~

Isabel rocked Willkyn as he whimpered and fidgeted. The noise was irritating her.

'I do not know what is wrong with him.' Isabel frowned at Milly, hovering anxious at her side. 'Here, take him.'

'Let me,' Alyce said. She lifted the child from Isabel and sat down, brushing her lips against Willkyn's silky head. She rocked him gently, crooning to him as he settled into her arms.

How did she manage that? It had not occurred to Isabel that Alyce might have some skill with children. No doubt this was something else Alyce would parade her superiority in.

'You must be dreading returning home.' Isabel could not keep the irritation from her voice. 'I would die of boredom if I were forced to live far from town.'

'There is as much to do in the countryside as in any town.' Alyce's colour rose as she answered. 'Weddings, christenings, lyings-in and churchings, wakes and harvest festivals, Christmas and Easter. All are celebrated just as you do here. Christmas last, Thomas had a troupe of players entertain the villagers in the hall of Ashthorpe. It was as good as anything you would see in London.'

'And how would you know that?' Isabel sniffed.

'I went to the playhouse when I was in London.'

Isabel pouted. 'And was it barge rides and banquets with Lord This and Lady That and visiting the tailor and having your portrait painted?'

Alyce did not reply.

'All of it?' Isabel gaped. 'Even a portrait?'

'A miniature and not a very good one.'

'You never used to be vain.' The gowns she had brought with her and the jewellery—even Isabel's friends commented on how fine Alyce looked. Dazzled by her attire, they did not see plain old Alyce beneath, nor did they notice what Isabel wore when she stood beside Alyce.

Alyce flushed. 'Thomas wanted the miniature.'

Isabel fought the laughter bubbling up. 'Oh, Alyce, you have become an old man's love.'

'Thomas is not old.' Alyce's eyes flashed. 'He is not much more than two score years. And he is a good, kind man.'

Isabel burst out laughing. 'It depends what you judge good to be.'

Alyce stared at her, those cold green eyes boring into her. Isabel's laughter dried up. If Alyce said a word about Will, she would tear those glittering earrings from her earlobes.

But Alyce gazed down at the sleeping child nestled in her arms and said, 'Willkyn is such a comely child.'

At least she acknowledged that. Doubtless Alyce's child would take after its parents—dark and graceless. They would need to spend a fortune on gowns, jewellery and a dowry to find her a husband.

~

Conversation hummed along the table as the household ate their evening meal.

Isabel sat silent. Beside her, Will was talking animatedly to her father of what he had heard of Sir Francis Drake and Sir John Norris's latest voyage to harry the King of Spain's ships. She pressed her lips tight. With his constant talk of Sir Francis and his exploits, perhaps he wished he were a seaman, hardly ever at home, women waiting for him in every port. And whenever her father spoke, Will's eyes strayed away from him to Alyce.

Alyce was boasting of her country life, pretending she had no interest in him. She never looked his way once. She was clearly hiding something.

'…and when I thought about it,' Alyce said, 'it was true. He came in nearly every second day in such pain I felt I had to give him aqua vitae before I could do anything for him.'

'The old rogue.' Mother laughed. She dabbed her napkin at her lips and folded it neatly. 'You are content with your life, Alyce?'

'I am.'

Mother reached out and touched Alyce's hand. 'I am glad. It has been a constant regret to me we took so little care of your future for so long.'

Alyce's eyes glowed in the candlelight. 'I could not imagine a better life.'

Isabel watched them, frowning. Just over a year ago Mother had as good as said Isabel was the most important to her; now here she was fawning over Alyce.

Mother glanced across at Isabel and quickly looked away. Isabel wondered if she was ashamed to be caught out.

'Your Jane seems to have won a couple of admirers,' Mother said.

Alyce's maid was sitting between two of the apprentices, each outdoing the other in an effort to impress her. At the other side of the table, a young groom glowered. Isabel wondered that Alyce allowed such lightness in her servants.

Father grinned. 'If we are not careful, Wat will start walking on his hands. He thinks it is the surest way to a girl's heart.'

'Has she a sweetheart at home?' Mother asked.

'Nay, but to look at Price, something might be brewing,' Alyce said. 'But I would have sworn that recently his main interest was Grietje de Jong's kitchen maid.'

'The realisation someone else is interested never fails to spark a lad's interest.' Will smirked.

Isabel pursed her lips and stared into her goblet.

~

Robin remained at the table as servants cleared around him. Alyce stood at the other side of the table with her mother, pretending to ignore her brother-in-law, Will Sutton. All through the meal, whenever he thought his wife was not looking, Sutton had had his eyes on Alyce. It showed the nature of the woman that she would attract the attention of her sister's husband.

Alyce walked towards the stairway.

Robin rose from his seat and greeted her with a deep bow. 'You leave us tomorrow, Mistress?'

'Ay, I return to Ashthorpe.'

'You look well indeed, Alyce.' His eyes travelled over the

brocade and silk, imagining the flesh beneath. She should be his. 'It appears marriage to a godless pirate has brought you satisfactions no honest merchant could.'

'My husband is neither godless nor a pirate.' Colour crept up her cheeks. 'He has done as much as anyone to protect this kingdom. Last year, while you were safe here in Norwich selling cloth, he was on the seas risking his life against the Spanish invaders.' Her eyes glittered as she said, 'And as for offers of marriage from honest merchants—I received none.'

'Do not play games with me,' Robin spat back. 'You and your father both knew I was interested.' He tasted the bitterness on his tongue. 'I am as good as any man.'

'Before God on Judgement Day, perhaps, but my father wanted a marriage that improved the family's fortunes, its connections. Could you have done that?'

The same argument his mother made.

'Given the freedom, I could enlarge your father's business.' He had never been given the chance.

'Well strike out on your own, make that profit for yourself.'

'Nothing comes in this world without birth. I work harder than Will Sutton.' He nodded to where Sutton sat beside Hugh Bradley. 'Yet he goes about like a lordling while I am treated no better than an apprentice.'

'It is the way our world is.' She spoke as if he were simple. 'If you want more, you must strive for it yourself. The world is changing. On the seas, in other lands, there are fortunes to be made. Invest judiciously, make partnerships, take shrewd chances. By the time you are Father's age, you could stand as high. If I were a man, I would make my own fate, not wait on the slim chance a merchant would permit me to marry his daughter.'

'It is rare for a man to rise solely by his own efforts. There is always a patron or an advantageous connection.'

'If you want an easy stepping stone, then find yourself a wealthy widow.'

Robin blinked. Why had he not thought of that? An older widow, no doubt eager for the attentions of a younger man and, better still, unlikely to live as long.

He stared at Alyce with her soft skin, her pale green eyes, her elegant clothing, her arrogance. 'We could have had a marriage of necessity had you been willing.'

'Do not be ridiculous. Neither of us cared for the other.'

'Then why did you lead me on?'

'Lead you on?' Her voice rose, as if she were shocked at the suggestion. 'I never did such a thing.'

Robin stared at her. Anyone who did not know her would be taken in by her pretended affront. 'Coming down into the shop. Always placing yourself in my way. Your false protestations of disgust intended to inflame me more.'

'I came into the shop because I had a foolish girl's dream that I could have a role in my father's business. And as for you—my disgust was real.' Her eyes blazed. 'I knew you only wanted me as a means to an end. Such a marriage would have been hell on earth for both of us. You neither liked nor respected me, nor I you. There was no…' she seemed to be seeking the right word, 'no magic.'

'Ah, magic. Always the heart of the problem. And have you worked magic on your husband?' he sneered. He reached out to grab her arm, to make her stay, to treat him with the respect that was his due.

Alyce stared back at him, her eyes cold and piercing. He heard again her voice in the garden. *If you so much as think of touching me, your manhood will wither.*

Robin shuddered, suddenly afraid. It was as if she had cursed him without needing to utter a word. 'You should have swung beside that old witch, you and your grandmother, vile old crone,' he mumbled.

Alyce turned and walked away from him as if he were of no account.

~

Alyce breathed in the cool evening scent of the garden, her heart still racing. She closed her eyes, her heartbeats easing with each breath she took, and forced Robert Chapman from her mind. Tomorrow she was leaving and need never see nor think of him again.

Alyce shifted back on the stone bench and leant against the

pear tree, closing her eyes. She tried to empty her mind of everything—the troubling glimpses of others' less than perfect lives, their disappointed hopes, her own sorrows.

She was tired of the hold the past had on her. It could not be changed and even if she could go back and live that day again, she would do the same. There had been no alternative, and she would rather her hands were bloodstained than her daughter harmed. Her nights had been peaceful these past few months, and with the passage of each day the guilt she felt was slowly draining away. She had done what she must. And Clifton was fading from her life. Nowhere at Ashthorpe reminded her of him, even the nursery. The first time she had walked back in there, it was as if it were a different room. The furniture had been rearranged to make space for the wet nurse, Maggie, and her son. The room had been filled with laughter and children's squeals as Elinor played with Maggie's son. Since she had been in Norwich, she had not once heard Clifton's voice whispering the criticisms she made of herself.

And Thomas? It was plain he cared for her as much as any other member of his family. She would heed Grietje's advice and reach out to him and see if there was more. She smiled. She was going home.

'Alyce.'

She jolted upright as Will Sutton sat beside her and grasped her hand.

'You have bloomed since your marriage.'

She tried to twist free but he held on and turned her hand over, kissing the palm. She sprang to her feet. 'Will. Stop!'

He stood and pulled her against him, groping at her breast as he nuzzled her neck.

Alyce struggled, her heart thumping. Over his shoulder, she saw a pale figure standing in the doorway.

'Isabel is watching us.'

'It will not work, Alyce.'

'See for yourself.' Alyce twisted away from him.

The figure disappeared into the darkened hallway.

Will swore as he strode towards the house.

Alyce dropped back onto the bench and gave a silent prayer

of thanks that she was leaving on the morrow.

~

Isabel lay curled in the bed, her misery too deep even for tears. She had closed her eyes to so much. But this. With Alyce. Had he deliberately wanted to injure her?

She watched Will through her lashes as he moved quietly around the chamber.

He came to the side of the bed. 'Isabel.'

She ignored him.

The candlelight glowed on his golden hair. His face was the picture of perfect contrition. 'Isabel, I have something to confess.'

Isabel rolled onto her back and stared up at the bed's canopy, her mouth a tight, bitter line.

'I cannot explain it. I must have been bewitched.'

She would not answer.

'Alyce invited me into the garden. I did not want to go, but I could not resist. It was as if a spell had been cast on me.'

Isabel gasped.

'She tried to seduce me, but God was protecting me—the image of you, Willkyn in your arms, rose up in my mind. Thank the Almighty but I found the strength to resist.'

She sat up. 'In truth?' That would explain why he would turn to Alyce of all people.

'Isabel, why would I want anyone other than you? I know I do not give you the attention you deserve, but my time is taken up with work. I want to give you and Willkyn every comfort you desire.'

Isabel held out her arms to him.

He climbed onto the bed beside her and gazed deep into her eyes, his hand against her cheek. 'In you I have everything a man could want.'

Isabel leant towards him and gently brushed her lips against his, a knot of worry still lodged in her throat. 'You are certain Alyce placed a spell on you?'

Will spoke carefully. 'What other explanation can there be?'

'She is dangerous. People should be warned.' Isabel's voice became shriller with each word. 'She may try the same with other women's husbands.'

'I am ashamed of my behaviour, even though I was not in my right mind, but do we want everyone talking about us?'

Isabel pressed her lips tight. 'Many would take gleeful pleasure in our misfortunes.'

She lay down again, Will's arms tight around her. They lay together in silence, minutes stretching on.

Why did he behave like this? He claimed he had everything a man could want in her, yet still he lusted after other women.

Will began to snore softly.

How could he sleep after this? Did it mean so little to him?

Isabel was not sure that she believed his tale of spells, but if Alyce were as virtuous as she pretended to be, Will never would have looked at her. With her fine clothing and rich jewels, she was courting men's attention, yet everyone thought of Alyce as a virtuous wife. It was a show—underneath she was still the same sharp-tongued, unruly girl with no care for who she hurt or how she broke her word. She had deserted Isabel when she needed her most, paraded her new position and connections and now had tried to seduce Will. It was the final step in an unbroken road of malice.

31

Alyce's mother kissed her and stepped back, holding both her hands. 'I will miss you.'

'And I will miss you, Mother.' Alyce was eager to be back at Ashthorpe but did not regret her visit to Norwich. The time spent with her mother had been a pleasure—helping her with the sewing and planning of meals, cooking and teaching her the skill of fashioning sweetmeats. The discords of Alyce's girlhood were now a faded memory.

Her mother brushed her fingers across her eyelashes.

Alyce looked away, blinking back her own tears.

'Mother.' She pointed to a sparrow sitting in the open window. 'If you are very still, sometimes they will let you close,' she said quietly.

She stepped carefully towards the window, her hand stretched out. The bird hopped from the windowsill onto Alyce's hand and sat, its head bobbing from side to side.

Isabel slammed the door open. The sparrow started up, its wings flapping frantically. It smacked into the window and tumbled to the floor.

'Isabel. What have you done?' Alyce bent down and cradled the bird in her hands.

'What have you done is more the question.'

The sparrow was alive, trembling. Alyce laid it carefully on the windowsill.

'What do you mean?'

'Playing the whore with my husband.'

'What?'

'Do not feign innocence—I saw you together.' Isabel's lip curled.

Milly sagged onto a chair just inside the door. Although her dress was neat, her hair escaped from beneath her coif and there were dark smudges under her eyes. She jounced Willkyn on her knee as he snuffled and whimpered.

Alyce drew herself to her full height. 'What you saw was your husband forcing his unwanted attention on me.'

'What would Will want with a cold piece like you?'

'A cold piece? A minute ago, I was a whore.'

'And you are a whore,' Isabel shouted. She dragged a chair out from the table and sat heavily, breathing through flaring nostrils. 'You have always wished me ill.'

Recognising Isabel's distress, Alyce forced herself to speak gently. 'Isabel, I would never harm you.'

'You already have,' Isabel spat. 'Last time you gave me a potion to make the baby sicken within my womb.'

A chill ran through Alyce. 'That is untrue,' she said quietly. 'I gave you poppy syrup to calm you, to help you sleep. You were distraught. I saw Grandmother use it often.'

'Grandmother was an evil old witch, lucky to escape the gallows.'

The ground seemed to fall away beneath Alyce's feet. 'Grandmother never did an evil thing in her life.'

'Ask Dame Katharine. She can tell you tales of Grandmother and the way she gave out potions to kill the unborn in the womb.'

Their mother groaned and sagged onto a chair beside Isabel.

'Lady Sutton is a liar,' Alyce said as calmly as she could.

'She warned me long ago you were a danger, but I did not believe her. You have always been jealous of me, and now you are trying to destroy my life.'

'Isabel, why would I be jealous? I am content with my life. You have nothing I would want.'

'Nothing you would want?' she scoffed. 'You are buried in the country, married to an old man who cannot give you sons, who is no doubt incapable. Is it any wonder you wanted to seduce Will? Were you hoping to pass his son off as Granville's?'

Alyce opened her mouth but did not know where to begin. It was all so ridiculous. As if she would ever choose Will Sutton over Thomas.

'You tried to ensnare my husband with spells. It was only the thought of me and our son that gave him the power to resist.'

Alyce rolled her eyes. 'Spells are not needed to get your husband into bed. If what I hear is true, he has lain with half the women of this town. Did they all trap him with spells?'

'Liar,' Isabel said through gritted teeth.

Their mother bowed her head, covering her face with her hands.

Milly sat with one arm around Willkyn, half-heartedly rocking him as she yawned, struggling to keep awake.

'I will leave now, Mother,' Alyce said.

Her mother looked up, her eyes glazed with despair.

On the windowsill, the sparrow stood, fluttered its wings and flew the short distance to the pear tree.

Alyce bent and brushed her lips against Willkyn's head as she passed him. 'God bless you and keep you, little one,' she murmured.

'You leave my child alone,' Isabel screeched.

'Isabel,' Alyce shouted over her. 'This child is burning with fever. He should be home in bed.'

'Quiet!' their father bellowed as he strode into the room. 'Stop your caterwauling. It can be heard halfway along the street.'

Isabel rose from her chair. 'Not content with destroying my baby last time, Alyce has now tried to seduce my husband.'

He scowled. 'Alyce had nothing to do with the death of your child.'

'See, witch,' Isabel hissed, 'you even turn my father against me.' She sailed out, her head held high, Milly running behind her, Willkyn on her hip.

Alyce's father glared at her.

She met his gaze and walked from the room.

He followed her into the street, where Alyce's servants waited with the horses.

Alyce stood beside her horse, her hands trembling as she pulled on her gloves.

'What is this about you and Will Sutton?' her father snarled.

Alyce lifted her chin, aware of the growing crowd of onlookers, apprentices and servants. 'Will Sutton tried his usual tricks with me. I refused.'

'You are sure you did not encourage him?'

Chapman stood in the doorway of the shop, smirking.

'You think that of me?' Why would her father even ask? Everyone in Norwich knew of Will Sutton and his women, though few spoke openly.

'All I want is the truth.' He crossed his arms, impatient.

'You know the truth—Will Sutton is a notorious adulterer.'

'Why would he mention it if he were in the wrong?'

'I assume Isabel saw him approach me in the garden and he sought to shift the blame. Ask him.'

Her father's scowled deepened.

'Of course you will not—you would not want to upset Sir William Sutton,' Alyce said bitterly. 'I will go.' She turned to her mother.

'Alyce...'

'Mother, it is best left unsaid.'

'It will die down.'

'Then there will be something else. It never ends.'

Stokes helped Alyce onto her horse.

'Take care of Isabel, Mother. She has her share of sorrow.' Her face set, Alyce rode away from her parents.

Once through the city gates, Alyce urged her horse into a gallop. She made no allowances for anyone, not even stopping to dine.

The afternoon was drawing on when Stokes rode up beside her. 'Mistress, we should stop soon. The horses need to rest, and I am not sure young Jane can keep on much longer.'

'How far is the next village?'

'Near an hour's ride. It is a sizable place and, if I remember right, has two inns.'

'Very well, we will spend the night there.'

Stokes kept pace with Alyce. 'Your mother is right, Mistress. People do forget.'

'People never forget,' she said, her voice harsh. 'They may not talk, but when the fancy takes them, they bring out the old stories and embroider them further.'

~

Isabel paced from one end of the parlour to the other, her

mouth pressed tight, breathing fast, fighting her almost over-whelming rage.

Julia kept her head down to her mending, not once wavering in her concentration, as if afraid that even a quick glance would bring Isabel's anger down on her.

Isabel stopped at the table and pressed her hands against her stomach. She closed her eyes. Her head was aching too. She had woken feeling unwell and Alyce's behaviour had only made things worse. Good riddance to her. She hoped she never saw her sister again. And to suggest that Will... Alyce's own husband was notorious. Who was she to throw stones?

Milly burst through the door, wild-eyed. 'Mistress, Mistress,' she screeched. 'You have to come!'

'What is it, girl?' Isabel snapped.

'It's Willkyn.' She convulsed with large wrenching sobs. 'He's... he's...'

Her mind empty of all but growing panic, Isabel pushed past Milly and ran up the stairs, stumbling near the top as her skirts caught beneath her feet.

The wet nurse knelt beside the cot, twisting her apron in her hands, her cheeks wet.

Willkyn lay in the cot, so still, his face perfect, as if carved from marble.

Isabel stopped. He was beautiful beyond words. She moved forward, one slow step at a time. He was only asleep, deeply asleep.

She bent over him and ran the side of her curled finger down his cheek. He was cold.

She turned to the wet nurse and snarled, 'What have you been doing? It is no wonder he is cold. He needs to be wrapped up.' She grabbed the blanket from the cot, wrapping him tight.

The woman stared at Isabel as if she were mad.

The ache in Isabel's belly strengthened, she felt the slip of blood down the inside of her thigh. It would be red, dark red like the life blood of her beautiful son, now still within his veins.

Isabel slid down to the floor, Willkyn held tight against her breasts. Someone was screaming—loud, swooping screams. Someone nearby.

Isabel's own throat was raw.

A cart rumbled by, a hawker called his wares, sparrows chattered in the tree outside, all as if life still went on.

~

Alyce rose with the first light, wakened by the sounds of the inn coming to life. She dressed with Jane's help before joining the rest of her servants in the taproom, where they were breaking their fast. Jane ate her bread and cheese hungrily, but Alyce picked at hers.

'Do any of you want this?' Alyce looked to the men. 'I am not hungry.'

Price muttered eagerly through his breadcrumbs. Alyce pushed her portion to him and sipped on her small beer.

As she wiped her lips on her napkin, she glanced through the open door. A group of horsemen wearing the livery of the Sheriff of Norwich clattered into the yard and dismounted. They marched into the inn, the captain making straight for the innkeeper. Alyce's stomach lurched when the innkeeper nodded towards her.

'Mistress Alyce Granville?' the captain asked. A tall well-muscled man in his thirties, he carried himself with an air of authority.

'I am.'

'Mistress Granville, I have a warrant for your arrest.'

Alyce gaped. This made no sense.

'You are required to accompany me to Norwich to answer charges of causing death by witchcraft and other related matters.' His face was impassive—no relish, no malice—a man doing his duty.

Alyce felt weak, the strength gone from her legs. 'Witchcraft?' She held her hand to her mouth, thankful she had eaten little breakfast. 'It is a mistake. What am I supposed to have done Master...?'

'Weatherby, Mistress. It is claimed you brought about, by means of witchcraft, the death of young William Sutton, otherwise known as Willkyn, and various other matters.'

'Poor little Willkyn is dead?' Alyce groaned. 'Oh, Isabel.' She could barely imagine Isabel's suffering. 'Why do they think I...?'

Her voice died away.

'All I know is that you need to be questioned about the child's death. Gather together what you need.'

Alyce forced herself to stand. No one could believe this of her. She must go with them to Norwich, explain that this was a mistake. Squaring her shoulders, she said, 'What will happen when I get to Norwich?'

'You will be examined by a justice who will decide if there is enough evidence to send you to trial at the Assizes.'

'Thank you, Weatherby.' Alyce spoke with a calm she did not feel.

She looked to Stokes. 'Get back to Ashthorpe as fast as you can. Mistress Beaumont will know what to do.'

Part 4
❧∘❧

Death and life are in the power of the tongue.
Proverbs 18:21

32

Late June 1589

The afternoon shadows were lengthening when the sheriff's men rode with their prisoner into Norwich. The castle stood stark against the sky. They trotted along the causeway and over the bridge across the rubbish-filled ditch that surrounded the castle. Before they passed the two round towers at the gateway to the inner bailey, Alyce turned in the saddle and gazed out over the town towards the market and St Peter Mancroft. She had never seen the town from here, never had need to come near the castle.

As they rode into the bailey, the keep loomed over them, faceless and impenetrable despite its air of neglect—flint at the lower level, grubby stonework higher, the beginnings of a crack high on the wall near the battlements.

Weatherby helped Alyce dismount and one of his men pushed her belongings into her arms. She gripped them tightly, something solid in what must surely be a dream.

'This way, Mistress.' Weatherby led her towards the keep.

The gaoler strolled down the staircase along the side of the keep towards them, a hard-faced, scowling man of fifty or so. Where, despite his task, Weatherby had an air of decency, the gaoler exuded menace.

Fear churned in Alyce's stomach as Weatherby turned to go. 'Master Weatherby?'

'Mistress?'

'Will you let my father know I am here? He is Hugh Bradley, the mercer. I am sure he will reward you.'

'I will see to it.'

The gaoler bellowed to a thin man in a grubby doublet lounging against the wall. 'Here Reeves, lock this one up.'

Reeves scurried over. He looked Alyce up and down. 'Down at the house in Golden Ball Lane?'

'No, although she does have the means to pay,' the gaoler grumbled. 'They are afraid she will escape. A room off the hall will have to do.' He marched back into the keep ahead of them, whistling tunelessly.

Reeves jerked his head towards the stairs.

Alyce followed the gaoler up, through two gateways along the stairs, to a portico with arched windows where she paused, staring out across Norwich towards the cathedral and the river. The trees and rooftops were a shaded patchwork of greens and yellows, browns and reds; the spire of the cathedral soared into the blue sky, and the Wensum glistened in the afternoon sunshine—Norwich at its most beautiful.

Reeves grunted and shoved Alyce towards the heavy wooden door set beneath a decorated arch. Inside the keep, yellowed light filtered from high, narrow windows; the air was stale and musty. The gaoler had disappeared, but Reeves was close behind Alyce. He grabbed her arm and propelled her deeper into the hall towards one of several wooden doors along the side wall. All had small metal grates embedded in them. Reeves stopped and threw open the door to a small chamber. It was bare except for a low pallet, a stool and a slop pail. One small window, high and barred, let in little light. The whole place stank of misery and neglect.

'In here,' he grunted.

Alyce stood in the centre of the room, clutching her bundle tight. 'What happens now?'

'Depends.' Reeves shrugged from the doorway. 'You'll stay here 'till the justice of the peace wants to see you.' He slammed the door. A key grated in the lock, and his footsteps faded into silence.

Alyce placed her bundle on the pallet and sat on the stool. She could hear, muffled by thick stone walls, faint shouts and sobs. After only a moment, she stood and paced the floor, fighting the swirling panic. No one could possibly believe she would kill a child. Cecily would send help from Ashthorpe. Her parents too. And Thomas, he would see that she was freed as soon as he heard. She clenched her fists, forced herself to sit again and to breathe slowly and deeply.

~

Robin walked Mistress Middleton to the door of the shop.

'Thank you, Robin. The broadcloth is exactly what I need. I will come back this afternoon with the measurements.'

He held the door open for Mistress Middleton and her maid, Susan, to pass through. Susan had not looked at him once but had stood quietly beside her mistress, her eyes lowered. She would have made a good wife who respected him. It was a pity she would not bring more than herself to a marriage. It would be worth humiliating himself and asking her forgiveness if she had a dowry large enough to help him establish his own shop.

Agnes Hall rushed up to the door, Robin's mother not far behind her.

'Maude, Maude,' she gasped. 'You'll not have heard—Alyce Bradley is locked up in the castle, charged with killing Isabel Sutton's baby.' Her small eyes glittered. 'By witchcraft. Didn't I tell you she was a witch?'

Mistress Middleton opened and shut her mouth. 'But... But... I cannot believe this.'

'It matters not what you believe. She will be tried for killing her sister's son and hanged for it. She cursed Isabel and that boy, and the boy died. He went to sleep and never woke up. And then Isabel lost the child she was carrying. Robin knows I am speaking nothing but the truth.'

Robin stepped into the street. 'I heard Mistress Sutton's child had died. Nothing else.'

He had known something more was afoot though. Sir William had been in Bradley's office, shouting, when Robin had arrived this morning, but Robin could not hear the argument. After Sutton had left, Bradley had slammed the door to his office and not come down since.

'Poor, poor Isabel,' Mistress Middleton groaned. 'But where did you hear this?'

'Edith had it from Dame Katharine just now.'

'Ay,' his mother said. 'I heard the child had died and went to offer Dame Katharine my condolences. She told me then.'

Hall took a breath and rushed on before his mother could say more, almost stumbling over her words. 'And you remember the year before last, the trouble Isabel had and how the baby was monstrous. That was Alyce and her spells.'

Mistress Middleton pressed her lips together and shook her head. 'No, that child was born far too early and Goody Godfrey said it wasn't monstrous, it was Dame Katharine exaggerating as usual. Sometimes these things happen—it is the Lord's will.'

'The Lord's will indeed!' Hall pursed her lips. 'We'll see what the Lord's will is at the next Assizes. Dame Katharine says Sir William is going to uncover just how much witchcraft Alyce has worked here. And there are plenty of other tales about her. I know a few going back a way about what they used to get up to on Mousehold Heath.' She caught both Mistress Middleton and Robin's mother by the arm, drawing them closer as if sharing a secret but speaking so loudly that others in the street turned as they passed by. 'A year or two before Alyce left, Alyce, her grandmother and that old witch Mason were all naked, dancing up there by the light of the full moon.'

'That is ridiculous,' Mistress Middleton said, her voice now as loud as Hall's. 'How could you possibly have seen anything like that?'

'They took me there on the back of a sow. They wanted to make me one of them but I refused.'

Mistress Middleton gaped at Hall. 'That is nothing but a disgusting dream. It says more of you than Alyce.'

That was Robin's first thought too, but it would not surprise him—he knew Alyce to be a most unnatural woman.

'I'm a decent woman,' Hall sniffed, 'I would never have a dream like that.'

'You have never said anything like this before.' Mistress Middleton shouted. 'And I am certain if it had happened as you say, you would have trumpeted it all over town. You can never keep anything secret.'

Robin watched the women arguing. Mistress Middleton was right: if Goody Hall had seen such a thing, it would have been no secret all these years. Still, nothing Alyce did would surprise him.

'Are you calling me a liar?'

'I am. This rubbish could see Alyce hanged. How will you feel with that on your conscience?' She turned to her maid. 'Susan, we have work to do.'

They walked away towards the market, Robin watching Susan. He wondered who was courting her now.

'I'll make sure Robin does,' his mother said.

What were they talking of now? Robin frowned. 'Does what?'

'Go to Sir William and tell him of the way Alyce cursed you.'

Robin stared at her. He had no wish to stand up in public and recount his humiliations.

'And what about the spell Alyce put on you to make you break your betrothal to Susan?' Hall nodded towards the market.

Is that what they were saying? They had not been betrothed and he had stopped seeing Susan weeks before Alyce returned to Norwich but, once she knew she was returning, she could have cast a spell from afar. It made sense and it was a measure of the depth of Alyce Granville's unnatural malice that, although she despised him, she had tempted him and, at the same time, she had destroyed his chance of happiness.

'I will think about it,' Robin said and walked back into the shop. He would have no choice if Alyce was to get what she deserved.

~

The door swung open into the darkened cell. A short, stout man stood silhouetted in the doorway.

Alyce rose warily from her pallet.

Sir William Sutton strode in. Close behind him, Reeves carried a torch, which he set in the bracket on the wall.

'You need not stay,' Sir William's voice rumbled. 'I will not need your help.'

'Whatever you wish, sir.' Reeves bobbed his head. The door thudded shut behind him.

Sir William stood at the centre of the room, fists on his hips. 'Alyce Granville.' He said her name as if it were an insult.

'Sir William, this is a mistake. I must see the justice of the peace.'

'I am the justice in this matter.' He drew his arm back and slapped Alyce across the face with such force she staggered back against the wall. He drove his fist into her stomach.

Groaning, Alyce doubled over and crumpled onto the floor.

Sir William lifted his boot but stopped. The gaoler stood in the doorway, Reeves behind him.

'Sir John Rogers has arrived. He is waiting in my office to assist with the examination.'

'That will not be necessary, Thorpe. I will examine the woman here.'

'Sir John is insistent.' The gaoler, Thorpe, stared at Alyce, curled on the floor, moaning.

Sir William grunted, 'She is dangerous. I want her manacled if we are to take her from this room.'

Thorpe called over his shoulder, 'Reeves, see to it.'

Reeves pushed past Thorpe, carrying the manacles.

Alyce pulled herself up against the wall and stood, unsteady, her arms folded around her middle, rocking with pain. She knew she had no hope of a fair hearing.

Sir William peered at Alyce through narrowed eyes. 'If ever there was a woman in need of correction, it is you.'

Alyce met his gaze, her eyes wide open, willing her tears back. 'Most men earn respect by honest deeds not by bullying with their fists.'

He clenched his fists but did not move. 'You will learn respect for me before you swing.'

'I may learn fear, but respect—never.' Her face stiff with self-control, she held out her arms to Reeves.

'If I had my way, I'd string you up tonight.'

Reeves locked the manacles around her wrists.

'No trial?' Alyce shuddered. 'Surely every person accused has the right to a trial?'

Sir William ignored her question and marched ahead with the air of a man who regarded the castle as part of his domain. Thorpe walked in front of Alyce, Reeves behind as she was led from her cell across the darkened hall to the gaoler's room.

A lantern threw light across a paper-strewn table where an elderly man sat, his bushy white eyebrows joined together in intense concentration. He looked up from the papers as Sutton dragged out the chair beside him.

'A word, Sir William,' he said, his voice lowered. 'This is a city matter. Should not Mistress Granville be held at the

Guildhall?'

Sutton glowered as he shuffled through the papers. 'Such a witch as this creature needs to be held securely. What better place than Norwich Castle? Her witchcraft is far-reaching. I am seeking evidence of the havoc she wrought on her journey here, and that, most certainly, is a county matter.'

Alyce strained to hear what they were saying. He seemed to be suggesting she had committed other murders. She swallowed hard. There could be no evidence of that.

'One other point, regarding your grandson's death,' Sir John spoke gently. 'The coroner could find no evidence of foul play.'

'This is witchcraft, Rogers, not poisoning or strangling,' Sutton snarled.

'Sir William. Courtesy please.'

'Forgive me, Sir John.' He bowed his head. 'In my grief, I forget myself.'

'Are you the best person to examine Mistress Granville?'

'Who better to get at the heart of the matter than one with a burning desire to see justice done?' Sir William shouted.

'We will proceed calmly. We will examine Mistress Granville, and if she does not confess, we will have her examined for the witch's teat. Keep in mind the High Sheriff himself will have a close interest in this case. Sir Robert Southwell is a friend of this woman's husband.'

Sutton breathed heavily through his nose. 'I will question her. You record what she says.' He glared at Alyce and barked, 'How did you become a witch?'

'I am not a witch,' she answered him as forcefully.

'What say you to the charges?'

'I do not know what they are.'

'You brought about the death of my grandson by witchcraft. You brought about a miscarriage on my daughter-in-law by witchcraft.'

'Isabel lost the child?' Alyce's voice cracked. She pressed her folded arms as tight against her stomach as the manacles allowed.

'You cursed her.' He took one of the papers, tilted it towards the light, squinting. 'You said to your mother: *Take care of Isabel,*

Mother. She has her share of sorrow.'

'How is that a curse?' She fought against tears. 'All it shows is that I cared for my sister.'

'It shows you knew the ill that was to befall her. She had no sorrow until that point. Further,' he stabbed a finger onto the papers, 'before you married, you gave Isabel potions to blight her unborn baby, to which end the baby was born early, was deformed and did not live more than a few hours.'

'That is a lie. I gave Isabel poppy to calm her. Once. That was all.'

'You say it was poppy, but it could have been anything. Who knows what else you were putting in her food and drink?'

Alyce moved away from the wall. 'Prove it, then.' She knew she must fight him.

'Oh, I will.' He watched her, speculation in his eyes. 'It will go easier for you if you admit to your evildoing, especially if in this you were the instrument of another.'

'And who would that other be?' She knew the answer.

'Your husband, Thomas Granville.'

Sir John paused his writing and glanced at Sir William.

'My husband is not a sly, base creature who would resort to attacking womenfolk to have revenge on a man. He would face that man himself.' She stared steadily at Sir William. After several moments she said, 'This muddle of lies is all I am charged with?'

'There is much more. You learnt witchcraft at your grandmother's knee. You bewitched Robin Chapman, drawing him away from his betrothed Susan Graham.'

Alyce's knees tremble. Wincing, she drew a deep breath and willed herself on. 'Robert Chapman was never betrothed.'

'He will swear they were to be married until you cast your spells on him and, against his will, he lost interest in her.'

'If he lost interest in Susan Graham, it was not my doing. And what does Susan Graham say?'

'You have bewitched her into such forgetfulness that she cannot remember she was betrothed. Chapman also says you admitted to him that you were a witch.'

Alyce laughed bitterly. Had she set this trap for herself when she rejected Chapman?

'You find that comical?' Sir William stood and moved around the table. With each step he took towards her, Alyce stepped backwards until she was against the wall. He pushed his face into hers. 'Do you?'

'I find it ridiculous.'

He held her face between his beefy fingers, squeezing hard. Alyce whimpered with the pain. 'You will take this seriously.' Close, his face was haggard, his eyes red-rimmed. 'You have committed heinous crimes and you will pay.'

He released Alyce and returned to his seat. 'You have boasted of your study of divination.'

'Whoever told you that misheard. I have an interest in astronomy, not divination.'

He snorted. 'A likely story.'

'You would do better to ask Master Harrison what I said than to accept an eavesdropper's carefully selected memories.'

Sir William grunted, 'You attempted to seduce my son using witchcraft and spells.'

'Your son is an adulterer,' Alyce scoffed. 'It would take no spell to get him into a woman's bed.'

'You are a whore, Alyce Granville.'

'I am no whore,' Alyce shouted. 'I have kept my marriage vows. Can your son say as much? Can you?'

Sit William's face flushed. 'You mind your slanders. They will be held against you.'

'And what of yours?'

'Do you not recognise the dire trouble you are in?' he said between gritted teeth.

'I recognise it very well. Tell me, Sir William, do you truly believe people can kill by cursing?' She took two steps towards the table. 'If you think I have the power to do that, are you not fearful I will do the same to you?'

A nerve flickered beneath Sir William's eye. 'A witch has no power once she has been handed over to a justice.'

'You are sure of that?'

'Of course I am,' he blustered. 'How else would we bring any of you creatures to trial and have you pay for your malice?'

'My malice? Or is it you saw the opportunity to turn your family grief to your own advantage by using it to strike at my husband. The beasts of the field have a stronger sense of family than you do.'

He bellowed, inarticulate, and sprang around the table, nimble for all his bulk, his fist raised.

Alyce stood her ground, staring into those desolate hate-filled eyes.

He stopped, dropped his arm as his face drained of colour. 'Have a care, or I will save the sheriff the cost of the rope.' He spoke without his earlier conviction.

He strode back to the table, breathing hard, and dropped heavily onto his chair.

'Thorpe, get her out of here,' he bellowed.

He slammed his hand down. 'Granville, do not think you will escape the consequences of your evildoing. No one, not even your father will raise a finger to save you.'

Sir John laid down his pen and stared at Alyce, his frown deeper than when she had been brought in.

Back in her cell, the manacles removed and the door locked, Alyce fell on her pallet trembling, rage and fear sweeping through her. She would not cry.

A key rasped in the lock and the door creaked open. An old woman, illuminated by the light falling from a torch behind her, shoved a dish and a tankard through the door, quickly slamming it shut again.

Alyce stared at the dish and tankard. She had eaten nothing since the previous evening, and hunger clawed at her. She rose slowly and picked up the dish, scooping a small amount of thin grey pottage into her mouth, but she could not swallow it. She spat it out and put the dish back down. She took up the tankard, sipping the weak, stale small beer. A pity it was not aqua vitae, but even the strongest drink could not obliterate this nightmare. Thought of the last time she drank spirits brought the presence of Thomas to her. She ached for him, the comfort of his arms around her. If he knew, he would not leave her here.

33

Alyce huddled on the pallet, wrapped tightly in her cloak, watching the weak morning light lessen the gloom of her cell. She had slept fitfully, jerking awake with every noise.

Easing herself off the bed, she stretched—tired, stiff, cold through to the bone. After straightening her clothes and combing her hair, Alyce lowered herself to her knees and rested her elbows on the seat of the stool. She emptied her mind of all but the psalms memorised through years of repetition. *The Lord is my shepherd; I shall not want…*'

She sensed she was being watched and raised her eyes to the door. Someone was peering in through the small grate in the door. Alyce shivered. Everything she did within this small cell could be observed.

The key scraped, and the door was opened just enough for the old woman of the night before to take the plate and push in a mug of small beer and a lump of hard bread. Reeves stood behind her.

'Goodwife,' Alyce called to her, leaning on the stool as she struggled to her feet.

The woman squinted, suspicious.

'Goodwife, how do I get better food than this?'

The old woman's face wrinkled into a toothless grin. 'You pay for it, lady.'

'Do I pay you?'

'Talk to Master Thorpe,' the old woman muttered as the door thudded shut.

~

Alyce could only guess at the time by the faint sound of bells pealing across the town. She supposed it was nearing midday when the gaoler, Thorpe, arrived. She remained seated, her turmoil hidden in her stillness.

'Time to pay, Mistress,' Thorpe scowled.

Alyce stood, her heart shuddering with fear. 'But there must be a trial. You cannot—'

'Pay for your lodging,' he said, smirking. 'I am to have the pleasure of your company until the Assizes.'

'Oh.' Her thudding heart slowed. 'When will they be?'

'In five weeks,' his small eyes glittered, 'and even if you offered a king's ransom, you'll not be bailed. There's no swaying Sutton on this.'

She drew herself up and stood, her hands clasped at her waist. 'Well, Master Thorpe, what is the price of a better-appointed room, one with at least a ray of sunlight?'

He named his sum. Alyce had only enough money for four weeks but by then Thomas was sure to be here. 'I want such a room. And I need blankets, writing materials. A small table, water and a bowl for washing. And a pie for my dinner today.'

He crossed his arms. 'Is that all?'

'I also need my linen washed.'

'Family usually take care of that.' Calculation in his dark eyes, Thorpe said, 'Reeves's daughter will fetch and carry for a price.'

'I'll wait until I hear from my family.'

'Anything else, your ladyship?' He gave a mocking bow.

'That is all, thank you.'

He named a sum nearly double his original price.

'It cannot cost so much.'

He shrugged. 'It costs what I say it costs.'

'And if I stay in this room?'

He reduced the price, but not by much. Alyce paid Thorpe for the first week, counting out the coins, careful not to show how much she had.

'Will I be examined further?' At the thought of Sir William, she wrapped her arms tight across her stomach.

'The examination by the justices of the peace is all that is needed, but as you are denying the charges, he may be forced to extract your confession.'

'Extract?' Her voice quavered.

'Ay, nothing too nasty—be glad you're not in Scotland. And as you are a witch, the minister may come to save your black soul.' He laughed as if he had told a new-minted jest and slammed the door.

~

Alyce had often been solitary, but she had never been alone. There was always someone nearby, someone in the next room, someone ready to walk in. Even when a door had been locked as punishment—as a child and at Dalstead—it had never been for long. Later, in an hour or two, or the next day, it would be opened and she could walk out and look at the sky and the hills, see the birds soar, feel the wind on her face. Now she had no idea of how long she would be locked away. The footsteps outside her door, muffled noises from the nearby cells, the sounds of men and horses carrying from the bailey held no hope of release. She stared at the tiny window, a window with no view, panic bubbling up at the thought that she would see nothing of the world for weeks on end.

She paced the room, stopping now and then to sit and read her Psalter but she could not keep the words in her mind. The walls pressed in on her, and her thoughts slipped away into panic. She clenched her teeth, fearful if she opened her mouth she would scream. She must be patient and wait—help would come.

~

For three days, Alyce had seen no one other than the old woman who brought her meals and Reeves, the gaoler's man, who let her out to empty her slop pail. She could have paid to have that done but she needed to conserve her pennies and it was a chance to step beyond her narrow room. She had tried to chat with him, but her comments were met with sullen grunts. The last real conversation, if it could be called that, had been when she had paid Thorpe for the room.

Reeves peered through the grate at her and unlocked the door, holding it wide as three women walked in. She searched their faces in the dim light, hoping her mother was among them.

Alyce's heart sank—she was not there. Three soberly dressed matrons stood facing her, Goodwife Godfrey among them. A small, neat woman in her sixties, she was the midwife who had delivered both Isabel and Alyce.

Reeves set a lamp on the stool and walked out the door. 'Yell when you are finished,' he called through the grate as he turned the key in the lock.

Once Reeves had gone, Godfrey said, 'Mistress Granville, we are to examine you for the witch's teat.'

'Ay, to find the place on your body where you have given suck to your imp or familiar,' a second woman spoke, tall, thin and narrow-lipped.

'Surely you do not believe this of me?' Alyce said to Godfrey.

Before Godfrey could speak, the thin woman said, 'You have quite a history. It is not only the death of young William Sutton that concerns us, but that of his brother two years past.'

Alyce blinked, not understanding. 'I was in London when he died.'

'That babe was born far too early,' said Godfrey, 'but you were foolish to meddle where you had no knowledge, Mistress.'

'I admit I know little but Isabel was distressed. She thought she was losing the baby. I consulted my herbal and gave Isabel a poultice of tansy applied to the navel. It is supposed to stay miscarriage.'

'I would have done the same,' said the third woman, round-faced and motherly.

Godfrey nodded in agreement.

'As well, I gave Isabel a single draught of poppy to help her sleep,' Alyce added.

The thin woman peered along her nose at Alyce. 'Mistress Sutton says you fed her potions throughout the pregnancy, potions that caused the baby to weaken, possibly bringing on an early birth.'

'I did not. My sister is—' Alyce stopped. Had this woman already judged her and found her guilty? Would it make matters worse to call Isabel a liar? 'Mistaken.'

'We should get on with our task, Goodwife Williams,' Godfrey said. 'Now, Mistress Granville, take off your clothing, all but your smock.'

'She should undress completely,' Williams said.

Alyce did not move. She did not want to stand naked in front of strangers, but refusal would be seen as an admission of guilt.

'Do as you are told, girl,' Williams snarled. 'Do you want us to call the gaoler's men to hold you down while we strip you?'

'For heaven's sake, Ruth, there will be no need for that,' said the motherly woman. 'Mistress Granville is cold. And no one wants to undress before strangers.'

Alyce reluctantly unbuttoned her doublet.

'Will I help you?' The woman glared at Ruth Williams. 'And we will leave your smock on.'

'Thank you, I can manage.' Alyce undressed slowly, folding each item and placing it neatly on the end of her pallet.

The women waited, Williams tapping her foot impatiently.

The motherly woman held the lamp as the other two moved near to Alyce. They searched her well, fingers poking through her hair, behind her ears. Williams was most thorough, making Alyce raise her arms as her nails scraped and pinched at her armpits. She tugged Alyce's smock forward to examine her breasts, the cloth tearing with the rough handling.

'Well, that would not have happened had you stripped,' she sneered.

Alyce flushed with embarrassment as Williams prodded her breasts, lifting them to search beneath. She was so close Alyce felt her breath on her skin. She seemed to be examining every pore.

Williams straightened up and said, 'Lift your smock above your waist.'

The motherly woman smiled at Alyce. 'No need to be coy, my dear. You can show us nothing we have not seen many, many times before. That is right, above the waist.'

The women peered closely at her belly, her legs.

Alyce stared at the wall, her face hot with shame.

'What is this?' Williams crowed as she prodded Alyce's buttock with an icy finger. 'So many marks.'

'Oh, Ruth, a witch's teat is raised and nipple-like,' Godfrey said, 'these are fleabites. You'll find them on everyone who visits here, even Sir Robert Southwell. What do you think, Harriet?'

Alyce felt the heat of the lamp on her skin as the third midwife held it close. 'Fleabites to be sure,' she said. 'Look, Ruth, you have three such marks on your wrist.'

Williams glared at Harriet and wrapped her hand around her wrist. 'I know what my eyes tell me.'

'You have a care, Ruth Williams.' Godfrey's face flushed. 'God will weigh any statement you make here on Judgement Day.'

'My conscience is clear,' Williams sniffed.

'It will not be if a woman dies because you have lied to please Sir William.'

'How dare you?' Williams turned on Godfrey.

'Ruth. Bess. Enough of this,' Harriet shouted over them. 'We have work to do.'

'Now, Mistress,' Harriet touched Alyce's forearm, 'lie on the pallet. We need to examine you further.'

Alyce lay down and squeezed her eyes tight, overwhelmed with shame as her knees were drawn apart. They whispered to each other as they poked and prodded her intimately.

After an age, a warm hand brushed Alyce's shoulder as another pulled the smock down to her knees. 'You may dress now,' Harriet said.

Shamed and angry at what felt like a violation of her entire body, Alyce struggled up from the pallet. 'Did you find what you were looking for?'

'You are an insolent baggage,' Williams said, her lips pursed and vicious.

Alyce drew herself up to her full height. 'You forget yourself, Williams. I am not convicted yet, and even if I were, you would still owe me the courtesy due to my husband's position.'

Williams opened and shut her mouth, stunned.

'Please Mistress,' Goodwife Godfrey said, 'this does you no good. When you come before the judge you must be demure and quiet.'

'I doubt the judge will treat me with the contempt this woman has. I fear I am to be hanged for no reason other than Sir William Sutton desires it. He sees it as a way of attacking my husband. Truth and justice have no part in it. If I am to die no matter what, I have nothing to lose by speaking.'

She turned her back to the women and pulled on her petticoat, tightening the laces of her bodice.

'Alyce,' Godfrey said gently. 'Is there any message you want me to pass on to your mother?'

'Nay.' Alyce struggled to keep her voice even. 'If Mother wishes to see me, she will come herself.'

Godfrey lowered her voice, 'She is ill with grief, not only at the loss of her grandson, but at what has happened to you.'

Alyce fought back tears. 'She could send Eliza to me even if she cannot come herself.'

'She cannot even do that. Whispers are your father has forbidden her because Sir William has threatened him in some way if they give you any help.' Godfrey gently rubbed Alyce's arm. 'Is there anything I can do for you?'

'Thank you, no. My husband will be here soon enough.' She looked towards the window, the brightest point in the dim room. 'Not unless you can convince them to let me leave with you.'

As the door banged shut behind the women, Alyce lay on the pallet and began to laugh. In danger of her life and naked except for a flimsy smock, she had reprimanded a woman whose goodwill was important because she had failed to show adequate respect. Three, even two, years ago, it would not have occurred to her. Alyce curled into a ball as her bitter laughter turned to silent, wracking sobs.

34

July 1589

Alyce stood on her stool in the corner of the room, her eyes shut as she drank in the warmth of a tiny patch of sunlight that covered no more than the middle of her face. It had been such an unexpected gift, lessening the gloom of the cell for a few fleeting moments.

A key grated in the lock.

'Get down from there,' Thorpe barked. 'Master Reynes is here to see you.'

Master William Reynes, curate of St Peter Mancroft, walked in behind Thorpe, carrying a Bible and a satchel.

Thorpe set a horn lamp on the small table Alyce had paid to have added to the furniture of the room. She had wanted, at least, to sit and eat her meals with a degree of dignity—an extravagance, she now realized. She had been held for five days and no help had come.

'Bring your stool over here, Mistress Granville,' Reynes said politely.

The sight of his neat clothing and immaculate linen shamed Alyce. Her own linen was grubby and her face poorly washed although she had done her best, scrubbing her face and hands that morning with the dribble of water left at the bottom of the jug. She could not afford to pay to have her washing done or soap and scents bought for her.

Alyce sat silent, her shoulders hunched with cold as Thorpe dragged a chair in from outside and set it beside the table where Reynes had placed his Bible.

'Thorpe, I will call when I am finished,' he said.

He picked up Alyce's Psalter, lying beside his Bible and flicked through the pages before taking his seat.

'Mistress Alyce Granville, I am here because you were once my parishioner and I want with all my heart to save your soul.'

Alyce looked at him, wary, her hands clasped tightly in her lap.

'I will find the truth, for I have God on my side.'

'Then I have nothing to fear.' There was no conviction in her voice. What most called the truth was what they wanted to hear.

'You do not fear the Lord?'

'Of course I fear the Lord.'

Alyce's stomach lurched as he took two small instruments from his satchel and placed them beside the Bible: a thumbscrew and a set of pincers.

'You see here the means to the truth used by our Scottish brethren.' He picked up the pincers. 'They call these *turkas* and use them to pull out the witch's fingernails. These are *pilliwinks*,' he pointed to the thumbscrews, 'which leave fingers as flat as the blade of a knife. There are other instruments too. Have you heard of the witch's bridle or the Spanish boot?'

Alyce shook her head, her mouth dry, her heart racing.

Reynes stood. 'I have a power greater than these toys to extract the truth from you—I have the power of God Almighty with me.'

He bent down until his face was an inch from Alyce's. She could not move back, fearful she would overbalance on the stool.

His voice was low, caressing. 'Now, Alyce Granville, tell me the truth.'

Alyce swallowed. 'What do you want me to say?'

Reynes straightened up. 'I want you to confess your evildoings.'

'I have never willingly done evil.' She pushed the face of Giles Clifton from her mind. She had been forced to that to protect her daughter.

He sat again and tugged at his sleeves, smoothing out the creases. 'If that is true, why do so many claim you are an evildoer?'

She shrugged. 'With some, it is pure malice.'

'The people who accuse you are not rabble but honest God-fearing men like Sir William Sutton.'

'Honest and God-fearing?' she scoffed. 'You do not know him well.'

His face hardened. 'Do not add slander to your crimes.'

Catherine Meyrick

'I have done nothing wrong.'

Reynes stared along his straight nose. 'Have you not?'

Again, Alyce thought of Clifton. She pressed her mouth tight against her uneven breathing. *I was defending Elinor*, she argued with herself. *Thomas said I had performed a soldier's task, that God had guided my hand.* Clifton's malicious laughter echoed in her head. *I will surely die, and Thomas too, if I do not accept God's mercy.*

'I see you hesitate.'

'I do not understand what you are accusing me of.' Alyce took a deep breath. The past was beyond repair. From here on she must trust in God's forgiveness and fight for her life.

'You deny you are a sinner?'

She straightened her back and sat upright on her stool. 'I know I am a sinner, but my sins are the petty failings of ordinary folk.'

Reynes drew a page covered with neat writing from his satchel, tilted it towards the lamp and searched it quickly. 'You deny that by means of witchcraft you brought about a miscarriage on your sister and the death of her two living children?'

'I do—I have never harmed Isabel. And how could I have killed either of her poor little boys?' Alyce groaned. 'I was miles away when each of those children died.'

'You killed those children by witchcraft.'

'But what does that mean? How am I supposed to have performed this witchcraft?'

'You wish to revel in your evil by having me repeat it to you?'

'No one—not the constable, Weatherby, not Sir William Sutton or Master Thorpe, and now not even you—not one of you will tell me exactly what I have done.' Alyce said, near to tears. 'If I do not know the steps I supposedly took to kill poor Willkyn, how can I defend myself properly?'

Reynes frowned and pressed his lips together. After a moment, he said, 'As you left the parlour of your father's house, you touched the child and whispered an incantation, cursing him.'

Alyce rocked on her stool, her arms tightly crossed. 'I kissed him and whispered a blessing as I said goodbye.' She sighed loudly. 'When did the poor mite die?'

'As you were riding from Norwich.'

'But how could I do it if I was not here?'

His frown deepened. 'You sent your familiar out to do it.'

'My familiar?'

'In the form of a sparrow. It flew from your hand as your sister entered the parlour and waited its chance. The child was put to bed, well and happy, but never woke from his sleep. The familiar was sitting in a tree outside the Suttons' house when he was found.'

'A sparrow in a tree?' She blinked rapidly, hardly able to understand. 'There are thousands in this town and they all look the same. How could anyone tell it was the same one?'

Reynes did not answer.

Alyce laced her fingers together and leant forward. 'Willkyn was fevered and whimpering when Isabel brought him to my parents' house. I told her to take him home. Mother will tell you the same, and the nursemaid.'

'Your mother is ill and has taken to her bed. She claims no memory of the day. The nursemaid supports what Mistress Sutton says, not that she has said much. Mistress Sutton was so overcome with grief she lost the child she was carrying.' He shook his head. 'You did your work well.'

'Poor Isabel.' Alyce fought down a sob as she imagined the desolation she would feel if Elinor died. She looked at Reynes. 'But why would I do these things?'

'Apart from an innate inclination towards evil? Jealousy of your sister's status and wealth.'

'My husband's status and wealth are greater than that of Will Sutton.'

'Sons. Mistress Sutton claims you used witchcraft to try to ensnare her husband into adultery to get from him the son your husband cannot give you.'

'That is ridiculous. I have only been married two and a half years and my husband has been away fighting for our country for much of that time, yet already we have one healthy child.' Alyce raised her eyes to the damp patches on the wall. 'Given time, I am sure we will have sons.' If she survived this, no matter how she had to embarrass herself, she would set things right with Thomas.

Reynes leant back in his chair, staring at her.

'It was he who tried to seduce me.' Alyce gave a bitter laugh. 'As minister of this parish you must know of Will Sutton's adulteries.'

'Do not presume to tell me my duty.' He glanced down at his papers. 'Nearing three years ago you gave your sister a potion that blighted the child in her womb.'

'On one occasion only, I gave Isabel syrup of poppies to calm her and give her sleep. She was upset and fearful she was losing her child. Poppy is often used to bring sleep to the distressed.'

'You say it was poppy. Can you prove it?'

'Can you prove it was not?'

'Do not play games with me, Mistress. We have irrefutable proof of your guilt. You have the witch's teat upon your body.'

'I do not.'

'It is a fact sworn to by a godly matron.'

'Goodwife Williams, I suppose. And what of the other two? What do they say?'

Reynes blinked. 'What other two?'

'I was examined by three women: Williams, Godfrey and another called Harriet.'

'Goodwife Brewer.' Reynes was thoughtful. 'Their testimony has, no doubt, been discarded as worthless.'

'And why would that be?'

'Sir William must consider you bewitched them to deny the evidence of their eyes.'

'But Sir William said once a witch has been taken by a justice, she has no power.'

'Hmmm.' Reynes tapped his fingers on the table beside him. 'You cursed Robin Chapman placing a spell on him making him impotent.'

Alyce laughed. 'That is ridiculous.'

Reynes's face mottled. He sprang up and struck Alyce hard across the face. 'This is no laughing matter.'

Alyce rubbed her cheek. 'I know it is not,' she said between gritted teeth. 'But tell me, how would an unmarried paragon of godliness such as Robert Chapman know he was impotent?'

'We are all sinners.' Reynes sat down again, rubbing the palm of his right hand.

Alyce was glad he hurt too.

'Why would you curse a man who offered you marriage?'

Alyce paused. She had meant to frighten Chapman. She had not cursed him but had threatened him out of fear.

Alyce chose her words carefully. 'I do not believe an ordinary person has the power to cause harm by curses.'

'Not unless that person had made a compact with the Evil One.'

'Are you accusing me of that?' A chill ran down Alyce's spine. 'I would never…. No. No. I try to live a godly life. I fear God and his judgement. I pray daily, alone and with my household. I attend church. I am raising my daughter to love God and do her duty.'

After a long, unblinking silence Reynes said, 'Why did you refuse Goodman Chapman's offer of marriage?'

'I did not consider his offer serious. I have no trust in Robert Chapman and that is no basis for a marriage. All I have ever felt for him is revulsion and fear.'

'Fear?'

'I feared he would force himself on me to get me with child so I would be compelled to marry him. Married to me, he would be heir to my father's business.'

'He could only get you with child if you took pleasure in the act. It is clear you had some feeling for him.'

Alyce shuddered.

'This is nothing but slander against Goodman Chapman's reputation.'

'As these claims of witchcraft slander me.'

Reynes watched Alyce, his face unreadable. Alyce met his gaze.

'Tell me, why did you choose a profligate like Thomas Granville? I would have cautioned you against this marriage had I been aware of the extent of his debaucheries.'

Alyce's eyes blazed. 'My husband is not profligate.'

'You cannot deny his reputation. Did he lead you farther along the path to evil? Was your evil done at his behest?'

Alyce leapt up from the stool, heat flooding her face. 'My husband is a godly man,' she shouted. 'Ask anyone who has sailed with him. There are prayers and services on his ships. He attends Sunday service like any other man. No matter what his behaviour as a youth, he is now respected by many men of high degree.'

Reynes rose from his own seat, unmoved. 'I will have the truth, Mistress.'

'I have no fear of the truth.'

'You will confess and pray for forgiveness, I promise you.'

Alyce met his fierce glare, refusing to show humility.

~

One day passed much like the next. Alyce read her Psalter when the light was sufficient, paced the cell reciting psalms from heart when it was not. She played memory games—thought of every stillroom she had used and, when she was hopeful, her room at Ashthorpe. She opened every drawer, every chest and coffer, remembering what each place held. She thought of Elinor and remembered her broad grin, the curve of her pink cheeks, her soft dark curls, her gurgling laugh. At first she called to mind Thomas too, in happier times—his grey eyes, crinkling at the corners as he gazed down into hers; the smile she could not help but return; his hands, scarred and competent yet gentle when he touched her; the way he stood, tall, legs firmly planted apart, forceful and protective of what was his; his arms, tight around her, the safest place on earth. But as the days passed, she began to doubt her memories of Thomas, saw them more as wishful dreams than reality and tried to push all thought of him away, relegating him to the crowd of those who had deserted her. Time enough had passed for anyone who wished to have helped.

She marked the passing days in the front of her Psalter. She had been imprisoned for nearly three weeks. Master Reynes had examined her four times. He had accused her, berated her, tried to trip her up. Each time it was something different: Isabel's miscarriage and babies, Robert Chapman and her early life, her knowledge of physic and of plants and cures, her marriage and her husband's influence. She answered carefully—anything she said could be used against her, twisted into an admission of guilt—yet she welcomed Raynes's visits. It was a battle of wills, and of all those ranged against her, she believed Reynes was the only one searching for the truth.

35

Alyce lay on her pallet, listening for movement outside her cell. She had written to her father three days ago but, as she had expected, no answer came. She had sold what she could of her possessions, her second kirtle to Reeves, who said he would give it to his wife. The old woman who brought what passed for food had paid her for a grubby smock embroidered with black work at the neck, and Alyce had eaten pie two days in a row. She had given Reeves her Psalter in exchange for carrying the letter to her father. The letter had been written with the last of her ink onto a blank page torn from the back of the book.

She struggled up from the pallet as the door thudded open. Thorpe stood, hands on his hips, filling the doorway. 'Your rent is due.'

'I have no money.' Each week the price of the room had increased, and now she had nothing left.

'It's the dungeon cells, then,' he growled. 'This is no almshouse.'

Alyce shrugged. There was nothing she could do.

'How long until the Assizes?' she asked Thorpe.

'Just over two weeks.'

As Alyce gathered up her cloak, she glanced down at her wedding ring. She supposed she could have sold that too but it would have been for a fraction of its value. She could not let go of it yet—it was a symbol of the shrivelled hope she had not managed to smother.

'I would hide that if I was you.' Reeves, who had followed Thorpe in, pointed to the ring. 'They'll tear the finger off you to get at it.' He pulled a grubby length of cord from his pouch.

Alyce threaded it through the ring and tied it round her neck. She pushed the cord beneath her bodice and felt the warm metal settle between her breasts.

'Thank you, Reeves. If I get out of here, I'll not forget your kindness.'

'No kindness,' he said gruffly as he manacled Alyce's hands together, 'don't want no trouble below.'

The reek of the dungeon cells rose up to meet them as they descended the winding staircase and walked through the gloom of the lower level of the keep: damp, excrement, unwashed bodies and plain ill health.

Thorpe stood back, a club in his hands, as Reeves unlocked Alyce's manacles and dragged the iron gate of the cell open. Alyce froze, her heart racing as she whispered a frantic prayer. *Lord protect me and preserve me.*

Shoved roughly from behind, she stumbled in. She pulled her cloak tight as the door clanged shut. The cell was barely lit, scant light coming from small barred windows high in the walls. Women shuffled towards her in the crowded half-light, nightmarish, unkempt creatures.

'You lot,' Reeves bellowed through the bars, 'you keep your hands to yourselves. Mistress Granville here has friends of high degree.'

'Not much good to her, were they, Davey love?' A young woman sidled up to the door and pressed herself against the bars. 'What she needs is a *friend* like you.' Her eyes on Reeves's face, her fingers reached through and played against his upper thigh.

'You mind yourself, Eva,' Reeves hissed and marched away.

Eva turned and stood in front of Alyce, hands on her hips. 'What are you in here for, my lady?' Her lip curled.

'I am unjustly accused.' Even to her own ears, Alyce's voice sounded prim.

'As we all are, eh girls?' She glanced at the women pressing close around them.

Eva shoved her face into Alyce's. 'What are you accused of?'

Alyce grimaced at the reek of her breath. 'Witchcraft.'

Hisses slithered around the cell.

Eva looked Alyce up and down. 'Are you a witch?'

'If I had such powers, would I be here?' Alyce snapped. She must show no fear.

Eva threw her head back and laughed, a rough sound without a trace of mirth. 'You'll get no special treatment here.'

She jerked her head towards the darkest corner. 'Sleep where you can find a space.'

Alyce picked her way through the mass of prisoners, careful to bump or tread on no one. Pressing her hand against the damp wall to steady herself, she sank down on the rank straw, drawing her knees up and pulling her cloak tighter. She rested her head on her knees and closed her eyes.

The room was alive with sounds and movement: sobbing, muttering, coughing, whispering. Alyce opened her eyes. Women crowded close around her: dirty, bedraggled and hungry-faced.

An old woman gingerly lowered herself to the floor beside Alyce. She stretched out a gnarled hand and stroked Alyce's sleeve.

'Pretty,' she croaked. 'If you give Eva something, she'll look after you.'

Alyce's first thought was of the ring hanging underneath her bodice. It was too much to ask.

Eva stood in front of Alyce, hands on her hips. 'What do you have for me?'

'You'd better give her something,' whispered the old woman.

Eva squatted down and took the cloth of Alyce's cloak between her fingers. 'This'll do.'

If she refused, Alyce knew Eva would take it anyway. She staggered to her feet and removed her cloak. Eva grimaced in a parody of a smile and bowed mockingly. She clasped it around her neck and walked away.

Alyce stepped back, the heel of her shoe pressing on to the foot of a woman behind her.

'Watch where you're going, bitch.' The woman thumped her hard in the back.

Alyce stumbled forward colliding with another woman who grabbed her by the shoulders and slammed her head against Alyce's forehead. Then there were bodies over her, scratching, pulling, gouging. She pushed back, fighting and struggling as she had never before. Punched, kicked, scratched on the face, her hair jerked back. She could not breathe—the cord, the grimy string that held the patterned gold band was pulled tight around her neck. Alyce's fingers scrabbled but could get no hold. It tightened, cut into her flesh. The world faded red. All that existed was the image of Elinor, and Thomas, as darkness overwhelmed her.

~

Air rasped in Alyce's throat.

Eva stood over her as she lay on the damp stone floor. 'Leave her alone,' she snarled. 'She's mine.' She stalked over to a woman pinning her hair with a comb and punched her in the face, grabbed a hank of hair and snapped her head back, wrenching the comb out.

Alyce crawled away to the wall and curled up careless of the damp and slime. One of her sleeves was missing, the other ragged, some of the lacings on her gown were broken, and her shoes were gone. Alyce pushed the cord and its treasure back beneath her smock, grateful that in the gloom no one had noticed it.

Eva shoved the comb at her. 'This is yours.' She squatted down. 'You are a sorry mess.'

Alyce touched her face: one eye was swollen, her lip split, scratches down both sides of her face. 'I suppose there's no way I can have these dressed?' The effort of speaking hurt her throat.

'Not unless you have money to pay.' Eva sat cross-legged beside Alyce, her ragged skirt tucked around her. 'And if you had that, you'd not be here with us.'

The old woman settled herself at Alyce's other side. 'So, dearie, what's your name?'

'Alyce Granville.'

'I'm Stella Knowles. I'm a witch too,' she said proudly.

Alyce leant her head back against the wall. 'I am not a witch.'

'So you say,' Eva snorted. 'What did you do?'

What had she done to provoke Isabel's wrath? Married Thomas at a time not convenient to Isabel? Taken pleasure in the life marriage had given her? Unwittingly attracted Isabel's husband's roving eye? Perhaps that was it—it was only then Isabel had shown her anger. Alyce leant forward frowning, her hand held at the front of her throat. 'Seduced my sister's husband, I suppose.'

Eva laughed, genuine this time. 'It does not take witchcraft to seduce a man, all you need is what we all have between our legs.'

Alyce lowered her eyes.

Eva poked her in the ribs. 'You're as coy as a virgin.'

Alyce winced with pain.

'You lay with your brother-in-law?' Eva smirked. 'Since when has that been a hanging crime?'

'I did not lie with him,' Alyce shouted, coughing as the air caught in her throat. 'He tried to seduce me.' She struggled to speak. 'I refused, but my sister saw us together. I expect he invented this feeble tale to excuse himself.'

'Is that all?'

'Nay,' Alyce said sullenly. 'Then, because I failed to have my way with him, I am supposed to have killed my sister's child by cursing and caused her to miscarry.'

Eva nodded. 'That is serious.'

'They say two years ago I blighted the child in her womb causing him to be deformed and weak. He died within hours of his birth.' Alyce coughed again. 'But I was in London with my husband then.'

Eva raised her eyebrows. 'Why has he left you to rot?'

'I do not know.' Alyce's voice cracked.

'Men are worthless.' Eva spat into the straw. 'You must have done something—none of us are here for nothing. I stabbed a faithless bastard. Stella here killed a miserly neighbour's cows. Then there's Esther, the slut that stole your comb, she's the best cutpurse in the county.'

'I have never deliberately harmed anyone,' Alyce said bitterly. She paused. Clifton did not matter—his death had not been by malice or design. She let out a long, slow breath. Somehow that burden of conscience had been lifted.

~

Alyce fought sleep, aware of movement around her: muffled weeping, intermittent groans and screams. She shivered with the cold and drew her bare feet under her skirt. Crossing her arms, she rubbed her hands up and down for warmth. Eva slept to one side of her. Stella had crawled alongside and Alyce relaxed between them, feeling a measure of safety in their closeness.

Sleep finally came and with it dreams of a fleeting life of clean clothes and solid food, of music and conversation, of the wind and the endless sky. She dreamt of riding out on Gleda, galloping along the lanes at Ashthorpe; of dancing in the hall, her husband's arms around her, his eyes smiling down into her own; of her arms tight around her beautiful child.

She woke with tears in her eyes to the rattle of the guards with the ration of rancid small beer and gritty bread. Alyce struggled through the crush of prisoners, pushing and elbowing as well as anyone, although each step was agony, her muscles bruised and stiff from yesterday's beating. Courtesy had no place in this pit of hell, not if she were to survive. She grabbed her stale crust through the bars from Reeves. He gave her a musing look, but there was no recognition in his face.

Alyce sat quiet in the corner, hoping her silence made her invisible in the darkness, noiselessly reciting the prayers etched in her mind.

'Out of the deep have I called unto thee, O Lord. Lord hear my voice...'

36

It was difficult to tell night from day, much less one day from the next. But soon enough the Assizes would begin. Thorpe had said a fortnight. Alyce was certain she had been here only three nights. Ten, eleven days at most—she could, she would survive.

'Alyce Granville,' Reeves shouted. 'Over here.' He set a torch in a bracket outside the cell and rattled his keys against the bars.

Alyce moved slowly, stiff with pain and the cold.

'Hurry up, woman.'

A group led by Thorpe stood at the other side of the bars— Sir William Sutton and Master Reynes and between them Isabel. She stood not three feet away in her clean gown of fine dark wool, her spotless ruff, her golden hair piled beneath a jaunty hat, her beautiful face wan.

Sir William spoke, his voice deep and resonant. 'What you see here is the true nature of the witch, filthy and disgusting as her very soul is.'

At the sight of Alyce, Isabel's eyes widened above the lace-trimmed handkerchief she held to her nose.

Sir William stepped closer to her, touching her elbow.

Screaming, Isabel collapsed, quivering and groaning, into Sir William's conveniently waiting arms.

Reynes sprang to the bars and shouted, 'Get back into your pit foul fiend.'

Alyce did not move. 'You are in his pay too?' Her voice dripped with disgust. 'I had hoped you, at least, were following your convictions no matter how misguided.' She walked back to her corner and sank onto the stinking straw.

Eva squatted beside her. 'Well. You are a witch.'

'I am not.' Alyce gritted her teeth.

'If the accuser comes before the witch and anything happens, it's proof she is a witch.'

'She was acting. Sir William was ready to catch her.' Alyce

drew a ragged breath and moaned, 'I have no hope.'

'None of us do.' Eva hugged her new cloak tight around her. 'The Assizes start in ten days. I had it from Davey Reeves last night as I warmed his lap.'

'Any idea who the judge will be?'

'Probably the same as last year. Makes no difference unless you have friends in high places.'

Thomas had said, before they were married, that by binding herself to him she would never be friendless. Like so much in her life, it was worthless—fine words that meant nothing. Nearly a month and he had not come. Alyce crossed her arms on her knees and lay her head down.

~

Isabel nursed a small beaker in her hands, staring around the gaoler's office.

'Drink up, girl. You have had a shock.' Sir William sounded more cheerful than concerned. He sat at the other side of the desk, his pen scratching furiously across a sheet of paper. 'Now we have the proof we need—the victim always faints in the presence of the witch.'

Isabel wanted to say, *But I did not faint, I only pretended like you told me to. Does that mean Alyce is not a witch?* She sipped the aqua vitae, grimaced, and placed it back on the desk.

The sight of Alyce, filthy and in rags in that stinking hole, had touched her in a way nothing else had these last few weeks. She had wanted Alyce punished but had not thought what that meant. A life for a life would not bring Willkyn back.

'Do you not think Alyce has been punished enough?'

'You have a kind heart, Daughter—you need to put that aside. Your sister is a dangerous woman. Do not forget she killed your son.'

Isabel sighed. 'I do not remember her cursing Willkyn. What she said sounded more like a prayer.'

'A few moments in her presence and she has befuddled you. On that dreadful day, you said she cursed Willkyn. Your memory was clear when I wrote down what you said.'

Isabel frowned. Other than the moment when she realised her poor boy was gone, her memories were unreal, dreamlike.

She vaguely remembered Sir William asking her questions, but she could not remember answering more than *yes* or *no*. Sir William's memory would be better.

'Besides Willkyn,' Sir William continued, 'she cursed you, and there are witnesses to that.'

'What did she say when she cursed me?'

'I will not repeat it—it will only pain you.'

Nothing would come near to the pain of her loss. And nothing would bring her baby boy back. She wanted to close her eyes and dream of him, not constantly dredge up the agony of the past with these examinations and statements and the ordeal that was to come in the court.

'Will says we should accept it as God's will, that Willkyn is in a better place.'

Sir William grunted, 'Will's mind is as addled with prayer as his mother's. It is not manly to have his nose stuck so much in the Bible.'

'But Will says he is a sinner.' She gazed at her father-in-law. 'He believes God is punishing us for his sins.'

'What do you mean?' Sir William snarled, his colour rising. 'It is disgraceful that you, his wife, would besmirch his name by accusing him of adultery. It is as great an infidelity as lying with a man not your husband.'

Isabel whimpered, tears spilling down her cheeks. Will had not said what his sin was. Why did Sir William assume it was adultery? And he used the same sharp words Dame Katharine had. She bent her head, her hand across her mouth, stifling her sobs.

Sir William came and sat by her, his anger gone. He gently pulled her hand away from her mouth and rubbed it between his. 'You have been confused by that witch's spells.' His voice was soft, comforting. 'You do not wish to think your own sister capable of such evil, but there are other charges, some going back to when she was a girl. Now dry your tears and drink the aqua vitae. And remember, I will keep you safe from the witch's influence.'

Isabel sniffed back her tears. Perhaps he was right. He had much more knowledge of the evil in this world.

~

'Alyce Granville,' Thorpe shouted.

Alyce got up slowly and shuffled towards the bars.

'My Alyce, you are honoured,' Eva's voice carried. 'If he wants something special, do not give it to him. He's got the pox.'

'Quiet!' Thorpe barked. 'Granville, you have a visitor.'

'A visitor?' Alyce stopped.

'Get moving.' Thorpe stood with a club, alert to trouble, as Reeves opened the door just enough for Alyce to slip through. Reeves manacled her as Thorpe locked the cell.

As they hurried Alyce through the darkness towards the stairs, Thorpe complained, 'A Dutch harpy has been raising hell. Even laying down the law to Sir Robert Southwell himself.'

Alyce's heart skipped a beat. Grietje de Jong. She had not been forgotten.

She walked between Thorpe and Reeves up to the hall and out through the great doors into the daylight. Alyce stopped in the portico, blinking hard, blinded by the brilliance of the sunshine. 'Where am I going?'

'Down to the house on Golden Ball Lane,' Thorpe grunted. 'The old woman has taken a room for you there. It's where we keep the better sort of prisoners.'

Alyce closed her eyes as hope swept through her.

She jolted to her senses as Reeves shoved her in the back. 'Move.'

She marched between the men down into the bailey and out along the causeway to a large house with barred windows on the lane opposite. The breeze caressed her skin; the warmth of the sun melted into her bones as they walked.

Alyce barely had time to notice the furnishings inside the house as Thorpe rushed her up the stairs, but the house felt warm and clean.

Halfway along the gallery, Thorpe jerked his head. 'In,' he grunted.

The room was filled with light, sun streaming onto the floor from a barred window. It was furnished with a narrow, curtained bed at one side, a table, two chairs, a close stool and a brazier in the corner.

The door slammed shut behind her.

Before she could stop blinking in the bright light, the comfortable arms of Grietje de Jong were around her, and Alyce was overwhelmed by her violet scent. She forced down a sob and tried to pull away. 'No, no. I am filthy.'

'It does not matter, *lieveling.*' Grietje held her at arm's length, her eyes wide with shock. 'But look at you. You are in rags. How can they have let this happen?'

Alyce kept her mouth shut, tears making tracks down her grimy face.

'Sit down, *Elsje.*' Grietje took a napkin from a basket from beside her chair and spread it on the table. 'You must be famished too.' She laid out chicken, bread and cheese, cake, a flask of beer. 'When I heard of this foolishness, I thought I would visit you, but I never expected this.' The colour in her cheeks was bright as she rushed on. 'I could not believe it when they said you were in a cell with common women.' She stopped and said, 'Eat, *Elsje*, eat.' She pushed a chicken leg into Alyce's hand and poured her a beaker of small beer.

Alyce looked down at her hands. They were filthy, her fingernails rimmed with dirt. Hunger had long overridden her fastidiousness. She fought the urge to cram the food into her mouth and nibbled on the chicken. She closed her eyes, savouring each mouthful.

'The High Sheriff, Sir Robert Southwell, I had to go to find him at his house. He was very angry when I told him. He believed you had a room of your own.'

Alyce swallowed her mouthful. 'I did, but my money ran out.'

'Why did you not ask your parents for more? Or me? You could have sent to me.'

'My parents have ignored my letters.' Alyce shrugged. She placed the chicken bone on the table and took a piece of cheese. 'I did not think to ask you.'

Grietje shook her head is if it were beyond understanding. 'And Sir Robert said you could not be bailed.' She breathed heavily through her nose. 'That Sir William Sutton, I could take a stick to him.' She stared at Alyce's blackened feet. 'No shoes. You have no shoes.' She rose from her chair and rushed towards the door. 'I will go now and get all you need—shoes, a gown, blankets.'

Alyce sprang up. 'No, wait.' This was too like a dream. If Grietje left, she would not come back. 'I want to talk a while. I have had no one…' Alyce swallowed a sob. 'How is Marieke? She must have had her baby by now.'

Grietje sat down heavily and groaned. 'My poor, poor girl. She had such a bad time. They came early, two of them, little boys—one far too small to live.' Her shoulders hunched. 'A wizened little man he was.' She blinked back her tears. 'The other is thriving, but we had to get a wet nurse for him.'

Alyce gulped. 'And Marieke?'

'My girl, she bled and bled. I feared she would die.' Tears rolled down Grietje's cheeks. Alyce ached to put her arms around her and comfort her but was aware of her filthy state. The stink of the dungeons wafted up with every movement she made.

'But my *lieveling* will survive.' Grietje sniffed back her tears. 'She improves every day.'

Alyce exhaled; she had been holding her breath as Grietje spoke. 'I am glad of that. Make sure you give her my love.'

'I will.' She stood again. 'Now I will bring all the things you need.'

'I am…' Tears caught in Alyce's throat. 'I am grateful to you, Mistress. I—'

'I would do the same for any of my children. You are mine now, *Elsje*.' Her tone allowed no contradiction. 'Your parents have cast you off, so you are mine.'

'They are not the only ones,' Alyce said bitterly. 'Thomas has deserted me too.'

'That I do not believe. There is a reason he is not here. He is a good man, and I know he loves you.'

'You cannot know that.'

She raised her eyebrows at Alyce. 'I am expert in matters of the heart. Now, child, do not contradict your mother.'

Alyce's heart thumped. Perhaps Grietje was right. She looked up at the clear sky through the window. 'Whether he comes or not, it is too late. The verdict was decided weeks ago.'

'No, your English justice is better than any—far, far better than what passes for justice now in my old country.'

~

Grietje bustled back about an hour later accompanied by her maid, Katrien, both laden with bundles containing fresh linen, a gown and smock and kirtle, stockings and a pair of shoes, blankets and sheets, even a Psalter. They were followed by guards lugging a heavy tub. Once they had dumped the tub on the floor, Grietje turned and said, 'Bring warm water. Eight, no—ten buckets at least.'

'Ay, m'lady.' One managed to combine a sneer, an ostentatious bow and a leer into a single movement.

After filling the tub, the guards left, banging the door behind them.

''Tis not much of a bath,' Katrien said in her heavily accented English.

'It is better than anything I have seen in weeks.'

'We'll leave your old clothing over by the door,' Grietje said as she poured scented oil into the bath. 'The guards can have them as a gift.'

'They should be burnt but no doubt they will sell them.' Alyce untied the cord from around her neck and held her wedding ring a moment before slipping it on. It still meant much to her.

She stripped off her verminous smock and stepped into the tub. It was only half full and the water was tepid, but it was clean.

Grietje stared at her. 'You are thin.'

'A diet of grey bread and stale beer is to be recommended if you want to achieve a fashionable slenderness,' Alyce said dryly.

'Nee. Women's bodies should be well-rounded,' Grietje said. 'I will feed you up.'

Katrien poured water over Alyce, scrubbed her back and soaped her hair, massaging her scalp vigorously. Alyce pressed her hand against the edge of the tub, feeling the wood beneath the linen lining, her fingers played in the water. This was not a dream. Smiling, she closed her eyes.

Washed and dressed in a clean smock, Alyce sat as Katrien tried to comb her hair. Patches were matted with tangled knots.

Grietje frowned. 'We must cut it.' She rested a hand on Alyce's forearm. 'It will grow back and meantime you can wear a coif.'

'Thomas hates coifs.'

'Tell him to buy you a wig.'

The lengths of hair fluttered to the ground. Although Alyce had rarely displayed it, her hair had been a source of pride. She was losing more and more of what she thought of as herself. By the time the final day came, she would have little left to connect her to this life. Perhaps it would be easy to go.

~

Alyce knelt by the bed in the darkness, her arms stretched across the mattress and her cheek resting on it, her mind empty of thought. The burdens of the last two and a half years weighed on her—fears of invasion, of Thomas's death at sea, the terror of Clifton's attack, her guilt at his killing, the accusations of witchcraft and murder, imprisonment, the living hell of the dungeon cell. She climbed onto the bed and curled into a ball, anguish slowly building in her. It burst into racking sobs as Alyce howled out her sorrows, her aching loneliness, her abandonment. And beneath it all, the greatest burden—hope, no matter how battered, that would not die.

37

Late July 1589

Thomas dismounted in the inn yard just on dusk and tossed the reins to the ostler. He strode into the taproom, Watkins and the rest of his party not far behind him. While Watkins organised their lodging for the night, Thomas looked around the room for an empty table.

'Tom. Over here.' Sir Philip Rossiter beckoned to him.

Sir Philip and his men moved along as Thomas's party sat down. Greetings were exchanged, food and drink ordered.

'Are you going or coming?' Sir Philip pushed a well-cleaned platter away and filled Thomas's mug from a jug of ale on the table.

'Returning home.' A trencher piled with a generous helping of rabbit stewed with bacon was placed before Thomas, and he began to eat.

'Fine fare here,' Sir Philip said. 'Almost as good as you get at home.'

Thomas swallowed before answering. 'Not quite that good.' He savoured another mouthful. 'I hoped to make it home tonight, but there are not enough hours in the day.' He felt the same urgency to be home he had last October. He was not a superstitious man. It had nothing to do with fear or portents. He wanted to be with Alyce, to set their problems right, to recapture what had been growing between them last January despite the looming war. He thought of her as he had seen her last, the longing in her eyes, the hunger of her kiss.

Sir Philip grinned. 'Still the impatient bridegroom?'

Thomas blinked. It was like the first time he had been in love—that disconcerting and delicious mixture of anxiety and exultation.

'I have been away far too often for the newness to wear off,' he said, sheepish, and picked up his mug. 'You are on your way home too?'

'Ay, I have been arranging a position for young Geoffrey in

Sir Christopher Hatton's household.'

Thomas raised an eyebrow. 'That will keep him busy.'

'It will relieve him of time for idle pursuits.' Sir Philip placed his mug down and sat back. 'Responsibility will be the making of Geoffrey.'

'I think his problem was poor company.' He did not meet Sir Philip's eyes. 'Lady Rossiter is happy with the arrangement?'

'It was she who suggested Sir Christopher. They are related somehow—Margaret is related to half the nobility.' He reached over and refilled his mug. 'She is off at the moment in Leicester, has been gone nearly as long as I have. She went for the lying-in of her niece and stayed on. Women love these celebrations.' He took a long draught of ale and smacked his lips. 'How did your business fare?'

'Very well indeed. I have acquired a coal lease in Wales and another manor, in Hertfordshire. Best not have the future tied to a single venture.'

Sir Philip nodded agreement.

As night fell, their conversation drifted to politics at home and abroad and the disappointing news of the failure of Sir Francis Drake and Sir John Norris's recent venture against Spain.

'You did not think to join their English armada?'

'Nay, I doubted the wisdom of it, and besides, I had more pressing matters here on land.'

Sir Philip drained his mug and said, as an afterthought, 'How did Alyce get on with that problem in Norwich?'

Thomas's heart thudded. 'What problem?'

'You have not heard?' Sir Philip frowned. 'Your man Stokes caught up with me in London to see if I knew where you were. There were messages for you flying everywhere a couple of weeks back.'

'None reached me.' Every fibre was alert as if he were facing the enemy in battle. 'What was it?'

'Nonsense of some sort concerning witchcraft. A baby died. No one of any sense would think such a thing of a woman of Alyce's position. Preposterous.'

Thomas lurched up and yelled along the table, 'Watkins. We

are leaving.'

Watkins remained where he was, not understanding.

'Now,' Thomas roared.

Feet and settles scraped as Thomas's grooms rose from their seats.

Sir Philip frowned. 'It is dark, Tom. Wait until morning. I am sure it came to nothing.'

Thomas's face had drained of colour, his mouth was dry. He could hardly get the words out. 'I pray you are right.'

~

Thomas rode so hard his men had difficulty keeping up. He had never felt fear so near the surface, even when surrounded by Spanish soldiers.

He thundered into Ashthorpe in the small hours. Bart, rubbing sleep from his eyes, wandered out, and had barely caught the reins before Thomas dismounted and was across the courtyard and into the house. Watkins and the grooms were nowhere in sight.

Thomas burst through the door calling, 'Alyce. Alyce!'

Marian Haines appeared at the top of the stairs, wraith-like in her pale bed-smock.

'Where is Alyce?'

'Oh Master.' Her voice caught. 'We did not know what to do.'

'Out with it, woman.'

'They took the Mistress to Norwich.' She burst into tears. 'Said she killed her sister's baby.'

He took the stairs two at a time, pushed past Marian as if she no longer existed and slammed into Cecily's room.

Cecily lay propped against the pillows. A candle flickered on the cabinet by the bedside but it barely lessened the darkness of the room. Shadows lay against Cecily's cheeks, in the hollows around her eyes. Her hands, resting on the bedcover, were gnarled and swollen. With effort, she raised her arms to Thomas, but he stood, unmoved, at the end of the bed.

'What has happened?'

'Tom, sit down,' she pleaded. 'You look fit to collapse.'

He remained standing, his knuckles white as he gripped a

bedpost, glowering. 'Tell me what has happened.'

'I believe Alyce has been charged with killing her sister's child by witchcraft. I suspect the trial will be soon.'

'You believe? You suspect?' he shouted. Had she not made the effort to find out? 'Why do you not know?'

Cecily jerked, fright in her eyes.

Judith, who slept by her, started to rise from the bed, but Cecily motioned her to stay.

'I have been ill with a lingering fever.' Her voice trembled. 'I wrote to her parents as soon as I heard. They have not replied but I am sure they are seeing to her immediate needs.'

'I would not count on it.' They were a family that had never put Alyce first.

'Did Stokes catch up with you? As soon as we heard, I sent him to find you.'

Thomas shook his head.

'You keep your own counsel too much—we had no idea where you were.' She swallowed, fighting back a sob. 'I sent Haines to Norwich over three weeks ago to see how he could help Alyce. He has not come back nor has he sent word.' She shut her eyes as if exhausted by the effort of speaking.

'I must go to Norwich.' He should have gone there first, but Ashthorpe was far closer and he had stupidly hoped Sir Philip was right and it had blown over.

'You need to sleep, otherwise you will never get there.'

'When are the Assizes held?' He stared at the ceiling. The darkness deepened as the candlelight flickered. 'July? Early August? I have to leave.' He rubbed the heel of his hand against his forehead, raked his fingers across his head and around his neck. 'Today you are to send someone along the road to Norwich to find Haines. They are to stop at every inn, every farmhouse, every hovel on the way. Sutton is behind this.' Alyce needed him. And, once again, he had left her to face danger on her own. 'If Alyce is dead, I will kill him.'

'Tom!' Cecily called after him, but Thomas strode away, the door crashing shut behind him.

~

Isabel stood with her maid among the crowd as the Assize

judges, William Peryam and Sir Christopher Wray, rode in procession to Norwich Cathedral where the Assize sermon was to be preached. They were escorted by the dignitaries of both the city and the county: the High Sheriff Sir Robert Southwell, the under-sheriffs, the bailiffs, as well as knights, esquires and gentlemen, pikemen and the livery men of the guilds. The procession glowed with opulent display, scarlet and purple cloth, furs and jewels and was accompanied by the music of the town waits.

Sir William had told Isabel that the Assize sermon would remind the judges of their duty to uphold God's laws in order to keep his people free from the taint of evil influence. There would be an especial reference to his exhortation that a witch should not be suffered to live.

Isabel had asked how he knew and he had said, the hint of a smile on his lips, that he had undertaken to bear the cost of repairing the choir loft in the parish church of the minister appointed to give the Assize sermon this year. Sir William's smile had given Isabel no comfort, nor had his assurance that the will of the Lord would prevail at these Assizes. All she wanted was her baby boy.

~

The sun was low in the sky when Thomas was led by a liveried serving man into Sir Robert Southwell's hall. The muted sound of conversation carried down the staircase from the dining chamber above. Sir Robert stood at the head of the stairs with a tall white-haired man dressed in the scarlet fur-trimmed robes of an Assize judge. Thomas swept off his hat and bowed deeply, aware too late that his dusty, stained clothing did not give the best impression.

'Thomas, just in time,' Sir Robert called as he and the judge descended the stairs. 'I wondered what had become of you.'

'I only heard two nights ago.' Relief washed through him. Alyce was alive.

Sir Robert turned to his companion. 'Sir Christopher, this is Thomas Granville, husband to one of the women charged with witchcraft.'

'One of the women?' Thomas raised an eyebrow. 'Who else

has Sutton snared?'

'We have two cases of witchcraft, but your wife's is the most serious. Sir Christopher Wray is the Lord Chief Justice who will hear the case.'

'This is absurd.' Thomas looked from one to the other. 'How can a case so obviously based on malice get this far?'

'A child died,' Sir Robert replied.

Sir Christopher stood silent, his bland face unreadable, watching Thomas.

'Children die every day across the country and charges of witchcraft are not laid,' Thomas scoffed.

'In some cases, they are.'

Thomas crossed his arms and glowered. 'You cannot have enough evidence—this is the word of one person against another.'

'The grand jury will consider her case, and if it is as you say, your wife will not stand trial but will be set free.'

'Not if Sutton has paid them to find his way.'

'Have a care,' Sir Robert warned. 'The jury is made up of respectable gentlemen and merchants, men not easily open to influence. You cannot make such claims without evidence.'

'The evidence is there, no doubt, but will the court have enough care for truth and justice to search for it?'

He saw affront in the judge's dark intelligent eyes and cursed his tiredness. He should have had the wit to try to gain Sir Christopher's goodwill.

'I am aware of my duties, Master Granville,' Sir Christopher said icily. He inclined his head towards Sir Robert. 'If you will excuse me.'

After Sir Christopher had returned up the stairs, Sir Robert shook his head. 'That was not wise. Sir Christopher is a thorough and well-respected judge—one of the highest in the country. He will examine both sides, but you should not antagonise him.'

'How has it come to this?'

'It is a long and sorry story.' He ushered Thomas into the small private parlour beside the hall. 'Sir William made a most persuasive case.' He went to the sideboard and poured two goblets of wine. 'There are other witnesses to this and other incidents, and your wife does herself no credit.' Incredulity was written on his face as he passed Thomas the goblet and gestured for him to sit. 'She jousts verbally with Master Reynes, the minister. Quotes scripture back at him. She has a sharp tongue.'

Thomas placed the goblet on the table beside him, relieved to hear that Alyce was not cowed.

'It may be her ungoverned tongue has brought her to this point.'

'She has the right to defend herself,' he snarled. 'Can she be bailed?'

'At this late stage?' Sir Robert raised his eyebrows. 'What plan are you hatching? Do you have horses ready to flee to the coast where your ship is waiting?'

Thomas blinked. He had not thought so far ahead and doubted he had time to organise it. 'You doubt my word if Alyce were released into my custody?'

'No.' Sir Robert paused as if he needed to think how to proceed. 'I do not doubt your honour, but if you were forced to choose between keeping your word to me and saving your wife, which would it be?'

Thomas glared at him.

'There is more I need to tell you.' Sir Robert leant forward, his hands spread wide on his knees. 'I am afraid your wife spent some time in the dungeon cells.'

'What?' Thomas exploded, lurching up from his chair.

'Only a day or so. She is suitably accommodated now.'

'Why?' He paced the room, his hands clenched. If he could get his hands around Sutton's pudgy neck...

Sir Robert ignored Thomas's anger. 'When a prisoner has no funds to pay for a private room, he or she is consigned to the dungeon cells,' he said evenly. 'I had no idea. If I had been told, I would have borne the cost of her lodging myself.'

Thomas kept his mouth tight shut, struggling to contain his rage.

'As soon as her Stranger friend brought it to my attention, your wife was moved.' He leant back in his chair. 'Sit down, Tom, and drink your wine. Your wife is comfortably lodged in a chamber of her own at the house we use for the better prisoners. She lacks for nothing but her freedom.'

Thomas took the seat opposite Sir Robert. 'Can I go to her now? Lodge with her until the trial?'

'Nay, it is too late in the day for that. And you cannot stay— Reynes, the curate from St Peter Mancroft, wants to examine her again. He hopes to bring her to a full confession.'

'She cannot confess to something she did not do,' Thomas said through gritted teeth.

Sir Robert raised his hands. 'Reynes persists because she has held fast against him. He has a burning desire to save her soul.'

'Her soul is saved. He would do better seeking to save perjurers and varlets such as Sutton who use their position to seek the death of innocents.'

'Thomas,' Sir Robert warned. 'You tread close to slander.'

Thomas sucked in a breath. Did Southwell believe in Sutton's honesty? Did he truly think Alyce deserved to stand trial? He stretched out his fingers, flattening his hands against his thighs. It would do no one good if he were to flatten the High Sheriff's elegant nose.

'You have been fortunate. The judges were delayed on their way here, so the trials will not begin until tomorrow afternoon. Given Alyce's position in the gaol calendar, her case may not be heard until Thursday morning. You may go to her tomorrow morning and stay until Reynes arrives.

'Sutton claimed there were other deaths along the route she had taken out of Norwich but nothing came of it. She will only stand trial for the death of the Sutton children and for spells and curses uttered against Robert Chapman. Sir Christopher is aware of all that has happened. He will see justice is done.'

'Can you guarantee that? Justice has not been done thus far.' Thomas picked up the goblet and drained it. 'Sutton tried this before, with more evidence than he has now—claimed I was a pirate. But I was never imprisoned. I was never tried. His claims were treated with the derision they deserved.' He stood up. 'I have lost faith in justice. All that is left is faith in God. Alyce has great faith in God,' he said bitterly. 'I hope he does not desert her as everyone else has.'

38

Alyce woke early and sat in the grey light of her chamber trying to pray for the strength to face what lay ahead. She knew her position was hopeless. Other than Grietje de Jong, no one had offered the slightest assistance. Her parents she could accept—they had never placed her interests first. But Cecily? And Thomas? She had believed they cared for her. And despite it all, hope still flickered. There had been a brief moment on dusk last night when it had soared. There had been a commotion in the street, shouting and the sounds of a struggle. She thought she had heard Watkins's voice. But she was mistaken.

No one could help her now.

She looked up with the scraping of the door.

It thudded shut and Thomas stood there, his eyes on her.

'Alyce,' he rasped.

'Thomas.' His name caught in her throat as she rose from her seat.

She took two steps towards him, aching for the comfort of his arms, but stopped. Anger surged through her. 'Where have you been?' She wrapped her arms tight against her bosom. 'Why have you left me here?' She pressed her lips tight against a shuddering sob.

Thomas moved towards her, but she held up her hands and stepped back. 'No.'

'I did not know.' His voice creaked. 'I heard less than three days ago.'

'But no one sent help, not even Cecily.'

For the first time she could read his face—anguish, pain and longing were written there.

'She has been ill but she sent Stokes to find me, and Haines was sent here to help you. Both have disappeared.'

'Why are you never at my side when I need you?' She knew she was unfair, that he had no way of knowing that Clifton would attack her or that Isabel's child would die, but she was tired of fighting alone.

His shoulders sagged. It was as if she had punched the breath from him.

'Forgive me, Alyce.'

She saw the glistening sheen of his eyes and recognised that the thought of her loss tore at him.

She had no memory of moving but she was across the room, Thomas's arms tight around her. She closed her eyes, welcoming the familiar scent of him, the brush of his beard against her skin, the touch of his warm lips on hers. All conscious thought swept away. Nothing else existed, not the past, not the future, only the two of them, equal in their longing and hunger.

~

Alyce lay alongside Thomas, tracing his face, his neck, his chest through his unlaced shirt. She could not have enough of touching him. She pressed her nose against his chest and breathed in deeply. No matter where they were, this was home.

Thomas laughed lightly, his breath still uneven. 'I did not expect such a welcome.' He placed his hand against her cheek.

She pulled his hand down to her mouth and kissed the palm. As she drew it away, she noticed on his little finger a ring set with rubies. Her heart twisted as she imagined the woman who had given it to him.

'You like the ring?'

She could not look into his face, could not keep the pain from her voice. 'It is beautiful.'

'It is yours.' She met his eyes. 'I had it made for you in London.' He pulled the ring from his finger and passed it to her. 'It is engraved.'

She ran a finger around the inside of the ring, rubbing the fine engraving as Thomas said, *'Her price is far above rubies. The heart of her husband doth safely trust in her.'*

Alyce fought back a sob as he took the ring and slid it down her finger.

'I love you, Alyce.'

Love? The word she had never believed he would say to her.

'I love you,' he repeated, 'more than life itself.'

Alyce stared at him, her lips parted, hardly daring to breathe.

'Since the day we married, there has been no one but you. When we married, I expected I would behave as many men do and be faithful when my wife was present but hold the vows less tightly in the months I was away. But when temptation finally offered itself, it was a tawdry thing beside what I have with you. And I pride myself at being a man of my word. Why, then, would the word I have given to you, who have put me before all else and suffered because of me, be of less value than the word I give to lesser men? I repeat my vow to you, Alyce.' He looked deep into her eyes. 'I will love you, comfort you, honour and keep you, in sickness and in health, forsaking all other, keep only to you, as long as I live.'

Alyce took a slow, deep breath and, looking up into his grey eyes, said the words she had held back for so long. 'Thomas, I love you, body and soul. All the days of my life.'

Thomas clasped her tight against him, and she buried her face against his neck. They lay together in silence, aware only of the beat of the other's heart.

His fingers ruffled through her shorn hair and brushed over her face, around her neck, across the shadows of bruises. 'Who hurt you?'

She looked away. 'It happened in the dungeon cell.'

'I do not understand how your parents stood by and allowed this to happen.'

'It is a question only they can answer.' Alyce shrugged. 'I no longer care.

'Sutton is behind it all. And,' he groaned, 'once again you have been caught between me and an enemy. I am sorry beyond words. I would give you up if it could keep you safe but I do not have the strength to let you go.'

'Thomas, Thomas.' She moved closer and kissed him. 'Never ever think that. Even without you, I could still be here facing trial. Had I not married you, Will Sutton would still be a lying adulterer, Isabel would still be a jealous woman who believes that no ill can befall her other than by malice or design, Sutton would still be a varlet mourning more the loss of his dreams of the House of Sutton than his grandson. To him it is simply an unexpected gift that he can harm you through me. And even if this is the price of being with you, I will pay it gladly. The joy you have given me far outweighs any pain.'

Thomas closed his eyes and brushed his lips against hers.

Alyce gave herself up to his touch as his kiss stretched on.

Heavy footsteps sounded in the gallery outside, moving back and forth. A door slammed farther along.

Thomas murmured, 'I think our time is almost up.'

Alyce smiled at him. 'Then we must finish this after I am set free.' She spoke more in hope than belief.

She rose from the bed and pulled her bodice up, tightening its lacings.

'I despaired of help ever coming.' She gathered her kirtle from the floor.

'Now we are here, we will do our utmost.' He stood beside the bed fastening his shirt. 'Sir Robert refused to let me lodge with you. He would not even let me come last night. Watkins tried to see you while I was arguing with Sir Robert and got a black eye for his trouble.'

'I heard his voice but thought it was my mind playing tricks.'

'You should see him—with his eye and the beard he has grown, he looks quite the brigand.'

'No matter how he looks, he is one of the best of men.'

'That he is. He has been by my side since he was little more than a lad. I could not have a better man.'

For all the hope Thomas had brought to her, Alyce still had to survive the trial. 'Do you know if I am to be tried today?'

'Sir Robert said either late today or early tomorrow. The grand jury will examine the witnesses first to see if there is a case to answer. If there is any justice, they will find your case *ignoramus*, and you will be set free immediately. If they find otherwise you will stand trial straight after.

'Watkins took himself to a couple of taverns after coming here last night. As many tavern-goers believe in your innocence as stupidly believe you to be a witch. But a number think there is not enough to judge either way. If the jury reflects this, all should be well.' Thomas frowned as he pulled on his doublet. 'I must ask you this—Robert Chapman's claims—the curses, what you would do if he married you, did you say them?'

'I cannot remember the words I used, but I know I did not use the word *curse*. I said I would poison him—I wanted to frighten him away.' She crossed her arms tight and shuddered. 'Death would be preferable to marriage to Robert Chapman.'

'If he appears sincere, his evidence may carry weight.'

Terror flared through her as she imagined the weight of the rope around her neck. 'If I am found guilty, will I be hanged straightaway?'

'It will not come to that. You have my word. I have already asked Sir Robert to seek a pardon if you are found guilty. And I will grease as many hands with gold as is needed to see you get it.'

Keys clattered outside the door as the guard was overcome by a coughing fit.

'The guard is warning us to make ourselves decent.' Thomas pulled her to him, less gentle now, and kissed her again.

To have him near, to breathe in the scent of him, to be held within his strong arms was to be safe at last. But Alyce knew that safety to be an illusion.

They turned together as the door swung open.

The guard slowly poked his head around the door. 'Sir, it's time for you to leave. Master Reynes is here to examine Mistress Granville.'

'I promise…' Thomas said.

Alyce put her fingers to his lips. 'Do not make promises. We will have faith.' She twisted the ring from her finger and gave it back to him. 'Mind this for me. When it is no longer mine, then it is Elinor's. Tell her that her mother wore it and, after Elinor herself, it was the most precious gift she ever received.'

Tears gleamed in Thomas's eyes. To wipe out the sight, she pulled his head down and kissed him with the passion she had contained over the past years, the passion she could hope to give him in the future.

Reynes stepped past the guard, his eyes flickering over the rumpled bed. He stood silent beside the guard, staring up towards the window.

Ignoring them, Thomas looked down at Alyce and said again, 'I love you, Alyce.' He squeezed her hand and walked past

Reynes without acknowledging him. The guard followed him out.

Alyce stared after Thomas, both heartened and despairing.

'Mistress Granville,' Reynes said.

Alyce blinked away her tears. 'Master Reynes, good morrow.'

Reynes walked to the table. 'I see your husband has finally arrived.' He dumped his satchel down. 'Do not think this means you will escape justice.'

'I have no fear of justice. It is its perversion that I fear.'

Reynes dragged the chairs together, one facing the other. 'Sit.'

He followed the well-worn path of questioning. Alyce had answered these questions many times, asked in so many ways.

'You mouth the words of faith.' His scorn was palpable.

'More than that, sir, I have faith in God.'

'Rehearse the articles of your belief.'

Alyce laughed. 'You would hear my catechism?'

'This is no laughing matter. The wicked cannot answer without stumbling.'

'*I believe in God the Father Almighty...*' Alyce repeated the Creed to its end.

'How many commandments are there?' Reynes continued.

'Ten.'

'Name them.'

'*The same which God spake in the twentieth chapter of Exodus, saying, I am the Lord thy God which have brought thee out of the land of Egypt, out of the house of bondage.*' Alyce leant towards him. 'And, Master Reynes, I dwell in Egypt, in a house of bondage, and I believe the Lord will deliver me by the means he sees fit. I will accept that, whatever it may be.'

Reynes scowled. 'Have a care, or you will have blasphemy added to your charges.'

'How is it blasphemy? When I say, *Out of the deep have I called unto thee, O Lord*, I am not blaspheming. I am praying for God to deliver me. When I say I dwell in a house of bondage, I am drawing strength from the example of the Bible.'

'I see you avoid reciting the commandments.'

'I do not. One. *Thou shalt have none other gods but me.* Two...'

Alyce recited the commandments clearly, without stopping to rake her memory.

'Very prettily said but how many have you failed?'

'I have never deliberately chosen to do wrong but, like most people, at times it is difficult to keep my tongue and my heart in check.'

'You admit to malice towards your sister?'

'No, no.' She could only guess at the depths of Isabel's suffering. 'I know my sister's actions come from a deep sorrow. I pray for her. I pray for myself. I do not want hate to steal my peace of mind.'

'You recite your catechism well,' he said. 'When and where were you confirmed?'

'Here, at St Peter Mancroft when I was fourteen.'

'You have employed some craft to remember the responses after this time.'

'Last year, I helped prepare children at Ashthorpe for their confirmation. And I pray daily and try to live by the commandments.'

'Yet you have a reputation for an evil tongue?'

'I know I speak sharply at times and, on occasions, I lack charity, but I eschew backbiting.'

'You have steadfastly claimed your innocence.' His belligerence fell away. 'If you are found guilty, what will you do?'

Alyce closed her eyes and bit her lower lip. She recognised how much she had been granted, how near she was to losing it all. She opened her eyes, her gaze unwavering. 'I will pray for the strength to face my end with dignity.'

'And those who have brought you to this?'

'I will pray for them all. It is no light thing to bring about the death of an innocent person, and in the secret places of their hearts they know I am innocent.'

Reynes frowned and blinked slowly. Her answer seemed to trouble him.

'You surprise me, Mistress.'

'What good will raging against my fate do? It will change nothing, and I must meet my Maker with a clean heart.'

Reynes jumped up and grabbed his satchel. As he banged on

the door, Alyce called to him. 'Master Reynes, will you be with me at the end?'

'It is my duty.'

'Pray loudly then. I would die with the words of God in my ears.'

39

Thomas stood outside the door to the Guildhall. Around him, dark-robed lawyers and clerks, witnesses, and men and women seeking an afternoon's entertainment came and went. Others stood patient at the stalls set up at the east end of the Guildhall where scribes copied legal documents for them.

He had been waiting over two hours, since the first blast of the trumpet signalling the beginning of the Assize trials. He kept his eyes on the corner of the market square from where he expected Alyce to come on her way from the castle's house. He thought of her, pale in that locked room, bruised, her beautiful hair cropped, and great waves of rage crashed through him. He clenched his jaw. He must keep himself in control. He would be of no use to Alyce imprisoned for lashing out at a servant of the court or a lying witness.

He turned at the sound of the elder Sutton woman's shrill voice.

She stood in the Guildhall doorway, berating someone within the building.

'You would think, young man, that this case would be dealt with first rather than having people of our standing wait around half the day and then be told to come back tomorrow.'

She sailed down the steps and out into the market, Isabel Sutton beside her, misery plain on her face.

Thomas pushed past others leaving the Guildhall into the dim entrance, almost colliding with the journeyman Chapman. Chapman glared up at him, but Thomas, fists clenched, shoved past him. The man was beneath contempt.

A clerk, a sheaf of papers in his hand, was at the turn of the staircase.

'Master Clerk,' Thomas called to him. 'The Granville case, when will it be heard?'

The man stopped and looked down at Thomas. 'Not until tomorrow morning—we have a long list this Assizes. Are you a witness?'

'Ay,' Thomas answered, 'a witness to malice, slander and misuse of power.'

The clerk blinked, surprised.

Thomas strode away and out into the market. Watkins fell in step beside him.

'Alyce will not be tried until tomorrow. See if Reynolds is willing to let us use his yard for half a day more.'

'I am sure he will be—anything can be bought in this town.' They wound their way through the marketplace. 'Times must be hard for grocers here when one is willing to rent out his yard for an afternoon or two.'

Thomas gave a dry laugh. 'I suspect it's more he would rather do Sutton an ill turn.'

'I'll do him an ill turn for free. And as for Chapman, I have an idea how we can deal with him. It is better if you do not know what I am planning.'

'Best not to kill him or beat him senseless—the finger would point straight at us.'

'Do not worry, Master, my plan is far more subtle.' Watkins's hand slipped to his sword as an apprentice stumbled into him. 'Drunken fool,' he muttered and kept walking. 'Haines has turned up—tossed from his horse near Thetford. Lay overnight on the road with a broken leg. He was wandering in his mind with fever for many days. The farmer who took him in had no idea who he was. And a number of men from Ashthorpe rode in early this afternoon. Took it on themselves to follow us in case we need to storm the castle, Collins the blacksmith among them. I doubt he has used a sword in his life but give him a halberd and there will be not a man left standing.'

Thomas threw his head back and laughed. 'I have no plans to storm the castle, but we may yet have need of them all.' He glanced around, aware he was being watched, and lowered his voice. 'My worst fear is if the verdict does not go Sutton's way, he may stir up trouble.'

'I should go now and slit his throat.'

'Not yet. It may come to that, but not yet. Besides, I reserve the pleasure for myself.'

They moved off towards the castle, Thomas hoping to bribe or browbeat his way back in to see Alyce again.

~

Isabel was waiting for an answer. 'What do you think?'

Her mother sewed three tiny stitches on the seam she was finishing and snipped off the thread. 'I am not sure Isabel,' she said quietly.

'That child has no hope unless she is brought up in a godly household.' Her eyelashes glistened. 'If only Alyce had been satisfied with her life. She was ever a discontented shrew.'

Mother concentrated on folding the unfinished smock and did not meet Isabel's eyes. 'Do you not feel some sorrow for her?'

'Why would I feel sorrow for her?' Isabel glared at her. 'She killed my babies.' She had nearly weakened seeing Alyce, grimy and ragged, in that foul dungeon. But Dame Katharine had said it was the devil playing on her kind heart to tempt her to let a sinner escape just punishment. If she could be strong and recite, one last time, all that had happened, God would reward her, perhaps with another child. But Isabel did not want another child, she wanted Willkyn.

'I find it hard to believe that Alyce would do such a thing.' Mother placed the smock in the sewing basket on the floor beside her. 'I saw no malice in her.'

Isabel sniffed back tears. 'Is that why you did not come to the Guildhall today as you were supposed to?'

'My head pained so much I could not get out of bed. It has eased a little now.'

'The court will not accept that excuse tomorrow. I am certain the grand jury will find that there is enough evidence for Alyce to face trial.'

Mother groaned.

'If you are so convinced of her innocence, why have you not visited her?'

'I cannot.' Mother closed her eyes and rubbed hard at her forehead. 'Sir William threatened your father. He says he has proof he trafficked with pirates—sold goods that were the product of piracy against English ships. Your father has never done such a thing but if Sir William pays witnesses to lie, your father could lose not only his property but his life.'

'Why would Sir William do that?'

'He hates Granville and will do anything to harm him. Alyce, all of us, are caught between them.'

'But Sir William is an honest man.'

Mother gave a mirthless laugh.

'He would not hold the high positions he does if he were not.' Isabel glared at her. 'And Alyce is where she is because she killed my boy.' She stared past her mother to the pear tree in the garden. Willkyn's life had been as short and delicate as the blossoms that had covered the tree not much more than three months ago when her boy was still alive. She closed her eyes. Even now she could smell his creamy skin.

Her mother rose and put her arms around Isabel, who rested her head against hers.

'Can you imagine what this child's life will be?' Isabel stepped back from her. 'Thomas Granville will not care for her. She will be a constant reminder of Alyce's wickedness. When he marries again, his new wife will have no love for her, especially once she has her own children.'

'No man willingly gives up his children.'

'A son would matter, but not a daughter. Elinor is our blood. We are the best to care for her.' She grasped her mother's hand. 'We should go and see him now.'

Her mother froze. 'Thomas Granville is here?'

'He arrived late yesterday. Will you come with me?'

'I... I... It is not...' she stammered.

'Have you no care for your granddaughter's future?' Isabel dropped her hand and jerked away. 'Do you not see? This has been ordained by God—no child of mine has lived and here is a motherless child. Dame Katharine said it would be the only good to come from Alyce's sin. She said to bring the child of a witch to live a godly life is a holy task. A soul saved.'

'You need to give more thought to this.'

'If you do not come with me, I will go alone.' Isabel raised her chin. 'And I will go with the knowledge of where your true loyalties lie.'

Mother's shoulders sagged. 'Where is he staying?'

'At the Maid's Head. He expected to stay with Sir Robert Southwell, the High Sheriff, they being such old friends, but I heard he turned him away last night,' Isabel said, smug. 'It is pleasing to know so many are eager to see justice done.'

'If you must go,' Mother sighed, 'I will come.'

~

The Maid's Head was the inn favoured by the better sort of traveller. A modestly dressed maidservant in a spotless apron and coif led Isabel, her mother and Julia up the stairs to the rooms Thomas Granville had taken.

His man opened the door in answer to Isabel's sharp raps. She could tell he recognised her, but he blocked the doorway, forcing Isabel to stand in the gallery while she explained they had come to speak with his Master. With a surly reluctance, he let them pass into the parlour. He disappeared through the door at the other end of the room without speaking a single word to them. The man was clearly a ruffian with his untrimmed beard and his black eye. No real gentleman would have such a servant.

Julia sat by the door. Mother seated herself at the window and gazed out into the street.

Voices rumbled behind the door, then silence.

Isabel walked over and stood with her head cocked.

'Isabel, come away,' Mother hissed. 'They will catch you eavesdropping.'

'I do not care.' Isabel tossed her head. 'He is every bit as bad as she is. And that servant—if any of mine were as ill-mannered to my guests, I would have him whipped and thrown into the gutter.'

'I doubt Master Granville will regard us as guests.'

Isabel arranged her skirts around her as she sat.

The minutes stretched out. 'What is he doing that we must wait so long?' she said tapping her foot rapidly.

'Perhaps he will not see us.' Mother looked hopeful.

'Nay, that churlish servant would have quickly shown us the door.' Isabel turned to her and said with something of her old spirit, 'He probably has a strumpet with him.'

Mother gaped at her as if she were mad. 'His servant is

present.'

'You do not think he is capable of such debauchery? No doubt Alyce...'

'Isabel,' Mother warned.

Granville stood at the doorway. His dress was severe but expensive—black brocade, his ruff and cuffs edged with pure white lace, his doublet fastened with a row of silver buttons.

Both women rose, but he nodded to them to sit. Silent, stony-faced, he stood in front of them.

It would be better coming from Mother. 'Master Granville,' Isabel said, 'my mother wishes to offer you our help in this sad time.'

'Isabel, no.' Mother stuttered, 'I... I...' She sat upright and drew a shuddering breath. 'Master Granville, we know how difficult a time this is for you. It is a sadness to us all. But there is one innocent in this, Alyce's daughter, Elinor.' She swallowed hard. 'Have you given any thought to her future?'

Why did she not get to the point? 'What my mother is trying to say is that Elinor will ever be a reminder to you of Alyce's wickedness. You may even come to hate her, fearing she is tainted like her mother. Any new wife you take will want nothing to do with her, fearing her children will be murdered as my own were.' What woman would not fear? But with prayer, Dame Katharine said, all evil could be overcome.

Granville stared at Isabel, showing no reaction at all.

Isabel rushed on. 'Elinor's life will be a misery. We would not want such a life for her no matter what her mother has done. We will bring her up—she will learn to live a godly and honest life with us. You need never give her another thought.'

Granville walked to the door and opened it. 'Ladies,' he said.

'You will need time to think on it,' Isabel said as she rose from her seat, 'but this is an offer that comes from the depths of my heart.'

'Of that I am quite certain,' Granville said, his voice harsh. 'A blacker, more malicious heart I have never seen.'

Heat flooded Isabel's face, but she dared not speak. Thomas Granville was the most menacing man she had ever met. She glared at him, her lips compressed into an angry line.

'You, Isabel Sutton, slander and defame my wife in an attempt to bring about her death, then you seek to steal her child away. The child would have more chance of a godly life amongst the whores in Southwark.'

He turned to Mother. 'And you, Joan Bradley, have you no shame? You desert your own child when she is in her greatest need, abandon her to the squalor of the castle dungeon, preferring instead to indulge this creature.'

Granville held the door wide.

Tears streaming down her face, Mother fled down the stairs.

Isabel sailed past him, her head held high.

He followed them and stood on the doorstep. 'If either of you comes near my wife again, I promise you most solemnly, I will snap your neck with my bare hands.' His eyes dark with contempt, he turned back into the inn.

'I will never see Alyce again,' Mother wailed.

'Why would you want to see Alyce?' Isabel sneered. 'If Alyce is a witch, then that man is Satan himself. He should swing beside her.' She marched off down the street, Julia running to keep up.

~

Isabel waited in her parents-in-law's parlour. She had come straight from the Maid's Head. Sir William would want to hear of Granville's threats and pass them on to the judge. But Sir William was still at the Guildhall and Dame Katharine nowhere to be found. Isabel strained to hear footsteps on the stairs above the sound of the servants readying the table in the hall for the evening meal.

She jumped as the door creaked open. 'Oh, Will,' she said, her shoulders dropping. 'I thought it would be your father.'

'Nay, only me.' He wandered over to a bench by the window and gazed out at the sky.

Isabel wanted to shake him. No doubt he felt the loss of Willkyn, but he had allowed it to unman him. If it were left to Will, Alyce would go unpunished. When he was not at work, he sat staring at nothing or else poring over his Bible. Perhaps when he heard of Granville's threats, he might finally shake off his lassitude.

Will gaped as Isabel told him of her visit to the Maid's Head. 'You what?' he shouted when she finished. 'You fool!'

'Shhh,' Isabel hissed, her eyes blazing. 'There are servants outside the door.' She kept her voice low. 'He was most vicious in his speech to me.'

'He was justified. Has it occurred to you Granville cares for Alyce? Think on it—you accuse his wife of witchcraft and then ask the man for his child.'

'Me accuse Alyce? You made the first accusation—that Alyce tried to seduce you with spells.'

Will closed his eyes. 'I did not mean it to come to this.'

'Well, it has.' The thought crossed her mind that Will had made up the talk of spells to shift blame to Alyce. No, that was ridiculous. She jerked her head to clear the thought. 'I was certain Granville would not want Elinor after this.'

'Isabel,' Will's face creased with worry, 'it gives strength to those who say this case was got up out of malice because Alyce has what you do not—a healthy child.'

The breath caught in her throat at the cruelty of his words. 'You must truly hate me.'

Will reached out and placed his hand on Isabel's. 'That is not true.'

Despite what Sir William had said, she still wondered if they were being punished for Will's sins. If the whispers she had tried not to hear were true, Will had ignored his marriage vows, taken every pleasure he could with other women over many years. No, that made no sense. God was not so cruel. Alyce was the cause.

'Alyce must be punished.' She flung his hand away. 'She killed our baby.' She spoke each word through gritted teeth.

'Did she?' Will said quietly. 'In truth, I doubt it.'

Isabel glared at her husband. 'Your parents know she must be punished. Your father is most active in seeing justice done.'

'My mother's mind is addled with overmuch praying. My father has other reasons for his actions.' He gazed back out the window to the high white clouds.

'What do you mean?' Isabel snapped.

Will looked back at her, his eyelashes wet. 'There is bad blood between him and Granville. It goes back a long way.

Father attempted to have Granville charged with piracy, claimed he had seized a cargo of his. There is only one thing on this earth that would cause my father's heart to break—the loss of money. He loves money and the power it brings above all else.' He sighed loudly. 'Granville denied the accusation, said he was sailing with the Dutch in their struggle against the Spanish, not pillaging English ships. Whatever the truth of it, Granville was believed and Father has never forgiven him.

'I know Father does grieve for Willkyn, but I doubt he would be as intent on his pursuit of Alyce were she not married to Granville.'

'That is ridiculous. Of course he would be—Alyce killed our son and must be punished.'

'Did not the Lord say, *Vengeance is mine*? Would it not be more godly to leave punishment to the Lord? Go on from now and try to live the life he has granted us?'

'No,' Isabel shouted. 'We must be active in rooting out evil. If this is not done, I will never raise a living child.'

'One does not depend upon the other.'

'It is God's test for me.'

'Isabel,' he groaned, 'you grow more like my mother every day.' He rose slowly from the seat. 'Have you told my parents of your meeting with Granville?'

'I have not had the chance.'

'As you are keen to do the Lord's will,' he spoke as if he carried a great burden on his shoulders, 'remember the vow you made to him to obey me. I am ordering you, as your husband, to say nothing of it to my parents.' He shook his head slowly. 'This must end.'

Seething with anger, Isabel watched him walk away, his face grey, his shoulders sagging. She saw him clearly now. He was weak—no strength to stand for anything, to care for anything other than himself and his pleasure. He did not even care enough to see justice done for his son.

40

Robin Chapman sat by the hearth of the taproom in the White Swan, nursing a mug of ale. He was oblivious to the cheerful noise around him: the singing and light-hearted banter of the men and a few women drinking or intent on hearty pottages and stews. The landlord, a brawny fellow with a florid face, stood with his thumbs hooked into his apron, alert to trouble among his customers.

Robin had expected the trial would be over by now and he could forget it all. Instead, he had to wait until tomorrow to say his piece. He would have to stand in court and tell the world how Alyce Granville had threatened to poison him and, by spells, had turned him against Susan Graham, but who on the jury would believe that? Half the town knew that from the very start his mother had no good word to say of Susan. Worst of all, he had to tell how Alyce had cursed him, and although he had not lain with a woman since he was a callow apprentice, no doubt as Sir William suggested, he would be impotent if he tried. He had wanted Robin to go to the castle and see Alyce, to scratch her and draw blood and then say he was cured of her curse. He shivered. He did not want to lay eyes on her again. It was easy to have Sir William write it all down, harder to stand and take an oath on it. The grand jury and the judge himself would question him, ask how he, an unmarried man, could possibly know that unless he had resorted to lewd women. He imagined the smirks on their faces. It would be humiliating.

He put his mug down and rubbed his fingers hard against his brow. He had been so sure of what he would say—he would be still if it were not for that curate from St Peter Mancroft, Reynes, pouncing on him as he passed the church on his way home. Reynes had been friendly enough to begin with, mentioning that they both would be giving evidence tomorrow, but then he had started on about the importance of speaking nothing but the truth. He had said three times that God knew the secrets of our hearts and that every word spoken tomorrow would be weighed on Judgement Day. Did the man think Robin was lying?

Sir William had said he needed Robin's testimony, that it would help the jury see what manner of woman Alyce truly was. But not everything Sir William wanted him to say was true. He considered himself a godly man because he did not fornicate, but to swear a false oath was ungodly too. If he spoke as Sir William wanted him to, would he be responsible if Alyce ended the day strangling at the end of a rope? Perhaps she deserved it for the death of the Suttons' child but did she for what she had done to him? How would that stand on Judgement Day? He picked up his mug and took another mouthful. Alyce was arrogant and heartless, but that was not a hanging crime. Murder of the child was. Surely Sir William had enough evidence of that crime alone without needing Robin's testimony. He stared into his mug. It was a tangle too hard for him to unravel.

He did not look up as a stranger seated himself on the settle opposite and stretched out booted legs.

'Why so glum, mate? The wife giving you hell?' He spoke with a Scottish burr.

'Not married.' Robin was terse.

'Well, 'tis sure a woman is at the heart of your troubles. Women,' he groaned, 'the cause of all man's woes on this earth.'

'In that, you are right.'

'What's the problem?'

Chapman scowled at the man. There was something about him. He was of middling height, wiry, a brawler too by the look of his black eye. Both his hair and his bushy beard were of a red more often seen colouring the heads of fashionable women.

'Do I know you?' Robin asked.

'I doubt it. I am passing through.'

'A pedlar,' Robin sneered.

'Am I dressed like a pedlar?'

Robin looked him up and down. Despite his untrimmed hair and beard, he wore a well-cut doublet with little adornment and boots of good leather.

'Harry Murdoch.'

Robin ignored his proffered hand.

'Sir Reginald Barrow's man. His sister is married to a local merchant.'

'Why are you here instead of enjoying her hospitality?'

'I prefer to taste the local cheer.'

'Whoring,' Robin said, contemptuous.

Murdoch shrugged. 'I'll wager by the time I leave, I'll know more of the pleasures this town offers than you do.'

'That I do not doubt.'

Murdoch caught a serving maid's eye. 'A jug of ale to share with my friend here.' He watched her move away through the throng, a pretty young woman whose modest dress did nothing to hide her charms.

'Careful, Murdoch. She's the landlord's daughter, and he will kill you if you even think of putting a step amiss.'

'I'm sure he would.' Murdoch's eyes followed her. 'A bonnie lass, though.'

When the maid brought the jug over, Murdoch took it and refilled Robin's tankard.

Robin drained the mug.

'And the problem is—the lady is married? The lady wants nothing to do with you? The lady is with child and you do not want her any more?' Murdoch sipped his own ale. 'Here, have another drink.' He refilled Robin's mug.

'None and all,' Robin said bitterly. He stared at Murdoch. 'But you would know this—the whole town now knows my business.' His mother had made sure of that, despite his protests, spreading an embellished story of Alyce's rejection of him.

'I arrived in Norwich this morning and have been busy all day—no time for idle chatter.'

Robin drained his mug and stood. 'I need the jakes.'

When he returned, Murdoch was still sitting at the hearth, a new jug of ale beside him. Robin walked past, heading for the door to the street.

Murdoch waved to him but Robin called, 'Time to leave. I have important business tomorrow.'

'One final drink.' Murdoch raised the jug.

One drink would not hurt. He did not want to spend the evening listening as his mother recited, yet again, all she wanted him to say in court tomorrow.

Robin sat and grabbed his tankard. He sipped, frowning. 'Is this ale?'

'Ay, must be a new barrel.' Murdoch drained his mug. 'Drink it down. By the second mug you'll not notice the taste.'

It was not unpleasant, so Robin drank. It must have been stronger than the last jug for it loosened his tongue and he found himself spilling out his woes to Murdoch. At least he was a stranger and would be soon gone.

'Sir William, grandfather to the child she killed, came to me and pleaded with me to tell my story. Said the more the court knows about her, the more likely she would receive just punishment. Said I was not valued properly by Hugh Bradley. Said he could find me a place with a mercer, friend of his, in London. Said within a year I would be managing one of his shops.' He blinked; his vision was swimming, his words slurring.

Murdoch forced another drink on him.

Robin gulped at it, spilling it down the front of his doublet. 'I do not want to go to London. There was this girl, Susan, better than that Alyce. She liked me too, but Alyce put a spell me...' He squeezed his eyes shut. He knew that was not true. 'No, not me. She put the spell on my mother, turning her against Susan.'

'I do not know that magic is needed to make an old woman hate the girl her son wants to marry,' Murdoch said.

Robin squinted at him. He thought he heard amusement in Murdoch's voice, but his face was serious. He was right. Mother had not suddenly turned against Susan; she had hated her from the start.

'Sutton did not tell me this mercer's name. Said he would arrange it when the trial is over. Tried to see him this evening. Need to be certain I have a secure place.' He stared into his mug, worry on his face. 'I am not sure he is an honest man.'

'Not if half what I have heard of him is true,' Murdoch said. 'I doubt that place in London exists.' He stood up. 'We need a diversion, mate, and I know just the place.'

'I need to go home. Tomorrow—'

'Forget your troubles for a time.' He grasped Robin's hand and hauled him from his seat. Robin rocked unsteadily. Murdoch put his arm around him and guided him through the doorway out into the dark street.

~

Dawn broke grey and cold over Norwich.

Robin woke befuddled. His head ached with the slightest movement. The room was dim, the small window in shadow. He eased himself up, puzzled by the sight of a naked woman lying beside him, her bright hair spread across the pillow. He had no memory of her at all. He shook his head to clear it and groaned as burning pain burst across his scalp.

The woman reached out sleepily. 'Leaving so soon?'

He heard disappointment in her voice. 'I have serious business today.'

'It's early—linger a few moments more.' She held out her arms to him.

Robin gazed at her naked breasts and forced himself to say, 'I should not be here.'

He could not understand how he had ended up in this woman's bed. He vaguely remembered drinking in the White Swan with a red-headed Scotsman. After that, his memories were hazy. Stumbling through an archway singing. A group of women crowding around him in a dimly lit room, their breasts on show. The Scotsman laughing behind him, speaking plain English. Nothing of this woman or of what he presumed, to his shame, had happened here.

'Robin, you disappoint me.' She pouted.

'I must go.' Wincing, he moved towards the edge of the bed.

She ran her fingers down his spine. 'Stay, Robin,' she wheedled.

He turned to her. It would be easy to slide into temptation.

She was kneeling on the bed now. She placed her hands on his shoulders, pushing him back against the pillows. 'It's early yet, no need to rush away. I'll get you something to break your fast.

He could see no harm and sank onto the pillows, watching through half-opened eyes as she pulled on her smock. His limbs were heavy. He had no wish to move from here.

That Scotsman last night was probably right—there was no position for him in London. Sutton was leading him on, using him for his own ends. What did it matter to him if Alyce walked free? She was nothing to him. He wouldn't have taken much notice of her but for his mother's ambitions. And that old journeyman urging him on, playing on his youthful ignorance of women, saying that Alyce's distain was a mask for lust. This was no better—his mother and Sutton had made him a laughing stock, publicly airing his private humiliations. They could all go to the devil. He would stay here and sleep, and his conscience would be clear. Tomorrow he would go back to Bradley's as if nothing had happened. If he did not stand up in court, Bradley would have nothing to blame him for. And Bradley was in no position to point the finger, having left his daughter to rot in prison. Robin pulled the blankets up and closed his eyes.

He was dozing lightly when the wench brought in a tray with bread, slices of cold mutton and small beer.

She sat on the bed beside him, her bodice loosely laced, her tousled hair spread around her shoulders. His eyes lingered on her breasts. A pity he was such a godly man.

She watched him, smiling, as he ate his breakfast. He did feel better with food in his stomach.

'Are you sure I cannot take your mind off your worries, Robin?' She fluttered her eyelashes.

He handed her his empty mug. 'No.' His eyes were heavy again. 'Wake me when court is over for the day.' He slid down under the blankets. As he drifted towards sleep, a voice echoed in his mind, *Find yourself a wealthy widow*. Now who had said that to him? He could not remember but it was good advice. Mother would not like a widow. He smiled sleepily.

~

Alyce woke in the cold dawn light, sick to the pit of her stomach. She dressed carefully. Grietje de Jong had provided everything—clean linen and stockings, a plain dark gown, a heavily embroidered coif and a bright confidence in the outcome of the trial.

Grietje had arrived late yesterday with the clothing and a

basket laden with food—ham and chicken, pies and tarts, cheese and cake and wine. Grietje's first words had been, 'He loves you, *Elsje*, never doubt that.'

Alyce had answered, 'I know that now.'

Grietje had smiled. 'Thomas sent this basket. He would be here to share it with you, but they will not let him near this house or the castle. He came here this afternoon, but that man Thorpe would not let him in. They would have come to blows, but Thomas's man, Watkins, stepped between them and forced him apart. They think Thomas has brought an army with him to break into the castle and steal you away.'

It was so easy for people, piece by piece, to embellish stories and alter supposition to decided fact. If Thomas had an army at his back, she would not now be sitting in what amounted to a cell, tracing her fingers over the pattern embroidered on a coif, wondering if she would ever hold a needle threaded with bright silk again.

She had no appetite for breakfast. She tried to pray, but it was as if the words had no meaning. She had lain down to sleep last night trusting in God and believing she would accept her fate, whatever it was. She had seen the depth of Thomas's love for her and realised that, briefly, she had tasted all life had to offer, possessed more than she had ever dreamt she would. And that knowledge had brought her peace. This morning she knew it was not enough. Hunger for life possessed her. She willed herself to live. She would leave this place with Thomas and spend the rest of her days at his side, in his arms, loving him. She would hold Elinor not once, but every day until she was grown and left to live her own life. She would hold her other children, those sons and daughters as yet unborn, and their children too. She would feel the sun on her face and the wind in her hair. She would ride Gleda, racing Thomas through the lanes at Ashthorpe to the hill at the far end of the manor. They would stand together and gaze out over the beauty of all that was theirs. She would not die.

With the sounds of the town stirring to life, Alyce thought of the trial, the townsfolk lining the street as she made her way to the Guildhall. Would they scream and pelt her with muck, leaving her to stand in the court bedraggled and muddy, a low woman capable of everything claimed against her? Her heart thudded, her head spun, her breath came in rapid shallow bursts. Alyce clamped her teeth together—she would not scream.

She forced herself to sit, motionless, her eyes closed, breathing slowly and deeply. Her slowing pulse jerked again as the door was flung open and Reeves strode in, another guard behind him carrying manacles.

Alyce rose from her chair. 'I will not try to escape.'

'Everyone gets chained.'

Alyce held out her hands, and Reeves locked the heavy manacles around her wrists.

She followed him down the stairs, the other guard behind her, and out into the street where Thorpe waited.

He glared at Alyce. 'I'll be glad to be rid of you, Granville.' He exhaled angrily. 'You and your husband are nothing but trouble.'

He turned and bellowed to a group of armed men lounging against the wall, 'Move yourselves.'

The men took up position around Alyce and, led by Thorpe, they marched in silence along the near-empty street away from the house. A biting wind blew up, twitching Alyce's skirts. The overcast sky threatened rain. She shivered.

As they turned the corner, she glimpsed Watkins standing against the wall of a house opposite, his hand resting on the hilt of his sword. Thorpe glanced across at him, and the guards pressed tighter around her.

When they reached the market, Alyce thought she saw Collins, the blacksmith from Ashthorpe, standing solid, his arms crossed, outside Middleton's shop. There must be some truth in Grietje's story of Thomas's army. It heartened her to think that they had come to help.

To Alyce's mind, the Guildhall with its high windows and chequered flint walls had always been a place of ceremony and of business, a place her father visited. She had never considered its courts and the prisoners crammed in below.

A trumpet blared inside—the day's business had begun

although it was not much past seven o'clock.

The guards shoved their way through the press of people surrounding the Guildhall.

Thomas stood inside the doorway. He tried to push his way towards Alyce but Thorpe blocked him. She could not hear what they were saying over the low roar of the crowd around her. Their eyes met over Thorpe's head. Thomas's look was enough to give her strength.

Thorpe had drawn his sword, and two of his men grabbed Thomas and forced him back out into the street.

Alyce was bundled towards the rear of the building, where a group of manacled prisoners waited outside the door to the women's prison. Reeves chained Alyce to the group and left her to be led with the rest upstairs to the court. A bedraggled group passed by coming down, their faces a mixture of despair and defiance.

Inside the courtroom, the crowd buzzed with a palpable excitement. Alyce gazed around the room. She could not see her parents, but Lady Sutton sat on the first of the public benches. Behind her, Edith Chapman scowled when she saw Alyce. An unlikely pair—Maude Middleton and Grietje de Jong—sitting close together, smiled encouragingly across at her.

At the front of the room, at the centre of the dais, sat two judges and, on the long benches beside them, the sheriffs and justices of the peace. Sir William Sutton glared out from his seat at one end. At a table before the dais were the ushers with their white wands and the clerks surrounded by their array of papers and pens, writs, indictments and records. To one side, an empty bench was set aside for the jurymen and a bar where the prisoners were to stand. Marshals, staffs in their hands, stood around the room, ready to maintain order.

One of the judges looked out across the courtroom to the prisoners. His bland, smooth face showed little of his thoughts and inclinations. He could be compassionate or severe and merciless—Alyce could not tell.

His voice carried through the room. 'The witchcraft case is to be tried separately.'

Alyce was taken down to the women's prison at the lower

level of the Guildhall and unchained. The room was crowded, some women lay huddled on their pallets, others sat on the floor, most silent as they waited to be called.

Alyce tried to keep calm through the interminable morning, but each time the gaol door was dragged open she started, her pulse racing. Women's names were called, and they were manacled and led up to the court. Others returned, angry and despairing, some prowling for an unguarded look, the chance to lash out. Alyce kept quiet, close to the wall in a darkened corner, as invisible as she could make herself. She closed her eyes and tried to calm her breathing. She could not pray. Each time she began, the words dried in her mouth, her mind empty of what came next.

'Alyce Granville,' a rough voice called.

Her heart pounding, Alyce rose and moved slowly towards the door.

41

Manacled, Alyce was brought into the courtroom. She stood at the bar to one side and looked around her. The public benches were packed with onlookers. The judges, grey-haired and serious, dressed in scarlet fur-trimmed robes, sat at the centre of the dais behind a table. The sheriffs and justices of the peace ranged beside them were equally serious, their eyes fixed on Alyce.

Alyce clasped her hands tightly together. She looked to the rear of the courtroom where Thomas stood against the panelled wall, his arms crossed. He nodded to her but did not smile.

The Clerk of Assize called her to the bar, and the jurymen were brought in. Twelve worthy and respectable men, they covered the range of human types—harsh and rigid, weak and vacillating, thoughtful and compassionate. Alyce objected to none.

She stood, her heart thumping as the long indictment was read in Latin. By the blank faces of most of the jurors, it was as incomprehensible to them as it was to Alyce. The clerk repeated it in English, setting out the claims against Alyce: that she did by charms and spells bring about the deaths of the sons of William and Isabel Sutton, that she did enchant and bewitch William Sutton with the intention of seducing him from his marriage vows and that she did at other times bewitch other men. The clerk looked straight at Alyce when he finished reading.

'How say you, Alyce Granville—guilty or not guilty?'

'I am not guilty,' Alyce answered.

The court crier called, 'If anyone can give evidence, or say anything against the prisoner, let them come now.'

The witnesses filed into the courtroom: Will and Isabel Sutton, Agnes Hall, Goodwife Godfrey, Master Reynes and the nursemaid, Milly Wyatt. One after the other, the witnesses each were sworn to speak the truth. They then sat together on a bench along the side wall.

Sir William ran his eyes along the assembled witnesses and glowered.

The examination made by the justice of the peace, Sir William Sutton, was read to the court. It was all Alyce feared. It listed the claims made against her and presented her as a wicked and unreformed creature who revelled in her sinfulness

~

Isabel was the first witness. She did as Sir William had advised and did not look at Alyce. He had come to her before he left for the court and, taking her hand in his, said he knew she had a forgiving heart, that if she looked at Alyce, sisterly love would weaken her resolve. No matter what Isabel felt, justice must be done today for the sake of her two innocent boys. She felt a sob building as she thought of them and forced it down; she had wept enough this morning.

After the examination taken by Sir William on the day of Willkyn's death was read, Isabel took a deep breath and began. 'My sister has borne me malice ever since we were children. But when she came to visit in May, I thought that was all past. I was glad she had married, finally, and had a child of her own, even though it was only a girl. I was so happy too.' Her eyes filled with tears. 'I had a healthy son, and I was with child again. But Alyce, discontented at her own lack of a son, could not bear to see me happy. She tried to seduce my husband.'

'That is a lie, Isabel,' Alyce called across the courtroom.

Isabel's nostrils narrowed, and for the first time she looked at her sister. The time in the castle dungeon appeared not to have harmed her. Who would believe Alyce was such a wicked slut, standing there in her high-necked gown, her white linen and her modest coif?

'I saw you with my own eyes,' Isabel spat.

'You saw us standing together. You were too far away to hear what was said.'

'Will told me, you vile creature.'

'He made up the story to cover his own licentiousness.'

Isabel held herself taut and looked ahead. 'My husband would not lie to me.'

Alyce rolled her eyes. Amusement rumbled from the public

benches.

Sir William jumped to his feet. 'Are we to allow this witch to defame decent men? She is using this court to further her own foul ends.'

Sir William, at least, defended her. Isabel glanced at her husband on the witness bench. He was staring at the windows, his thoughts miles away.

The older judge, Lord Chief Justice Wray scowled. 'Sit down, Sir William. We have not yet determined whether the woman is a witch. The accused has the right to defend herself.' His heavy-lidded eyes fixed on Alyce. 'Alyce Granville, have a care what you say.' His face softened as he spoke to Isabel. 'Mistress Sutton, continue your account.'

'The next day I went to my parents' house and upbraided my sister. She said foul words to me, claimed my husband tried to seduce her. Before she left the room, she bent over my son, cursing him and me.'

'You are lying, Isabel,' Alyce shouted. 'Tell them my exact words.'

The second judge, Justice William Peryam, a sharp-faced man about their father's age, glared at Alyce. 'I will not permit you to abuse witnesses.'

Alyce froze, open-mouthed.

Isabel allowed herself the smallest of smiles. Sir William was right, despite the pain it caused her to talk of her loss, the judges were doing their best to treat her kindly—they would make sure Alyce got what she deserved.

'Alyce screamed at me to take him home, that he was burning with fever. That was part of her curse. There was nothing wrong with my boy, but we left because I would not stay a moment longer under the same roof. Milly, his nursemaid, put him to bed, but when she went to wake him later, he was cold.' Her face crumpled, her eyes filling with tears. 'Then I lost the child I was carrying. That was Alyce's doing too.'

'Mistress Sutton,' Justice Peryam leant forward, a paper in his hand, 'the words of the curse are not set out here. Repeat them for us now? And remember, you are on oath.'

Isabel shook her head. 'I cannot. But I remember Alyce had

a bird with her. She whispered to it and sent it out the window just before she cursed us. It was sitting in the tree outside our house when we found...' her voice trailed off, 'my son.'

Alyce called to her, 'How do you know it was the same bird?'

'I sensed it—the sight of it sent shivers through me. And there were always sparrows in the garden whenever you were outside.' Sir William had suggested Alyce must have had a creature to do her bidding and the incident with the sparrow had been strange.

'But there are sparrows everywhere,' Alyce said.

A murmur ran through the courtroom.

Isabel kept her eyes on Justice Peryam. 'Then there was the time two years ago when she killed my first child.' She hurried on, afraid she would break down again. 'She gave me a potion that made my child sickly. He did not thrive in the womb. He was born deformed and did not draw breath for more than an hour before he died.' Isabel's shoulders sagged, a single tear rolling down her cheek. She did not brush it away. No matter how hard she tried, there would be more to follow.

'Isabel,' Alyce spoke again. 'I gave you syrup of poppy in small beer to calm you and help you sleep. Only once.'

'That is what you say.' Isabel paused, silent a moment. She was on oath; she must tell the truth. 'Ay, it was only once, but I doubt it was syrup of poppy.'

'Why do you think that?' Justice Wray asked.

Isabel sniffed back her tears. 'The fact my child was born weak and died.'

'Mistress Sutton, are you now claiming your sister poisoned you rather than used witchcraft? You do not mention the nature of any spells in your examination.'

'I do not know what spell it was she said when she made the potion, but she must have said one because my baby died soon after birth.'

'What ill effects did you suffer when you took the potion?' Wray asked.

'My baby died,' Isabel sobbed.

'Your baby died months after that. What happened at the time you took the potion your sister gave you?'

Isabel glared at him. Why was he asking these questions? Did he not believe her? She could feel the eyes of every man sitting on the judges' dais watching her.

She had thought the judges kind, but now she noticed hardness in Justice Wray's smooth face—the truth was more important to him than anything else. 'You may not accept she killed my first child, but she killed my second,' she said sullenly.

Isabel glanced to the back of the courtroom where Thomas Granville stood, his arms folded across his chest. Sir William was right: he had probably urged Alyce to kill Isabel's boys because of the ill will he bore Sir William. But Alyce had been his willing instrument.

Justice Wray said, 'You may go now, Mistress.'

Isabel did not move. She would tell the judges that Granville had said he would break her neck. Will had only ordered that she not tell his parents. She looked directly at Justice Peryam. 'There is more you should know. Thomas Granville threatened to kill me.'

The judge scowled towards the back of the courtroom. 'When was this?'

'Yesterday afternoon. My mother and I visited him. We offered to help him by taking that poor motherless child to care for.' To have a child to hold in her arms, even Alyce's child, would help ease this pain.

She heard Alyce's strangled cry, the gasps and muttering of the crowd. Did they not understand she was offering that child the chance of a happy and godly life?

The marshals banged their staffs and shouted for silence. Justice Wray bellowed, 'Quiet, or I will have the public cleared.' He turned his attention to Isabel. 'This is the child of Alyce Granville?' Isabel nodded. 'I would point out, Mistress Sutton, the child is not yet motherless, and the guilt of Alyce Granville has not yet been determined. It is this court, and this court alone, that will decide whether she is guilty.'

'He said he would snap my neck with his bare hands,' Isabel said sulkily. Why were they pretending Alyce was not guilty?

'We will keep it in mind, Mistress,' Justice Peryam said. 'You may go now.'

Isabel glared at Alyce as she walked across the room to sit beside her mother-in-law. Perhaps Alyce was weaving a spell on them and would escape justice. She wished Sir William could come and sit beside her, hold her hand and tell her, as he often did, he would see justice was done.

~

Milly Wyatt, the nursemaid, stood wringing her hands as her examination was read.

Alyce tried to question her, hoping that if she could get her to say that she had heard no curse, it would count with the jury. But Milly mumbled her answers, even though Justice Wray ordered her to speak up. Each time she spoke, she cast terrified glances to the end of the bench where Sir William sat.

Justice Wray picked up a pile of papers and shuffled through them, frowning.

'Was the wet nurse examined?' he asked.

'No, my Lord,' Woolmer, the Clerk of Assize, faced the judges' table. 'She was a country wife and returned home as soon as the child died. Sir William Sutton, the investigating justice, said she knew nothing more than Wyatt.'

'Hmmm.' Wray tapped his fingers on the bench.

Milly was dismissed and Joan Bradley called. Minutes passed, the noise of the crowd increasing. Necks craned as she was called a second time. A messenger came into the court, bowed to the judges and spoke to Woolmer, who turned and said, 'Joan Bradley has taken to her bed. She says she is too ill to attend.'

'Do we have her examination?' Wray asked.

'Nay, my Lord, she claims she heard nothing.'

'It is a cruel thing for a mother to be forced to choose between her children but we are seeking the truth here.' The judge looked out across the court. 'The constables are to go to her home and bring her here—carry her bodily if need be.' Answering the gasp from the public benches, he continued, 'A woman is on trial for her life, and justice will not be served if we do not strive to the utmost to uncover the truth.'

Alyce moved from foot to foot, already tired from standing. She did not understand her mother's absence. She had thought it clear which side her mother had taken from the moment of her imprisonment.

The cryer called Robin Chapman, and again the court waited. Wray raised an eyebrow. 'Has Chapman sent an apology?'

'No, my Lord,' Woolmer answered, 'but we do have his examination.' He passed it to the judge.

After running his eyes over the sheet, Justice Wray passed it to Peryam. He looked out across the courtroom. 'Some in this town are treating this trial as if it were a trip to the playhouse. Chapman too is to be found and compelled to appear.'

Alyce was certain Robert Chapman would be as fierce against her as Isabel had been. She wondered if Thomas had a hand in Chapman's absence. She dared not look towards him, fearing it would be misinterpreted by the judges or the jury.

'Master Clerk,' Justice Wray said, 'who has come to court?'

'William Sutton, the children's father, is here.'

Will Sutton took his place and stood, staring at nothing in particular as his examination was read.

'You do not mention the words Alyce Granville used when she cast her spell on you,' Justice Peryam said. 'Tell the court now what they were.'

Will shrugged. 'In truth, I cannot remember.'

Alyce held her breath, wondering why he seemed reluctant. It was his lie that had set all this in motion.

'My Lord, I remember what happened,' Isabel called from her seat.

'You have given your evidence, Mistress Sutton,' Justice Peryam said, not unkindly.

'But I remember what my husband does not.'

'I will keep that in mind.' He turned back to Will. 'What do you mean, you do not remember?'

Will gazed around the courtroom as if he did not understand why he was there. 'There has been so much sorrow since. I cannot remember anything clearly.'

'You remember nothing of the evening in question?' Peryam seemed perplexed.

'No.' Will shook his head slowly. 'I know my son died. Beside that, the memory of all else has paled.'

'In your examination, you say Alyce Granville tried to seduce

315

you by using spells.' Peryam frowned. 'Do you stand by that?'

Will ran his finger between his neck and his ruff, adjusting it and staring into the soft light falling from the window.

Justice Wray raised his voice. 'Sutton, answer the question.'

Will blinked. 'The question?'

'Do you stand by the examination taken on the day of your son's death?'

'No.' Will gave a long, shuddering sigh. 'I tried to seduce Alyce, but she was unwilling.'

Alyce gasped. The oath had power to force people to the truth. She grasped the bar, her knees suddenly weak. If others felt the same, there was hope.

Justice Wray leant forward. 'Why did you say otherwise?'

'My wife saw us, and I was too craven to tell the truth.'

Alyce glanced over at Sir William. He was glaring at his son, his face almost purple.

Even Justice Wray's colour had risen. 'Sutton, you may go,' he said tartly. 'Consider yourself fortunate that, in view of your recent loss, I do not have you answer for your lies.'

Will walked away, his head held high, his shoulders straight as if a weight had been lifted from him. Isabel rose from her seat and hurried after him.

Whispers slithered through the courtroom.

Sir William was on his feet, his voice booming out. 'See how this woman works her spells. Here in this court, even before you, my Lords, she has bewitched a man away from the truth.'

Justice Peryam went to speak, but Wray cast him a warning glance. He turned and glared at Sir William. 'Sit. Down. I suggest you control your outbursts. It is unbecoming in one charged with maintenance of the peace.' He gazed out over the courtroom, 'I believe Master Sutton's testimony is honest.'

Beside him, Justice Peryam's frown deepened.

~

Isabel followed Will down the stairs, calling to him, but he strode on, out towards the market.

'Stop! Will!' she screeched.

Two lawyers near the entrance to the Guildhall turned and stared.

Will kept moving as if he had not heard her, disappearing down a crowded path between the market stalls.

Isabel sped after him, struggling to keep up. Shoppers kept moving in her way, stopping to view the produce displayed on the stalls. When she caught sight of Will again, he was too far ahead. She could have wept with anger at him. He had proclaimed his unfaithfulness to the entire world. It was as if he had stripped her naked for all to laugh at—a woman who could not keep her husband faithful.

She called to him again but her shout was drowned by the noise of the market-goers, and merchants, apprentices and pedlars calling their wares. Will's pace increased once he was beyond the market, clearly making towards their house.

Isabel slowed to catch her breath. He would not be able to run away from her at home. There she would tell him exactly what she thought.

She slammed the heavy door to the street behind her and ran up the stairs to the hall.

Will stood at the window, staring into the street.

'Did you not hear me calling you?' Isabel's voice was harsh.

He turned to face her. 'I did, but I had no wish to be berated in public and provide entertainment for all those in the market.'

He was so calm Isabel wanted to scream at him, shake his composure. 'Why did you stand up in court and shame me?'

He closed his eyes a moment and said wearily, 'I did not mean to shame you, but I had to tell the truth.'

'The truth. When have you cared about the truth?'

'I care now. My lie started this. I hoped the truth would end it. I could not bear to think Alyce would die for my falsehood.'

'She is not on trial for trying to seduce you,' Isabel hissed, 'but because she killed our sons.'

'I do not believe she did that. Why would she?'

'Because Granville cannot give her sons. She was hoping to get a son by you and pass it off as her husband's.' Isabel knew it was true. It had been her first thought when she saw Alyce and Will together. Sir William had said that would be the reason, and Dame Katharine had agreed.

'Listen to me.' Will walked towards her. 'Alyce did not try to seduce me. She was as she always has been—sober, modest and practical. I was the one with adultery in mind.'

Isabel winced at the word. It made no sense. 'So why did Alyce kill Willkyn if not for spite? And what about our baby two years ago?'

'I do not know why they died.' Will's voice caught as he answered her. 'Our baby came too early—all except my mother believe that. And Willkyn? Sometimes children die for no reason we can fathom. I do know Alyce was always gentle with him. She looked the image of the doting aunt.'

Isabel remembered. She had been jealous of the way Willkyn would stop crying when he was in Alyce's arms. And when Alyce had bent over her boy on that last day, she had been gentle, brushing her lips against his silky hair. She had whispered to him. Alyce said it was a prayer. That would be like her, more like her than to curse an innocent child. And Isabel had screamed at her because she thought Alyce had tried to steal her husband and, if she were honest, she thought she would steal her son's heart too.

Isabel placed her hand over her mouth. Alyce did not kill her boy.

She had known it all along but, willingly seduced by Sir William and Dame Katharine's malice dressed up as concern and virtue, she had pushed the knowledge to the darkest corner of her heart.

She felt weak, her legs unsteady.

Will caught her around the waist and drew her close. It was the first time he had held her since they had buried Willkyn. She wanted to bury her face against his chest and forget it all. But if she did not explain it to the court, Alyce would die.

'I must go back, tell them I was mistaken. If Alyce dies...' Her voice broke.

'By the time you get there, it will all be over.' Will said, his eyes glistening.

Isabel saw her sister's face as that old witch's had been, contorted in agony as she slowly choked. Isabel slipped towards the floor, her skirts spreading around her. She felt ill, ill to her soul—if her sister died, she would be the cause.

42

Now, Master Clerk, who have we left?' Justice Wray asked. Woolmer glanced at the list on his table, then at the witnesses. 'There is Agnes Hall, who claims longstanding knowledge of both the accused and her sister; Elizabeth Godfrey, a midwife; and William Reynes, curate of St Peter Mancroft. Joan Bradley, mother of the accused, has finally presented herself too.'

'May I see Hall's examination?' Wray said.

Woolmer handed it to him.

Wray frowned, reading rapidly, and passed it to Peryam. There was a whispered exchange between them, Peryam glowering as Wray crumpled the document. 'We will forgo Hall's testimony.'

Agnes Hall jumped up from her seat and barged over to the clerk's desk. 'I have long knowledge of Alyce Bradley and her grandmother and their witchcraft.'

'Go and sit on the public benches,' Wray ordered. 'Your testimony is laughable—decades' old rumour and a lurid dream of naked cavorting on Mousehold Heath no one else has reported. Nothing remains secret. If it was as you say, others would have known of it.'

'Ay,' a voice from the back called. 'And Agnes Hall would have made sure all Norwich knew by nightfall.'

The rumble of laughter from the public benches died quickly as Justice Wray raised his voice. 'This dream tells more of your own imagination than anything Alyce Granville has done. The facts are you fell asleep in your own bed and you woke to find a cat sitting on your windowsill. It is telling you have remained silent on this matter all these years, conveniently remembering them now at Sir William Sutton's prompting.'

Sutton sat, mottle-faced but silent, at the end of the bench.

'I will have my say.' Agnes Hall thrust her chin out.

'Have a care, Hall. Your examination shows a detailed knowledge of the uses of rue and pennyroyal and the effect they have on a child in the womb. Perhaps *you* deserve to be investigated further.'

'Oh! No. No. It's just what I was told.' She scurried over to the public benches and elbowed her way through to a space beside Edith Chapman.

'Now,' Wray said, 'we will hear the midwife, Godfrey.'

Woolmer faced the judges. 'My Lords, three midwives examined Alyce Granville for a witch's teat. But the only examination presented to the grand jury was that of Ruth Williams which suggested that Alyce Granville carried a witch's teat upon her body—irrefutable proof that she is a witch. The depositions of midwives Godfrey and Brewer appear to have been lost. They presented themselves at the grand jury and have now made formal statements. Both attest that Alyce Granville has no such mark upon her body. Williams has withdrawn her examination. When it was read to her, she said it was not what she had said to the justice of the peace. She agrees with Godfrey and Brewer.'

'I smell witchcraft here,' Peryam said. 'These women have been bewitched to change their testimonies.'

'And I smell the use of influence in the first place,' Wray answered sharply, ignoring Peryam's rising colour.

'I would have Williams here to explain herself, but I have no wish to prolong this trial.' Wray looked across at the jury. 'We will hear the rest of the evidence before deciding guilt or innocence.'

Goodwife Godfrey's examination was read, and Justice Wray asked, 'Are all three of you of one mind, Godfrey?'

'We are. Alyce Granville has no witch's teat upon her body.'

Peryam snapped, 'Not even on her privy parts?'

'Indeed not!'

Alyce thought quickly. She believed Goodwife Godfrey to be an honest woman, and she had said, when she had been in Alyce's cell, that she did not believe Alyce had killed Isabel's first baby. If she could get her to say that here, perhaps they would set that charge aside. 'Goodwife Godfrey, why do you think Isabel's first baby died?'

'That child was small and weak, born two months before its time.'

There was a rumbling from the courtroom and someone yelled, 'What about the potion to cast infants from the womb?'

Godfrey glanced up at Wray.

He nodded. 'You may answer that.'

'Mistress Sutton said earlier that she was given a potion, only once, early on. If it was a potion to bring about a miscarriage, it would have done its work then, not months later.'

'But the child was monstrous.' This time it was Edith Chapman and Lady Sutton together.

Red-faced, Godfrey turned and shouted back, 'That child was not monstrous, as well you know Lady Sutton.' She turned and faced the jury. 'There was a web of skin between the fingers, more than most of us have. It was a slight imperfection I have seen before on healthy living children. It had nothing to do with the child's death—few infants survive that come so early from the womb.'

Wray stared down at the document on the table in front of him. 'What do you know of Mistress Sutton's recent miscarriage?'

'Very little. Ruth Williams said Mistress Sutton had not asked her to attend her next childbed yet. It was too early—she had not begun to show. You cannot know for certain you are with child until the baby quickens within the womb. Some poor women, who dearly want a child, believe themselves to be with child when they are but a few days late. When their monthly courses come, they call it a miscarriage.'

'You think this was the case with Mistress Sutton?'

Godfrey shrugged. 'It is possible.'

'That is merely your opinion, Godfrey,' Peryam pronounced. 'It is as open to question as any of the evidence presented in this court today.'

'Ay, it is my opinion as a midwife who has attended many, many women in all their travails.'

Peryam grunted but said no more.

'Thank you, Goodwife,' Justice Wray dismissed her.

~

Three years ago, Alyce had thought her mother a beautiful elegant woman. Today, although neatly dressed, she appeared old, thin and harried.

'Mother,' Alyce called to her. 'Did you hear me curse Willkyn?'

For the first time since she had entered the courtroom, her mother looked directly at her. Her tear-filled eyes pleaded for understanding. 'I cannot believe you would harm poor Willkyn,' she answered in little more than a whisper. 'Yet Isabel said she heard you curse him.'

'Speak up, the court cannot hear you,' Justice Wray said, impatient.

Alyce tried again. 'What did you hear me say?'

Her mother raised her voice. 'I cannot remember.'

'Witches can confuse those who would speak against them,' Justice Peryam said.

'I am not confused,' Alyce's mother said firmly. 'I know my daughters argued. I know my grandchild died.' She swayed. A tear trickled down her cheek. 'Other than those incidents, who would remember such a day clearly?'

'I see little to be gained pressing Mistress Bradley further,' Justice Wray said. 'You may leave, Mistress.'

Alyce watched her mother walk slowly from the courtroom and felt nothing.

'Has Goodman Chapman arrived?' Wray asked.

'No, my Lord.' Woolmer rose and faced the Bench. 'No one has seen him today. He is not at his place of work nor is his at his home.'

Edith Chapman stood and called out, 'I am his mother. He did not come home last night. I am worried what has become of him.'

Someone behind her laughed. 'Lying drunk in a ditch somewhere.'

Another answered, 'Ay, he was well in his cups last night at the White Swan.'

Wray paused and closed his eyes as if praying for patience. He opened them and stared out across the court. 'These proceedings are not being treated with the seriousness they deserve. We will make do with Chapman's examination.'

Woolmer selected a sheet from the pile on his desk and read. *'I, Robert Chapman, journeyman mercer, of the parish of All Saints, say here that Alyce Granville confessed to me that she was a witch. In the month of August in 1586, I proposed marriage to her. In answer, she said she was a witch and cursed me, making me incapable of relations with women. She repeated this curse last June merely by looking at me. She did not speak, but I clearly heard her say the words in my head. I was relieved of her curse only after scratching her and drawing blood.'*

'He never scratched me,' Alyce shouted. 'I have not seen him since I left my father's house.

'Granville,' Justice Peryam bellowed. 'You will keep quiet. You may speak only when I say so.' He nodded to the clerk to continue.

Alyce leant against the bar, and stared up at the carved ceiling beams as Woolmer read. The room was hot and stuffy. She was tired and her legs ached. She did not know how much longer she could stand here, listening to these lies.

'Before her return to Norwich three years ago, she cast spells from afar to estrange me from my betrothed, Susan Graham. As a girl, Alyce Granville was complicit with her grandmother, also a witch, in making potions and spells to make men quick with desire and to cast babies from the womb. I was present in the month of June last when Alyce Granville cursed her sister calling down all the ills that have befallen her.'

Peryam began as soon as Woolmer finished reading. 'The scratching is important. When a bewitched person gains relief by scratching and drawing blood, it is another sure proof that the accused is a witch.'

Justice Wray tapped his thumb against his lips. 'Chapman does not say when this scratching occurred—it is why he should be here so we can question him.' He glanced to the end of the table. 'Sir William Sutton, did this occur in your presence?'

Sir William stood, blinking rapidly. He cast a quick glance at

Sir John Rogers seated beside him, the other justice of the peace who had been present at Alyce's initial interrogation. Sutton cleared his throat. 'No, my Lord. Chapman advised me that he had gone to the castle himself.'

'Is the gaoler in court, Woolmer?' Wray asked.

'I believe he is outside, my Lord.'

'Get him in.'

Alyce watched as Thorpe was sworn, wondering if he would tell the truth or had been paid to lie.

'Are you aware of any visits by Robert Chapman, journeyman mercer, to Alyce Granville while she was in your keeping?' Wray asked.

'I do not know who he is, my Lord. Granville's only visitors in the castle were the curate, Reynes and the midwives. At Golden Ball Lane, her husband, and a Dutch friend visited too.'

'Could others have visited without your knowing?' Peryam asked.

Thorpe twisted his mouth. 'I doubt it. I take my duties seriously.'

Peryam leant back in his chair. 'This is concerning. The scratching is important evidence.'

'But the accused denies it, there are no known witnesses and Chapman is not here to be questioned,' Wray countered. 'And, once again, curses are claimed but the words are not reported and no witnesses mentioned.'

'Are there witnesses to the older claims of witchcraft?' Peryam asked.

'No one has come forward, my Lord,' Woolmer said. 'No one other than Agnes Hall has provided any information on that. And while Hall gives detail of the potions that will do as Chapman describes, she provides no names of those who claimed to suffer from Granville's or her grandmother's spells.'

'Usually, in these cases, we have no shortage of those who can attest to the evil done by a witch,' Peryam said, thoughtful.

Wray turned to the jury. 'Chapman needs to be questioned and give explicit detail of these spells, potions and curses so you, the jury, can form your own opinion. We cannot judge these older claims of witchcraft or even the relief from the more recent curse without Chapman's evidence.' He looked toward Woolmer. 'Was Chapman's betrothed examined?'

'No, my Lord.'

'Is she here in the courtroom?' Wray asked.

There was murmuring in the public benches as necks craned and heads swivelled to see if Susan Graham was present.

'We must forgo her testimony too.' Wray scowled around the courtroom. 'We will speak to the minister, Woolmer, and that will be the end of it.'

Panic sparked in Alyce, her heart racing. Reynes would be damning. She needed to answer these charges. She would speak out, no matter what the judges' objections.

After Reynes's examination had been read, Justice Wray said, 'Your examination dates from when Alyce Granville was first charged. Have you questioned her since?'

'Many times, my Lord. The last time was yesterday afternoon.' He held his head high and looked straight ahead. 'Alyce Granville could not be brought to confess her witchcraft. She has remained resolute in her conviction she played no part in the deaths of the Sutton infants. She could not be swayed from this. She denies all charges brought against her. This is unusual as, in most cases of witchcraft, over time there is some wavering. In the end these creatures want to boast of their evildoing.'

'Do you believe her to be a witch?' Wray asked.

'There is much evil report of her, but no one has related any specific incidents from her youth. Yet Mistress Sutton, when brought into her presence, collapsed—this happens often when the victim faces the witch. But...' he shook his head, took a deep breath and continued, 'I prayed with Alyce Granville. Witches will baulk at this. She is a most obstinate woman with an unruly tongue. She does not know her proper place, but for all of that, when I examined her yesterday on her catechism, I found her knowledge to be complete. As good as any I have ever examined although she was confirmed many years ago.'

Peryam slowly tapped his fingers on the judges' table. 'Satan's creatures are subtle.'

'No minion of Satan could answer as she did. I do not believe her to be a witch but I am firm in the belief she is in need of strong correction. Her husband would do well to chastise her regularly.'

'Master Reynes,' Wray said sternly, 'why did you not bring your views to the court's attention as soon as you had formed them?'

'I needed to pray and be sure I was of the right opinion. I believed there were other matters to be examined by the court and my opinion was only one among many.'

'As a witness who does not bear personal animosity towards the accused, your opinion is of great importance.' Wray scowled. 'You may go.'

Agnes Hall jumped up from her seat and called out, 'What about the Lord's Prayer?'

Reynes stopped and looked towards the judges.

Agnes Hall called again, 'Witches cannot say the Lord's Prayer.' There were murmurs and nodding from those around her.

'Master Clerk, may I see Sir William's initial examination?' Justice Peryam asked. He drummed his fingers on the table as Woolmer sorted through his papers. He bowed and handed it up to Peryam.

Peryam ran his eye down the page. 'It says here Sir William had her say it but she could only say the prayer in Latin.' He sat back, satisfied. 'This is solid proof she is a witch.'

'That is not true,' Alyce shouted. 'I know no Latin, and Sir William never had me pray. It is a lie.'

'Quiet, Granville.' Peryam shouted over her.

Sir John Rogers stood up from beside Sutton. 'My Lords, I transcribed Sir William's examination of the accused. There has been some mistake—Alyce Granville was not asked to pray or recite scripture.'

Peryam looked down at the page. 'It is written in a different hand. It is no matter. We will have her say it here.' He stared hard at Alyce. 'Alyce Granville you will repeat the Lord's Prayer, in a loud voice, for the court to hear.'

Alyce hesitated. Surely her guilt or innocence would not depend on her ability to recite a prayer she could never remember not knowing? But would the slightest stumble or slip of the tongue make her a witch? Earlier today she could not remember the psalms she had tried to recite.

Agnes Hall shouted, 'See, she cannot do it. She is a witch.' Others took up the chant, 'Witch. Witch.'

'Silence,' Wray bellowed. 'The next person to speak out of turn will stand in the pillory next market day regardless of his or her degree.' He turned his attention to Alyce. 'Repeat the Lord's Prayer.'

Alyce drew a deep breath. *'Our Father which art in heaven…'* She spoke clearly and evenly. She did not rush. Her voice rang out around the hushed room. *'…but deliver us from evil. Amen.'*

'Right, that was correct.' Both judges seemed satisfied.

'Master Reynes, in a word, do you believe Alyce Granville is a witch?' Wray asked.

'No. I do not.'

'You may go.'

Justice Peryam leant toward Justice Wray and whispered to him. There followed a short but uneasy conversation as the courtroom rumbled around them.

Both judges sat erect, their faces grim. 'We will see justice done openly here,' Wray said to the jury. 'The only charge that Alyce Granville has to answer is that of killing her sister's child in June. You cannot give heavy weight to the testimony of Robert Chapman, who has not deigned to present himself to this court. You have heard what all other witnesses say against the prisoner. Master Reynes says, in his opinion as a man of God, Alyce Granville is not a witch. You have heard Goodwife Godfrey say Alyce Granville bears no witch's teat upon her body—there is nothing about her person to indicate she is a witch. If she is not a witch, then she does not have the powers of a witch—she has not the ability to bring about death by a curse which only Mistress Sutton heard, the wording of which she cannot remember. Keep in mind there is no evidence the death was brought about by ordinary means, by suffocation or poisoning, only by cursing. The verdict is clear.'

It was not clear to Alyce. So much had been said against her that she doubted Reynes and Godfrey's opinions would count for much when set beside Isabel's testimony. And even though the judge had said that Chapman's and Hall's examinations could not be counted on, she was certain there were many on the jury who would take notice of them.

'But,' Alyce called out, 'I have not had my say. I have not been given the chance to defend myself.'

'Granville,' Peryam glowered at her, 'you speak out of turn.'

'I have a right to defend myself,' she persisted.

'Others have defended you, woman,' he barked. 'Keep silent or I will have you gagged.

Alyce gasped and shut her mouth.

Wray set his hard, cold gaze on Alyce. 'I am convinced Alyce Granville has an ungoverned tongue that has stirred up malice against her. But equally others have cast about for reasons for their misfortunes rather than accepting the mysterious workings of the will of God. These have used malice to assuage their grief. This town appears to be a nest of backbiting and pettiness. Many have not dealt honestly with this court and should tread warily in the future.' He stared along at Sutton. 'I warn all present not to use the courts lightly to further their petty feuds. We are here to see justice is done. God visits misfortune on us all, and we do well to accept his chastisements and right our lives rather than to cast blame on others for them. Witches live more easily among us when the innocent are accused and put to trial.' He turned back to the jury. 'Good men of the jury, remember your oath and your duty and do that which God shall put in your minds to discharge of your consciences, though the right verdict is plain. There is no need to leave the court. You may discuss the matter here.'

The jurors huddled together, whispering to each other, some casting back looks at both Alyce and the judges. Alyce looked towards the rear of the court but could not see Thomas. Her heart thumped in her chest. Her mouth was dry. Surely Justice Wray had directed the jury to find her not guilty. But what if they ignored him?

'Have you reached your verdict?' asked the clerk.

The first juryman sworn rose. 'We have.' The rest nodded as one.

Woolmer told Alyce to raise her right hand as he set out

again the crimes with which she had been charged. He turned to the foreman of the jury. 'What say you? Is Alyce Granville guilty or not guilty?'

'Not guilty, sir.'

The public benches erupted, cheers and boos in equal strength.

'Silence,' Justice Wray bellowed, the marshals banging their staffs for order. The noise subsided to a low mutter.

'Alyce Granville, you are free to go,' Justice Peryam said. 'Be of good behaviour and forsake the devil.'

Alyce stood where she was, her knees trembling. She held on to the bar, doubting she could move.

The noise from the public benches mounted as the onlookers spilled out from their seats, swarming across the courtroom. Wray nodded, and the marshals pushed their way through the crowd and took position around Alyce. Thorpe was in front of her, unlocking her manacles. 'Your husband has already paid your gaol fees. You may leave, and good riddance to you both.'

The judges rose, and to the sound of trumpets, left the court, the rest of the dignitaries following them in procession.

The marshals, Alyce in the middle of them, forced their way through the surging, shouting throng. She could see Agnes Hall standing on a bench, her face contorted, screaming with the rest. Here and there individual voices carried above the rest, 'Kill the witch!' The law had set her free but the crowd had judged her otherwise.

Out into the hallway beyond the courtroom, still guarded by the marshals, the mob pressed close. Alyce let out a cry as her arm was grabbed from behind.

'Quick, Alyce, follow me.'

Her pounding heart steadied at the sound of Thomas's voice.

He pushed her through the door opposite the courtroom into the empty council chamber where the civil cases had been heard by Justice Peryam yesterday. The noise of the crowd was hardly muffled by the door.

Thomas passed Alyce a bundle of clothing. 'Put these on.'

She shook out a man's shirt and breeches, a canvas jerkin

and a cap. Her fingers fumbled at the lacings on her gown.

Thomas stepped close and ripped through them with his dagger.

She stripped off the gown and petticoat, dumping them on the floor.

Thomas scooped them up and bundled them under one of the public benches, out of sight.

Alyce shivered as she pulled on the breeches and dragged the shirt over the top of her bodice and smock. She rolled up the smock and tucked it in, buckling the belt Thomas had given her, and put the jerkin over it all.

'Take this too.' He handed her a long dagger. 'Use it if you have to.'

Alyce swallowed hard as she fixed it to her belt. She pulled the cap down, shadowing her face.

Thomas walked to the nearest window and leant forward, one knee against the bench in front of the window, watching the crowd in the marketplace.

Alyce stared up at the small glass window panes, trying to ignore the noise of the rabble surrounding the Guildhall. It was the noise of a massive, mindless beast. Alyce's breath shortened with panic, a scream swelling within her. She opened her mouth, but nothing came. Her throat burned as she struggled for breath. A strong calloused hand clamped her mouth shut.

Eyes wide with terror, she looked up into Thomas's face.

'Shhh, Alyce, shhh.' His voice was soft but urgent. He removed his hand from her mouth and, gazing deep into her eyes, bent close and kissed her. His lips, the prickle of his beard against her cheek, the scent that was Thomas alone were all that existed in that moment. As the kiss lengthened, Alyce's fear faded. Together, they would make it through this final trial.

Thomas drew away, but Alyce pulled his head back down and kissed him fiercely.

'I am ready now.'

Thomas rested his hand against the door. 'Stay close behind me, but if we are separated, make your way to the yard at the rear of Reynolds the grocer's shop. You know it?' Alyce nodded. 'The mob will be looking for a woman, but it will also have its eyes on me. If I think we are followed, I'll lead them away from you.'

Thomas stepped out into the crowd, which was thinner now, most having spilled down the stairs. Marshals still stood outside the door.

Alyce kept her eyes on Thomas's back as they strode into the street. The entire town appeared to have gathered outside the Guildhall. They were as frenzied as the day her grandmother's friend Bridget had died. Familiar faces made unfamiliar: grimacing, leering, eager, distorted with anger and hate. Ordinary, God-fearing folk dressed in their Sunday clothes transformed into malevolent strangers jeering, spitting, screaming, 'Whore, witch, murderer!'

Alyce kept close to Thomas as they struggled against the flow of the crowd. She kept her head down, her heart thumping so loudly she was sure those around her could hear it.

'Kill the witch!' 'String her up!' 'Kill the witch!' 'Kill the witch!'

As they reached the edge of the crowd, Alyce noticed three grooms from Ashthorpe, Nick Price among them, lounging like a group of idlers at the entrance to a narrow laneway. Thomas and Alyce slipped past them as a cry went up, 'There she is!'

Alyce stopped, rigid with fear. Surely that was Price shouting.

Thomas grabbed her arm and broke into a run. Alyce stumbled after him.

The crowd surged past the lane. The noise faded as she raced behind Thomas through a warren of narrow lanes until they came to a passageway that was no more than a space between the buildings.

'Here,' Thomas said.

They were in an open courtyard that seemed to be full of horses. Watkins stood holding the reins of three; Collins and one of the younger grooms from Ashthorpe waited to one side of the courtyard each with three more. Beside them, Stokes sat on the mounting block, his head in his hands.

Alyce pulled off her cap and smiled around her.

Stokes gaped, bewildered, and said, 'Mistress?' as the rest of the company broke into a cheer.

'It is good to see you all.' Alyce grinned.

'And you, Mistress,' Stokes said as he rose from the block. He turned to Thomas. 'You set such a pace, sir. No matter how hard I rode or where I went, I was always a few days behind you. I feared I would never catch you, that I would be too late.'

'I know that fear only too well Stokes,' Thomas answered.

Thomas helped Alyce into the saddle as Price and his companions pounded through the main gate, laughing.

'The mob has gone in the direction you wanted, sir,' Price gasped.

They mounted up and left the yard, Thomas leading, Stokes and Watkins either side of Alyce, the rest behind. The crowd still roared in the distance.

They galloped through the near empty-streets. The faster they rode, the more willing others were to get out of their way. And then they were through St Stephen's Gate and out into the open countryside.

The clouds broke apart to reveal a sky washed blue.

Alyce smiled widely, exhilarated. She twisted in her saddle and looked towards Norwich.

Thomas dropped back beside her. 'You'll be turned into a pillar of salt, Alyce,' he said, 'frozen by the past. Forget them all—look only to the future.' They rode on together, side by side. 'We will stay tonight at a manor of Lord Reading's a couple of hours' ride from here.'

'I will go wherever you want, Tom,' Alyce said. *Whither thou goest, I will go also…'*

She raised an eyebrow as she dug her heels into her horse and said with a playfulness she had not felt since childhood, 'I'll race you there.'

Epilogue

Let sea-discoverers to new worlds have gone,
Let maps to other, worlds on worlds have shown,
Let us possess one world, each hath one, and is one.
'The Good-Morrow'
John Donne

Christmas 1589

The hall was strung about with swathes of ivy, box and holly; candles lit even the darkest corners; logs glowed in the great fireplace. Outside, dusk fell gently, snowflakes lightly dusting the windowsill.

Cecily and Lady Rossiter sat near the hearth, the new wife of Lionel Metcalfe with them, cheerfully submitting to their friendly interrogation. Lionel and John Wyard stood together near the sideboard, goblets in hand, laughing as Sir Philip, his own goblet set aside, recounted what Alyce took to be a hunting tale as he play-acted a man inexpertly riding a horse.

Alyce sat farther along, the Wyards' three-year-old son asleep, stretched along the settle beside her, his head resting in her lap. A consort played a lively courante as the rest of the company danced, including the two older Wyard boys and Lionel's younger daughters. Eloise Wyard danced with Elinor, though mostly she carried her in her arms, capering through the steps, Elinor crowing with delight. Amy Metcalfe skipped along beside Thomas. She was Lionel's eleven-year-old daughter, recently arrived at Ashthorpe to begin learning from Alyce the myriad skills required of a manor wife.

Alyce sighed. The day had been everything she could hope for—family and friends, good food, pleasant company, the house ringing with the squeals and laughter of children. Not a single mishap, not even in the kitchen. And while the first part of the year was best forgotten, these last five months had been the happiest she had known—she was where she belonged.

Clifton crept into her mind only occasionally now, but when she thought of him it was with sorrow for a wasted life. There were still fleeting moments when the walls of the prison closed around her but each time, as she knotted her hands tight together, she felt the engraved ring Thomas had given her press into her skin and knew it was not reality.

Young Ned Wyard whimpered in his sleep and turned over.

Alyce gently brushed the hair back from his forehead. She looked across the room to where the nursemaids sat together and nodded to them. It was time the children were in bed.

Eloise danced Elinor over to kiss her mother good night and went off with the children and their maids.

Thomas came and sat beside Alyce. 'Now that the children have gone, it is time you danced with me.'

'Will Amy allow it?'

He frowned. 'Amy?'

'I think you have won a heart there.'

'Nay.' He grinned, shaking his head. 'I suspect I was her good deed for the day. She believes elderly men rarely get the opportunity to dance.'

'Elderly?' It was Alyce's turn to frown.

'Ay. She has misunderstood her father's jest. Although there is only six months between us, he was born at the start of King Edward's reign and I at the end of old King Henry's. She asked me if I had met the Queen's grandfather.'

'Oh dear,' Alyce laughed. She stood up and caught Thomas's hand. 'Do you think, then, that you could manage a slow pavane with me?'

He rose from his seat and drew her closer. 'An energetic galliard might be more to my liking.'

Alyce raised an eyebrow and stepped away.

Thomas did not move. He caught her other hand in his and pulled her close. 'I know New Year is a few days away, but you could give me my gift today.'

'Your gift?'

'The news that you have been nursing these past few weeks.' He rested his hand against her stomacher.

Alyce placed her hand on his. 'How did you guess?'

'The way you smile to yourself when you think no one is watching you.'

'How do you know I was not thinking of you?'

'Oh, I know that smile too.' He bent in close and brushed his lips against hers.

Alyce closed her eyes and whispered his name.

'We should dance,' he murmured, 'rather than provide our

company with an excellent illustration of the bliss of marriage.'

Thomas led her to the centre of the room and bowed as the music began.

Alyce curtsied to him and took his hand.

They moved between the other dancers, in harmony, together possessing one entire world, new made.

Historical Note

The Bridled Tongue is set between August 1586 and December 1589 within an accurate historical timeline. The story and the major characters are all fictional, although they occasionally brush shoulders with historical persons in their known roles. When this occurs, I have tried to keep my depiction of the historical characters in keeping with what is known of them. But, as this is fiction, where there are gaps, I have used my imagination. Lord Chief Justice Sir Christopher Wray (1524–1592) and William Peryam (1534–1604) did sit at the Norwich Assizes in the summer of 1589. Wray was a highly respected judge but, as I have been unable to determine his views on witchcraft, I have presented him as a man of his time who, while believing that witches exist and can cause harm, is concerned to ensure that the processes of the law are followed and justice served. Peryam, later Lord Chief Baron of the Exchequer, had stronger views on witchcraft and was a member of the committee of the House of Lords involved in redrafting the bill that became the 1604 Witchcraft Act. As I was unable to discover the names of the curate at St Peter Mancroft or the gaoler at Norwich Castle during the years in which the novel is set, William Reynes and Ralph Thorpe are my own creations.

Henry VIII's 1542 *Act against Conjurations, Witchcrafts, Sorcery and Inchantments* was the first Act to define witchcraft as a felony, a crime punishable by death at the first offence and forfeiture of goods and chattels. Prior to this Act, most cases of witchcraft and sorcery were dealt with by ecclesiastical courts; such cases were generally infrequent, and punishments were relatively mild. The 1542 Act was repealed in 1547 during the reign of Edward VI and not replaced until 1563. Any cases of witchcraft in this intervening period were again heard by the ecclesiastical courts. Under the 1563 *Act against Conjurations, Enchantments and Witchcrafts* the invocation or conjuration of evil spirits or the use of witchcraft to bring about death received the death penalty on a first offence. Using witchcraft to harm people or property, to find treasure or lost or stolen items, or to provoke a person to unlawful love earnt a year's imprisonment and six hours in the pillory on market day four times in that year. Second offences could receive the death penalty. This Act was replaced in 1604 by James I's *Act against Conjuration, Witchcraft and Dealing with Evil and Wicked Spirits* which extended the death penalty to those using witchcraft to harm people in any way at all and introduced it for the new crimes of covenanting with evil spirits and taking up the dead from graves for use in witchcraft. This was the first time an English Act referred to a pact with the devil; previous laws had concentrated on the damage done through *maleficium*. The Act was finally repealed in 1736.

Various tests were used to determine if the accused was a witch. A witch's confession or identification by another known witch were of primary importance. The inability to say the Lord's Prayer without mistake, or to only be able to say it in Latin were also considered strong proofs. The presence of a mark or growth anywhere upon the body could be considered to be an extra teat used to suckle the accused's familiar spirits. These familiars were a uniquely English phenomenon and were commonly small animals such as cats, rats, dogs, ferrets, birds, frogs or toads and were believed to assist the witch in her magic. If a person afflicted by a witch's magic gained relief by scratching the suspected witch and drawing blood, it was clear proof she was a witch as was the afflicted fainting when brought into her presence. Witch pricking and swimming were not used in sixteenth-century England although pricking was common in Scotland. Witches were believed to have a place, or mark, on their bodies that would be insensitive and not bleed when pricked with a needle. It appears not to have been used in England until the reign of James I. Swimming involved throwing an accused witch into a body of water in the belief that if the person sank, she was innocent; if she floated, it was proof that she was a witch. The first reported incidence of swimming occurred in Northamptonshire in 1612. Torture was not sanctioned in witchcraft investigations, though, to the modern mind, some of these tests are extraordinarily close to it.

An accusation of witchcraft did not automatically result in conviction and execution. Records no longer exist for all counties, but at the Home Circuit Assizes (Hertfordshire, Essex, Kent, Sussex and Surrey) from 1570 to 1609 witchcraft accusations resulted in execution at a similar rate to other crimes (around 24 per cent). Only 44 per cent of those accused of witchcraft are recorded as having suffered punishment of any sort. These statistics are examined in chapter four of *Instruments of Darkness: Witchcraft in Early Modern England* by James Sharpe (1996). Even those who were found guilty of causing death by witchcraft were sometime granted a special royal pardon. During her reign, Elizabeth I granted thirty-six such pardons to people convicted of witchcraft; nineteen of these were on the Norfolk circuit.

For the most part, those who were brought before the court in England were poor old women with reputations for a nasty tongue that they used to get begrudging charity from their neighbours. English witches did not fly, nor did they meet in Sabbats. Agnes Hall's dream of naked cavorting on Mousehold Heath was not the usual way of things in sixteenth-century England, but it is the sort of spiteful imagining of which Agnes was capable. Witchcraft was believed to run in families, passing from mother to daughter, witches being trained at their mother's knee, almost like an apprenticeship.

The spread of witchcraft accusations was not uniform across Europe. There were far fewer trials in countries such as Italy and Spain compared to France and central and southern Germany. Within the British Isles, England had around five hundred executions over the period covered by the Witchcraft Acts compared to Scotland, where from 1563 to 1727 over fifteen hundred people were executed. Wales and Ireland had few cases of witchcraft as personal setbacks were more often ascribed to fairies or the little people rather than to witches. In England, the punishment received by those found guilty of causing death by witchcraft was hanging, the usual penalty for murder. Burning was reserved for the crimes of heresy and, for women, for both high and petty treason (the murder of either a husband, or a master or mistress).

The Elizabethan courtroom differed from what we expect today. Cases were tried in batches and usually involved disputation between the accused and the accuser and witnesses. Judges were interventionist, asking questions and involving themselves to a degree that would be considered improper today. Rules of evidence were not yet fully developed and hearsay was freely accepted. The accused was unrepresented and a prosecutor was rare. Elizabethan jurors usually did retire to another room to reach their verdict but I have them remain in the court because the judges consider the verdict clear and wish to waste no more time. The procedure I set out is that described by Sir Thomas Smith in *De Republica Anglorum* (1583). I have also drawn on J.S. Cockburn's *A History of English Assizes 1558–1714* (1972) and *The Office of the Clerk of Assize: Containing the Form and Method of the Proceedings at the Assizes and General Gaol-Delivery* (1682).

Norwich Castle was originally built as a royal palace but used as a prison from 1220. It gradually fell into disrepair and by the seventeenth-century wealthier prisoners with the means to pay were kept in a house with barred windows on Golden Ball Lane near the beginning of the causeway to the castle. This arrangement could have been in place in the latter half of the sixteenth-century. As there are no detailed descriptions of the interior of the castle before the latter part of the eighteenth century, I have resorted to my imagination to fill in the gaps. It is possible that the prisoners held in the castle were chained, particularly in the dungeons. I have ignored this possibility because I felt that the story gained more by having the female prisoners free to move about.

Quotations from the Psalms and church rituals are drawn from the 1559 Book of Common Prayer and biblical quotations from a 1580 printing of the Bishops' Bible. I have chosen to use the later King James translation for Proverb 31:10, 'Death and life are in the power of the tongue', and Proverb 18:21, 'Her price is far above rubies', because the later translation is more poetic and familiar to the modern reader. The song Isabel sings in chapter four is 'The Lowest Trees' by Sir Edward Dyer

(1543–1607), best known through its musical setting by John Dowland. The song Alyce hears in Lord Reading's garden is 'Orpheus with his Lute' by William Shakespeare. This song is from the play *Henry VIII*, first performed in 1613; however, some scholars believed it was written around 1603. Although this is later than the years in which *The Bridled Tongue* is set, knowing the way writers reuse old ideas and unpublished writing, who is to say that Shakespeare did not write the song during his 'lost' years and permit a friend to perform it at a noble patron's feast? It is a fictional possibility.

Many of the sources I have consulted in writing this novel can be found on my website as well as posts on the historical background from the making of marriages and the role of the manor wife to the legal process in Elizabethan witch trials, the gaol at Norwich Castle and surprising snippets of information I have discovered during my research.

I have tried to walk the middle road in the use of language as it is impossible to write a story set in the sixteenth-century that sounds fluent to the modern ear without drawing on the words that have enriched our language in the intervening centuries. I have attempted to avoid the use of thoroughly modern terms but have included some terms common in the sixteenth century rarely used now to give a uniquely Elizabethan flavour. I hope the result is a novel that is enjoyable to read but that also gives a believable sense of time and place.

Acknowledgements

I would like to thank all those who have helped me on the road to publication.

Thank you to Juliette Godot, Sarah Ormerod, and Linda Hardy whose comments on earlier versions of *The Bridled Tongue* encouraged me to think that this was a story worth telling. Particular thanks to Samantha Edwards for her extremely helpful critique of the novel and to Janine Smith for not only reading it but, as a work colleague, for showing both forbearance and good humour in dealing with my random and out of the blue questions at times when I should have been concentrating on the task at hand. Thanks also goes to Sarah Kirby for her patience and meticulous proofreading. I would particularly like to thank Steve Arber of the Norfolk Museums Service who kindly answered what I thought were unanswerable questions about Norwich Castle in the late sixteenth century. Thanks also go to Denise McKay for her advice on all things equine, any mistakes in this area are solely due to my misunderstanding. Immense thanks to Jenny Quinlan of Historical Editorial whose insights and advice were critical in adding depth to the story. Without Jenny, *The Bridled Tongue* would be a shadow of itself. My greatest thanks is to my sister Gabrielle who has been an unfailing support on this journey almost from the beginning. Last but not least, I am indebted to my husband and children for keeping me in touch with reality— without them I would, most likely, have disappear completely into the sixteenth-century.

About the Author

Catherine Meyrick is a librarian with a love of history and fiction. She has a Master of Arts in history and is also a family history obsessive. Although she grew up in regional Victoria, Catherine has lived her adult life in Melbourne, Australia.

You can find out more about her at her website catherinemeyrick.com

Also by Catherine Meyrick

Forsaking All Other

Love is no game for women; the price is far too high.

England 1585.

Bess Stoughton, waiting woman to the well-connected Lady Allingbourne, has discovered that her father is arranging for her to marry an elderly neighbour. Normally obedient Bess rebels and wrests from her father a year's grace to find a husband more to her liking.

Edmund Wyard, a taciturn and scarred veteran of England's campaign in Ireland, is attempting to ignore the pressure from his family to find a suitable wife as he prepares to join the Earl of Leicester's army in the Netherlands.

Although Bess and Edmund are drawn to each other, they are aware that they can have nothing more than friendship. Bess knows that Edmund's wealth and family connections place him beyond her reach. And Edmund, with his well-honed sense of duty, has never considered that he could follow his own wishes.

With England on the brink of war and fear of Catholic plots extending even into Lady Allingbourne's household, time is running out for both of them.

Made in the USA
Coppell, TX
06 April 2021